"A vivid and detailed portrait of the life of the legendary Lucy Duff Gordon. Tessa Arlen has crafted a transporting and beautiful homage to Lucy Duff Gordon's creativity, perseverance, and influence on the fashion industry."

—Chanel Cleeton, *New York Times* and
*USA Today* bestselling author of *Our Last Days in Barcelona*

"Tessa Arlen delivers a fascinating tale based on the real-life fashion icon, Lucy, Lady Duff Gordon, who went up against a male-dominated industry and revolutionized it. Her daring designs were worn by royals, aristocrats, and the celebrities of her day. Be prepared to google your way through this captivating novel, filled with its glorious ensemble cast of characters. Rich and atmospheric, Arlen's descriptions of haute couture are simply breathtaking. A must read for fashion fans everywhere."

—Renée Rosen, *USA Today*
bestselling author of *The Social Graces*

"Tessa Arlen's novel is as elegant as a Lucille gown, full of movement, color, and beauty. It brings to life some of the most important and fascinating people and events of her generation, from Nijinsky to the *Titanic*. For anyone interested in fashion; in the Gilded Age; in stories about strong, visionary woman, Tessa Arlen's novel is a must read!"

—Jeanne Mackin, author of *The Last Collection*

"The epic story of a self-made woman, and a fresh and captivating look at the birth of fin de siècle runway fashion. From cramped, terraced house-sitting rooms to ballrooms, readers will be enthralled by the parade of notable historical figures whose appetite for clothing allows a single mother to not only raise her daughter but to do so in growing comfort, style, and notoriety. Arlen doesn't shy away from hardships and tragedy, but with a bright, hopeful, industrious protagonist like Lucy Duff Gordon at the forefront, the reader is never burdened. A true pleasure from start to finish."

—Erika Robuck,
national bestselling author of *Sisters of Night and Fog*

"A sumptuous treat of elegant prose, evocative descriptions, and compelling emotions. Arlen's writing absolutely shines. . . . She succeeds in making fashion designer and *Titanic*-survivor Lucy Duff Gordon both relatable and sympathetic, and stirs the senses with her lush depictions of clothing and settings."

—Anna Lee Huber, *USA Today* bestselling author of *A Perilous Perspective*

# A DRESS of VIOLET TAFFETA

Tessa Arlen

BERKLEY
New York

BERKLEY
An imprint of Penguin Random House LLC
penguinrandomhouse.com

Library of Congress Cataloging-in-Publication Data

Names: Arlen, Tessa, author.
Title: A dress of violet taffeta / Tessa Arlen.
Description: First edition. | New York: Berkley, 2022.
Identifiers: LCCN 2022006412 (print) | LCCN 2022006413 (ebook) |
ISBN 9780593436851 (trade paperback) | ISBN 9780593436868 (ebook)
Subjects: LCSH: Duff Gordon, Lucy, Lady—Fiction. |
LCGFT: Biographical fiction. | Novels.
Classification: LCC PS3601.R5445 D74 2022 (print) |
LCC PS3601.R5445 (ebook) | DDC 813/.6—dc23/eng/20220211
LC record available at https://lccn.loc.gov/2022006412
LC ebook record available at https://lccn.loc.gov/2022006413

First Edition: July 2022

Printed in the United States of America
2nd Printing

BOOK DESIGN BY KATY RIEGEL

*For my sister, Debby*

# A Dress of
# Violet Taffeta

# CHAPTER ONE

*March 1893*

LUCY

The cup shook in Lucy's hand, slopping tea over the tablecloth. *Damn.* She blotted the spreading stain with her napkin, trying not to catch her mother's critical eye.

Mrs. Kennedy wrinkled her nose in fastidious disdain. "Not like you to be clumsy, dear," her mother said. "Are you feeling quite well?"

She was spared an explanation. "Oh, for heaven's sake! Will you look at the toast—quite burned—*and* they have forgotten the marmalade!" Lucy's mother rang the bell at her elbow. "Where *is* Palmer? What on earth is going *on* in this house?" She jangled the bell again, her eyebrows raised at the careless attention to their breakfast.

Lucy leaned her hot forehead into the palm of her hand. *Please,* she begged whichever god was responsible for deep, dreamless sleep. *Just one night—is that too much to ask?*

"Really, my dear, you must speak to them—they get worse every day." Her mother shook her head at the misery of poorly trained servants and opened her embroidered reticule. Lucy watched the sal volatile make its first appearance of the day and stifled irritation. *If only all of life's real catastrophes could be righted with a sniff from a cut-glass bottle with a silk tassel*, she thought as she hung on to silence. The signs were clear: her mother was having one of her bad days.

"I waited half an hour for my early morning tray, and it was brought up to me by an untidy-looking girl who I don't believe I have seen in the house before today. It's rather frightening, Lucy, to wake up to find a complete stranger in one's bedroom even if they are offering you tea." She took a delicate sip from her cup and put it down again, her lips pursed in a moue of distaste. "It's cold, and the milk—the milk has turned." Her voice sank to a martyr's whisper. "It's quite un-drink-able."

Lucy looked down at clotty clouds floating on the surface of dishwater gray tea. She took a mouthful and swallowed in defiance. "Yes, Mama, the milk's off."

Her mother's exasperation at Lucy's inability to supervise her servants drifted across tired table linen, mismatched china, and the offending toast. "They won't exert themselves if you don't take the time to *correct* them, Lucy, will they?" Her tight smile of grievance struggled against outright disapproval at her daughter's handling of her domestic staff.

All Lucy wanted to do was grope her way back up the stairs to her room, lay her aching head down on her cool, smooth pillow, and drop into sleep, but it was time to brief her mother on the uncertain future of her household—the House of Hell, as James had called it the last time he had slammed the front door on his way to his club.

She straightened her back and met her mother's gaze. "You are absolutely right, Mama. But I'm afraid that the servants won't exert themselves at *all*—because they have gone, all of them. I gave them notice two weeks ago." She tried to make her voice light, as if dismissing a houseful of servants was an everyday occurrence to be remedied by the Slade Domestic Agency. "Yesterday was their last day, which is why . . ." Her voice faltered as she saw the faces of women who had been her servants and companions for the past nine years when they had said goodbye. As they had held her hands or enfolded her in their arms and wished her all the best in the world. *At least they found new, grateful, and hopefully stable employers. Well, nearly all of them.*

Her mother's hand flew to the single strand of pearls around her neck and held on to it for dear life. "You let them *go*? My dear child, then who was that *person* in my room?"

"That was the scullery maid—I agreed to keep her on for another week or so . . . She is very willing."

Dismissing her maid, Clotilde; the housekeeper, Mrs. Jackson; Cook; the parlormaid, Palmer; Esmé's admirable but intimidating nanny, Mrs. Cameron; and the odd job man who came on Fridays had had a strange effect on Lucy, and its outcome lay upstairs in her chest of drawers, wrapped in tissue paper.

It was a complete waste of energy to try to put an optimistic gloss on what she must say next. "You see, Mama . . . James . . . It seems that James has left me."

Her mother held her breath. Her eyes closed for a brief flutter of a second. "Oh, Lucy, not again."

*She might as well say: Which James?* Lucy thought as she watched her mother struggle for composure. *She never had time for him in the first place—no wonder she didn't notice when he left a month ago!*

As she waited for her mother's "Whatever are you going to do, dear?" the skin on her arms seethed in a sting of unease so close to fear that she was amazed she could string two words together. Without a husband, or the necessary means, deserted wives simply did not survive, and if they did, it was not in a way that polite people recognized. *We are equipped for marriage and bearing children but not for desertion.* It was not a new realization. Lucy had known the moment James had stormed off into a rainy February night with a badly packed valise that she might very well be destitute within six months. Three if her plan did not work.

Her mouth was as dry as toast. She took another mouthful of sour tea. *I'd give anything in the world right now for a whiff from that blasted bottle.* She felt the familiar stirring of resentment and welcomed it as an alternative to dread. Why didn't she have a comfortable mother? A kindly woman with a soft bosom on which she could lay her tired head and cry out her crushing fears and the deep aching despair of being abandoned?

Mrs. Kennedy did not encourage outward displays of emotion: swollen eyes and red noses were vulgar—even if the love of one's life had been carried off in three days, as in Lucy's father's case, by typhoid.

"I can't imagine he will be gone for long, dear. James tends to be unpredictable. I expect he'll be back when . . ." A dismissive wave of her elegant hand. From the moment Lucy's mother had met James she had considered him irresponsible: lacking in all reliable masculine virtues.

*The money runs out?* Lucy knew how her mother's mind worked. *Is that the best you can do?* Irritation rescued her from self-pity. "I'm afraid that this time it *is* for good. Even if he wanted to come back, I would say no. So, it seems I have no husband!" Lucy heard defiance in her voice. Her mother, no doubt, heard her remark as brazen.

*I have no husband!* A month ago, the dreaded words had left her trembling. Saying them aloud, she felt her fear begin to subside. A surge of something akin to excitement prickled in her throat with the exhilarating effervescence of champagne. *Stop it*, she told herself. *Not enough sleep has made you light-headed.* But the feeling of giddy elation persisted. Even if she couldn't pay the bills, and they were turfed out of the house, she was free of James: his erratic and badly timed disappearances, cold sarcasm, and two-day hangovers.

"He ran off with a pantomime dancer." She pressed the tips of her fingers to her lips to stop herself from laughing. *I sound like a heroine in one of my sister's stories.* She gulped another mouthful of sour tea. "Her name is Gilda, Gilda La Vie—I believe she pronounces it Lavvy." Laughter rippled upward, met cold tea coming down, and rushed it back the way it had come. She pressed her napkin over her mouth to prevent more damage to the cloth.

Her mother looked away. "I am not surprised that you are overwrought, dear. I always said that James—" She lifted a hand, palm outward. "Perhaps we should not discuss that now." Her mother's fragile bone structure, fine gray hair, and soft voice belied a deeply practical nature. "I am sure he has made adequate provision." She tugged a scrap of lawn and lace from the cuff of her sleeve and handed it to her daughter.

Lucy blew her nose. "There is no money—he took the last of it." She watched her mother's hands reach for each other: two terrified children seeking comfort. "I had to let the servants go so I could pay the rent." She didn't mention her other extravagant purchase the day before yesterday. *Have I completely lost my mind?* she asked herself.

"My dear child, whatever are you going to do?" Her mother twisted both of her wedding rings on her thin fingers. Twice widowed, she had married once for love to Douglas Sutherland, and the second time for financial security. When her second husband died of chronic dyspepsia, Mrs. Kennedy discovered that she had not married for an assured future after all and had come to live in Davies Street (just off the fashionable end of Berkeley Square, she told her friends) with Lucy and James.

Lucy knew exactly what her mother was thinking: *I would be welcomed everywhere as a widow: no one wants an abandoned wife hanging around, particularly if there is no money.*

She met her mother's gaze: *She's hoping that if I am ever lucky enough to find myself a second husband, I'll choose one who is wiser with his investments, or, at least, easy on the brandy.*

Her mother's expression intensified into one close to rebuke. *And now she's worried that I am closer to thirty than to twenty.*

She stared across the untidy table at her mother's pale, powdered face. "I would rather die than marry again." It was a challenge, quickly tempered by her mother in the graceful tit-for-tat she excelled in.

"Well, you can't marry again, can you, dear? You already have a husband." And then to cap it: "Have you told your sister?"

Lucy's resentment intensified. Her younger-by-a-year sister, Elinor, with her spectacular marriage to the heir of a rich family, was every mother's perfect daughter.

"No, not yet," she lied and crossed the fingers of both hands.

When her mother left the dining room she would go upstairs to put on her hat for her morning walk. The guest room door was directly opposite the door to Mrs. Kennedy's room. Lucy could see her mother jogging her sister awake in a flurry of concern and whispered lamenting

as she announced Lucy's abandonment and looming financial catastrophe.

She glanced at the dining room clock. It was half past nine. Elinor
was volatile at the best of times; if she were awoken too early, it would
be fatal. In her eagerness to be rid of their mother's desperate need to
discuss Lucy's dilemma, Elinor might give away everything she and
Lucy had planned together last night.

Lucy reached across the breakfast table, took her mother's hand, and
went to the heart of the matter. "There is nothing either you or Elinor can
do to help, Mama. I have started divorce proceedings against James—for
desertion. My decree absolute will be granted in a few weeks."

Her mother snatched back her hand and brought it down on the tablecloth with a slap that made the cups quiver in their saucers. "Divorce?" She
hauled in air like a drowning woman. "Have you completely lawst your
senses, Lewcy? If you divorce James, you will lose *every single one of your
friends*. The scandal will be unimaginable. You will not only be destitute,
an exile from all decent society, but your child will have *no* father! Have
you thought of that? No, of course you haven't. Well, think of it now: if
you proceed with this insanity, Esmé will be made a ward of the court."

LUCY PUSHED OPEN the door to her sister's bedroom with her shoulder
and, followed by her Pekingese, NouNou, and her plump puppy, Minou, maneuvered the breakfast tray into the dimly lit room.

A head lifted itself briefly from the pillow. "Oh, it's you. I thought it
was Mama again." Elinor turned over onto her back, her long hair
spread out on either side of her beautiful, grumpy face.

"She's gone for her walk, with Esmé."

Elinor's brows came down as Lucy dumped the heavy tray onto the
bed. "You should never have told her about your divorce. She's frantic—
unstoppably frantic. What you should have done . . ." Two hands pushed
hair back from her forehead. "What you should have done was wait

until it was final. You could have made up a story—and she would have believed you. James was hardly ever here anyway."

Lucy's head throbbed. Last night she and her sister had finished off the remnants of a decanter of brandy that James had somehow over-looked. She had hoped it would make her sleep—but it had kept her awake all night, tossing and turning in a depressed state of what-ifs.

"Yes, I know that she would far prefer me to be widowed than watch me stand up in court and tell everyone that 'my hubby ran off with a Gaiety girl.' But if I don't divorce James, there is nothing to prevent him moving back when he tires of this woman. And if, in the meantime, my scheme is successful, then he'll drink away any money I might have in the bank before he runs off with another dancer. It has to be divorce."

Elinor pressed the heels of her hands against her closed eyes. "Dogs off the bed." Lucy picked up both Pekes and put them outside the bed-room door. "You surely didn't tell her about Gilda Lavvy, did you, Lucy?"

"Whyever not? She needs to hear it from me rather than one of her gossipy friends. I didn't tell her anything else, by the way, did you?"

Elinor turned onto her side with her back to her, and Lucy swallowed down alarm—had Elinor told? "Elinor, *don't* go back to sleep, it's nearly eleven o'clock. Mama will be back soon, and I have a favor."

"Another one?" Elinor pushed herself upright to loll against her pil-lows and accept tea.

"I want you to take Mama back to Grosvenor Square with you. I have so much to do, and you know how demanding she can be. Anyway, I don't think she can survive without a crew of servants. She has to be given time to adjust, and I would prefer her to do it in your house and not in mine. It would be kinder."

"Kinder to whom? Certainly not me." Elinor sorted through the of-ferings on her breakfast tray with an irritable jabbing finger. "You seem to forget, Lucy, that Clayton is redoing the drawing and dining room. The house is in chaos, which is why I am staying *here* with you." And under her breath: "What on earth made me think that was a good idea?"

Lucy remained silent: at this hour of the day, it was always best to let Elinor lead the way.

"What about Esmé? Mama could look after Esmé for you now that you have fired Nanny."

Lucy was already shaking her head. "No, I can't have that. Mama scolds and corrects her. If Esmé makes the slightest noise she is sent to her room. I need time; you have to give me more time. And isn't she due to you for a visit? You promised me you would take her this year." *I must not*, Lucy reminded herself, *start an argument with Elinor. I need far too many favors.*

"What *possessed* you to get rid of her nanny?"

"Too expensive, but the scullery maid is—"

Elinor bolted upright, green eyes wide with disbelief. "*No one*, Lucy, absolutely no one trusts their daughter to the care of a scullery maid. If you were going to keep one servant, it should at least be someone useful, like the cook"—she waved a piece of scorched toast—"or Nanny."

*Yes, why did I agree to keep on that sad fright with her chapped hands?* Lucy asked herself. "She had nowhere else to go."

"And that's a reason?"

"Elinor, she is only sixteen: Cook hired her two weeks ago. She has no family, no one at all."

"And no skills, except washing pots and pans and sweeping the floor. You know nothing about her, and you entrust your little girl to her care?" Elinor, annoyed at being woken twice by her family, was now in a quarrelsome mood. "Where is she from? Did she produce references? No, of course not. She is probably a workhouse girl." She threw her arms wide and tossed back her hair. "Why don't you hire a butler from the rookery while you are giving room and board to all the riffraff in London?"

*Always such histrionics; she should be on the stage*, Lucy thought.

She saw again the thin face of the maid crumple when she had told her that she could no longer keep six servants and that she was to be let go with five shillings and a reference. *I can't even remember her name. Francis? Frank? Franklin!*

"She is from Northumberland. She was obviously from a decent family before she was made an orphan. She is polite, she can read and write, and her mother was a dressmaker. Yes, Elinor, she came to us from a workhouse, but Cook was nobody's fool and she told me that Franklin was a decent, clean, God-fearing girl."

A flash of gunpowder from the bed—Elinor had after all drunk most of the brandy last night. "Rubbish, absolute and complete and utter rubbish. She is a workhouse menial, willing to tell any tale to keep her place. That God-fearing scullery maid is probably packing up the silver in one of your hand-embroidered coverlets at this very moment."

Lucy shook her head. "There is no silver—James sold it all last year. If a pleasant young woman will accept food and shelter as compensation for hard work, and you are in my position, you jump at it. Do you imagine for one moment that Mama will put on an apron and produce breakfast, lunch, and dinner?" Her voice cracked and tears streaked down her cheeks. "Why on earth would I turn out a girl onto the streets to fend for herself? Franklin and I are in the same damned boat." *That's twice that I have sworn this morning.* She felt her self-control begin to fray around the edges. *I must get a grip*, she told herself as tears started to splash in earnest.

Elinor's anger evaporated as quickly as it had crashed into the room. She took her sister by her shoulders and pulled her close. "I'm sorry, Lucy, please don't cry. I didn't mean it. Everything will work out, I'm sure of it. We have a plan. I didn't tell Mama, I promise," she whispered as she stroked Lucy's disheveled hair. She pulled back to wipe away her sister's tears, and imitating the high, fluting voice of their mother, she added, "We don't use that sort of language, Lewcy, we are not a family of tinkers."

Lucy pulled away, laughing through her tears. "You can't tell her *anything*—she would never understand."

"Well, she will find out, eventually. So be prepared." Elinor took her sister's hand and held it tightly.

"I am not sure I understand what I am about to do, either." She squeezed Elinor's hand to emphasize something they had agreed on last night. "You will ask Clayton to open a bank account for me, in my name, won't you? I have enough money to open an account—but they won't give a bank account to a woman, divorced, married, or single, without the guarantee of a responsible male."

"Yes, yes. I will make him do it first thing tomorrow morning. But"—Elinor pointed her forefinger—"this venture has to be carried out with tact and discretion. Otherwise, Clayton will be angry."

"I wouldn't dream of doing it any other way. If it doesn't work . . . then I'll have to try something else."

Elinor lazed back on her pillows and smiled. "I can't wait to see what you come up with. Come on, darling, no more dread and panic; it will be fun, you'll see."

*The last thing in the world it will be is fun,* Lucy thought as she remembered the lawyer whose fees she couldn't afford, the tradesmen who were already impatient to settle February's accounts, and a landlord with a short fuse. Not to mention parting with some of her precious few pounds on a reckless purchase that made her wonder if she had lost all judgment.

Her sister sat forward. "Stop worrying. Our plan will work. And anyway, I will tell Clayton that he has to lend you some money—to tide you over."

Lucy started to shake her head. "No . . . please don't. I have enough to get me started. I would rather—"

The door flew open and Esmé came into the room at a run. "We are back from our walk, and Grandmama wants to talk to *both* of you!" She threw her arms around her mother's neck and kissed her cheek. "She says I am not to play in the garden with Celia because she has to make lunch, and *I* have to stay out of the way in the nursery, *all alone,* and be good." Tears welled up and spilled down her cheeks. "And I heard her tell Celia that we were all going to stay with Aunt Elinor, and that we wouldn't need her anymore. Which is *wrong* because Celia is my nanny now, and I like her much more than Grand."

Elinor sank her head into her hands, her shoulders shaking with laughter. "Not an Ethel, or a Mabel, but a Celia? How poetic: you have a scullery maid who calls herself Celia! I think you've got trouble on your hands, sister."

Lucy pulled her daughter up onto the bed and into her lap. "Her name is Celia Franklin and she and Esmé are friends, aren't you, darling?" She tied up a trailing ribbon, smoothing silky dark curls back from Esmé's round, damp face. *You see*, she telegraphed with raised eyebrows to her sister. *This is why you have to take Mama home with you.*

Elinor threw back the covers and got out of bed. In her fine lawn nightgown, she was a stirring sight with her magnificent breasts, her long supple back ending in a round bottom as firm as a young girl's, and a neck like a column of alabaster. She was taller than Lucy, with vivid coloring and the confident allure of a woman feted for her dramatic beauty. Lucy remembered James telling her on their wedding night that she looked like a delicate fawn poised for flight. *What a pity I didn't pay more attention to that remark*, she thought.

Elinor picked up her wrap. "How long must I keep Mama?" she asked as she thrust her arms into the sleeves.

"For as long as you can stand it."

Elinor bit the top of her thumb as she calculated. "Two days—three? Absolutely no more than three." Esmé giggled and snuggled deeper into her mother's lap. "Oh, for pity's sake! A week, no longer than a week. After that Clayton will put his foot down." Elinor clapped her hands. "Now, off you go, both of you, and leave me in peace. If I must take Mama home with me, I need to dress and leave before you give me a disgusting lunch."

*April 1893*

LUCY

Lucy turned the envelope over to read the sender's address on its back. It was from her solicitor's clerk, Mr. Wilfred Clemens. Using the tip of her scissors she slit the envelope and pulled out two pages: an official document and a letter. The letter, written in black ink, confirmed that the marriage between Lucile Christiana Sutherland and James Charles Stuart Wallace, solemnized on the thirteenth day of September 1884, had been dissolved on the thirtieth of April 1893. She could see Mr. Clemens's long, clean-shaven face, his lips pressed together in disapproval as he had written in his even copperplate hand: *Your decree absolute has been granted and you are now legally divorced.*

She stared down at the document releasing her from her marriage to James. What had she expected to feel now that the nine years of her marriage were over? Elation? Joy? Guilt that she had not been a worthy wife? Gratitude that she would never smell the sour odor of stale brandy on James's breath as he lay beside her in their bed, or feel him fumbling at her nightdress, his legs thrusting hers apart? She shook her head to rid it of his slurred command that she lie still when she had tried to pretend she was turning away from him in her sleep to avoid the brutality of his nightly assaults, until, bored of her, he had pushed her away and told her she was frigid.

She sat down at her dressing table and looked at the serious woman gazing back at her in the looking glass. *Where has that eighteen-year-old girl gone who fell so completely in love nine years ago? That laughing, happy girl?* She saw for a fleeting moment the skinny tomboy who swam in the icy water of the Gulf of Saint-Malo off Jersey island, who fished in the pond for tiddlers in spring and skated on its surface in winter. *Is she still in there somewhere?*

She searched her reflection for lines. Yes, there they were at the corners of her eyes. Her mother reminded her not to frown; her sister dismissed them as laughter lines. Lucy traced the edge of her jawline with her forefinger: *My face is too thin.* She pulled the lamp closer and leaned into its light. Her skin was still firm, her mouth full-lipped. At least she hadn't become grim and tight from nine years of disappointments and the indifference of a husband whose interest lay only in women who drank gin and kicked up their legs in a pantomime chorus. *Did he ever really love* me? she wondered. Had that younger, superficially charming man ever felt any emotion deeper than the need to gratify momentary physical pleasure?

She felt no joy that she was free—not a quiver, not a shred—simply relief. If relief was all she felt, so be it! Perhaps joy of a sort would come in its own time. She bent and opened the bottom drawer of her chiffonier and lifted a parcel onto her lap, peeling away layers of tissue paper. A bright flash of indigo and violet gleamed in the lamplight as she held the silk up to her face. *Violets and heartsease:* women of her mother's generation believed flowers were symbolic. Violets represented faith, and heartsease peace. The rich hue made her skin look porcelain smooth, pearl white. She shook out the folds of taffeta around her like a cloak and walked slowly around her room, feeling its heavy rustle pull behind her.

Wrapped in silk, she threw the two pillows on the right side of the bed onto the floor, pulling her own into the center. She lay down and stretched her arms and legs out as far as they would go to the bed's four posts. *This is my bed now, my room, and if I can hang on to it, my house!*

She smoothed her hands down over the taffeta and looked around the pretty room she had created in the weeks she had waited for her divorce, obliterating all evidence of a masculine presence. A swathe of fine white muslin embroidered in white roses looped around the crown of her bed, softened its thick mahogany posts. Gone were the heavy red brocade curtains blocking the light from the windows, replaced by simple dove gray linen over sheer white muslin that she kept open at night. She had re-covered the maroon velvet cushions with silver-gray silk. To her mother's horror she had painted over the burgundy wallpaper with a tinted wash of lavender. The pale south-facing walls reflected the slanting rays of the rising sun in the morning, flushing them rose pink, and in the evening the cool grayish tint of lavender intensified. She lay quite still on her bed, her hands folded behind her head, breathing in the late-night air as it belled the muslin curtains inward.

For the first time in weeks she was hungry! *No more half-raw joints of beef squatting on the sideboard in my house!* Tomorrow morning she would order a roast chicken for lunch. Surely Celia would be able to manage something as simple as roasting a chicken? What a pity James had emptied the cellar; her meager budget didn't extend to wine. She ignored the niggling voice that whispered in her head: *If it doesn't work, what will you do? What will you do?*

"It will work!" she said to her room. "Most certainly it will!"

After breakfast she would put on her hunter green broadcloth and walk to Farmers & Rogers in Regent Street, where she would buy ten yards of the sheerest gray mousseline de soie and a length of deep indigo silk for the sleeves of the dress. Sleeves were important in any gown, and these sleeves would be sublime.

Lucy could see it now as if it were already hanging in her wardrobe. She reached out to the table by her bed for the tablet of drawing paper and a pencil. Sitting up against her pillows, she started to sketch the bodice of the dress. "Smooth, boned so it fits tightly . . . with a plunging vee neckline," she instructed herself, "ending between my breasts." She looked down and laughed. They were not as mountainously glorious as Elinor's snowy prow, but they would look impressive enough if she pushed them up with her corset. "The décolletage trimmed with the lace from my wedding dress and secured with . . . a bow?" She tapped her pencil. "No, dark blue appliquéd flowers . . . here and here and here." Her pencil traced lightly over the page: "Soft, bouffant gray chiffon sleeves, set over indigo silk, and gathered into frilled cuffs of long lace above the elbows: lace sleeves half covering slender arms are irresistible." She drew the line of a flowing skirt. "Simple . . . feminine." She corrected herself. "*Alluring* and feminine."

When she looked up from her drawing the sun was streaming in through the windows. It was the first day of her new life.


CELIA CAME INTO the dining room as Lucy laid out the double length of taffeta on a white sheet pinned to the Turkey rug.

"What a color," the maid marveled at the sheen of silk on the floor.

"I don't think I've ever seen anythin' laike it. What sort of material is it, ma'am?"

Lucy sat back on her heels. "Do you like it?" In the days that her only servant had managed to achieve a flawlessly clean house, deplorable food, and a contented child, Lucy had come to enjoy her maid-of-all-work's curiosity and her inability to keep her thoughts to herself. She found her slow Northumbrian accent soothing: the long flat vowels and the complete absence of hard consonants at the ends of her words had a rhythm and musicality that made Lucy think of quiet country villages and fields of grazing sheep.

"It's called taffeta. Look at the way the color deepens and changes in the light." She picked up a handful of silk and twisted her hand in the sunlight. "See?" She moved the hand holding the silk. "Dawn and dusk. That's the beauty of this type of silk; it's alive with iridescent color."

Celia turned to the dining room table, pushed against the wall to make more space on the floor. "Is this part of it too, ma'am, the dress?"

"Yes, this is chiffon. The French call it mousseline de soie." She lifted a length and held it up to the light and smiled at Celia through it. "So sheer it's like mist. I'll use it as an overskirt; the colors of the taffeta will gleam through it. When I move, the chiffon will slide over the taffeta and these violets will look as if they are flowing across the dress."

Celia picked up a silk violet and studied it carefully. "You made these, ma'am?"

"Yes. Like this." Lucy picked up a narrow dark green ribbon and a violet one. She filled a needle with silk thread and, twisting and crimping the ribbons, fashioned a violet with two tiny leaves. She pinned it onto a piece of ink blue lace net. "These will be scattered in a panel down the front of the skirt." She glanced up at the girl standing absorbed as she watched Lucy's fingers. "Do you see?"

Celia nodded. "Th'ur laike real flowers." Her admiration was delightful. She turned the silk flower in her hands, absorbed in its intricacy. Her skin was no longer papery and pale but firm and flushed with health. Her hair was clean and glossy, concealed under a perfectly ironed cap. But the parlormaid's old dress hung from her thin shoulders. *It needs to be taken in; no, it needs to be turned into dusters; that sickly pink is hideous with her pale skin and fair hair.*

"We need to see about a new dress for you, Celia." It wasn't right to call a servant by her first name; it was too familiar. Her mother had told her that she was asking for trouble. Lucy shrugged off her mother's often-voiced opinion. What had she to lose? She had already broken the rules. She was a shameless woman: a divorcée. She had a scullery maid to look after her daughter and make her something called pease pudding for lunch and dinner, but the last thing in the world she could bring herself to do was to call this diminutive fairy Franklin.

"That dress has seen better days, and it is far too big for you. I have some cloth somewhere that will do. You know how to sew, don't you?"

Celia bobbed a curtsy. "I do, ma'am. Me mam was a seamstress, but she could do anythin': cutwork, embroidery, fagoting. Fine shirts she made for genelemen and luvely undergarmints fer the ladies." She threaded a needle and, picking up a green and a violet ribbon, twisted and tucked the fabric into a commendable imitation of Lucy's violet. "I can come down later in the evenin', when Miss Esmé is in bed, and help you with yer dress . . . tha' is, if you wish me to, ma'am." She blushed at her presumption and Lucy heard her mother's voice: *I told you she would take advantage.*

She nodded, making her expression grave to mask the pleasure she felt. "Yes, thank you, Celia. As soon as you have finished your duties and given Esmé her bath, I will be up to read her a story; then we'll work on the dress. Now, you had better run along and make lunch. It's nearly noon."

# Chapter Two

May 1893

## Celia

Never, ever use a cloth from the kitchen to dust my room. I can't imagine why you would do such a thing." Lucy's mother, Mrs. Kennedy, had surprised Celia in the pantry. She had seemed to come from nowhere to loom over her as she wrote out her shopping list.

"Yes, ma'am. I mean, no, ma'am." Celia dipped a respectful curtsy. *The owd witch in't finished wi' me yet*, she thought as she bowed her head in contrition, and waited.

"I can't begin to imagine who trained you. Didn't they teach you anything at the workhouse?" She could feel Mrs. Kennedy's hard eyes boring into her. She was holding a duster between her finger and thumb as if it was a dead rat.

Celia didn't say the workhouse had given her board and scrape: just enough food so that she could make hemp flour sacks for fourteen long hours a day. She stared down at the floor, reluctant to share the shame of parish charity with this cold woman.

"I see you are off to buy comestibles. Try and remember, *if* you can, that respectable people do not eat salted, yellow fish—or cabbage." Mrs. Kennedy's voice was low, with a bite behind every word. Celia looked up into eyes narrow with contempt and a thin mouth turned down at the corners. "If we must eat fish, then buy *white* fish: halibut or Dover sole. We are not a family of costermongers."

*Costermongers? You should be so lucky! If you turn up your nose at a nice bit o' haddock, then it will have to be minced mutton—full of tasty fat and a big helping of cabbage to keep you regular.*

Celia waited on the two ladies at luncheon and dinner, watching their reaction to the food she had prepared through half-lowered eyelids. Mrs. Wallace ate her food with graceful thanks, while the old lady sniffed and picked like a fussy old cat, her eyebrows raised in disgust, dabbing at her mouth with her napkin as if it would take the terrible taste away.

"Don't stand there staring at the floor! If you are going shopping you had better be on your way. No dawdling—you will be back by half past eleven. I have my eye on you, Franklin." Celia tucked the list in her pocket, picked up a basket for the fish, and fled through the scullery door, her feet light and quick up the area steps to the street above.

"Life was grand without you around," she muttered as she clanged the iron paling gate shut at the top of the steps. "Why did you have to come back and make everyone miserable?"

The warm sun on her back banished the misery of the scullery, and Celia skipped down Davies Street toward Berkeley Square. Swinging her basket, she crossed into the center of the square and inhaled the sweet freshness of the tree-filled gardens laid out in its middle. She twitched the right side of her new royal blue shoulder cape over her shoulder, the way she had seen other servants do, to show off her dress of light wool. The cape had been cut down from an old coat of Mrs. Wallace's. The Melton wool felt supple and smooth to the hand, but it was her new slate blue dress with its tall, starched linen collar and folded-back cuffs that enthralled Celia. The skirt swirled around her ankles as she walked and made her feel tall, stylish, and supremely elegant.

She slowed her pace to a saunter in defiance of being told not to dawdle. There were pink and red tulips and blue forget-me-nots to admire in the rectangular flower beds, and all the fine folk out taking the air. She sat down on a bench in the sun to watch a tall, dark-haired woman sweeping along the gravel path toward her. The plum red of the woman's merino dress caught the light as she walked through patches of bright sun and dark shade. Celia's quick eyes admired the detailed black trim of the skirt and the fitted black velvet jacket that emphasized a tiny waist. With a swing of her paneled skirt and a quivering black ostrich plume in her hat, the vision swept by.

Celia had never noticed what people wore before—she had never had the time. What was the point of yearning for pretty things when your day was spent bent over a sink full of pots and pans, or sitting on a narrow wooden bench in a cheerless workroom with windows so high they only let in the light and shut out the world? When you flopped into bed at midnight, too tired to take off your stockings, only to be woken at first light, you certainly didn't dream of violet silk gowns and plum merino walking costumes. But now with nights of untroubled sleep, her afternoons spent playing with Esmé in Green Park, Celia had time to notice what ladies wore. And they wore wonderful things in heavenly colors that made you hungry for more.

*It all started with making this dress*, she thought as she stroked the smooth wool twill of her skirt. She hadn't worn anything so fine in years, not even when her mother made pretty clothes for her.

Esmé had arrived, with the dogs, in her attic room this morning to see her in her new dress.

"Ooh, Celia, you look so pretty," she had cried as Celia adjusted the detachable collar and buttoned the crisp cuffs. "Don't use that mirror—it's too small. Mama is in the morning room with Grandmama, come on." She had tugged Celia down the back stairs to the second floor of the house, throwing open the door to her mother's room and standing Celia before the pier glass. "Look!" She had held up her doll to inspect the new dress. "Anna says you look so much prettier now."

*Is that really me?* The slate blue made her gray eyes darker, almost the same color as the dress, and her freshly washed and braided hair gleamed like spun silver; even her pale skin had brightened: flushed with excitement and pride.

Mrs. Wallace had appeared in the doorway of her room and nodded her approval. She'd picked up the hem of the dress to inspect the needle-work. "Yes, that will do very well, Celia. Your stitches are small and even, and whoever taught you to do French seams, and buttonholes?"

"My mother, ma'am. She was reet handy with a needle." She hadn't said that her mother's skill had kept them housed and fed after her father had died in a carting accident. She couldn't bear to remember his pallid, sweating face frowning in pain, his pale lips pressed together so he wouldn't cry out when the doctor tried to splint his legs. When her father's desperate struggle for life had ended, the doctor had said her da had been injured inside and that it was a mercy that he had gone to God, as he would never have been able to walk again. Celia remembered pain so cruel and sharp, she could hardly breathe when he had died, followed, five years later, by the agony of watching her mother quietly fade away.

She wouldn't think of the heartbreak of those distant days again; she had a new family now. You couldn't find a kinder woman than Mrs. Wallace, and Esmé was like a little sister to her.

"Thank you, ma'am, thank you for this dress," she had said to Mrs. Wallace.

"Don't mention it, Celia. Remember that it is to be worn in the afternoon when you take Esmé for a walk in the park, or when you go out to run errands for Mrs. Kennedy. We will make you some pretty lavender blue dresses for the summer. And from now on you leave the pots and pans and the heavy cleaning to the new daily woman, Mrs. Clark. Your job is to keep the house clean and tidy and prepare our meals; for that you can wear Palmer's cotton morning uniform. I have cut it down to fit you—all you need is to sew it together."

Celia stroked the smooth fabric of her dress and watched another glorious creature swan past in an olive green frogged jacket that emphasized her soft-bosomed front, narrow waist, and provocatively arched back. *It's all about the curves.* Celia admired the pronounced shape of the woman's torso, wishing she had more "up there." *If they don't have much bosom or bottom, and too much waist, the dress is cut to make the best of what they do have. That and those terrifying corsets.* She had seen Mrs.

Wallace's whalebone corset—an iron cage, strong and unforgiving—
lying on her chair when she made the beds in the morning.

The procession of ladies dressed in their elegant outfits thinned to
two nannies with large black perambulators. Celia got to her feet and
made her way to Slade Street to join servants and housewives bustling
along the pavement. She pulled out her list to concentrate on her pur-
chases for the family. Pennies had to be watched, and corners trimmed.

"That's a nice new dress you got there. Proper elegant you look." The
fishmonger was a cocky fellow with a straw boater perched at a jaunty
angle on the side of his perfectly combed head and a full-lipped, very
red mouth. Celia couldn't bring herself to look at him. Instead she gazed
resolutely at the silver of freshly caught fish arranged in perfect overlap-
ping rows on a table of ice. "What can I do for you today, miss?"

Remembering Mrs. Kennedy's demand: "'Ow much is the 'alibut?"
she asked.

"A shilling a pound." He laughed at her recoil of horror. "Cod. That's
what you want. Affordable, tasty. Fourpence a pound and any leftover
you can make fish cakes for breakfast." He slapped the front end of a
codfish on the scales; its flat dull eyes and huge mouth gaped up at her.
She must have looked confused. "You new to this cooking lark, or what?
Bake it, not too long, with chopped onions, parsley, and a lump o'
butter—just the way me ma makes it. Squeeza lemon before you serve
it up with plenty of mash pertaters. They'll love it."

"There's only three o' them, and the weather is warm, so it won't
keep. I'll jus' take a pound off a tha' piece, thank you. And please fillet
an' descale it an' include the head and the bones fur stock in a separate
parcel." *There*, she thought, *I might be new at this, but I am quite capable
of reading Mrs. Beeton's cookery book*. The fishmonger's jaw dropped.
Celia decisively counted coins into his outstretched palm, pulling her
hand back before he could close his fingers over hers. "If I am payin' fur
a piece o' fish, I want all of it, includin' the bones."

The fishmonger put his hands on his hips and grinned. "Tell you
what, I'm picking up some plaice from Billingsgate in the morning. Fresh

as fresh it'll be. And I'll throw in some whelks for your tea. The name's Bert, by the way." Celia nodded. "Fancy coming to the flicks?" She frowned. "The cinema tomorrer night?" He tucked a lemon and a bunch of parsley in her basket. "No charge for them," he said and winked.

She glanced up at him from under the brim of her hat. Black eyes stared impudently back at her as he tossed the coins she had given him in the palm of his big red hand—there were fish scales stuck to his knuckles.

She tried not to shudder at the thought of him trying to put his arm around her in the dark of the cinema. "Thank you, but I don' think I will—g'day."

"READ ME A STORY." Esmé was tired, and it made her imperious.

Celia raised her eyebrows. "I'm sorry, I didn't quite . . ."

"Celia, *please*, will you read me a story?" Esmé wheedled. She nodded, and Esmé hauled a large book off the bookshelf and opened it to her favorite fairy tale and then snuggled NouNou into her arms.

"Rapunzel again?"

"It's my favorite."

"It was mine, too, when I was a little girl. Me mam read it to me, an' it was the fust story I ever read fur mysel'."

"Where is she now, your mam?"

"In heaven, wi' my da." Celia saw her mother propped up against her pillows, her eyes red-rimmed, lips dry and cracked from fever. She closed her eyes to shut out the image.

"My father ran off. I heard Cook telling our housekeeper," said Esmé, stroking NouNou's long silky hair. "He didn't really like us much anyway."

Celia wasn't sure what to say. "Do you miss him?" was all she could come up with.

"No, he was always grumpy in the morning. And if you did something wrong or were noisy, he got cross—like Grandmama. Will you read to me, please?"

Celia smiled as she listened to the clear little voice and decided that she would try to sound less flat and hard. All three of the ladies in the house sounded like silver bells when they spoke.

She opened the book and Esmé rested her head on Celia's shoulder to look at the illustration of Rapunzel leaning out of her tower, a riot of golden curls falling to the ground.

"Don't you love her hair?" Esmé stroked the illustration with the tip of her forefinger. "I want hair like that when I grow up."

Celia tried to enunciate rounded vowels. "Yes, I do. I aw—always used to ask why Rapunzel's hair din't . . . did not get all tangled, with the prince climbin' up and down it all the time."

Esmé laughed. "You sound funny when you talk like that. How did she get the tangles out?"

"My mam said it was with great diffi-culty, and lots o'—of—brushin', so perhaps you will stan' still when we get yours out. Now we will take it in turns to read. But I think"—she stroked back Esmé's dark curls the way her mother had stroked hers—"I think you know this story by heart."

MRS. WALLACE TAPPED her chin with her thimble finger as she circled the dressmaker's dummy. She shook her head and her eyes slid over to Celia and then back to the dress. "My original thought was that the netted violets would come down the front from the waist, catching the overskirt to the taffeta." She frowned. "But then the chiffon doesn't move the way I had planned."

Celia stood back from the dress, her head cocked to one side, and waited for the final verdict. Mrs. Wallace looked tired; her eyes were strained, her shoulders slumped. She massaged her neck with one hand. "I simply don't know about that panel. Is it too . . . stiff for such a soft, floating dress?"

"Symmetrical?" Celia heard herself and instantly wished she had kept her mouth closed.

"What did you say?"

"Nothing, ma'am." She was not here to venture her ignorant opinions.

"No, you said 'symmetrical.' That's it—it is too balanced, too equal." She had already started to slip out the tacking that held the panel in place. "This is a dress that flows like water, or mist at the end of the day. The flowers shouldn't look like they are lining a straight garden path but scattered in the grass along the edge of a woodland the way wildflowers . . ." The rest of her words were obscured by a mouthful of pins, as Celia watched the dress transform before her.

"Pull up the hem of the taffeta and pin it, yes, there. I want it to reveal a glimpse of ankle. The chiffon hem should be four inches above the taffeta so we can see the embroidery. Do you know how to embroider, Celia? No? I'll teach you." Mrs. Wallace's directions were clear, often brisk, but most of the time they worked in silence. A week ago Celia had a job to keep up with her quick, deft movements, but this evening she felt like another pair of Mrs. Wallace's hands.

"There now, what do you think? Bit of an improvement, wouldn't you say?" A swathe of violets rippled from the right side of the waist in a fluid stream to the left seam at the hemline.

Celia reached out and swiveled the dummy slowly back and forth on its one-legged stand. The skirt was a mist of flowers. They flowed with the movement of the chiffon, and from underneath it the taffeta flashed violet and indigo in the gaslight, and then as it turned away from the light: lapis, sapphire, and amethyst. "It's a dream of a dress. A perfect dream."

"A dream of a dress." Mrs. Wallace's voice was low, and she, too, turned the dummy to watch the violet fire. "I think you might be right, Celia. It *is* a dream."

*But when*, Celia asked herself, *when will she ever wear such an exquisite gown?*

THE CLOCK CHIMED in the hallway, four deep bongs. Celia's back ached. In two hours she must be belowstairs to light the kitchen range to make breakfast.

"Help me," was all Mrs. Wallace said as she turned her back. "Unbutton me; I have to see it on." There was a detached quality to her as Celia's fingers, no longer roughened and clumsy from scrubbing floors, flew down her back.

Undressed, Mrs. Wallace was almost perfect. Delicate bones, a diminutive waist, and rounded hips. Nothing like her own straight-up-and-down boyish shape. *She needs a bit o' weight on her*, Celia thought. *It's the worry of those unpaid bills.* They were mounting up. Celia had seen them in neat piles on the bureau: a bill from the solicitor, the coal merchant, a City of Westminster demand for rates and taxes, a polite reminder from the landlord that the rent was due.

"Bodice first: start with the top button." There were twenty-one tiny buttons, each covered with silk. Celia had made every one of them.

"Yes, that's right, leave the last two undone until we have the skirts on." Mrs. Wallace looked over her shoulder as she smoothed down the front of the bodice, tugging at the bottom and pushing her breasts outward to fill the plunge of the neckline with a mere froth of lace for modesty's sake. "Yes, a good fit. Put the skirt on the floor, yes, that's the way."

She was barely breathing as she stepped into the pool of silk at her feet. Together they drew up the taffeta skirt to her waist, and Celia started to hook it to the bodice. "It's a perfect fit in the waist, ma'am . . ." *It should be*, she thought. *We took it in twice, now.*

"The overskirt," Mrs. Wallace directed. Her brows were down as she stared at herself in the mirror. Celia threw a cloud of chiffon over her head. She smoothed and hooked the overskirt under the bodice and buttoned the last two buttons.

"Now, where did we put the belt?"

Celia searched among the pieces of silk on the dining room table and found a midnight blue velvet boned belt, which fastened at the front with an ornate gilt buckle.

"Turn up the gaslight!" Mrs. Wallace ordered. Her face was pale, her eyes fixed on her reflection. "Bring over the lamps from the sideboard and the table." Celia organized the lamps in a circle around Mrs. Wallace and the pier glass. One on the edge of the sideboard, another on the plant stand. She held the third one up as high as she could.

"Ah," she said, as her mistress stepped into the light. The rich bay brown wings of her hair framed a face severe with concentration as she gazed into the mirror at a woman of delicate beauty and elegance.

The skin of her arms, neck, and bosom glowed as lustrous as fresh cream. The deeply plunging neckline emphasized her long, graceful neck and the roundness of her breasts. The cut of the bodice made her waist as narrow as that of a sixteen-year-old. All severity gone, Mrs. Wallace laughed and tilted her head to one side, swaying in waltz time.

"It is absolutely perfect!" she cried. "As light as a summer breeze. And the color, oh my God, Celia, look at the color—it's mesmerizing!"

The lamp in Celia's hand shook with fatigue, the dress shimmered in the quivering light, and the sound of Mrs. Wallace's voice sent a shiver up her spine to prickle in her scalp. "A Dream of Endless Summer," Mrs. Wallace cried. And to her dismay Celia saw there were tears standing in her dark eyes. "Do you think it will sell?"

"Sell?" Surely she had lost her reason. Women did when their husbands ran away and left them, and nothing stood between them and the workhouse. Celia had watched her mother slide away from reason when her father had died in that terrible accident, and grief, poverty, and illness had overwhelmed her.

"Yes, sell! Do you think they'll like it?"

Celia did her best to reassure her mistress. "Oh yes, ma'am, of course they will. It is the most lovely . . . It is all light and shadows and as ethereal as gossamer."

Mrs. Wallace turned, and triumph still shone on her face, but there was curiosity there too. "Celia," she said. "Where did you come by such a vocabulary? 'Ethereal'? 'Gossamer'?"

She had no idea; the words had simply come out of her at the sight of the dress, and then she knew. "The Brothers Grimm," she said. "It is a fairy-tale dress."

———

CELIA COULDN'T BEAR it a moment longer. She had to know. "Ma'am, please may I have a word?" Mrs. Wallace paused from pairing stockings and waved her into her bedroom. "The dress—what did you mean by 'sell' it?" Celia couldn't let herself believe that she would never see it again. She knew which of the violets she had made, and it had been her hands that had basted the lace into the décolletage and helped to appliqué the flat faces of the pansies. In some way it had become her dress too. She must know what would happen to it.

"Didn't I tell you? No, I suppose I didn't. My sister, Mrs. Glyn, has many fashionable friends—they were mine, too, once, when I was first married. She has invited me, and our dress, down to her husband's country house for a party. There will be many women invited for the weekend, most of them are quite well-off, and I am hoping that they like the dress. If they do, perhaps they will commission me to design similar ones for them."

*She is selling the idea of the dress!* This made complete sense to Celia's practical mind. More dresses would rescue them from an impatient landlord and tradesmen who were refusing to make deliveries unless they were paid in cash. She stepped across the tissue paper toward the open dome of the trunk that sat in the middle of the bedroom floor.

"And then?" she asked.

"Then I will design and make dresses for anyone who is rich enough to afford one. And, if I am lucky, there will be enough interest and orders for you to help me." Mrs. Wallace put stockings and underclothes into the trunk. "Everything hangs on the next two days, Celia. If the dress is a success, then it will change our lives."

*Our lives? Oh, please make it my life too!* Celia looked down at the polished tips of her boots peeking out from under the hem of her pretty new dress and prayed. A deep fervent prayer that a Dream of Endless Summer would turn heads, lift pulse rates, and ultimately seduce even the most prudent husband to open up his checkbook and demand that his wife buy a dress like the one Mrs. Wallace was dancing in . . . no matter the cost.

❋

# CHAPTER THREE

*May 1893*

LUCY

Lucy felt strange to be out in society again, without the distraction of her tiny household in Davies Street. There was no need to be anxious or awkward, she told herself; she was here at her brother-in-law's invitation to make her future secure, and that meant she must be relaxed and at ease.

"Ready to come down?" Elinor wafted into the room in a rustle of silk to tuck a sprig of stephanotis blossom into Lucy's hair. "The Wentworths are here, but don't waste too much time on Freda; she always has her dresses made over. Clayton has invited an American business friend—some sort of robber baron, I think. Are robber barons in railroads or do they make their money in something else? I can never quite understand what they mean by the term. Anyway, new money and eager to make an impression." She frowned. "Unfortunately I can't remember the wife's name. Oh, and pay attention to Lizzie Featherstone—she loves to dress. Then there are the Mecklens—you remember them— pots of money and love to spend it; Edith Brand could certainly do with some help with *her* wardrobe. And then there is the prize of the group: Emmeline Lancaster. If anyone is a complete clotheshorse, it's Emmeline. You know them all, I think . . . most of them were down for the shooting the last time you were here."

That had been nearly four years ago. Lucy had almost refused the invitation because James had made a fuss that he needed the carriage and he wasn't going to spend time with a patronizing bastard like Clayton Glyn.

"Sadly, I had counted on Daisy Brooke, particularly since Lady Brooke, the Countess of Warwick, is now Prince Albert's new *favorita*. She goes everywhere with him. Next time perhaps. Once they break into the Marlborough set, those girls never look outside it again."

Her sister drew back from the mirror and looked Lucy over. "You look a little pale; pinch your cheeks." Elinor opened a heavily embroidered purse. "I know James sold all your jewelry . . . so I brought these along." She draped a triple strand of pearls with a diamond clasp around Lucy's neck. "Wear the clasp at the front. Oh yes, that looks wonderful. You've always had such perfect skin . . . Mine gets so dry, I have to use oceans of rose cream. And here—" Elinor held out a gloved hand cupping pearl and diamond earrings, and Lucy's eyes swam in gratitude. "The house is hotter than a Turkish bath—Clayton does so hate cold rooms—so no need to worry about not wearing a fur."

*She's tense*, Lucy thought. *Clayton can't be happy about his newly divorced sister-in-law at one of his splashy country house parties.*

"Do you think they all know . . . about—?"

"Bound to, darling. They can manage to read the newspapers even if they never pick up a book. But they won't care *if* you don't refer to it. It is hardly as if James was popular among our friends."

Lucy stood up and smoothed the front of her bodice, looking for her sister's approval. "Oh, Lucy." Elinor put her arm across her sister's shoulders. "You really outdid yourself. It is sheer perfection. And that color . . . is *you*."

The color was perfect for everyone: delicate redheads who freckled in the sun, luscious brunettes with dark flashing eyes, tender blondes from silver to gold, and everything in between. *That is why I chose it.* Lucy smiled at her reflection in the pier glass. *This dress would look delicious on any woman here tonight.*

"Now, remember what we discussed?"

"Don't say anything about the dress, and don't respond to Clayton if he offers to lend me money?"

Elinor tugged Lucy's elbow in time to her words. "If Clayton offers to lend you money, just smile and be evasive."

Lucy wasn't at all sure that borrowing even a small sum of money was a good idea, but her sister had a strong mind, and now that she had Lucy in her house, she was determined to make things happen.

"*I* will talk to Clayton about money. And, yes, say everything about the dress, but *not* that you made it—that you designed it. Leave everything else to me. Come on now, best foot forward, as Nanny used to say."

IT WAS QUITE clear that Clayton Glyn had not only refurbished his London house but had had a go at his country seat too.

"Good heavens, what have you done to the drawing room?" Lucy had barely glimpsed the newly decorated downstairs of Wardley House on her arrival as she was sped up the stairs to her room by her sister. Elinor loved secrets and conspiracies, hiding away for hours to confide and scandalize. "It is completely different: so light and airy."

"You mean what haven't we done to the drawing room. It's Clayton's work—don't forget to praise his efforts—it cost a packet," Elinor muttered in her ear before lifting her voice. "But the very last thing you can accuse Clayton of is being stingy. He's such a generous man, aren't you, darling?"

Clayton Glyn was barely thirty, but his startling shock of thick white hair gave everyone who met him for the first time pause. He wore it unfashionably long and slightly tousled à la Lord Byron. Elinor claimed that he had blown off all his hair in a science experiment at school and it had grown back completely white. Women adored Clayton: his shoulder-length silver-white hair; his slightly protuberant dark eyes and long lashes; and his soft, sensual mouth had them all behaving in either a flustered or challenging way, depending on their age. Lucy found

Clayton Glyn's rather smothering charm disturbing and had difficulty not laughing outright at his romance-novel name. When he was being particularly attentive he gave her a slithery feeling, as if she were lost in a wood at night and wasn't quite sure what she would meet around the bend in the path.

"My dear Lucy." Clayton's manners were as extravagant as his taste for fine furniture. He picked up her hand and she felt his lips brush its back. "*Ravissante*, as always, *ravissante*." He continued to hold her hand as he stood back to admire her. "And the dress . . . a sensation. But I wouldn't expect anything else." Lucy brushed her hand down the fine fabric of the skirt. There was nothing insincere in Clayton's tone: his gaze held genuine approval. If there was one thing she could rely on, it was his connoisseur's eye, his aesthetic appreciation of true beauty, and his veneration of the rare and costly.

Now it was Lucy's turn to admire, as Clayton, with his head modestly to one side, waited. "You have made the house splendid, Clayton. It has always been a lovely old place, but my goodness!" She turned slowly to take in every detail. Gone was the character that only centuries of family living could give a house. The oak wainscoting had been ripped out to be replaced by pale gold damask wall coverings. The jewel colors of Persian carpets, the dazzle of electrified chandeliers, and the hushed luxury of soft furnishings were almost overwhelming. Wardley House had been a tired but gracious Queen Anne country house surrounded by a generous park when it had come to Clayton Glyn. Its transformation had resulted in unashamed aesthetic luxury. To her delight Lucy had discovered that there was a bathroom attached to her room, and she had spent a heavenly hour up to her neck in a tubful of hot water that had come gushing out of the mouths of two shining silver dolphins, but she found all this new lush grandeur oppressive.

"I knew *you* would appreciate it." Clayton smiled his gratification. "It seemed to take forever—I thought they would never be done! We are celebrating the season with a ball . . . Nothing but hard work, of course, but you must come. You will, won't you? Now, let me see, you know everyone, of course, even if James never let you spend time with us!" A quick sideways glance, a slight lift of his upper lip at overbearing husbands, as he drew her toward the crowd at the other end of the room. "Poor silly fool, what on earth was he thinking? I give him six weeks with that pantomime dancer!"

"He's had more than that already!" Lucy said, and Clayton tossed back a silver lock and laughed as he drew her arm through his and slowed their pace to a lazy stroll down the length of the room. Lucy allowed herself to be drawn into a bit of Glyn pageantry. She almost expected her host to bow to the left and right as if he were attending his own *levée*. How he loved to take center stage!

While smiling graciously at his admiring guests, Clayton said, "Ivor and I were saying earlier what a fool James was," as they approached a tall man with bowed shoulders and a hooked nose. "Weren't we, Ivor?"

"A complete fool." Sir Ivor Wentworth smiled at Lucy. "My dear. How delightful! You are looking remarkably well. Please tell us that you will be staying in town for the season?"

Lucy did not say that she had never left it, that her Davies Street house was her only home now that she was the head of her family. Sir Ivor was a perfect choice to be landed on and she nodded her thanks to Clayton as he swanned off to greet arriving guests.

Sir Ivor reminded her of a dilapidated bird, with his untidy black feathery hair and beaky nose, but he was a good-natured man, immensely well-connected, and loved to chatter with attractive women. Nevertheless, there was a look in his eye that Lucy hadn't seen before when she had been James's wife. His glance lingered a little too long and with far too much concentration on her bosom. *The dress is working its charm!* Lucy smiled to herself as she answered him, "I will be in town all this summer, Sir Ivor."

His eyebrows rose and he stroked his full lower lip. "Then how very pleasant the season will be, my dear. You must come to dinner when we open up the house. Now, where on earth is that fella with the champagne?" He signaled to a footman and drew Lucy farther into the group of chatterers.

"Lucy Wallace will be in town for the season too, Freda. I was just saying how jolly to have her to dinner!" Heads turned and inclined in greeting. Speculative feminine eyes swept up and down Lucy's dress, and after the slightest hesitation there were cries of welcome and delight.

"How well you look—dear Lucy—how positively radiant!" Gregoire Mecklen, always so consciously Continental, bowed.

Eileen Mecklen, too short for her colossal diamond tiara and overwhelmed by a heavily bustled dress the color of mustard flowers, was at Lucy's side in a flash. If Sir Ivor thought her jolly, then so did she. "It has simply been too long, Lucy. Are you in town at present?"

Lucy thought of the last months in not-quite-fashionable Davies Street, living on stodgy dishes prepared by Celia, of lighting a fire only in the drawing room and being frugal with the gaslight. Unlike the country in winter, at least London was lively, the parks full of beautifully dressed women swathed in their furs as they took the air, and the thrill of spotting an electric brougham cluttering up a busy crossroads when it broke down.

*Thank God I'll never have to spend a winter in the country again*, she thought as she saw in her mind's eye the rain pouring steadily down on the sodden fields surrounding her husband's neglected country estate, where he now lived. Surely this crowd of old friends knew that she, her mother, and Esmé had not been near James's house for more than a year? Longlawn Hall had been horrifyingly damp in the winter and midgey in the summer. Once a place of prosperity and pride, it was now shelter to a man who soaked up third-rate brandy and sternly corrected Gilda Lavvy's faulty grammar. She had heard from her lawyer that James intended to lease Longlawn and move to the French Riviera.

"We have been in London all winter, Freda. My mother has been poorly, and it is far too chilly for her at Longlawn," she said, accepting a glass of champagne.

"Then I must come and call on you. We will be in town next Thursday!"

Bright, curious female eyes rested briefly on her face and then traveled downward. Lucy moved farther into the light and lifted her glass of champagne. When she had everyone's attention, she turned ever so slightly to the left and then back to the right, her glass lifted in greeting. A Dream of Endless Summer shot violet fire. "How lovely to see you all again; it has been far too long." She laughed, banishing any thought they might have that she was an abandoned wife without a penny to her name.

She caught her sister's eye across the room. *Thank you*, she telegraphed. *Everything is going to be all right; I'm back in the fold.*

DINNER WAS SERVED in a dining room that was unrecognizable from the comfortable understated baronial hall of yesteryear. Its walls had been redone in gleaming emerald silk and crowned with a molded ceiling with gilded cornices and a painted central medallion. Pinky white cherubs, linked together by ribbons of cerulean that covered their private parts and wound around their plump bottoms and thighs, romped among gold-edged clouds. Lucy glanced upward throughout six exquisite courses to imprint on her mind's eye the exact shade of summer blue of the ribbons.

"No, not that peach." Clayton had seated her next to him. "It's not quite ripe. May I?" He selected another from the silver epergne. Holding it inches away from his nose, he shook his head and picked up another. "This one is ready—you can tell by its scent." He deftly cut the peach away from the pit with his knife and sharp-tined fork, putting it piece by piece onto her plate. "Did I ever tell you that I sat at this very table, all through a night last September, to wait for a pear to reach perfection? No?" He laughed. "Eccentric, I know, but there is nothing more disappointing than an overripe pear and nothing more tasteless and woody than an unripe one. At twenty minutes past four in the morning I knew it was ready: the scent was sublime—it completely filled the room."

Clayton had a reputation as a character, a wealthy dilettante who went to a great deal of trouble to please his expensive appetites. Lucy speared a piece of peach and put it into her mouth. It was the crowning glory of a remarkably good meal. She had eaten everything that had been put in front of her, from the Orkney oysters to the truffle-stuffed squab. She put another piece in her mouth and straightened her back, her eyes staring ahead of her, as her brother-in-law's hand slid up over her knee and came to rest on her inner thigh.

"Delightful little kneecaps—like seashells," he murmured as he reached toward the fruit epergne, his hand still caressing, his moist eyes glowing in the candlelight.

Lucy froze, repressing the impulse to slash downward with her fork. *So, this is what happens when you are a divorced woman,* she told herself. *A woman who needs to borrow money from her brother-in-law.* She would rather scrub floors than borrow a penny from this insinuating little viper.

*And Esmé?* she asked herself as his grip tightened. *Would you borrow money to keep Esmé from becoming a ward of the court? Taken in by Aunt Hester to be bullied and patronized and made to feel obliged?* Lucy realized she was standing on the cusp of her future. If she politely ignored Clayton's creeping hand, she would be doomed to countless insults perpetrated by every crawling toad. The hand on her thigh tightened in a quick, powerful squeeze. She turned her head and looked straight into Clayton's bulging eyes. "Clayton," she said through barely moving lips. "Your hand is sweating through the silk." A flicker in those shallow depths was the only sign of life. She smiled as if in response to a witticism and held up her fruit fork, its sharp tines glinting in the candlelight. "*Now,* Clayton, otherwise I will puncture it." The hand slipped away as if it had never been there. Clayton's polite smile froze on his face, the pupils of his eyes constricted to two black pinpoints.

Lucy could feel her legs shaking. She turned to talk to Sir Ivor on her left, praying that the interest she thought she had seen earlier that evening did not manifest itself on her left thigh.

"Sir Ivor, am I right in saying that you hunt with the Quorn and not the Pytchley?" she asked.

———

THEY HAD BEEN dismissed from the dining room, leaving the men to their after-dinner rituals. Lucy looked around at the group of expensively dressed women whose clothes did nothing for them and who had congregated in the center of a drawing room that was as hot as a furnace. Freda Wentworth sat down at the piano, begging Eileen Mecklen to sing.

In spite of the overpowering heat, Lucy's hands and feet were ice-cold. She could still feel Clayton's hand on her. Had she really threatened him with her fork? A pulse of anxiety and fear beat in her throat. Supposing Clayton tried to get into her room tonight? She shivered with fear as she remembered James's late-night arrivals in their bedroom when she was asleep and he was drunk. She would put a chair under the handle of her bedroom door tonight even if there was a key to lock it with. What woman could possibly trust that the master of this house didn't have his own passkey to his guests' rooms? *Pull yourself together,* she told herself. She must put Clayton Glyn out of her mind; her future depended entirely on the dress and which of her old friends would place an order with her. With the sweat beading on her forehead, Lucy stood by the flickering fire and waited to see who would come to her first. Would it be Edith, Emmeline, or Lizzie?

"Are you at home on Tuesday afternoon, Lucy? Lizzie and I would love to drop by so we can talk about dresses. Your sister told us that when you were a little girl your dolls' clothes were the envy of all your playmates! And that you might even consider . . . designing something for close friends." Emmeline Lancaster rustled to her side the moment Alice began to sing, with Lizzie a close second.

*Don't ruin it now,* Lucy instructed herself as she lifted her chin in defiance of Clayton's dinner-table assault. *You have worked too hard to be angry now.* She nodded, remembering those carefree nursery days. "They certainly were! I collected scraps of lace, silk, ribbons, and beads . . . and goodness knows what else to make ball gowns for my dolls! I suppose, in a way, it was those dresses that inspired the one I am wearing tonight."

A genuine gasp of admiration from Lizzie. "And then you turn the design over to a dressmaker. How extraordinarily clever you are, Lucy. The detail is exquisite." Emmeline stood back to feast her eyes on hopefully affordable features, and Lizzie's eyes gleamed with the treasure she had discovered tonight. Behind the sparkle, Lucy imagined that she was totting up the cost of Lucy's design and a London seamstress, rather than flogging over to Paris to patiently wait for Doucet or Worth to grant her a consultation. Her mental arithmetic over, Lizzie lifted Lucy's hand to show off the bouffant sleeves. "No scraps of lace and silk here, Lucy. These sleeves are so charmingly original, and so . . . feminine." She turned to include their friends. "Aren't the colors sensational?"

A chorus of love for the colors, the lace, the décolletage. Lucy thought of the hours she and Celia had labored over the gown. "I can't imagine how I would spend my day, if I weren't thinking of one dress or another." She lowered her voice and transferred her gaze to the medallion of the Persian rug at their feet. "But as you know, now I have my little girl to support. So my designs are no longer something I do to while away the evening hours!"

"Do you mean"—Emmeline, never one to mince words, could be trusted to come straight to the point, saving Lucy any further explanation—"that you have actually become a couturiere? How wonderful! Do you have an atelier?" Emmeline had most of her clothes made by the top couturiers in Paris, so she was aware of the vocabulary used by the great fashion houses.

Lucy hesitated. She would not lie, or pretend she had become a successful fashion designer, or even intended to be. "Oh good heavens, I hardly dare think of it that way. You make it sound so professional, and my mother would certainly not approve. I simply love to design beautiful clothes. I call them my dresses of emotion." She turned to welcome

the American woman who had been sitting at the top of the table. They
had not been introduced, but she had not taken her eyes off Lucy all
evening.

Now she came forward in a rustle of orange silk and gold fringe.
"Dresses of emotion? What a lovely description. And this . . ." Her frank
and open smile of appreciation was a relief after the interrogation of
"old" friends trying to be tactful. "Is this one of your creations? Why, it
is simply the most beautiful gown I have ever seen in my life!"

"Thank you. I think of it as a Dream of Endless Summer. I am so
pleased you like it."

She smiled at her sister as Elinor joined them.

"Like it? My dear Mrs. Wallace, I could hardly breathe when I saw
you being taken in to dinner. Your sister told me that it was you who
created her wedding dress. I call that charming. My name is Martha
Guttenberg, so very pleased to meet you. My husband, Harris Guttenberg, and I are here for the London season. We are from Pittsburgh: a
little town in Pennsylvania. Do you happen to have a card, and may I
call on you?"

This was the American couple Elinor had told her about—Harris
Guttenberg had made his massive fortune in rolling stock. Lucy had
heard him gently bragging to Edith Brand that there wasn't a locomo-
tive, railroad car, coach, or wagon that moved from east to west that had
not been made in his factory in Pittsburgh. *He must be worth an absolute
fortune.* Lucy could hardly breathe. And Mrs. Harris Guttenberg's dress,
while its deep orange tone did not flatter her pretty skin, was certainly
this year's model and made with the finest silk.

Lucy gazed into the earnest face in front of her. *She should wear clear
colors with that delicate fair skin*, she thought. Her mind went back to
the cerulean blue ribbons painted across the dining room ceiling. The
clean, fresh colors of the old Italian masters when they had adorned
Rome and Siena with their vibrant frescoes would complement the soft
gray of her eyes and the fading blond of her lightly graying hair. She was
a handsome woman, no doubt lovely in her youth. Lucy tried not to

sound as breathless as Mrs. Guttenberg as she said, "I am at home on Thursday afternoons, Mrs. Guttenberg—23 Davies Street near Berkeley Square. I do hope you will come to tea!"

Elinor cut her away from the group as soon as she could.

"Such a success, and who would have thought that my sister could be so skilled a saleswoman."

"I was rather hoping that the dress would speak for itself." Lucy found she could not look her sister in the eye. She shuddered at the thought that Clayton's foolish lechery might cause a rift between her and Elinor. She steered her sister farther away from the group. "I have been thinking things over, Elinor. I don't want to sound too optimistic. But if all our friends come to me for just one dress, I think it will solve my immediate financial problems. It is so generous of you to offer me a loan, so incredibly kind of Clayton. But unless I am on the brink of catastrophe, I would rather not borrow any money at all." She crossed the fingers of both her hands. If these admiring women were merely being polite, she would be unable to pay the rent and put food on the table. If they came to her, she would be teetering on the brink of becoming a dressmaker.

She found the courage to look into her sister's clear green eyes. Elinor's brow was furrowed. She was silent for a moment or two, and then she nodded, slowly, as if she was agreeing with something that had not been said. "Of course, Lucy. I completely understand. There is no need to explain." And in that moment Lucy realized that Elinor knew. She knew that her husband had used his generosity as an opportunity.

Lucy was not the first and would probably not be the last woman Clayton made his sly advances to. She slipped her arm through Elinor's and leaned forward to kiss her cheek. "Helping me the way you have is more than enough. If you send me your friends to dress, that is all you need do for me, and I will never be able to repay such kindness."

"Oh yes, you will! Imagine how many dresses you are going to make for me!"

## Chapter Four

*November 1894*

Celia

"The fog is so thick you could cut slices with a knife. It will take a gale to clear that lot." Celia came into the drawing room, her eyes smarting from an acrid November pea-souper.

Fog had shrouded the city in a blanket of perspiring damp the night before. In the muffled silence only those who truly needed to be out groped their way along the pavements. Even Mrs. Kennedy's distant sneezes were muted. She was suffering from her first cold of the season, confined to her bed, fretfully demanding bowls of hot water with eucalyptus oil to clear her head.

"A moment please, Celia." Mrs. Wallace held up her hand as she counted. "Forty-two pounds ten shillings and sixpence and thirty-six pounds eleven shillings is . . . seventy-eight, no, seventy-nine pounds—oh, bother!"

"I think you will find it comes to seventy-nine pounds one and sixpence, ma'am. I made malted milk to help you sleep." *If you can tear yourself away from your account books.* Celia put a glass down on the side table next to Mrs. Wallace's desk. She waited as her mistress wrote her total before she offered the advice she had come to give—a bit of north-country straight talk was what was needed when it came to Mrs. W. and money matters. "It might be easier if you charged in guineas, ma'am. Round everything up to twenty-one shillings instead of all those pounds, shillings, and pence."

Mrs. Wallace rubbed her forehead in irritation. "No, it would make it harder, Celia. I would have to do a sum for pounds and another for shillings . . . and then . . . all that adding."

Celia looked over Mrs. Wallace's shoulder at a column of scratched-out numbers; not one total was accurate. "Guineas sound so much more elegant than pounds. I spend one pound on groceries for a week. You create a vision in silver silk and lace that is worth ten guineas."

Mrs. Wallace sipped her malted milk in silence. Celia decided this was an indication she would welcome more information.

"I have looked over the cost of making the different types of dresses you design and come up with a price list. It covers everything from hats to tea gowns."

Mrs. Wallace blinked up at her. "A price list?"

Celia knew that she had proved herself useful months ago when they had made a Dream of Endless Summer together and its cousins had gone out into the world in a variety of colors and styles. Now that she was no longer confined to domestic duties, she had become Mrs. Wallace's right hand. But not all her talents had been exploited. She hesitated.

"Please go on, Celia."

"Our new seamstresses are fast workers, but it's the detail and the trim—the feathers, the lace, the silk ribbons—that drive up the cost of each piece and add hours to the labor. So, I have made a basic list and then we can add specific items. If we cost out each dress in stages—how many yards of silk, the fabric for the underskirt, the bodice—then add the various trims, the hours of work that went into it, we will be better able to estimate the final costs for each garment we make. Presently, I think you might be undercharging your friends." Mrs. Kennedy had forbidden the words "customers" or "clients" to be used in what she considered her daughter's shameful new occupation. She insisted that

Lucy give her friends guidance: teach them discernment in selecting their immense wardrobes.

Silence. The face looking up at her was neutral, as if Mrs. Wallace hadn't heard a word Celia had uttered. But this apparent inertia was deceptive. Mrs. W. had a way of appearing passive when her mind was at its most agile.

"In other words, I think we could make more out of each gown." Celia put five pages of detailed lists into her employer's hand. "This is just a start, of course . . ."

Mrs. Wallace took a sip from her glass and looked through the pages and coughed. Whether it was at the exorbitant price she was expected to charge for a hat or because her hot milk had gone down the wrong way, Celia couldn't be sure. But some explanation was evidently needed. She waded in, choosing her words as carefully as her honest nature would allow. "For example, the ball gown you made for Mrs. Guttenberg cost fifteen pounds and ten shillings in materials, which included some beautiful Brussels lace and hours of labor. We let her have it for twenty-pounds four shillings and tuppence. I think she would have been just as delighted if we had charged her thirty guineas."

Mrs. W. raised startled eyes from the pages in her lap. "But I priced out the materials and the workmanship myself."

*Which left us a very meagre profit. How she hates to talk about money.* Celia nodded in agreement. "But the House of Paquin charges more and their gowns are not as well made, or as original, ma'am. And I am sure you have noticed that the line of the skirt and bodice of a Dream of Endless Summer is now appearing all over London." A pause. "You are being *copied*, ma'am. A dress you designed over a year ago is now being made by some of London's top dressmakers. So it is not only your clients who are delighted, but the dress itself has set a style that is clearly popular."

"How on earth do you know?"

Celia cleared her throat. "Lady Featherstone's maid came to pick up her last order. She said that her ladyship went to Paquin because we were so busy with Miss Webster's wardrobe, and she was scandalized about how much a tea gown costs over there. They turned her gown out very quickly, charged her fifteen guineas, and the workmanship was shoddy. Her maid said it won't last the season!"

"Fifteen guineas for a tea gown? We charge half of that!" Her boss's head came up, the look of shock on her face so palpable that Celia wondered if she had gone too far again. Mrs. Kennedy would have put her in her place in an instant for being so outspoken.

"Yes, ma'am. Doris's embroidered panels for Miss Whitfield's tea gown took hours of work, and the underskirt is French silk. I know we have a lot of business, almost more than we can handle, but I do think we are undercharging."

Mrs. Wallace finished her milk and sat back in her chair, her feet up on a footstool, her head thrown back, and her eyes closed. The last two weeks had been a hectic rush to complete the orders on their books, and Mrs. Wallace had put in as many hours as her employees.

"Celia," she said at last. "We have to be twice as good, twice as original, but, most of all, twice as affordable as anyone else in the city."

"But why, ma'am?"

"Because Reville and Rossiter are court dressmakers headed up by William Reville—he does the designing; Miss Rossiter merely oversees the workrooms. The rest of them—Kate Reilly, Elspeth Phelps, Helen Metcalfe—are all very good at what they do, which is making dresses. They buy models from Worth, Poiret, and Doucet in Paris and then copy them. Do you see the difference, Celia?"

She didn't but she knew she would be enlightened.

Mrs. Wallace counted on her fingers: "*William* Reville, *Charles Frederick* Worth, *Paul* Poiret, and *Jacques* Doucet. See a pattern? Yes, that's right, every single one of them is a man. In haute couture houses men do the designing—they are the artists. Their models are then turned over to be made by women. I want to be known as a designer, not a dressmaker. I want people to come to me because my gowns are innovative, original, and exciting—not copies of the big fashion houses in

Paris! But"—she held up her forefinger—"no one outside of my circle of friends has any idea who I am—not yet anyway. My dresses may be copied by provincial dressmakers, but no one utters my name alongside the House of Worth, which is why I must not charge haute couture prices."

"The House of Paquin, the one that opened in London, is run by a Frenchwoman who is the designer. Miss Vionnet."

Mrs. W. shook her head. "Yes, a designer called Vionnet working at the House of Paquin: an employee, not an owner. And what did you tell me about Lady Featherstone's tea gown? Cost a fortune and will fall to bits. Miss Vionnet will not be here beyond a year, but I will. Because I am not going to rush people for a few extra pounds on the way to establishing a respected institution."

*Well, there is a point in there somewhere,* Celia thought. *What it comes down to is confidence.* "You are already a designer, ma'am. You were from the time you were a little girl dressing your dolls. Now you have to become a successful one. And nothing spells 'not top drawer' like affordable prices."

A long, patient sigh. The damp air outside had seeped into the room through the gaps in the window frames and under the doors.

Mrs. W. put aside her inaccurate ledgers. "I was wondering about approaching *The Queen* magazine; perhaps they might consider featuring one of my gowns in their spring edition." She was clearly not in the mood to talk about her finances. Celia's revolutionary idea for making real money must be left for the while and taken up again later. *She knows how to economize, to go without, but she is timid about asking her clients to pay more for dresses they are overjoyed with.* It was a puzzling attitude from a woman who worked to attain such exquisite perfection. But there it was: to people like Mrs. Wallace, talk of making a profit was a squeamish business; it was what people in trade did. She could hear Mrs. Kennedy remonstrating, "No more talk of money, Lewcy. We are not a family of shopkeepers."

Celia didn't have such scruples. Her ambition was to help her mistress become one of the most renowned designers in London. *But we won't get anywhere at all if she keeps dressing her friends at less-than-reasonable prices*, she thought. *To her it's "art"; to me it's doing more than getting by.*

But even in Celia's deeply pragmatic north-country soul she had to admit that never in her short hard life had she dreamed she would jump out of bed every day eager to get to work. She made appointments to consult with Mrs. Wallace, or afternoon tea as Mrs. Kennedy insisted on calling client consultations; she stood at Mrs. Wallace's elbow to record measurements as they were made in each client's notebook; and she organized fittings. She even helped to supervise the workload of their seamstresses and had learned different sewing techniques from each of them.

Ivy from Hackney was a quiet woman who had come to them one day with a little bag of exquisitely made lawn blouses. "I heard about Mrs. Wallace from my sister who is a personal maid to Mrs. Asquith, and I have come on the off chance that there might be an opening."

An affronted Mrs. Kennedy had said, "Be off with you—I've never heard such rubbish," and Celia had had to run up the street to bring Ivy back, where she had been hired on the spot by Mrs. Wallace. Ivy had taught Celia how to make perfect French tucks and seams for fine lawn blouses—and the undeniably tricky skill of fagoting lawn and lace together with delicate embroidery.

Then there was Little Mary, who arrived every morning at six o'clock on the dot and was a close friend of Ivy's—and the reason why she was hired for her own particular skill. If Celia had wondered how small bosoms and lean hips could be made to emulate the curves of an hourglass, the answer was padding. Little Mary showed her how to pad the shoulders of walking costumes and round out boyish hips and flat chests with buckram. She was particularly skilled in "inflating" the sheer bouffant sleeves of ball gowns and dinner dresses with light flexible frames made of feather bone.

An advertisement in *The Lady* had brought them Annie. Upright, square shouldered, and brusque to the point of being curt, Annie was a tailor. Bent over the cutting table until her back ached, Celia spent hours every morning practicing the art of cutting cloth on the bias under Annie's capable tutelage and weeks learning how to embroider the finest feather stitch.

And effervescent, bespectacled Doris was their embroidery queen, whose fine stitches were the envy of Davies Street.

If Celia had craved the closeness and companionship of a family in her workhouse days, she had one now. It was sheer delight to sit down with the other girls to work together to complete a dress that would transform the homeliest of women into an elegant woman of fashion. The companionable gossip, the gentle teasing as the women gathered together every day to work, was like having four older sisters—and a little sister: Esmé would sit at their feet, piecing together scraps of silk and wrestling the protesting NouNou into "such a pretty little cap for bedtime. No, Nou, stop wriggling. You'll love it when it's on."

But more exciting than dressmaking was the discovery that she had developed a head for figures, and she yearned to take over Mrs. W.'s account books.

She gazed down at her boss on this dull, foggy afternoon and heard herself say, "I could help you with the books. I've always been good at sums."

Mrs. Wallace continued to stare at her ledgers with distaste.

*Bigmouth*, Celia scolded herself. *Why don't you come out and say she's done a botched job?*

Her boss picked up her pencil and then laid it back down. "Celia, why don't you sit down here and tell me how you would make this side of things more efficient. You have come up with some really good suggestions: hiring our page, Robbie, was a fabulous idea. He gives us such an air of professional hospitality when he greets our guests, serves tea, and then delivers the finished clothes to their houses. You are more than welcome to take over the bookkeeping side, but what were you saying about how to make a little more money? Will you show me?"

Celia pulled up a chair and planted herself down. *Go easy, now—don't terrify the poor creature.* "If you take the sum from this column as the amount of money it costs to make the dresses, which includes the materials you use, the rent, and the girls' salaries, you can subtract from the total from this column, which is the amount you charge. And this figure shows you exactly how much money you make in a month. Do you see?"

The head next to hers nodded. "Yes, I was trying to do that, but my arithmetic is very weak. We are not doing too badly at all, are we?"

"Right now we are working to full capacity. If we raised our prices— just a little bit—say, by ten percent, we could hire a part-time girl, which would give you more time to prepare for the spring collection—a larger collection."

Mrs. Wallace's eyes flicked sideways to look at her in surprise. "More time to prepare—that would be very pleasant." She subsided into silence, her face contemplative, her hands folded quietly in her lap. Someone in the street called out a greeting and was answered by the cook from next door. Minutes ticked by. "*If* we increased our present prices by ten percent, how much more do you think we would make?"

Celia was ready for her. "After all our expenses I think we would make close to seven hundred a month—in the season."

Her mistress sat up straight. "Without making more gowns?"

"We can't take in any more work unless we employ at least four more girls, and we can't do that because this house is bursting at the seams already. Crammed in like biscuits in a tin we are upstairs. And then there is the problem of how many clients have to wait around because we don't have enough fitting rooms. The other day, Mrs. Wentworth must have drunk four pots of tea while she waited to be fitted. And Lady Featherstone only went to Paquin because we were overloaded."

It had been a shocking few minutes for her, but her boss seemed to be taking things in her stride.

Celia produced a newspaper folded into quarters from the pocket of her apron. Without saying anything she handed it over, pointing to two lines in the margin of the column headed RESIDENCES FOR LEASE.

"What have we here?" Mrs. Wallace read. "Aha!" She glanced up at

Celia. " 'Superior gentleman's residence in Old Burlington Street, London W1. Comprises light and sunny south-facing drawing room and salon on ground floor. Second-floor morning room, dining room. Four bedrooms. Large belowstairs servants' hall. Servants' quarters top floor. All amenities: gaslight, cellarage included. Five hundred and twenty guineas per annum. Minimum one-year lease. Inquiries to Mr. George Smart, etc.' "

She watched Mrs. Wallace quickly fold up the page. "It is more than twice the cost of our rent here," she said.

"And more than double the size, ma'am, at a much more fashionable address."

"I worry about the end of the season, Celia. When the Americans go home. They pay promptly and order larger wardrobes than my friends."

Celia understood the very real fear of having no orders. How quickly the fad could change: next year a modiste or glove maker would recommend a new and exciting dressmaker. London was full of them, competing frantically for top clients.

She pulled her appointment diary out of her pocket. Perhaps the next fortnight's activity might give Mrs. Wallace more confidence in her up-and-coming popularity and the need to charge more realistic prices.

"Yes, the London season ends in August, but not for everyone. Mrs. Guttenberg's good friend Miss Louise Whitfield has an appointment on Tuesday. She is staying with friends in Mayfair and needs an extensive wardrobe, as they will be going down to Gloucestershire as guests of Lady Rawdon Berkeley for Christmas and the Berkeley Hunt ball. I understand from Mrs. Guttenberg that Miss Whitfield is a very shy and retiring woman who is intimidated at the idea of going to that snooty Madeleine Vionnet, who behaves as if she is Jeanne Paquin herself."

Mrs. Wallace nodded. "Yes, Mrs. Guttenberg told me that she is the fiancée of the very rich steel baron, Mr. Carnegie, and feels like a fish out of water in fashionable London society. I think dressing her will be quite a business; she was wearing an ill-fitting muddy brown walking costume when I met her—I wondered if perhaps she was one of those Quakers—and you are quite right; she wants a complete wardrobe."

Mrs. Wallace pushed back her chair and got to her feet. "Have everyone waiting in the wings. I'll have a much better idea of what it is she needs after our first consultation. Then I think that perhaps you and I had better put our heads together over our prices." She closed her account book and handed it over, together with Celia's lists. "Perhaps we are indeed undercharging, Celia. I know you are far more adept at arithmetic than I am. I never had any real education for that sort of thing." She paused. "And perhaps you would take Esmé under your wing again—a couple of lessons a week? Her new governess is talented in every area except mathematics. Why, I wonder, do we think that women don't need to develop that side of their education as thoroughly as learning conversational French, writing a clear hand, and playing the piano?"

Celia had to look away to regain her composure. She made a vow in that moment that she would do everything in her power to help this creative, intelligent, and artistic woman free herself of the minutiae of running a company so she could concentrate entirely on designing her captivating gowns. *If we are to succeed, then we must lure in the fashionably rich in high society, and no one courts clients like Mrs. W. She has to be free to design for women who go everywhere in London; then she will never have to think about buying advertising in* The Lady *or* The Queen.

Did she dare take it a little further? "What about this place in Old Burlington Street, ma'am? Would you like me to write to the landlord and ask him for an appointment to view?"

The worried frown was back, and the caution. "Let's see where we are in December, Celia. I don't want to rush in and end up over our heads."

*November 1894*

LUCY

Doris, Ivy, Little Mary, Annie, and Celia sat in a circle around the dining room table, surrounded by rich silks and the finest challis and worsted wool. It was dark outside the dining room windows, but the gas lamps were turned up and their bright light fell on the soft sage greens, rich Holbein blues, and deep wine reds of the fabric they worked on.

It was ten o'clock at night and Lucy could see how tired the women were, shoulders slumped forward, eyes close to their work. All chatter and gossip had stopped two hours ago, but their needles flew, steel bright in the lamplight.

Ivy lifted fabric to her mouth and bit off the thread, but Lucy wouldn't dream of asking her to use scissors. "This one is nearly done. I need to trim the sleeves with burgundy net." Ivy lowered the soft wool into her lap and rotated her shoulders, glancing across at Celia hemming rich blue silk velvet. "That color would make any woman look beautiful— even a giant like that Miss Whitfield."

Celia continued hemming. "She is not a 'giant' at all. She is Junoesque."

Ivy laughed. "Twice your height at least!"

"Mary, I need those panels for Miss Whitfield's dinner dress," was all Lucy had said in the past hour. She looked across the room at her daughter curled up asleep under the dining room table with NouNou and Minou in her arms.

"Esmé looks like one of the babes in the wood," she said. Celia got up from her chair and, bending down, tried to gather the little girl into her arms. "Come on now, sleepyhead, it's time for bed. You can't possibly sleep here all night. Yes, yes, NouNou is coming too."

Esmé lifted a tousled head. "Mama said she would read me a story." Her eyes were barely open.

Lucy didn't look up from the rose silk tea gown she was working on. "I'll read you a story tomorrow morning after breakfast."

"You said a *bedtime* story, not a breakfast one."

"A bedtime story at nine o'clock in the morning will have to do. Now please go upstairs and let Celia pop you into your nice warm bed." Lucy lifted her head. "But come and give me a good-night kiss first!"

Lucy gathered Esmé to her and rubbed her cheek against her daughter's glossy hair. "Softer than silk," she said and kissed her round cheeks.

"What are you calling this one?" Esmé asked, lightly stroking the soft sheen of the satin.

"Miss Whitfield doesn't like fancy names." Celia tried to turn Esmé toward the door, but she remained obdurate.

"What name, Mama? You don't have to tell Miss Whitfield."

Lucy laughed and, taking an embroidered panel from Doris, she quickly tacked it into place. Miss Whitfield was a tall, broad-shouldered woman with a kind plain face. But she emanated good nature and had been particularly sweet with Esmé and showed her appreciation to everyone at Davies Street, from Robbie, the little page boy, to the indifferent Mrs. Kennedy—until the old lady had learned the size of the American's planned wardrobe.

"This tea gown, fit for a princess of extraordinary goodness, is called Serenity." Lucy glanced over to the heap of gleaming velvet on Celia's chair. "What do you think, Celia? What name would you give the blue velvet?"

Celia took Esmé by the hand and tugged her toward the door. "That one, I think Stubborn Determination would suit."

"No, Celia, she meant the dress, not me! I think you should call it Bright Eyes. Miss Whitfield's eyes sparkle when you show her pretty things!"

"OH, MY GOODNESS gracious me. Why, it's the most beautiful thing I have ever worn." Miss Whitfield stood rooted to the spot in front of the pier glass. Lucy had pulled the heavy curtains back to the walls, and winter sunlight came through the window. "It is the same color as the stained-glass window at St. George's Church in Gramercy Park, where I grew up." She looked down at Esmé. "I used to stare at the robe of the Madonna right through the pastor's very long sermons—a naughty thing to do. I am sure you listen to your sermons very carefully."

"Yes, but they are always very long," Esmé said.

Miss Whitfield turned to Lucy. "My dear Mrs. Wallace, I have never felt so pampered, so looked after, in my life, and that is before I even put on one of your glorious gowns. Now I don't feel quite so terrified of meeting all those lords and ladies in their grand houses. But thank you for listening to me and not making me look too daring in the . . . my front."

*A pity*, thought Lucy, because her large firm breasts were easily one of Miss Whitfield's most attractive physical qualities. *Just wait until you see yourself in your wine red tea gown*, she thought. *That will show off your embonpoint to perfection.*

The fitting continued with visiting costumes, dinner gowns, and walking outfits. Lucy's mother, who had come into the room, could hardly contain herself. Her attitude had changed toward the tall American woman the moment she had had a surreptitious peak at the bookkeeping ledger: "Breathtaking . . . quite superb . . . oh yes, that color is perfect on you, Miss Whitfield," she gushed. But it was the Holbein blue velvet dinner gown that had brought everyone to silence.

Louise Whitfield surveyed herself in the mirror. "The color is exquisite, and the embroidery so fine and so very feminine. But I am such a galumph." She cast another despairing glance in the looking glass.

"No, no, not at all; you have a wonderful outline. But I've noticed," Lucy said, "that tall women tend to take longer steps when they walk—simply because of course they can. I think if you were to shorten your stride—like so—it would make a huge difference." She took a few steps forward and turned, encouraging Miss Whitfield. "Yes, yes—even shorter. You see what I mean? Let's try it again. Not so fast; walk very slowly. There now!"

Miss Whitfield crossed and recrossed the room. "It sometimes helps to count!" Mrs. Kennedy advised. "Allow yourself fifteen steps—and turn." Miss Whitfield obediently spun on her heel like a woman who feared she was being followed by a hungry wolf.

"Let's see, how best to describe?" Lucy took two steps and turned. "Rather than halt . . . try drifting to a stop. Yes, a complete stop, that's right. Keep your feet together and now pivot on your right foot, turning your hips and shoulders together—that way the hem of your skirt will flare a little—so graceful. Let's try it."

Slender Lucy's gliding steps made her look as if she were being pushed forward on silent wheels. She came to a stop and, lifting her skirts to show her feet, pivoted on her right foot to make her turn fluid and graceful rather than the abrupt maneuver Miss Whitfield managed. She floated back again across the room to her client.

"Of course it takes practice, but imagine that there is a book balanced on your head. Yes, that's right, Miss Whitfield, exactly! Keep your chin up, look straight ahead, and glide. Not difficult at all when you know how, is it? Well done." She clapped her hands. "My poor daughter has to practice every day. Go on, Esmé, show us how perfectly you glide these days—thanks to Grandmama."

Esmé walked around the room with her head erect; she stopped and curtsied to her grandmother, then to Celia, before floating to a stop in front of Louise Whitfield. She curtsied and said, "*Enchanté*, Mademoiselle Whitfield."

Miss Whitfield was *enchanté* with her lesson, her ability to glide to a halt and sit down slowly with a straight back instead of bending in the middle and sticking out her bottom. Within days she could effortlessly rise from her chair to float around the drawing room that she almost managed to contain the shock of seeing her décolleté in all its splendor when she tried on her wine red tea gown. "Good grief," she said as a sunbeam lit up her cleavage. "I think perhaps a little more lace . . . here?"

"Not at all." Mrs. Kennedy had not missed a single fitting. "This is a dress to wear when you drink tea with Lady Rawdon Berkeley and her friends in the privacy of her sitting room. At five o'clock we relax, drink tea, and enjoy the freedom from stays. And your figure is so firm and so feminine that it would be wicked to cover it with layers of lace."

Lucy had difficulty not catching Celia's eye. If she did, it would be a disaster. Mrs. Kennedy had harrumphed at the top of the stairs every time she heard Louise Whitfield's clear American voice, but the moment Lucy had informed her mother that their American client had insisted on paying her bill for ten different outfits on their penultimate fitting, Mrs. Kennedy, dressed in her most elegant afternoon dress, had greeted Louise Whitfield herself and had insisted on pouring her tea with her own graceful, lavender-scented hands.

When every dress and gown was ready and packed in its pasteboard box, the entire atelier said how much they would miss their American client. They exclaimed over every outfit and assembled in the hall to bid her a tearful farewell. Miss Whitfield inclined her perfectly coiffed head, adorned with a saucy little hat and its flat black velvet bow—Lucy did not approve of plundering the natural world for bird feathers. "Good-bye, dear Mrs. Wallace, and Mrs. Kennedy." Tears shone in her eyes. "Esmé, what a wonderful instructor you are, my dear, in the discipline of deportment. And, dear Celia, thank you, thank you so much!"

Louise Whitfield's final bill came to four hundred and eighty-nine guineas—an astonishing sum. Lucy had never imagined that when she had sold her first gown for eight pounds six shillings and sevenpence that just over a year later she would be in possession of such a vast amount of money from just one client.

"How we will miss dear Miss Whitfield," said Mrs. Kennedy when she had closed the front door. "If only all our American clients were as gracious. Come on, my dear, it's time for tea!"

"But they are gracious, Mama, every single one of them." And to Celia under her breath: "It is time to write to Mr. Smart to make an appointment to view Burlington Street. If it is suitable, I suggest we move our premises after the New Year, when we return from my sister's New Year's Eve ball."

# CHAPTER FIVE

*December 1894*

LUCY

Lucy and Esmé were blown in through the front door by a blustery autumn wind, with rosy cheeks and streaming eyes. Their new parlormaid, Townsend, pushed the front door closed and the three of them burst out laughing.

Lucy undid the buttons of her coat at the neck. "Will you look at us? What wrecks we are! Esmé lost her hat, and just look at my hair . . ." Wisps of it had escaped from under her hat and had plastered themselves in wet strands across her face.

"We were blown right up the steps to the front door like leaves!" Esmé was clutching her sodden toy boat with a bedraggled canvas sail in hands that were still showing traces of pond mud.

Townsend nodded, but her manner was inattentive and her deep blue eyes shadowed with concern.

"What is it? Has something happened?" Lucy felt her heart skip. "Townsend? Is everything all right?"

"Yes, ma'am. Miss Franklin asked to see you as soon as you came home. I think it is something important."

"Is it something terrible?" Esmé was convinced that Townsend, with her exquisite raven's-wing hair and azure blue eyes, was really Snow

White taking refuge as their parlormaid at Davies Street from her wicked stepmother.

There was an urgency in the maid's tone, and Lucy noticed that she had changed into a formal black dress and that her apron and cap were freshly laundered to a crispness that was rare on a common or garden weekday.

"Then tell Miss Franklin that I will see her now; please bring tea into the drawing room."

The maid hesitated, as if tea was not something Mrs. Wallace should be thinking about in the face of Celia's news.

"Esmé, will you please go upstairs to Nanny Edwards, take off those muddy shoes, and wash your face and hands. I will ring for you when tea is ready." As Esmé started up the stairs, she ran into Celia coming down.

*Something is brewing*, thought Lucy as she saw her assistant's flushed cheeks and bright eyes. Celia had schooled herself to be what she imagined was a model of decorum when clients came to call. Her face was composed, her carriage upright, and even if there was an emergency, such as there obviously was now, she walked slowly and with dignity.

She arrived in the hall and stared gravely at her disheveled boss. "I have good news, ma'am. We received a telephone message from the Countess of Warwick." She corrected herself. "Lady Brooke, the Countess of Warwick, has made an appointment to see you this afternoon at half past five. In fact, she should be here at any moment. She wants to consult with you about a dress." There was no trace of the Northumbrian in Celia's low-pitched, well-modulated voice, and unlike Townsend, who was vibrating with nerves at the thought of opening the door to a real countess, Celia was as cool as a glass of water.

"Coming here?" Lucy heard Celia's careful enunciation, and her own voice wobbled. "Good heavens, do I have time to change? Look at me! My hem is muddy—my hair's a fright." She struggled to regain calm, to be dignified. "Esmé must stay upstairs with Mrs. Kennedy. We will offer Lady Brooke tea in the drawing room. I see you are ready for any eventuality." Celia had a tape measure around her neck and a fresh notebook to record their new client's statistics in her hand. "Now, Esmé, on no account must you tell Grandmama who is visiting today. It is your job to tell her I have a consultation and that I must not be disturbed." The thought of her mother's effusive greeting to the leading light of the Marlborough House set—who had attained the coveted position of *la favorita* with the Prince of Wales—made her heart slam against her ribs in panic.

"Now, I will run and change, and let's hope that the countess will be a few minutes late, as they always are." She was halfway up the stairs when something made her stop. "Perhaps I am getting ahead of myself. Did the countess say anything else?"

Celia beamed reassurance. "All she said was a dress she ordered had arrived and it would not do. And something about a presentation at court."

"Court? On my goodness, court!" And without another word Lucy sped on up the stairs into her room.

"Lady Brooke, the Countess of Warwick," Townsend announced, her head bent as she made a shaky curtsy.

The creature that came through the door was clearly used to being called riveting. She swept into the room and stopped in a swirl of silk and fur, a perfect example to the American Miss Whitfield, had she been there, of grace, dash, and poise. Lucy in turn floated forward to drop a curtsy of welcome. Everyone who had met Daisy Brooke described her as either tantalizing or so overbearing that her manner bordered on arrogant. As Lucy took in the shining vision that was Daisy Brooke, all she could think was that she wanted to dress her.

The Countess of Warwick's rose-gold hair was piled high on her head, with shining tendrils clinging to her pearl white forehead. Two large blue-gray eyes gazed at Lucy as if the countess was trying to ascertain if she was Mrs. Wallace or if it was the smaller fair-haired young woman standing beside her. She stopped and looked from Lucy to Celia and back to Lucy; then she laughed and threw out a hand to her. "You are undoubtedly Mrs. Wallace. Unmistakable style and such elegance. You must have guessed why I am here?" She didn't wait for a reply but ran on. "Your gowns are the most thrillingly elegant, the most femininely alluring creations I have ever seen." She drifted into the middle of a room that seemed to have shrunk in size. "How many times have I admired a beautiful dinner gown or a walking costume, to be told it was the creation of Mrs. Wallace?"

Lucy started to respond, but the countess rushed on. "I saw your lovely sister the other day at the Cassells' for dinner." She shook her red-gold curls and closed her eyes at the vulgarity of Ernest Cassel—financial adviser, wealthy banker, and dear friend to the Prince of Wales. "Elinor was wearing the loveliest gown. She told me that it was you who had designed it. So of course, when this horrifying catastrophe occurred—" She turned to a stout woman with a round face who had followed her into the drawing room and was now standing sentinel by the door. "Vickers, show Mrs. Wallace the dress . . . I don't think you will believe it when you see it, my dear Mrs. Wallace. The color is vile. I aged ten years when I put it on."

A footman carrying a large dark green pasteboard box that advertised that its contents had come from the venerable House of Worth, rue de la Paix, Paris, was waved into the room by Vickers. The box was set down on a low table, the lid removed, and out of a heap of tissue paper Vickers lifted a flame-colored satin evening gown.

Lucy's eyes widened: it was the most vivid shade of magnificent scarlet imaginable, and the last color in the world that would suit the countess or should be worn at a court presentation. She took the dress from Vickers and held it up against the countess's rich bronze hair and pink-and-white complexion. The hair and gown shouted at each other for a brief second. Lucy nodded. "A vibrant color, but not—"

The countess launched into speech again. "*Absolutely* not. And look at the sleeves. Anyone would think I was trying to hide sagging upper arms or thick wrists." She lifted a rustling balloon of satin and let it drop again. "The presentation . . ." She sank down onto the edge of a chair and gazed up at Lucy. "A week away . . . Can you imagine what I am to do?" She didn't pause for a reply. "I have to be perfect; otherwise I will not be forgiven.

"His Royal Highness the Prince of Wales always stands in for Her

Majesty for court presentations, and he is very particular about the right dress for an occasion like this, and I can't bear to be dressed like every other woman. Such a dilemma." Her tone became wheedling. "I am hoping that you will rescue me." She waved a hand to conjure the right words. "Elegant, feminine, a color that will flatter." She dropped her eyes briefly and laughed at her faultless perfection. "My coloring"—her carmine lips parted in a smile showing even teeth—"is difficult, I know. But what do *you* think, Mrs. Wallace?"

Lucy paused to make sure that the torrent of information had come to a halt. Her practiced eye had noted the countess's greatest attributes—ones that had undoubtedly captured the prince's eye. Lady Brooke had ideal proportions: the sort of figure that dressmakers hungered to design gowns for. Not to mention the tender complexion that had never seen the summer sun and the glory of gleaming, abundant hair. Lucy saw a hundred shades of blue that would enhance Daisy Brooke's natural coloring and prayed that she didn't have her heart set on pink.

*Lillie Langtry has nothing on this woman.* She remembered the last beauty the Prince of Wales had been besotted with for eleven years—another woman she ached to dress. Her eyes made a further inventory of the countess's lovely bosom, still heaving with the exertion of describing her predicament, and saw it swathed in the palest of blues: lace the color of ice water supported by a boned satin bodice of cobalt watered silk. Her clothes should be fragile, delicate. The bodice and the waistline should cling to that voluptuous figure. A palette of azure blues and silver embroidery. Lady Brooke should shimmer but never glitter.

Lucy pulled herself together. "Yes, of course we must do something that will bring out your glorious coloring, Countess. I can only imagine that someone"—she wondered if it was Charles Frederick Worth who had designed this catastrophe; the old man was well over sixty—"has mistaken you for a brunette with dark eyes and a rich complexion." Before her prospective client could rush in, she continued. "A palette of blues from Prussian to sapphire would suit you superbly. But, please, let's make ourselves comfortable. Will you take tea? I would like to find out more about what you would enjoy wearing. Do you have time to talk now?"

*Talk*, she thought. *It will be difficult to stop her.* Daisy Brooke was called the Babbling Brooke in society—after some scandal or other. Lucy reminded herself to ask Elinor about that particular part of the countess's life. It was important to understand one's client's character as well as her physical attributes. But all she really needed to know now was that Lady Brooke had influence—abundant influence—as the reigning queen of the smart set that surrounded Prince Albert, the heir to the British throne. She entertained lavishly for him, went to immense trouble to amuse a man who hated to be bored. And most important, Daisy Brooke was invited *everywhere* the prince went. And now she was going to be formally presented to him at court and had no new gown for the occasion. No wonder the poor woman's bosom was heaving. Lucy tried not to lick her lips.

"I was hoping you would be free this evening." The countess waved to her footman. "Take this awful thing away, Henry, and, Vickers, find yourself a chair—over there. Yes, Mrs. Wallace, tea would be delightful. And who is this young woman?" She turned to Celia, who had retreated to a corner and was waiting to be of assistance.

"This is my assistant, Miss F-Franklin, Countess." She saw Celia smile as she stumbled over her rarely used last name. "If you decide that we shall make your gown for the presentation, then Miss Franklin will record your measurements so we can organize a first fitting. Ah, tea," she said thankfully as Townsend, her face crimson with anxiety, maneuvered the tray through the door.

Lady Brooke seated herself and took a proffered cup of tea. A delicate sip and she was off again. "Elinor told me that you designed her wedding dress." She smiled her pearly smile and took a more substantial mouthful from her cup. Her shoulders relaxed against the back of her chair. "Ah yes, that's better. I can tell just by walking into your charming drawing room that you have the sort of eye for style and line that I do, Mrs. Wallace. No clutter, no tables crowded with hundreds of little things collecting dust. A sense of space, of stylish comfort without stiff formality. Delightful!" Daisy Brooke's eyes came to rest on Lucy's face as if she had discovered something rare and wholly irresistible in a shop. "How long have you been a couturiere, Mrs. Wallace?" The blue-gray eyes sharpened as she looked at Lucy over the rim of her cup.

"Since I was a little girl, I made gowns for my dolls. Nothing gives me greater pleasure than to dress beautiful women. Color is one of the most superb things about being alive, don't you agree?"

The countess sat forward a little in her chair. "I *love* to dress. There simply aren't enough changes in the day for me." Lucy admired Lady Brooke's evening gown; the silver was perfect for her. Perhaps too much lace at her décolleté—and far too much trim around a bust so splendid that it needed nothing to enhance its imposing magnificence—but that was the Worth brothers: Gaston-Lucien and Jean-Philippe, who had taken over the business from their father only recently and who simply loved to load on the feathers and the fuss. But the lines were good, the shimmering silver silk and black velvet perfect for her complexion. It was thoroughly clear to Lucy that Lady Brooke had exceptional taste.

They sipped their tea and talked, or rather Lady Brooke talked, of her children, the trials of continually organizing social events, and the hard work it was to be fashionable, sophisticated, and never, ever to wear the same dress twice to a grand occasion. "And now that Lord Brooke has inherited, there is the business of doing something to that great pile of stone we have to live in when we go to Warwick. Ancient and so romantic, perched on a bend in the river. But bitterly cold in the winter: chills you to the marrow just to walk into the place."

While the countess described Warwick Castle and all its impractical attractions and discomforts, Lucy was thinking of the fabrics she would choose, the range of hues, the trimmings, and the lace that she had put by for the ideal client, a client with connections to the tightly closed-off world of privilege and wealth that every designer and dressmaker in London would give anything for an entrée into.

*And here she is—sitting in my drawing room!* Lucy took slow, even breaths. *This is my chance to go forward and upward—what a gift!* she thought as she gazed at the woman in front of her.

She looked over at Celia, sitting up straight in her corner. *She is thinking the same thing!* Lucy smiled to herself. *But being the prudent, practical girl she is, she is also thinking that this is a woman who does not tolerate being disappointed—if her disgust with poor Charles Frederick Worth is anything to go by.* Celia's hopeful expression tightened to stern gravity. *Yes, Celia, you are right: woe betide me if I disappoint.* Lucy squared her shoulders for business.

"Countess," she said when Lady Brooke drew breath. "Shall we talk about details? I would love to dress you in a palette of blues. Sapphire for the bodice, a deeper cobalt blue for the underskirt, with soft drapes of steel blue chiffon panniers embroidered with silver thread." She nodded to Celia, who was already on her way out of the room. "Since we only have a week, we might have to cheat and use chiffon that has already been embroidered. But we will add some interesting touches to make it completely unique—a dress for your personality. A gown that expresses the emotion of a woman of originality and beauty."

"Not pink? I had thought perhaps a wonderful burnt rose pink, in velvet."

Lucy couldn't quite imagine why anyone would want to burn a rose, and she resolved to tread carefully. "But of course if you would prefer, we can do pink. I just thought how certain shades of blue would emphasize your coloring. I believe I have the ideal silk taffeta that will not only match the color of your eyes but emphasize their deep allure."

There was no hesitation. "Blue, yes, blue! How thrilling."

"I am thinking that the bodice should have a low décolletage edged in little velvet flowers—over a lace chemisette, of course." She traced the line of its plunge in the air. "The skirt will be one shade deeper than the bodice, and do you see a short or full train?"

The countess's expression became wistful; her eyes gazed into the distance. *She can see herself sweeping up to the throne, sinking into a deep court curtsy that she will hold, without a quiver from her fine strong legs.*

"Hm, yes." The countess drifted back to the present. "I will be wearing sapphires and diamonds. So, I think a long train. It is a very *formal* occasion."

Lucy rose to her feet. "Let me show you what I see. Such a delicious slate of blues," she said as Celia appeared through the door carrying bolts of bright silks in her arms. She draped them across the table and onto the floor next to Lady Brooke, in puddles of gleaming iridescence.

"When you use a range of hues of a color, it is not immediately apparent to the eye that they are different, but they have the effect of making the entire ensemble shimmer." Lucy pulled swathes of silk into a loose knot in her hand and held them up to the countess's face as Celia slid a pier glass to her side. "Perhaps this sapphire watered silk for the bodice—it will be boned to emphasize your tiny waist and lift the bosom—embroidered with daisies in silver thread. Do you see the effect this shade has on your eyes? The result will be electrifying. We must do something very special for the sleeves—off the shoulder in cut layers that flutter a little, again the embroidered daisies perhaps with dark silver bead centers. And then this glorious deep ocean blue for the underskirt, with this steel embroidered chiffon floating . . . but I really love the idea of soft panniers—so that we catch glimpses of the underskirt as you walk." Lucy let the silks fall back on the table and then arranged them in layers. "Do you see how they play against each other? There is a subtle difference between the colors that will look, from a distance, as if the dress is simply dancing with light and shade. What do you think?"

The countess stared at the silk spilling out of her lap. "I had never thought of using a range of one color before. Yes, it does look like it is moving, doesn't it?"

"I am so glad you approve. Will you leave it with me for a few days? We can arrange a first fitting in linen to make sure we have everything right, and I can show you the lace I want to use for the chemisette, and the dark silver beads."

The countess got to her feet. "Yes, absolutely yes. I have to say, I don't think I have ever enjoyed planning a dress as much as I have this afternoon. Really, Worth is getting past it, isn't it, now that the old man has retired? And Doucet? Quite old hat now, poor chap." She got to her feet, as did her maid. Two brilliant eyes fixed themselves firmly on Lucy's face. "But will you have it *completely* finished by next Tuesday? I do so hate to be anxious before a grand occasion."

*If I have to sit up every night for a week.* "Completely ready, Countess. We will have a first fitting this Thursday with a final fitting on Monday afternoon for any minor alterations that we think necessary." She extended her hand toward the door and the dining room. "Will you come through so we can measure?"

# CHAPTER SIX

*January 1895*

LUCY

Mrs. Kennedy's forehead puckered; her lips clamped tight in a pencil-thin line. "This is ridiculous, Lucy. Utterly ridiculous—I doubt very much if the trains are even running in this weather." They stood in the hall, surrounded by two suitcases, a dome trunk, hatboxes, and countless little bags and packages that belonged to Lucy's mama, and gazed out the window at a gray winter sky. As if to prove Mrs. Kennedy's point, three delicate snowflakes drifted past the window.

Lucy knew better than to contradict her mother on something as important to her as the winter weather.

"Two minutes out there—and my throat is already sore—it will be downhill for the rest of the winter. How can you be so terribly inconsiderate?" Mrs. Kennedy sniffed her outrage.

Lucy smiled away her mother's penchant for chest colds and said nothing. Mrs. Kennedy was a robust old lady despite her vagaries and addiction to spirits of ammonia.

"We should think twice about a journey to Elinor in this terrible weather. Though I do so hate to disappoint her."

Despite her mounting irritation, Lucy's face remained impassive. It was entirely typical of her mother that she should raise objections to going to the Glyns' in Essex minutes before they were due to leave.

"But Esmé does so love to spend time with her cousins, poor little thing. So hard to be an only child."

Lucy nodded in complete understanding. "If you would rather stay—all the servants will be here. So . . ."

Her mother began the business of relenting: "Are our costumes packed? We can't be the only ones turning up for dinner in our ordinary evening wear."

"They most certainly are, Mama. How lovely you will look in your powdered wig." She looked at her watch. They had twenty minutes before their train departed. "Come on now, let me tie that scarf up around your neck."

She helped her mother into her coat, found her hat, gloves, and muff, and opened the door as a hansom cab drew up to the pavement. "Liverpool Street Station, please, cabbie. Hardly the blizzard we thought it was, Mama. Look, the snow is only two inches deep. Esmé, stop playing and get into the cab, please." Esmé threw a snowball at Celia running up the area steps to see them off.

"You will take care of NouNou, won't you, Celia? Let her sleep in your room in her basket, otherwise she will be lonely and cry all night long." The old Pekingese was smuggled into Esmé's room every night to sleep in her bed. "And remember to take Minou out after breakfast, otherwise . . ." She nodded to acknowledge puddles on the floor.

Celia helped her up into the cab. "They will both sleep in bed with me and we'll be as warm as toasted crumpets."

Mrs. Kennedy took the opportunity to admonish. "Don't blame me if you get fleas."

Esmé turned an outraged face toward her grandmother, and Lucy hastily closed the door. "Happy New Year, Celia!" she called as the cabbie clucked to his horse and they set off down the street.

"Happy New Year, Celia, and give my love to Nou and Min." Esmé hung out of the cab window waving both hands.

Mrs. Kennedy pulled her fur collar close around her ears. "Esmé dear, please close the window, the wind cuts like charity."

CRIES OF DELIGHT and exclamations of pleasure greeted the gilt brace-
lets engraved with *Auld Lang Syne Wardley House 1895* gleaming at each
lady's place at dinner on New Year's Eve.

"Oh, Clayton." Lizzie Featherstone congratulated her host—
everyone knew that Elinor spent very little time on domestic details.
"How charming."

Mrs. Kennedy stood, entranced, at the top of the table. A garland of
white hothouse roses and chrysanthemums entwined with ivy wove its
way down the length of the table, bright with silver and crystal, inviting
twenty guests to feast on eight sumptuous courses.

Mrs. Kennedy had unfolded like a flower in the luxurious warmth
of Wardley House, the meticulous attention of perfectly trained servants, and the smiles of their welcoming host. She had giggled like a girl
when, dressed for dinner, they assembled in Elinor's room to admire
their eighteenth-century finery.

"I didn't make the skirts as wide as they wore them then." Lucy's
mantua silk gown was the color of pale jade. "But I do love these fan-
shaped skirts. And so light because of the hoops. Elinor, you have to
walk sideways around the furniture. Oops!"

Mrs. Kennedy, in silver brocade, managed her wide skirts perfectly.
"How I wish these graceful dresses were still in fashion. Life was so
beautiful then—so full of courtesy and charm." She sighed for a gracious age long gone. "So much bustle and rushing about nowadays—
and everything is so frightfully expensive, and no one seems to know
their place in society any longer."

Elinor rolled her eyes. "It was a wonderfully charming time all right,
Mama: children hanged for stealing a loaf of bread, streets full of pick-
pockets and cutpurses, and prostitution rampant. I am all in favor of
reform myself."

"Elinor—what an awful thing to say. Criminals should be treated
harshly—they know the law!"

Elinor pursued her theme on Georgian brutality. "We mustn't forget slavery. People selling themselves into bondage for a new life in the Americas . . ."

"Elinor, you are confused, you are talking about Tudor England."

Her youngest daughter laughed. "Oh, no, I am not, Mama. King George III—mad as a loon—was on the throne when they started deporting men, women, and children to penal colonies for the slightest thing."

"Elinor—how you exaggerate." Nothing could detract from their mother's enjoyment of the New Year festivities. She had flirted decorously with Sir Ivor, beamed approval and delight at her son-in-law for his lavish hospitality, and even taken a stately turn around the ballroom floor for a slow waltz with him.

"Clayton was made for the eighteenth century," she had proclaimed more than once. "He doesn't even have to wear a wig." She had smiled up at her son-in-law, flawlessly attired in more embroidery and lace than any other man present.

Clayton had rushed to agree. "My dear Mrs. Kennedy, it is a sad day for England when silk breeches are only required at court."

"AH, CLAYTON, SUCH an accomplished man. Lucy, did you know that he is going to tear out the old rose garden to create a vista? You didn't tell me that you were going to rejuvenate the gardens this spring, Elinor!"

Lucy had spent the past three days keeping out of Clayton's way. Careful to wedge a chair back under the handle of her bedroom door every night, and selfishly grateful that there were younger and prettier women for Clayton to clutch under the tablecloth.

Elinor picked up the silk and velvet cushions that the children had heaped in a corner as a fort and tossed them back onto sofas and chairs. "I can't imagine why he told you that, Mama. We are still trying to pay the bills for our new ballroom!"

"And such an elegant room—heated! So luxurious."

*We have stayed one day too long.* Lucy put the book she was trying to read to one side. *These two are impossible after the first flush of being together wears off.* "I am desperate for fresh air and exercise." She got to her feet. "Come on, let's take the children to the lake to skate. Yes, Mama, you can come too. Don't forget your fur muff, but there is a brazier lit each day at the edge of the lake to keep you warm."

Her mother was on her feet. "Clayton thinks of everything!"

"Yes, doesn't he."

"HAVE YOU HAD your gamekeeper test the ice thoroughly, Elinor? I think it is very irresponsible of you to take your sister and the children skating if there is the slightest danger." Mrs. Kennedy, holding on to Esmé for balance on the perfectly swept path, peered mistrustfully at the lake.

"Clayton skated yesterday. It has been frozen for weeks, Mama. Of course it is completely safe." Elinor's voice was abrupt, causing hurt feelings.

"If you don't want me to come and watch you skate, then by all means say so, Elinor."

"Mama, of course we want you to come." Elinor had lost her patience with her mother more than once this morning.

Esmé, catching the sharpness in her aunt's tone, wriggled free of her grandmother's restraining hand and raced down the path to join her cousins. "Margot, Juliet—wait for me." She sat down on the bench with them as their nanny laced up their skates.

Lucy could hear their voices, shrill with excitement, and marveled at how agile they were as they took to the ice. "Perfect balance!" She smiled but couldn't help calling out, "Slowly now, Esmé—wait for little Margot!"

"Daisy Brooke is over the moon about the dress you did for her, Lucy. She hasn't stopped talking about it to everyone! With her as your patroness, I think we can say that you have arrived!" Elinor linked arms.

Lucy's natural caution had prevented her from being too carried away by the countess's effusive note the day after her presentation. "Natural beauties are so easy to—"

"It should have been a success," Mrs. Kennedy rushed in. "I don't think Lucy had one single night's sleep until it was finished. Oh, Elinor, do call the children back—they are too far out in the middle." Shrill cries of excitement came from the lake as Nanny and three little dots circled in the center of the lake holding hands.

"I am just grateful Lady Brooke was satisfied. Oof, how we worked." Lucy laughed remembering the long hours she had spent with her sewing women, listening to their gossip, their stories about their families. "Around the clock. But she looked simply lovely in it—and she is very well connected."

After her falling-out with Elinor, Mrs. Kennedy was in a fretful mood and found nothing about Lady Brooke's gown to be happy about. "And it would have been even more of a success if she had actually paid for it. The silk: yards and yards of the stuff. I hate to think how much it cost us." Mrs. Kennedy waved her muff in the air. "The finest trimmings, not to mention the lace! Nothing but the best. And of course the seamstresses had to be paid—even if Lady Brooke didn't offer up one penny in payment. If we are going to be a family of tradespeople, it would be nice to make some money!"

"Mother!" Lucy had given up on explaining that Lady Brooke's dress was an investment in her future.

"And yet"—Elinor narrowed her eyes at her mother—"every single one of the Prince of Wales's set talked about how magnificent Lady Brooke looked at her presentation. A presentation, Mama, that included some of the best-dressed women in London. All of whom will no doubt wonder why they have not heard of Lucy Wallace before now."

Mrs. Kennedy drew herself up to her full height, her eyes shining with outrage. "You are missing the point entirely, Elinor. If Lady Brooke did not pay for her dress, how many more spendthrift clients will be attracted to Lucy? I wonder. She worked her fingers to the bone for a woman who probably never pays her bills. The aristocracy never do."

"Dear God, give me strength!" Elinor shouted so loudly that her mother jumped and the little skaters stopped their ice races and looked up at them.

"Elinor! There is no need to scream like a . . . like a fishwife! You are married to a very rich man—poor Lucy here has no one and nothing. She needs every penny she can squeeze." Somehow amid the layers of scarves and shawls wrapped around her, Mrs. Kennedy found her coat pocket and dabbed at the end of her cold-reddened nose with her handkerchief.

Elinor stared down at the ground breathing like a bull. If she had pawed at the frozen earth, Lucy would not have been surprised. With a long inward breath to either roar or calm herself, Elinor lifted her head. "I apologize for losing my temper, Mama. So terribly rude of me, but Lady Brooke will bring Lucy wealthy and influential clients. You simply don't know what you are talking about."

"I am going back to the house to my room. I will stay there for dinner and breakfast—until we leave tomorrow." Mrs. Kennedy turned on her heel and marched solidly up the path toward the house.

"Best to leave her . . ." Lucy said. "She will be down for tea—it is her favorite meal." Elinor linked arms with Lucy and marched down to the lake. "Darling, I don't know how you can put up with it day after day—sometimes I could strangle her!"

"She gets fidgety if her routine is interrupted or she is worried. Most of time she is quite kind."

They walked on in silence until they reached the lake's edge and sat down on the bench to put on their skates.

"Why is she so angry with you, Elinor?" Lucy asked. "She wasn't that upset when she wheedled the information out of poor Celia that Lady Brooke hadn't paid her bill."

Elinor bent down to lace her skates, her voice muffled in her scarf. "She is angry at Clayton, not Daisy Brooke. And since she adores him, she is taking it out on me." She tightly tied the knot of her skate laces with an emphatic tug. "She pokes and pries into our business, finds something she doesn't like, and gets terribly upset. The worst of it is that, as usual, she is absolutely right when she alludes to people not paying their bills. Clayton is floundering at the moment. It won't take much for him to lose his financial footing. Honestly, darling, I can't believe how much money he squanders. He doesn't seem to understand that there is a bottom to the well." Elinor stood up in her skates. "Come on, I need exercise. Too much rich food, too much champagne." She giggled. "And far too many lectures from Mama."

A low sun gleamed on the pewter surface of a lake ringed with fir and the silver filigree of naked beach trees glittering with frost. *Evergreen*, Lucy thought as she stepped onto the ice. *Dark, almost blackgreen; gray and silver, bound with the purest white. What an exquisite combination: perfect for blondes and redheads.* Her sister flashed past her, and she set off after her. They were both laughing as they reached the end of the lake and skated in a circle to slow down.

"Please, don't think you won that one," said Lucy. "You cheated by taking off before I was ready."

Her sister draped her arm across her shoulders as she caught her breath, her green eyes shining with health and good humor. "Heavens! Far too many French sauces. Come on, we need to work off all those ridiculous dishes Clayton's chef made us eat."

They completed another circuit of the lake, their voices echoing across the ice.

"Stay away from the reedy end; the ice is thin there," Elinor called as Lucy shot past her. "If you fall through it, I'll have to look after Mother for the rest of her long and complaining life."

Lucy turned to skate back to her. "Is it really that bad, El? I mean about Clayton."

"It's worse than bad, darling. Clayton lost a lot of his money in the financial panic. Most of it has to do with the agricultural depression here in England, and in America too. And then last year he invested in American railroads, and they hit a trough . . . so we are in pretty bad shape. But I'm afraid that Clayton doesn't look to the future: he lives very much for the moment. I don't suppose I am much better." She saw the anxiety in Lucy's face and reached out to smooth her hair back off her face. "Don't worry, darling. We will recover—we always do! Come on—there are the girls—I can't believe how tall Esmé has grown. Let's race over to them." And she was off before Lucy could ask her to forgive her mother for her outspoken observations on people who didn't let little things like money stand in the way of getting what they wanted.

Lucy organized their tour of the Old Burlington Street house to show it to its best advantage. Mrs. Kennedy walked behind her in silence until they reached the hall. "It is a beautiful house, isn't it, Mama? Do you see how it would work for us? The business would be on the ground floor, and we would live on the second and third floors, with the maids and workrooms in the attic." Lucy tried not to mind that she was speaking to a back rigid with disapproval.

*I love this house! I love it!* How heavenly it would be not to have to juggle their space: clients arriving for appointments; finding a place to store their materials; their seamstresses' work area; and private fitting rooms. Lucy wondered how she could feel so carefree, so ready to expand and fill her horizon with Lucy Wallace creations, when her mother was such a damp squib.

"Well, it is certainly large. However much is it costing?"

She couldn't see her mother's expression under her hat, but Lucy knew she was trying too hard to convince her that this house with its graceful staircase ascending to three generous floors above its ground floor was a gem—and an affordable one thanks to Celia's dogged negotiations with the owner.

Mrs. Kennedy sighed, a long drawn-out exhalation in memory of gracious and genteel days long gone. "What it amounts to, Lucy, is that you are opening a *shop*. Advising old friends, from our house, on their wardrobe is one thing, to help us live in reasonable comfort. But you are now proposing to go into *trade*, with your name advertising as much on the front door. Blazoned there"—she swallowed and whispered her shame—"for any Tom, Dick, or Harry to see—in brass! My dear, don't you see? You will be treated like a shopgirl. None of your friends will invite you to their houses." And to Lucy's dismay she lifted a handkerchief to her eyes and wept silent dignified tears. "What happens if you fail?" Mrs. Kennedy gave up on dignity and sobbed her fear into damp lace and lawn. "What happens if your friends find someone else, someone new and exciting, and you cannot pay your rent? What will we do?" She leaned against the mahogany newel-post for support; clearly her daughters gave her none.

"Mama, please. Don't cry. It will be all right. Everything will be all right. You mustn't worry." Lucy put her arms around her mother's slight shoulders and rocked her the way she did when Esmé had bad dreams and sat up in bed crying out to be rescued.

Her mother turned away, dabbing with her handkerchief. "I wish we could just be a family again." Her shoulders shook. "It is wrong that you should have to work for a living. Absolutely wrong. Gentlewomen don't open shops and put their names on their front door, and they don't sue their husbands for divorce. I don't understand what has happened to us."

Lucy produced her own, more solid handkerchief and wiped her mother's eyes. "Ladies do all of those things now, Mama. Our world has changed . . . is changing. Women are demanding their right to vote, and many live independently from their husbands if they can afford to, and sometimes even divorce them. I have more money in the bank now, more than poor James ever managed to keep in one place." She stood away, holding her mother at arm's length so she could see her face. "But I don't just do this for money. I *love* it. Love every moment of what I do. I wake up each morning eager to design beautiful things for women who are enthralled to wear them. It gives me pleasure and a sense of purpose. I can't imagine living any other way!"

Her mother's red-rimmed eyes searched Lucy's face. "Working all hours of the day and night? With people coming and going. There is no rest—the house is like Euston Station." She lowered her voice and muttered, "It can't be good for Esmé to see her mother with a tape measure around her neck."

Lucy struggled not to laugh as her daughter appeared at the top of the stairs with Celia.

"I like my room." Esmé did a twirl of pleasure. "It looks across the rooftops to the park. I can climb out of the window onto the flat bit and pretend to be a squirrel—if I want to."

"Esmé, you will fall to your death!" Grandmama cast a stricken look at her daughter, begging her to chastise her wayward child.

"No, Mama, she will not. It is quite flat and there is a parapet." And to Esmé: "Yes, darling—how lovely. Come down now." Lucy watched her pretty little girl bounce down the stairs. *She is a tomboy just like Elinor and I were.* "There is another reason we are taking this house, Mama. There will be absolutely no need for you, or Esmé, to see any of my clients. The house is so large you will never come across them, if you wish not to."

Her mother's face took on the old disgruntled look. "What about when I have to go out? Do I have to use the back stairs, like a domestic menial?"

Lucy knew her mother would enjoy swanning down the sweep of the stairs and being gracious to the titled and the wealthy. "Of course not. I am quite sure you wouldn't mind bumping into Georgina Ward, the Countess of Dudley; the very beautiful and artistic Violet Manners, Duchess of Rutland; and I believe that Lady Angela Forbes's maid telephoned and made an appointment to see us too. All three of these lovely ladies are incredibly well connected, and each one of them has requested a consultation in our first week of opening! You can't imagine how much I have to thank Lady Brooke for her many recommendations."

Lucy's elation made her catch her mother's hands to include her in her joy. "Between Mrs. Guttenberg's American friends all coming to London for the season, and the Marlborough set, I think we are going to be very busy—so busy, we will have no problem at all in paying our rent, our coal bill, or any of the servants' wages." She kissed her mother on the cheek. "We can afford to have a really good cook, at long last. I was hoping you would contact the Slade Domestic Agency . . . if you are not too busy, or should I ask Celia to take care of it?"

Her mother harrumphed as Celia walked down the stairs to join them. "What would that girl know about good food?" she said under her breath. "I'll do it."

Esmé sprang down the last steps of the staircase and hopped from square to square of the black-and-white marble floor. "Isn't it teatime?" she asked. "I am awfully hungry."

"Ladies don't use the word 'awfully,' Esmé. It is vulgar."

Lucy laughed. "Yes, Esmé, that's exactly what we need: tea. Come on, Mama. Let's go back to Davies Street and celebrate. After I signed the lease on this house I bought a chocolate cake from Gunter's."

"WHAT DO YOU think, Elinor?" Lucy threw open the double doors into the drawing room.

Elinor stood rapt on the threshold. "So elegant, Lucy. And you have Papa's portrait on the wall. Doesn't he look dignified?" The red-haired Mr. Sutherland, standing in the perpetual pose of lord and master of all he surveyed, with his left hand holding his pocket watch as if to perennially chide the women in his family for tardiness, gazed down on his daughters with mild disapproval.

Elinor turned in a slow circle in the center of the room. "The colors are divine: silver-gray linen walls—how sophisticated! White paintwork, and I love this very dark, almost black, green you've used for the curtains and coverings. Such a subtle backdrop for your lovely clothes." She plumped herself down on a sofa. "This is luxurious. Even Clayton wouldn't turn his nose up at this lovely room." She looked around her. "And it is such a perfect size. Is this where we wait?"

Lucy nodded. "I wanted somewhere where friends could gather for tea and to maybe try on hats. They will look so ornamental on stands placed here and there—the hats arrive tomorrow. And the day after that, when it doesn't smell of paint anymore, we open. Lady Brooke has been such an incredible help. She introduced me to Elsie de Wolfe— who has an eye for doing up rooms without spending the earth—and she recommended a secondhand shop for the chairs and sofas; we reupholstered them. I made her one dress and my client list is bulging, and she has made an appointment for next week; she wants to talk about her

wardrobe for summer. Thank you for sending her to me, Elinor. I feel
we have really turned the corner."

Elinor laughed and pointed her finger. "Don't be too quick with your
thanks. She will expect 'special rates,' you know."

Lucy shook her head. "Yes, I am quite sure she will. But my book is full
of new clients—all of them desperate to visit Lucile Wallace Fashions."

Elinor patted the space on the sofa next to her. "There is one other
thing you should know, about Daisy Brooke. She is a generous-hearted
woman, and I have no doubts at all that she will send everyone she
knows your way. But whatever you do, never, ever trust her with a confidence. She simply can't help herself. She is addicted to gossip. And she
has in the past caused havoc . . . if you remember Charles Beresford and
what happened to him."

Lucy shook her head. "I recognize the name and that's all. I know
the countess is called the Babbling Brooke, but I thought that was because she talks so much."

Elinor threw back her head, her eyes half-shut with laughter. "Talks
so much about *other* people's affairs, you mean. Let me tell you a cau-
tionary tale so you are not lured by Daisy's undoubtable charm into
sharing *any* secrets with her.

"In her early marriage, Daisy fell in love with Charles Beresford—a
serial lady-killer with a long-suffering, plain wife who is extremely rich:
far richer than her husband. Daisy was so infatuated with Lord Charles
that she burst into Lady Charles's bedroom at a country house party and
announced that she and Lord Charles were passionately in love and were
going to elope." Elinor shook her head, her eyes shining. "Lady Charles
put up with a lot from her husband, but this forceful attack from his
mistress was simply not to be tolerated: rich wives carry a lot of weight
with their husbands. She didn't say a word to Daisy but collected her
husband and took him off home.

"Inevitably the incident doused Charles's ardor for the reckless Daisy,
and he abandoned her to concentrate his energies on women who did

not specialize in histrionics. In the meantime, his wife became pregnant. Daisy found out, of course, and was outraged that her lover had been *unfaithful* to her—with his wife! She had no doubt that the child was Charles's because in her outspoken opinion no one else could possibly be interested in the dowdy and unattractive Lady Charles. In a fit of temper—another of Daisy's little faults, by the way, so don't say I didn't warn you—she wrote a letter to Charles. It was quite a graphic piece. How could he, she demanded, have gone from her to his fright of a wife? Unfortunately, she took the opportunity to reminisce about how passionate they had been together in their intimate moments." Elinor nodded as Lucy shook her head in delighted horror, beginning to see where this irresponsible act would end. "Yes, you are right. In the way letters rashly written in the heat of the moment often do, it was delivered to the wrong person: *Lady* Charles. Who not only opened the letter and read it, but the very next day consulted her solicitor, who insisted on keeping it safe for her, in his strongbox.

"In a panic Daisy realized that her letter in the wrong hands would be her downfall. She went to her dear friend Bertie the Prince of Wales for help. It was during a very tearful scene with the gorgeous Daisy begging for his intervention on her behalf that Bertie fell in love with her!"

Lucy stopped laughing and her eyes widened. "No, really? Even though it was quite clear that Lady Brooke is so dangerously impetuous?"

Elinor put her hand on Lucy's arm, head bent as her shoulders shook with laughter. "Oh, I am quite sure that he found her dilemma absolutely enchanting: all those passionate tears and frantic hand-wringing. Being the consummate gallant that he is, and now completely besotted with Daisy, he went into action immediately. At two o'clock on a rainy morning he rousted the unfortunate solicitor from his bed and demanded to see the letter. Once he had read it, Bertie knew the dreadful thing must never come to light. But the solicitor refused to hand it over. So later that day Bertie went to Lady Charles. Now, Lady Charles may be a plain Jane, but she is a woman with a strong character. She agreed to return the letter to Daisy, if Daisy would agree to take herself off to the Continent for the rest of the season. Banishment—can you imagine?"

Lucy could imagine and resolved to handle Lady Brooke's explosive side very tenderly indeed. But in the meantime, she wanted to understand a little more about the man who was the Prince of Wales. "What did the Prince of Wales say? I mean, he could hardly make her give him the letter!"

"Bertie is not a man to threaten; he told Lady Charles that if she used the letter in any way whatsoever, it might be her who would be ostracized by society. To the complete delight of everyone, who were now fully aware of what was going on, Bertie made sure the Brookes were invited everywhere and then cut Lady Charles from any function that involved him until she finally agreed to destroy Daisy's letter." Elinor finished to peals of laughter from Lucy.

"No, no, it can't all be true. Why haven't you told me this before?" Lucy wiped her eyes with her handkerchief. "Oh, I have a stitch from laughing. You are not making this up—it is not the plot of one of your romance novels, is it?"

Elinor shook her head. "Every word is true. There now, is that a good enough reason to be careful what you say to Lady Brooke?"

They were interrupted by their mother. "Goodness, girls, I could hear you shrieking from my room. Tea is ready. We are taking it in the upstairs drawing room." She linked arms with her daughters and walked them up the stairs.

"Lovely, graceful staircase, isn't it, Elinor?" Her mother smiled at Lucy. "Has Lucy shown you around? Such a charming house. From the moment I walked through the front door, I said to Lucy that she would be a fool not to take it. So much space, and so very comfortable! I can't tell you how pleasant it is to be out of that crowded little house in Davies Street."

❆

# CHAPTER SEVEN

*June 1898*

CELIA

She stood discreetly in a corner of the fitting room, her client book open, as Mrs. Wallace slipped the tape measure around the jutting prow of Mrs. Evelyn Willie James's splendid bosom.

". . . thirty-eight and a half inches, please, Celia."

*She has the sort of figure they call "statuesque" in books,* Celia thought as Mrs. Willie James burst into enthusiasm for the play she would be appearing in at Warwick Castle. "The only thing I am *terrified* of is that I will forget my lines on the *night*. Now, Daisy, tells me that the Prince of Wales is *definitely* going to be there—so *terrifying*. Your sister told me to pretend I was acting for my own little family at West Dean. But I can't, I simply can't believe that the prince will be sitting in the audience—watching me."

*She sounds like a little girl who has been promised a treat,* Celia thought as Mrs. Wallace slid the tape down to a tiny waist. "Twenty-five inches . . . thank you, Celia. Do we have all we need?"

"Yes, ma'am." Celia jotted the final figure. *How can they bear to be constrained in that dreadful cage? She has five children and still she laces herself in as if she were eighteen!* Celia lifted her head from the notebook to gaze at Mrs. Willie James's curvaceous shape. She couldn't imagine wearing something that molded her form into such savage obedience. Her own figure—straight up and down, with boyishly slender hips and no bosom whatsoever—felt light and fluid as she ran up- and down-stairs, climbed ladders to search for a box of long white kid gloves, size seven, and stretched up on the tips of her toes to pull down a heavy bolt of linen. Being twenty-eight inches around her bust and hips meant that there was no need for a corset at all.

Mrs. Willie James sat down on the daybed. "Elinor is so clever—so versatile. How does she do it? Such a wonderful actor, such an inspiring director—and her confidence! If only I had such poise."

Mrs. Wallace turned her head, but Celia saw her quick smile. "Elinor has always been drawn to the theater. She should have been on the stage," she responded.

But Mrs. Willie James gushed on as if Mrs. Wallace hadn't spoken. "Your mother must be *so very* proud of you both—such creativity. I am in awe, simply in awe! I have never been particularly good at doing anything at all. I arrange the flowers for the house, of course, that is one thing I insist on doing myself. But I never thought I would be in a *real* play, other than the silly things we do on Boxing Day—charades, or a tableau vivant—for amusement, for the family. Under Elinor's direction I feel as if I actually have talent! And it is all such fun!"

Mrs. Wallace stood back from her client and came out of the trance-like state she went into when she was dreaming up silky possibilities for them to wear. It astonished Celia that she managed to keep track of Mrs. Willie James's exclamations and enthusiasms for her part in an amateur performance. How did she manage to say yes one moment and no the next, all in the right places, when she wasn't even listening?

Mrs. Wallace had told Celia when Lady Brooke had recommended her: "Mrs. Willie James takes precedence over any other client, Celia—apart from Lady Brooke. She is one of the most elegant society hostesses in London, and she never tires of talking about her wardrobe. One might almost say she lives in it."

Mrs. Wallace smiled at Mrs. Willie James the way she smiled at

Esmé when she had practiced her piano. "I have two of your costumes for the play ready to try on this afternoon. I think you are going to love the one I have for the second act. No, that's right, you have not seen that one yet. Then we must decide on an evening gown for the first night of your arrival at Warwick Castle—for the ball. I have some ideas and we can discuss those when we have finished with your costumes."

Mrs. Willie James rushed into excitement again. "You are coming to the castle for the play, aren't you, Lucy? If you are there I know it will help me relax—" *Her expression*, Celia thought, *is almost beseeching. How much reassurance does one woman need?* she wondered.

But Mrs. Wallace was all business in the fitting room. "I wouldn't miss it for anything!" was her only comment. "Ah, here is Alice with your costumes! I hope you like these lovely things as much as I do." Celia marveled at the ease with which her boss introduced new gowns to her clients. She was as light as a feather duster with Sèvres. No pomp or ceremony, merely a pretty, breezy woman who you would never guess had spent hours staring at fabrics, rejecting a boxful of tiny ivory buttons as too large, or inspecting pieces of lace with her arms folded in judgment.

*But once her decision is made, she is brisk and clear in her instructions as she manipulates yard upon yard of fabric into a dress so marvelous, it makes you want to go down on your knees and thank the good Lord for silk.*

Mrs. W. slipped the tea gown out of its sleeve for her client's inspection and awaited the verdict: cries of delight or a brow wrinkled in concern at a neckline that revealed too much, or not enough, bosom. *There are very few furrowed brows*, Celia thought. Nothing was too much trouble and no client ever left without a face wreathed in smiles and fervent thank-yous.

The delicate lace of the gown had been carefully steeped in weak tea to soften its white to blend perfectly with deep rose silk. "The kimono style is perfect for you, Evelyn; loose, comfortable, but timelessly chic. What do you think of the sleeves? Not too wide? They look . . . almost medieval—perfect for your first scene? Yes, I thought so too." She buttoned the gown and Celia arranged the two pier glasses to help Mrs. James look at the back of the dress.

"It's me. Dearest Lucy, it *really* is *me*. If you were inside my head you couldn't have understood what I wanted more perfectly. I'm overjoyed, absolutely overjoyed. Simply glorious!"

Mrs. Wallace busied herself with slight alterations, and the tea gown was handed off to Alice.

There was an enthralled moment of anticipation as they waited for the finale. Mrs. Wallace's demeanor was as reverent as if she was in the front pew at church. She stood in thought for a moment, one finger on her lips, her head bowed. Then she straightened up, her tone measured and grave as if this was a moment of national importance. "Now, to the second gown. It wasn't ready when you last came for a fitting. Do you remember, we talked about how some gold and green colors together are reminiscent of ripe greengages? There now, I knew you would!" Like a conjurer she slid the dress out from its sleeve. "Well . . . what do you think?" A cloud of green-gold hung in the air for a gauzy moment before settling around the head and shoulders of the almost delirious Mrs. Willie James. "Oh yes, oh absolutely a hundred times yes."

A quickly muffled squeak from the sewing assistant; Celia shot a glance at Alice, but the girl's head was down, her lower lip caught between her teeth as her fingers organized the pins on the cushion on her wrist.

*None of us ever get used to this part*, she thought, as she waited to see Mrs. James's uplifted face as her head emerged from the brilliant cloud. *We never, ever tire of the joy when they see themselves in their dress for the first time.*

When the exclamations of elation died to a whimper of delight, Celia remembered what Mrs. Wallace had told her. "When some of our clients appear to lose their heads at the sight of a dress we have created for them, it is important to remember that these women spend most of their lives not just thinking about their wardrobe but *worrying* about it. They change their clothes five or six times a day, spending hours in their dressing rooms. Some of them truly believe that the clothes they wear during their long day and evening are who they really are. The right dress gives them a feeling of security, that they belong on the august perch their marriage to a wealthy man, a duke, or a great landowner has given them. They are not just dressing for themselves but as a representative of a powerful, rich, or noble family. They must never look at themselves in their dressing room mirror and feel anxious or unsure." This had all made perfect sense to Celia once she had actually witnessed one of their clients overwhelmed to tears by a new ball gown.

"Then of course there are the rare few who understand the importance of the right dress but have other things in their lives that tell them who they are: they write, they paint, they create spectacular gardens. Lady Cunard, for instance, is an accomplished pianist and patroness of the arts—I just wish she would stop asking me to trim everything with swan's down and bird of paradise feathers—the carnage in the bird world has simply got to stop. To some of them music or the arts are as important as the food they put in their mouths; to others the preservation of beautiful and rare paintings is their life's work. But these women are rare: they are fun to dress because talking about a new dress is time away from the things that really matter. They are not our bread and butter, not the way women like Mrs. Willie James are, but they are just as important, as they are seen everywhere."

Leaving Mrs. Willie James to purr over her gown, Mrs. Wallace turned to Celia. "Do you remember we discussed the wine mousseline de soie and the chocolate lace? You said at the time you thought it perfect for Mrs. James's delicate coloring." Her voice was as triumphant as if she were reassuring herself, as well as Mrs. Willie James, that she had found perfection. "Would you bring them to us? Oh, and the plum French silk too. I think it will be ideal for the first evening at Warwick Castle, a blend of understated elegance and the rich ripe days at the end of summer." For a moment Celia wondered if her boss was referring to Mrs. Willie James's mature and womanly shape—but fitting-room talk was always reverent.

"I will bring them immediately, ma'am," she said in her best posh home counties accent.

In the corridor the glowing pleasure she felt at working for one of the most talented dress designers in London was interrupted as she made her way back to the hall. She stopped, mid-step, with her head on one side, and then glanced at her appointment book: *Lady Ottoline Cavendish-Bentinck consult. 3:30 p.m. Debutante.*

A murmur of sound from the fitting room on her left: a soft feminine exclamation of pleasure and a low, seductive answering laugh. She paused only for the brief second it took to register that the laughter was deeper in pitch because it was male.

Another glance at her appointment book. *Ottoline? Debutante?* She hurried on, her eyes wide with disbelief at what she thought she had heard. Was Mrs. Wallace aware that the adolescent Lady Ottoline Cavendish-Bentinck was entertaining a friend to tea, as if she were a married woman with children in the nursery and too much time on her hands?

Celia came to a halt before she reached the hall. "Pull yersel' together, gurl!" she instructed herself in a growl that came straight from Tyneside docks. She knew that some of Mrs. Wallace's more worldly married ladies entertained a "friend" for tea as they waited in their fitting room for a consultation, and occasionally light flirtation strayed into breathless silence.

Affairs were an accepted fact of life in high society but never, ever referred to. This was the unwritten law that governed those who worked on the ground floor of the house. In Mrs. Wallace's establishment, gossip about clients was absolutely taboo. Celia's next thought stopped her in her tracks, causing her to cover her mouth with her hand. Only a month ago she had found a group of seamstresses on the back stairs peeking through a hole in the wallpaper into Lady Gwladys Robinson's fitting room, where she was entertaining a gentleman to tea as she waited for her appointment with Mrs. W. Celia had given them all a thorough scolding and sent them back up the stairs to their workrooms, and the next day had called them one by one into her tiny little office—a cupboard really—at the bend of the stairs between the second and third floors. Her lecture, delivered in a stern voice and accompanied by a forbidding frown, had started, "I would never have expected this of you," and had ended with, "Do not disappoint me again."

The hole in the wall had been repaired and Celia liked to think that she had established an understanding among the staff that whatever they might believe happened in the fitting rooms was a figment, a suspicion, and absolutely nothing more.

The sounds she had heard in Lady Ottoline's fitting room were far from being a mere figment. The girl was certainly unmarried and for some reason—Celia couldn't imagine why—unchaperoned. If she were not alone in that wretched room, the consequences could be a disaster, both for Mrs. Wallace in the face of an angry mother and for the salon's reputation.

*Her elder brother, perhaps?* Celia grasped briefly at a straw and then let it drift away; nice brothers did not laugh like that. Nothing could save this situation. Even if Mrs. Wallace had referred to Lady Ottoline as her little bohemian friend, well-brought-up girls from good families did not meet gentlemen in fitting rooms.

"Bohemian," Celia repeated the name out loud to herself. *And the good Lord only knows what that means—a fancy name for a wayward baggage, if you ask me.*

Mrs. Wallace's bohemian friends belonged to either the artistic or the literary set. Some of them were new friends like Lady Manners, the Duchess of Rutland, who floated in through the door in a billowing velvet skirt, with her head done up in a brocade turban, forgetful of the time of her appointment for a consultation, but quick enough to correct if the teaspoon was set awkwardly in her saucer. But not as terrifying as Mrs. Margot Asquith, the central figure of an aristocratic group of intellectuals called the Souls, who talked in a sharp, hard staccato voice and pounced on those who kept her waiting like a hawk on a mouse.

*Bohemian my eye!* she said to herself as she crossed the hall. *Affected and full of themselves.*

She paused to check on two courteous and very rich American ladies trying on hats in the drawing room. Real ladies, who would no more dream of welcoming a gentleman friend into their fitting room than running through Mayfair in their nightgowns.

Where Celia came from, girls of Lady Ottoline's age were married with their first baby clinging to their skirts and another on the way. She had learned very quickly that the daughters of the aristocracy were shielded from the world—kept safe in a nursery with a strict nanny or governess to see to their manners. At seventeen or eighteen, these shockingly ignorant young things were taken out of the nursery, their hair piled up on top of their heads, laced tightly into a corset and decked out in haute couture costing hundreds of pounds, to spend a season in London being taken to balls, parties, and gala events, at the end of which each of these young ladies was hopefully married off to some lucky man who took over her care, so that she might dedicate the rest of her life to adorning his world, having his children, and ensuring that the wheels of his domestic life ran smoothly. It was then, and only then—and this to Celia was the puzzling part—that ladies of good name and impeccable lineage might throw all morals aside and look to their own pleasure, with a young admirer who discreetly dropped in on them between the hours of five and seven o'clock—no doubt when their husbands were off indulging in their own discreet pleasures.

Celia, her head reeling with panic, found herself in the fabric room, and to calm her nerves set about finding the silk Mrs. Wallace wanted to show Mrs. Willie James—and she had better be quick about it. She found what was needed and walked back down the corridor—past the now silent fitting room. What if someone other than herself discovered that wicked little girl misbehaving?

She caught Mrs. Wallace's eye as she opened the door. "Will that be all, ma'am?" she asked as Mrs. Wallace spilled ruby plum silk into Mrs.

Willie James's lap. "Thank you, Celia. Who else do I see this after-noon?"

"Lady Ottoline, ma'am, is waiting in the Iris Room."

"Ottoline?" Mrs. Wallace frowned at the name. "Oh, yes, of course. I did agree to see her, didn't I? Well, you had better tell her I am running late. That's all, thank you, Celia."

Celia closed the door and leaned on it for a brief moment to steady herself. Of course dressing that girl would be a headache. The hoyden's nose was too long, her brows too dark, and they emphasized her heavy-lidded and brooding hazel eyes—eyes that shone with intelligent deter-mination one moment and then fixed themselves with cold arrogance on members of the servant class who told her to behave herself and say goodbye to her handsome boyfriend.

Standing in the corridor that served the fitting rooms, Celia could think of no other way this situation could be handled. She went hot, then cold, as she remembered Beryl, Ivy, and Moira sniggering on the back stairs as they took turns peering through the peephole.

She moved toward the door of the Iris Room and listened. Silence. *What will I see if I throw open the door to that room?* she asked herself. She shook her head to rid it of a kaleidoscope of embarrassment. Her wildest visions were interrupted by a loud exclamation from inside the room, followed by laughter and a frantic shushing.

Feeling like a cheap servant looking for an opportunity to blackmail, Celia put her ear to the panel of the door. She listened for the briefest moment. *Yes, I was right!* She put a clammy hand up to her hot forehead. *She's got a chap in there with her. How do they get them into their fitting rooms without them being seen?*

Almost immediately she knew the answer. They came in through the garden gate and through the conservatory. *There is no other way!* No one would see; no one would suspect. The conservatory opened into this room, or rather what had been a large drawing room before it was di-vided so cleverly into fitting rooms. There was no need to ring the front doorbell, hand your hat to the parlormaid, and embarrass anyone within sight or earshot by asking what fitting room you would find Lady What's-Her-Face in, and yes, she was expecting you.

Celia glanced at her watch; she had better get a move on if she was going to deal with this disaster now. She trotted down the corridor across the hall and pushed open the green baize door to the china pantry.

Minutes later, she lifted her hand and rapped smartly on Lady Ottoline's door. The sort of silence that follows hurried activity answered her. She put her ear close to the door's surface. Silence. She knocked again and listened. An audible exclamation, a hissed conversation, and a young voice lifted in irritation. "Yes, what is it?"

Celia took a long breath and opened the door a crack.

"Yes?" Two large, fierce eyes and a mass of dark brown curly hair. Lady Ottoline was sitting in her camisole, corset, and pantalettes, long stockinged legs stretched out in front of her.

She glared at the tray Celia was holding. "I didn't say I wanted tea."

"Nor did you, m'lady, and I am afraid you won't have time for it either. Your mother, the baroness, this moment sent word that she will meet you here at half past four . . . in about five minutes." Celia paused; supporting the tea tray in her left hand, she pushed against the door. It appeared to have jammed—something prevented her from opening it fully. She gave the door a couple of strong shoves, her forehead creased in perplexity. "Something's made this door stick," she said as if to herself, and, "Oh, and Mrs. Wallace begs your pardon, m'lady, but she will be a little late for your consultation. Would you like me to show the baroness to your fitting room when she arrives?"

A toss of long curly hair. "I don't have time to wait!" And a scowl from the formidable brow. "For either of them!"

"Then if you will give me a moment I will look in Mrs. Wallace's appointment—"

"I *told you* I don't have the time: either for my mother, Mrs. Wallace, or your appointment book."

*Nothing shrinking about this little violet.* Celia nodded and gave the door a couple more shoves with her right arm. She could have sworn she heard a sharp inhalation and a muttered curse.

"No tea, then? What a pity. Are you quite sure you don't want to make another appointment?"

Ottoline got to her feet; she was remarkably tall for a girl.

"May I help you dress?" Celia made as if to come into the room.

A sneer of derision. "I have been dressing myself since I was six, thank you! And no, no appointment." And as if to herself: "This coming-out business is such a farce." Ottoline Cavendish-Bentinck slammed her fitting room door shut, leaving Celia on its other side with her rattling tray. *Next time that nice little girl comes for a consultation, I must remember to lock the conservatory door before she arrives.*

"CELIA, WHERE IS that little girl?"

"Lady Ottoline, ma'am?"

"Yes, that's the one. You said the Iris Room?"

"I did, m'lady, but she left the salon. Said she couldn't wait."

Mrs. Wallace turned, her eyebrows raised; then she glanced at her wristwatch. "I am only ten minutes late, for heaven's sake! I practically bundled poor Mrs. Willie James . . ." There was such a scandalized expression on her face that Celia had to bite the inside of her cheeks to stop herself from laughing.

"How very impolite of her."

"Arrogant, I would have said, ma'am. The younger generation, eh?"

"No more appointments for little Lady Ottoline."

## Chapter Eight

*June 1898*

Lucy

Lucy smoothed the collar of her dove gray traveling coat and turned to count her luggage. "Trunk for costumes, and one suitcase. Hatbox." She pulled on her gloves as she turned to Celia. "Ivy and Doris should have Lady Cunard's visiting costume and afternoon dress ready for her fitting by Thursday. Don't forget that she is the most impatient and careless woman in the world and will not stand still for a moment. So you have to be quick and deft; otherwise she will walk out and her clothes will look terrible. I honestly don't know why I bother with her; she wears something once and it is covered in cigarette burns. One day she'll go up in flames." She turned to her sewing girl, Alice. "Did you remember to pack the train we added to my sister's costume for the second act?"

Patient Alice didn't hesitate. "Yes'm, it is in the dome trunk with all the other costumes."

Alice's inability to be excited about anything at all had a steadying effect. "Thank you, Alice, I know I can rely on how thorough you are." She bent to straighten her hat in the hall looking glass—her hat brim quivered with excitement. She was off to Warwick Castle to a house party. A big event that offered tremendous opportunities because the

Prince of Wales and his fashionable friends would all be there—guests of Lord and Lady Brooke. The possibilities to lengthen her client list were endless!

"And here is my little Esmé!"

Esmé came down the stairs carrying NouNou. "Oof, Mama, Nou-Nou is getting heavier and heavier every day." She put the squirming animal down.

"Then don't feed her your breakfast egg when Nanny isn't looking, darling! Give me a kiss goodbye."

Esmé planted the fat Pekingese on the hall floor. "Now, why aren't I coming? Is there a really good reason?" At thirteen she had a will of iron and an ability to argue a point with such a clear, cool head that the wishy-washy wilted into obedience. She reminded Lucy of her sister, Elinor.

"Because it's grown-ups only. Aunt Elinor is not bringing your cousins. I can't imagine how bored you would be all alone in the Warwick Castle nursery."

Esmé's lower lip protruded. "But I am all alone in the nursery here."

"You will have me!" said Celia, her mouth pouted in pretended hurt feelings, as she pulled Esmé to her and did up the ribbon in her hair.

"Yes, yes, and I love you dearly, but it would be so much fun to sleep the night in a real live castle, Mama—Celia would like that too. She could look after me. And doesn't this Daisy Brooke have children too?"

Lucy bent down and put her arms around her daughter. "First of all, she is 'Lady Brooke' to you, and second of all, I want you to be very good while I am away. Please listen to your grandmama and do whatever Celia and Nanny ask you to do, without arguing! Now, kisses, lots of kisses."

Robbie opened the front door. "Ma'am, the hansoms have arrived." He picked up the suitcase and hatbox as horses clattered to a stop in the street.

Two cabbies carried out the dome trunk and stowed it in the rear cab. "I'll see you on Monday, Celia. Remember, be deft and quick with Lady Cunard." She blew a kiss to her daughter and walked down the steps.

She was about to get into the cab when she noticed a tall woman dressed in a striking black walking costume, with a hat in a stunning shade of turquoise. The woman was standing quite still and it seemed to Lucy that she was looking at her intently.

"What a lovely color," she said to Alice. "Do you know who she is? A neighbor perhaps?"

Alice shook her head. "No idea, ma'am. Never seen her before." They climbed up into the cab.

"What will you bring me?" Esmé called out to her mother's retreating back.

"Something interesting!"

"You always say that and it never is!"

The cabbie clucked to his horse, and off they went.

"Warwick Castle looks a bit intimidating when you arrive, doesn't it?" Lucy saw her seamstress's anxious face as they bowled across the castle's dry moat, through its barbican and gatehouse into an immense inner courtyard. "But all it really is, is a nice old country house, surrounded by castle walls. A bit on the primitive side, but I am sure you will be comfortable. We'll make sure that your room is close to mine so there will be no need for you to tramp about for hours between stairs looking for me." Lucy stuck her head out of the carriage window. "There's my sister! Elinor, Elinor!"

Her sister's flaming hair and apricot tea gown were a beacon of bright light against the stone walls of the castle. "Lucy! Oh, thank heavens you are here. Evelyn and I have been praying you didn't miss the three fifteen. There isn't a train after that for two hours!" Lucy could feel her sister simply vibrating with excitement in her arms. "First we must go up to your room so you can wash and change, and then tea. Alice, you have the dressing room next to Mrs. Wallace, and a maid will take you down to tea in the servants' hall and bring you back up again to unpack. Now, Lucy, did you remember that the hem is too long on my dress for the second act? Alice did you turn it up?"

"Yes, ma'am." Alice, reassured that she would not be turned loose in this vast castle, had returned to stoic calm.

Up the great sweep of the staircase they went. Large oriel windows looked out over the river Avon and its tumbling, frothing weir. Lucy stood still for a moment to see if she could feel the thrum of the great wooden mill wheel under the castle walls. She raised her eyebrows and clapped her hands together as she felt the deep tremor far below the tread of the stairs. "How wonderful to have a working water mill underneath your house!" She leaned to look through the windows down at the wide expanse of river, glittering in the afternoon sunlight. "Elinor, after tea let's go for a walk along the river and see the mill."

"Why? It's just a mill. And there isn't time: after tea Evelyn Willie James and I are coming to your room so we can have one last fitting for our costumes for the play. And then I want to take you to the Cedar Room, which Daisy has turned into a theater—it is absolutely spectacular. Did I tell you that Evelyn managed to catch a cold—silly woman. I think it's nerves. I am quite sure she will be all right on the night, but Daisy is standing by to understudy just in case." She put her hand on Lucy's forearm and lowered her voice. A quick sideways glance: "I was up half the night rehearsing with Horace Brand; he really is coming along frightfully well." Lucy's glance at her sister's glowing eyes told her everything she needed to know about dress rehearsals with the dynamic Sir Horace. It also told her that she did not have to worry about Clayton appearing at odd and inconvenient moments while she was enjoying Lord and Lady Brooke's hospitality. "We are quite exhausted, but the effort was completely worth it—he has such talent!" Elinor threw open the door to Lucy's room. "Look, a lovely view of the river. Alice, you are through that door. Now, darling, do you really want to go down to tea? We can take it in Evelyn's room, so much more fun."

Lucy took off her traveling coat and smoothed down her garnet red afternoon dress. "No," she said as she washed her hands. "No, little cups of tea as an afterthought as you and Evelyn gas on about the play. I want lots of sandwiches, hot buttered toast, and cake. I haven't eaten a thing all day. Ring for a maid, Elinor. We must make sure that Alice is taken care of." She sat down at the dressing table and took off her hat. "No, the hat will have to stay on. My hair is a mess."

Elinor opened Lucy's traveling case and took out two silver-backed brushes. "I will brush it out and make it look lovely; the prince hates it when women wear hats to tea."

Elinor watched her sister's brisk movements as she brushed out tangles and skillfully arranged her back hair in a coil low at the back of her head, pushing a cluster of curls toward her forehead. "What sort of silk is that you are wearing? Such a lovely sheen."

Lucy glanced in the looking glass to remind herself what she was wearing. "Yes, it's perfect for the afternoon. It comes from China; it's called shantung. I love it for day dresses. Now I'm ready for tea."

AT LEAST THIRTY people were gathered in the Green Room, as Elinor swept her sister down the stairs and across the great hall with its towering barrel roof: "Daisy hates the castle, poor lamb, but she has to spend time here because of you-know-who.

*That will be Daisy's long-suffering husband*, Lucy thought as she smiled at the popular misquotation that was currently doing the rounds: "Greater love has no man that he should lay down his *wife* for his king."

There was a huge fireplace burning brightly that did nothing at all to ease the cold of late afternoon, with windows long deprived of sunlight. Weapons were ferociously displayed along its stone walls, and the earl's armor collection stood to attention, gleaming in the candlelight. *Why*, Lucy wondered, *do people who own castles always go in for such savage displays of weaponry? Some lovely Gobelin tapestries would take some of the ice out of this massive cavern.*

The door to the Green Room was open, and Lucy relaxed in anticipation of tea and hot buttered toast, as they left the icy hall for the comfort and warmth of deep sofas and sunlight streaming through western windows that looked out over the Vale of Avon. A great shout of laughter came from a group gathered by the fireside around a fat man standing at its center, puffing cigar smoke.

*That is undoubtedly the prince*, thought Lucy, trying not to stare. *I had no idea how overweight he is. And this is the man who is considered to be the lady-killer of the Marlborough set? How odd people are about royalty.*

Albert, the Prince of Wales, was short, wide, and dressed in flawless tweeds with a gold watch chain looped across his protruding stomach. Lucy thought he looked as if he ran a successful greengrocery, but his bright blue eyes shone with good humor and he was clearly enjoying himself. He turned to a willowy woman next to him. "And that is vy we always haff to haff the redoubtable Ernest Cassel with us whenever we go to Baden-Baden. He knows efferyone there—efferyone."

*Good heavens, he speaks English with a German accent!*

Elinor caught her surreptitious glance at the royal Bertie. "Hard to believe, isn't he? Such an unattractive man, really. The Marlborough set all call him Tum Tum—not to his face, of course." She bent her head to murmur in Lucy's ear. "I mean, when you look at how lovely Daisy is, can you imagine having to do 'it' with him? I mean, his corpulence would make things a bit cumbersome, don't you think? Daisy told me that is why they use a *siège d'amour*."

Lucy smiled up at her sister. "*Siège d'amour*? Love chair?" What on earth was a love chair?

Elinor moved closer and whispered.

"Really? How very practical! Elinor, don't you ever think of anything else?"

"Isn't that all anyone thinks about, really? Come on, Lucy, don't you miss it at all?"

"No, El, I really don't. I don't think I am made that way. Someone in our family has to keep her head when it comes to sex. And, oh, would you look at that cake—and there is Lady Brooke." She had identified her hostess in the crowd by the tea gown she had made for her. *Soft blues and grays. Those are the colors she should wear; she looks too bandbox in pink.* She made her way across the room to thank her hostess, stopping en route for a smoked salmon sandwich or two.

"Lucy Wallace, whenever I see you, the first thing I want to say is, What a stunning dress." Daisy Brooke leaned forward and kissed her cheek. "How lovely you look in red. So you have heard that poor Evelyn has a cold? Great gusts of eucalyptus oil wafting out of her room and down the corridor!" They stood together in front of a tea table, where a tall dark-haired man was standing with his back to them. "Do you know Cosmo Duff Gordon? I am sure you do. His cousin Cynthia Antrobus came to you for her presentation dress, didn't she? Such a pretty girl." She tapped the tall man on the shoulder. "Sir Cosmo, do turn around and meet Mrs. Lucy Wallace."

The tall man obliged, and Lucy found herself looking up into brilliantly dark eyes under straight black brows and a ferociously dramatic mustache.

The dark eyes smiled down at her. "Lucy Wallace? Now, where have I heard that name?" She liked his voice; it was deep, with the slightest lilt of the heather moors and craggy outcrops of the Scottish Highlands. *Careful now,* she instructed herself, *the last time you fell for smiling dark eyes, you spent the next nine years suffering through hell.*

"Perhaps from your cousin, Miss Antrobus?" she reminded Sir Cosmo. "I designed some dresses for her when she came out last year."

The dark eyes crinkled at the corners. "Gorgeous dresses. And you designed them? Of course, I saw you come in just now, and I thought, 'Now there is a woman who knows how to dress and what color suits her.'"

Lucy felt her cheeks warming. "The right color is the most essential part of a dress," she said.

"Cynthia told me you give names to your favorite dresses. Do you have one for the one you are wearing?" He was flirting outrageously now—*so typical of someone who runs with this set,* Lucy thought.

The words were out before she could stop herself. "The Sigh of Lips Unsatisfied," she said, and inwardly cringed with embarrassment. Elinor could say something like this and get away with it, but Elinor was an accomplished flirt and Lucy knew she was not. She felt awkward and clumsy.

"Oh really?" Cosmo said, his voice so thoughtful, she realized that he had taken her seriously. "That's rather a tragic name for such a lovely dress. I am bringing my cousin down to London in a fortnight at the end of June. I am sure she has made an appointment to see you." Lucy heard a voice like a soft foghorn behind her. It was Mrs. Willie James holding a plate piled with sandwiches and brandy snaps.

"Lucy darling!" Evelyn Willie James handed her plate to Cosmo, and Lucy was engulfed in her strong arms and the reek of camphorated oil. "Come along, my dear. Elinor will not leave me alone until we have tried on our costumes. I am so sorry to pull her away, Sir Cosmo, but duty calls—she is dressing our play." She retrieved the plate and Lucy turned to say goodbye, but Sir Cosmo was talking to a tall woman with hair so deeply black, it couldn't possibly be real.

"STAND STILL, EVELYN, otherwise your eyebrows will be all crooked." Elinor stood back to admire her handiwork and applied rouge to Evelyn Willie James's already feverish cheeks. "We are making a list of girls who have what Lucy and I call 'It.' Girls we know." Elinor blew cigarette smoke all over her friend, and in an aside to her sister, she said, "Poor Evelyn's a bundle of nerves; we have to distract her." And then back to Evelyn: "So, we've got Daisy, of course. Who did you say, Gwladys Ripon? No, darling, she's too old, but nobody had more 'It' than Gwladys ten years ago."

"The actress, the actress Lily Elsie," Evelyn said as Lucy tacked up the cuff of her green velvet sleeve.

Elinor shook her head. "How do you know that she has 'It'? Do you know her?"

"Because she is very beautiful." Evelyn winced as her hair was pulled back by Elinor's strong hands. "Nice and tight, so we can put your wig on at the last moment." Evelyn's wide gray eyes shone out of a face lurid with stage makeup. *Diplomacy* was about to make its debut in twenty minutes.

"Beauty doesn't come into it. Look at Lucy here; she is a lovely woman, but she doesn't have 'It.'"

Lucy laughed. "No, I am sure I don't. I have no interest in attracting." *Then what was all that about in the drawing room yesterday? Whenever I try to flirt, I am so heavy-handed.*

Lucy decided that if she came across Sir Cosmo Duff Gordon again this weekend, which would be highly unlikely because there was such a crush of guests at the castle, she would be her normal self: polite and distant. Trying to fit in with the Marlborough set was not her at all. She half listened to Elinor instructing Evelyn on the finer points of "It." "It" was a game the two sisters had played for years.

"You see, Evelyn, Lucy and I have a list."

"No, you have a list, Elinor. I sometimes add to it."

"Don't interrupt, Lucy. We call it the 'It' list. And we are very particular who we put on it. This is how it works: Daisy is not quite as lovely as Lily Elsie, but she attracts. Men are drawn to her—she could wear a bag over her head and she would still attract: it is the pitch and tone of her voice, the way she walks, the way she *is*. She has what people used to call je ne sais quoi when what they really mean is that she has allure. Not in an obvious way, of course; that would be quite awful."

"Five minutes to curtain, everyone, five minutes." Georgina Ward wafted past their dressing room and Evelyn started to cough.

"Elinor has 'It,'" said Lucy, snipping off a loose thread on the sleeve of Evelyn's costume. "By the bucketful. Now, put this on, Evelyn. There now, look how lovely!" She practically had to shout over Evelyn's hard, tight cough.

"A sip or two of something." Elinor put a glass into Evelyn's hand. "Try saying 'keep a copper kettle in the kitchen.' That's what Lily Elsie does; it loosens the tongue and relaxes the throat."

Lucy sniffed Evelyn's glass. "And try saying it after you have drunk that."

Elinor stubbed out her cigarette and pulled Evelyn to her feet. "That dress looks divine on you, Evie. What a figure you have. Lucy, let's put Evie down on our 'It' list." She held the glass to her friend's lips. "Little sips . . . darling. Little sips."

Georgina Ward put her head around the door. "Places, please, curtain up in two minutes. Who is prompting? Did Daisy arrange for someone to prompt? Of course not! Never mind, I'll find someone."

Evelyn's hands started to shake, and Elinor took her firmly by the shoulders. "Stop it now, Evie! You will be brilliant—the moment you say your first line."

They walked up the corridor from the anteroom and through the servants' entrance of the Cedar Room to backstage, interrupting Harriet Mordaunt and Charles Kinsky doing a bit of rehearsing on a silk sofa.

*God save us from amateur theatricals,* Lucy thought, and, to her surprise, out from the wings strolled Sir Cosmo Duff Gordon. "Georgina asked me to sit here and be prompt." He smiled at Lucy. "Did you dress everyone?"

"No, just the two female leads."

"You aren't taking part?"

"Oh, good heavens, no. I can't act to save my life."

"Curtain call, curtain call." Georgina Ward shooed everyone offstage. "Take your place, please, Elinor."

Lucy's sister stood center stage, her head thrown back and her eyes closed. She dropped the embroidered shawl she was holding at her feet.

Cosmo sat down rather abruptly in a chair that was shoved up against his legs, and Lucy stepped back to find herself hemmed in by the rest of the Castle Players of *Diplomacy* behind her.

The lights went up and the curtain swept open to applause from the audience as Horace Brand strolled in to join Elinor onstage. *Ah yes,* Lucy thought, smiling to herself, *there it is, the result of thorough "rehearsing,"* as Brand came to Elinor's side and smiled down into her glistening emerald eyes.

The play began.

"You will catch cold, Barbara. Have you left your shawl indoors?" The pitch of Brand's voice was intimate—caressing, her sister would have said.

"Oh no, I shall not. How very soon you are leaving; you have scarcely stayed ten minutes," Elinor/Barbara replied in a voice husky with emotion and the last of Evelyn's medicinal whisky.

"But you forget, Barbara, that I have a home. A wife and a family . . ."

*You most certainly have*, Lucy thought as she watched Elinor turn from him in a swirl of rich blue, the back of her hand pressed gracefully to her forehead.

"Oh Lord," Lucy heard Cosmo mutter as he rustled through the pages of the script. "I had no idea it was a ruddy melodrama."

She laughed under her breath and he raised his head from the play on his lap. "I am so sorry," he whispered. He pulled the corner of his mouth down in mock contrition and, getting to his feet, offered her his chair.

LUCY CAME DOWN to the great hall early the next morning, in her warmest coat, determined to walk down to the river and watch the great grist mill at work under the castle walls.

As she crossed the floor to the open front doors, a figure emerged from behind a rack of African spears.

"Good morning, Mrs. Wallace." It was Sir Cosmo, who had done such a sterling job of prompting Evelyn Willie James from his corner, stage left. "Are you out for your morning walk?"

"I want to see the old mill underneath the castle ramparts. I saw the weir from the staircase when I arrived. You can feel the wheel turning if you stand on the stairs."

He turned and cast a thoughtful look at the display of swords and rapiers on the wall, as if trying to decide what to do. "May I accompany you?" he asked with a formality that Lucy's mother would have admired as "considerate."

Lucy started for the door. "Of course." And off they went into the courtyard with the sun shining through the tops of the trees and the shout of early morning birdsong. It took them a while to find their way out of the courtyard and down the steps to the banks of the Avon.

The tumbling river shone in the early morning light. Willows graced its edge, and a vee formation of a female pintail with her ducklings moved effortlessly forward on its surface. The castle's walls rose steeply above them, its cathedral-like windows glinting in the sun.

"The castle is so much more beautiful outside than in," Lucy said as she gazed at the scene before her. The woodland on both sides of the river came down to its edge, fringing the bank with the bright, fragile greens of June.

"There is a bridge further down where we can cross and come up to the weir on the other side. That way you'll get the full benefit of the castle standing above the mill house. Then we can cross back to the castle side, above the weir. It's a perfect place to fish." Sir Cosmo stepped aside for Lucy to walk ahead along the narrow path.

"For eels, the butler told me." Lucy shuddered. "Apparently they catch eels above the weir."

He shook his head. "No, I was thinking of trout. A bit more fun than an eel. All you need for them is a net."

Lucy was grateful that he became silent as they walked. After three days of the endless energy of her hostess, her sister, the Marlborough set's frantic need for entertainment, and the demanding bonhomie of the Prince of Wales, she craved the solitude of a quiet early morning walk.

The air was clear and cool, and the delicate scent of blooming dog roses reached them on the sunlit path. Ahead, a narrow stone bridge had become a riot of late-blooming honeysuckle, alive with bees. It took them to the other side of the river, where the trees thinned out to the castle's parkland and sheep grazed under the canopy of ancient beech trees. Nibbling the grass, they lifted their faces, their fleece glowing like fresh milk in the morning light. Lucy was transfixed by any scene that blended the colors of nature. *Cream, lime, and gold*, she thought as she gazed across the parkland to the woodland and the rich stone of the castle. A perfect blend of tints and hues that complemented one another, with an edging of pale rose-pink along the path.

"I see what you mean about the castle's beauty from outside," her companion said.

"Yes, the stone looks so rich in this light. What I love about the country most is the delicate color of spring as it turns into summer. Before everything becomes dark and dusty and loses its freshness. I don't think there is a country in the world that is as beautiful as England in spring."

"You've traveled?" he asked as the path widened and he came alongside her.

"Oh, no, not really. Elinor and I were born on Jersey island, and when our father died, my mother was so devastated she simply couldn't cope, so we were sent off to Canada to our grandparents—we were only away for a couple of years, while my mother found us a house in St. Helier." She did not say that their mother had also found a new husband. "My grandparents had a cattle ranch—we could ride for hours and not see a soul."

"Canada, that's a pretty large canvas. Mountains, lakes, prairies, and the great forests of the West," he said.

Elinor nodded. "It was vast and magnificent; Elinor and I were good at giving our grandmother the slip to explore. I remember when we came back to Britain, it seemed tiny. Everything in miniature. Black-and-white villages, stone churches, fields and meadows with hedged-in lanes. I was my daughter's age: twelve or thirteen. England has perfect scale for a child."

"Do you miss the country, living in London?"

"No, not really. I love London and I enjoy visiting the country for its beauty and serenity. But it is so cold in winter, and I find days of endless rain, mist, and dark depressing. I am the worst guest at a country house party because I don't hunt or ride to hounds, but I do enjoy walking. This weekend was enough country for me."

He was laughing. "Rain and mist. Have you ever been to Scotland?"

"No, but I've heard it's very lovely."

He stopped and waved his arm at the horizon. "Rivers, crags, and mists, with hills red and purple with heather. It is empty and, as you say, very lovely. But like you, I am happy to live in London."

They resumed their walk, skirting the meadow and dropping back down to the river's edge. "What keeps you in town?" She knew he wasn't in politics, and somehow he didn't seem to quite fit in with the Prince of Wales's pleasure-seekers.

"I fence."

"With a . . ." She frowned not sure what the correct term was. "Sword?"

"An épée or a foil, and sometimes a saber."

"That sounds dangerous."

When he laughed, his eyes were two crescents of shining onyx. "We are protected by a padded jacket and a wire-mesh face mask. Fencing is about balance, timing, and concentration—rather than hacking away at your enemy in battle. There is a strict code of behavior, of honor."

*And that*, Lucy thought, *is why he moves with such grace for a tall man.* She looked at his hands, long palms and fingers. She saw him wearing a wide-brimmed hat with a curling feather, a short cloak swinging from one shoulder, and a pointed lace collar.

*Dashing*, she thought, as she watched the cavalier doff his hat and make a graceful bow. *Elegant and*—she glanced up from under her hat at his rather flamboyant handlebar mustache—*and debonaire, with more than a touch of male vanity.* She saw him in a solid gray granite house in Scotland setting out to stalk deer in the heather, while his wife sat in the drawing room stitching at her tapestry and gossiping with friends. But why did he bring his young cousin down to London to shop for her coming-out wardrobe? *That is a wife's job*, she thought.

Fencing? She had no idea that people still did that—for sport. Sir Cosmo certainly didn't fit in with the Marlborough House crowd, with their delight in practical jokes and sledding down the stairs on trays. When not eating, drinking, or gambling, the Prince of Wales's cronies had broken the tedium with soda-siphon battles and other boisterous games. Lucy yawned. It had been fun to venture out into the world of fashionable society, but she already missed her studio and planning next season's models.

*If he's not part of the prince's coterie, he undoubtedly belongs to the tweedy set,* she thought—*how predictable.* "Hunting, shooting, and fishing," she said to a surprised laugh, and then realized she had blurted.

"No, I don't enjoy foxhunting—seems rather unfair for twenty men on horseback, with a pack of well-fed hounds, to run a small animal to death for sport. And shooting is an abysmal waste of a beautiful morning in late summer or autumn . . . but I do enjoy fishing. Staring into water all day—contemplative solitude."

"Is it fair to sneak up on a fish and yank it out of its home? I wonder."

"If you are hungry, I think it is perfectly fair to take your shotgun or fishing rod to hunt for food. It is a reasonable exchange: life for sustenance. When I fish for sport and catch a crafty old trout, I let him go. Who knows, if I am lucky I might catch him again!"

Her glance was quick enough to see his expression. His eyes were alight with pleasure—this wasn't an anti-blood sports lecture from some citified crank. He was quite comfortable sharing his views. In spite of her fatigue, her desire to be home with Esmé snuggled up next to her as she read to her, she smiled. He was the least affected man she had met this weekend: pleasant, thoughtful, and kindly. She looked up as they came within the sound of the crashing weir and the great wooden mill wheel. Walking onto the narrow footbridge they leaned out over the railings and gazed downward.

He touched her arm and pointed at fish—trout—leaping in the water as it spilled over the weir. She saw another and another. Silver, gray, and white soared in the air for a split second, and as the sun caught them, their scales glittered in iridescent sequined color before they plunged back into the river. Exclaiming in delight, she turned to him and saw in his eyes a flash of complete recognition, of understanding. "Are they grinding wheat?" she shouted, looking at the great wooden wheel.

He shook his head and walked her off the bridge. "Not now; they are

making electricity—for the castle. The lights for the castle and last
night's play were generated from a dynamo powered by this wheel."

She was disappointed. *How practical*, she thought. She had imagined
golden wheat kernels being ground to flour. She looked at her watch and
walked past the mill house.

"Thank you," she said, "for such a pleasant walk." Her mind was
already calculating the time it would take to drive to the local railway
station. "We have to catch the half-past-nine train back to London.
Thank you for keeping me company." She went on ahead as they climbed
the steps to the castle courtyard, grateful to see Alice was already waiting for her, surrounded by their luggage.

# CHAPTER NINE

LUCY

*If one more person says, "Ma'am, do you have a moment?" I don't know what I'll do.* Lucy returned to the business of tacking silk velvet around the décolletage of a dress for her autumn collection. The knock came again, more insistent. Lucy pricked her thumb. "Damn," she said under her breath. "What is it *now*?" she called out.

"Celia, ma'am."

Lucy didn't hesitate. "Come!" she called out—Celia never interrupted unless it was vital. "I hope you are bringing good news . . ." And as Celia came into her studio: "Whatever it is."

"A bit of both, ma'am." Celia was wearing her new spectacles; they looked enchanting perched on the end of her tiny nose. "A message from Mr. Charles Wyndham . . ."

"Wyndham—do I know him?"

"The actor-manager of the Criterion Theatre, ma'am. He is putting on *The Liars* and he would like you to dress his two leading ladies, Miss Vanbrugh and Miss Moore. He says there is not a moment to lose, and he wants to know if he should come to you, or will you go to him?" It was quite clear that Celia had made up her mind that she would be dressing *The Liars* leading ladies.

Lucy licked a drop of blood off her thumb and tried to collect her thoughts. Dressing Mary Moore and Irene Vanbrugh? She felt too stunned to speak. She sat down, holding her hands tightly together between her knees.

"Yes, ma'am. Mr. Wyndham wants you to dress them. He says he won't take no for an answer!"

"He wants me? Oh my goodness, Celia, this is tremendous news. Tremendous. Between Lady Brooke and this wonderful, wonderful play. I think more doors are opening!"

"And your answer, ma'am," Celia pressed.

"What? Oh yes, of course. I will go to him at the theater, as soon as he likes. I can't believe he wants me." Lucy tried to remember Mary Moore from her last play: petite, light, a bright candle flame of a girl. And Irene Vanbrugh . . . how she would love to dress that stately brunette with her thrilling voice.

"And the other news? Please make it good!"

"I can't, ma'am, because it isn't good." Celia bit the bottom of her lip. "I contacted the agent about renewing our lease, and he says that the owner, Mr. Buchanan, wants his house back."

Lucy stood up and lifted both hands to her head. "Bother, bother, and bother all landlords."

"Not immediately, ma'am, not immediately. I told him that you were run off your feet, what with the autumn collection, and now this theatrical commission. He says he is happy to put us on a monthly arrangement until we find new premises. But he asks us not to delay too long."

Lucy sat back down in a chair and stared out the window. "Celia, a moment, please." She held up her hand to stop the flow of her landlord's needs. "Do you know that woman? I used to see her walking in Davies Street, and then we moved and here she is again."

Old Burlington Street was a busy thoroughfare; shops sold flower essence and distillations, every possible face cream that could be concocted from lavender, roses, chamomile, and mint; Mr. Padre's shop next door made embroidered kid gloves; and there were three modistes who made hats and parasols within yards of Lucile's front door. "There . . ." Lucy lifted the window and leaned out. "Now do you see her? She is wearing a dark blue coat, beautifully cut, and a turquoise hat. You can't miss her. I feel as if I might know her. Do I know her?"

Celia poked her head out. "You mean the one with the dark turquoise parasol?"

"Yes, she put it up as you looked out."

"Never seen her before, ma'am. I'll describe her to Robbie. He knows everyone. Very quick eyes that boy has, and such a memory for names and faces."

"Goodness, with all this news. I am most certainly not thinking straight. She is probably shopping like a hundred other women in Old Burlington Street." Lucy pulled the window sash down. "Now back to business. Where were we? Ah yes, it always comes down to one thing, unfortunately: money. And a move is always expensive. How much have we got in the bank?" It was a question she never asked directly. It was Celia's job to pay the bills and their seamstresses' wages and fuss about clients' timeliness with their payments.

"Well . . . if everyone paid us—"

Lucy waved away her words. "The aristocracy never pay on time: it is dinned into them from earliest childhood: don't pay the tradesmen unless they threaten to cut you off, and then find another who is more cooperative. They pay in the end, of course, but we must never press them. So . . . how much money do we have in the bank?"

It was a trick question, and Lucy smiled, knowing that Celia would answer her in a way that made sense. "We are solvent for the next eighteen months—even if no one places another order with us and if no one pays their outstanding bills to us."

"As much as that? Thank heavens for the Americans and my old friends; they always insist on paying the minute their orders are complete. Write to our landlord and thank him for giving us some time to find another house.

Then we will put out the word for a new one. Here is what we are looking for: a large house in a fashionable area with a ballroom."

Celia had been on her way out, but her head whipped round as if she had been smacked on the jaw.

"A ballroom?"

"That is what I said." Lucy sat back in her chair. "And you want to know why, don't you?" She laughed. "Ah, Celia, if you could see your face. I have had an idea brewing for quite some time—it needed the right moment and the perfect place. Tell me, what do you think of this new walking outfit?" She waved at the canvas-and-horsehair dressmaker's dummy.

"It is lovely." Celia's answer was automatic.

"No, no. What do you really think of it?" Celia stared at the dummy, closely watched by her boss. "What are you thinking?"

Celia laughed. "I would like to eat the colors: chocolate and raspberries."

"And you got that from looking at an outfit on a dummy."

Celia nodded. She knew what was expected of her. "And it will be perfect for a woman with fair or red hair and a pale complexion."

"Yes, I designed it for a very fair complexion. A dress always comes alive on the right woman, doesn't it?" Celia nodded. "So . . . picture several young women, lovely young things, the prettiest girls in London actually, wearing my dresses for the autumn collection. Imagine a large room full of all our clients sitting on comfortable chairs and sofas: relaxed, in the company of the friends, enjoying tea together, and one after the other these glorious creatures walk into the room and stand in its center. They turn this way and that to show off one dress and then another. What sort of impact would this walking outfit have on you then? I wonder."

Her assistant didn't hesitate; the walking costume was made for women with her coloring. "I would say yes, make me one immediately!" Celia was quite carried away by the prospect. "And I think we should serve champagne instead of tea. A little bubbly always helps loosen the purse strings, ma'am."

Lucy's eyes were wide. "Could this be Celia Franklin? Giving away the best wine!"

She watched her assistant imagine the moment. Her brow puckered. "But who would wear . . . ?"

"Beautiful young women, Celia. We could make our autumn and spring collection into a series of little stage productions. Just like going to the theater. And there is no reason to restrict the guest list to women only—perhaps at first it should only be a show for our clients. But later on, we should invite their husbands too. Some men love to watch their wives dress up. Haven't you noticed that more gentlemen have been popping into Old Burlington Street recently?"

A look of horror flashed across Celia's face. "Lord forgive me, ma'am, I completely forgot with all the excitement. There is a gentleman downstairs in the drawing room. He is with Miss Antrobus; he says his name is . . ." Her hand flew to her forehead. "Sir something Gordon?"

"Cosmo Duff Gordon, quite a mouthful, isn't it?" *He is here, downstairs . . . in my salon?* It was entirely the last thing in the world she had expected to hear. "Thank you, Celia. Please tell Miss Antrobus I will be down directly." And Lucy turned away to hide her confusion.

WHAT A MORNING! And if all the exciting news wasn't enough, the arrival of Sir Cosmo had certainly increased Lucy's pulse rate.

Where did Sir Cosmo fit into this remarkable day? After the first moment of alarm that he was actually downstairs, Lucy told herself off. *He said he might be coming to town with his niece . . . so why are you so surprised that he's here?* There was nothing for it but to deal with her two guests. And downstairs she must go to say good morning. Lucy automatically brushed stray threads from her skirt and leaned into the looking glass to tidy her hair in the light from the window. *Surely I would do this for any visitor,* she thought as she smoothed the wings of hair on either side of her face. But would she pinch her cheeks until they were rosy for a consultation? And what about her work coat: plain, drab, and serviceable? It wouldn't do for someone paying a social call—or a client.

*Well, it is too late to change now—they could have at least made an appointment.* She felt harassed by the impromptu call when she wanted to sit and enjoy her good news and wonder how she would find another house.

She pulled off the jersey wool coatee she wore for work and prepared to go downstairs. Turning at the door, she returned to flip the delicate lace shawl adorning her dressmaker's dummy over the shoulders of her white blouse. It was a fine piece of lace, and the coffee color contrasted well with the crisp lawn of her blouse, bringing out the rich color of her hair. *That's a bit more presentable,* she told herself before she descended to the ground floor of the house.

Cynthia Antrobus was trying on a hat that made her look like a little mushroom. "Mrs. Wallace," she said. Without the hat Cynthia was a handsome young woman, with the clear-eyed, healthy complexion of someone who spent a good deal of her time out of doors. *How active young girls are these days: how bright and pretty they are,* Lucy thought as she looked from Miss Antrobus to Sir Cosmo, standing half-turned to the window, watching the street with his hands clasped behind his back.

"How lovely to see you, both of you!" She walked forward, hands outstretched to Cynthia. "Now, what brings you to my shop?"

"An engagement . . . and . . . a new wardrobe." Cynthia Antrobus was laughing as she stood with the hat in her hands.

"And I have come with her, to say hello!" Sir Cosmo turned his back on the window.

"How very nice! Congratulations to you, Miss Antrobus. When are you to be married?" She kept her gaze fixed on Cynthia. Conversation was effortless when there was a trousseau to plan, even with this tall man gazing at her.

"This October to Giles Sinclair. In Scotland. Do you have time to fit me in today just for a quick chat? I know it's short notice." Miss Antrobus was still holding the hat, and Lucy gently took it out of her hands.

"A narrower brim for you, with a tall crown. And yes, we can always make time to discuss a trousseau and the perfect dress for an October wedding." A quick glance at Sir Cosmo. "Sir Cosmo, can you bear to listen to all the fabrics and the fuss? It can go on for quite some time."

His smile was genuinely thankful. "I am off to my club, but perhaps if you are free this evening I might take you to dinner?"

A dinner invitation? Lucy ate dinner at the houses of her friends, but she had never in her life been taken *out* to dinner. *How would I know what is done these days?* she thought as she realized how reclusive her nighttime habits had become.

"In a restaurant?" She had eaten luncheon at the Savoy, certainly, with her sister and her friends, but an invitation to eat dinner in the company of a gentleman—now, here was a novelty.

His confusion was greater than hers. "Yes, in a restaurant. Perhaps you are engaged this evening?"

"Oh, no, it's a lovely idea, but I have never . . ."

"Eaten in a restaurant?" Perplexity turned to stunned astonishment.

"Yes, yes, I have for luncheon. Of course, for luncheon."

His look was hopeful. "Well, it's the same as luncheon . . . only there are more courses and we normally dress up." He was laughing now. "Shall I make a reservation for us at Rules, or perhaps the Savoy?"

"Wherever you think best." She felt her ears growing hot and she wished this awkward exchange would end. *He must think me a complete fool!*

"Well, I am glad that's settled." Cynthia Antrobus gave her cousin a peck of approval on the cheek as Lucy rang for tea.

LUCY FELT ABSURDLY nervous as she was led to Sir Cosmo's table in a quiet corner of the Savoy Grill. She saw several of her clients enjoying dinner with friends, which made her feel completely out of place and even more self-conscious.

She nodded to the actress Ellen Terry, who was wearing one of her gowns. *What on earth is Maud Cunard doing here with someone other than her husband?* She smiled and lifted a hand in greeting to Lady Cunard's parrot screech of recognition. *And there is dear Mrs. Guttenberg, thankfully eating dinner with her husband and that lovely friend of hers from Chicago.* Lucy stopped at Mrs. Guttenberg's table to say hello and for introductions to be made.

*I have dressed most of the women in this restaurant.* Thoroughly at ease after Mrs. Guttenberg's affectionate greeting, Lucy floated back across the dining room to Sir Cosmo, standing at their table to greet her.

Before she could say good evening to him, Lucy caught Margot Asquith's eye and they exchanged polite bows. Margot's eyes glistened with barely concealed curiosity, and she lost no time informing everyone at her table that Mrs. Lucy Wallace, who was rarely seen outside her shop, was eating dinner with—raised eyebrows and little smiles were exchanged—Sir Cosmo Duff Gordon, who rarely strayed outside his fencing club.

"Well, this is exciting!" he said as he seated her, but she could tell that his natural reserve told him otherwise. Now half of the dining room was buzzing.

Lucy took a sip from her water glass. She was nervous enough about dinner with Sir Cosmo without being the talk of the evening. *I don't have to live like a nun in a cloister because I divorced my husband,* she thought, and then told herself off for being defensive.

"Do you always lead such a busy and exciting life?" Cosmo glanced around at the gossipers.

"It is certainly busy," she said. "But rarely exciting."

"My cousin Cynthia told me that you were dressing Mary Moore and Irene Vanbrugh for the Charles Wyndham production of *The Liars.* I have to say I know nothing about the theater." He laughed. "But it is rather a step up from the Castle Players putting on *Diplomacy.*"

*He is very nice,* Lucy thought. *Really very nice indeed, but he is not my type—far too conservative, and he's probably only interested in fishing and fencing.* "I am still struggling to believe that they want me to dress them

at all. Amateur theatricals are fun—probably more fun for the cast than
the audience. But I am really excited about *The Liars*..." She shrugged
away making dresses for a West End play and half acknowledged possible success.

He laughed. "So, you are on the brink of something really thrilling."
The waiter poured champagne and he lifted his glass. "To new paths...
wherever they may lead."

"Thank you," she said, and then, conscious that she had dominated
all the attention since she had arrived, she asked, "Do your family live
in Scotland?" and prepared herself to listen to the Duff Gordon family
history.

"A branch of the family live in Wales. But yes, my two younger
brothers and my sister, Flora, are all entrenched up there in the heather.
We are a very proper Scots family, hidebound Presbyterians every
one of us," he said, confirming Lucy's guess that a man like Sir Cosmo
was a traditionalist. "Actually, I am considered the black sheep of the
family."

Lucy raised her eyebrows.

"Not in that way." His laugh was self-deprecating. "I just don't wake
up every day eager for the kill. My brother should have inherited, not
me. I enjoy living in London and visiting when I feel the call of the
wild—salmon fishing." He smiled at what was evidently the only country sport he pursued.

More champagne was poured, and with it came Orkney oysters. "I
ordered dinner for us earlier, so we wouldn't have to waste time with the
menu. I have a feeling you don't mind what you eat."

It was true she picked like a bird all day, existing on a glass of milk
at noon if she was working on her latest design, but by dinnertime she
was ravenous. "I am very fussy about what I eat, in fact. I don't follow
the fashion of eating nine courses at dinner. How can anyone sleep afterward? I find the formality tedious, especially if you end up between
two dull old men whose only interest is in politics. Dressing for dinner
is a bit tiresome too."

"But you make glamorous gowns for just that purpose."

"Yes, but it doesn't mean that I want to wear them at the end of a day at work." He looked almost startled by her reference to the fact that she worked for a living. "Designing clothes takes concentration, and often my days are very long." She didn't want to be a bore with the details. "Well-brought-up girls do not let the conversation center on themselves," she heard her mother's voice say. "My sister told me that you were the best épée swordsman in England. But I had no idea what she was talking about." Elinor had also been quick to inform Lucy that he was not married. "Not even a widower, darling."

He started to shake his head. "Oh, you can't describe something like fencing—any more than I am sure you can't describe how to design a dress. Fencing has to be seen; otherwise it sounds like two old fogies pretending they live in medieval France."

She scooped an oyster into her mouth. "What sword is used for dueling?" She pursued her polite inquiry.

"An épée. There are two other types of swords in fencing: the foil, which is used for training, and the Italian saber, which is used in the sport of fencing—unlike the cavalry saber . . ."

He leaned forward as he talked about a sport he was clearly obsessed with, and Lucy nodded along; her face expressed polite interest, but she was barely listening to a word he said. She was too busy thinking that Sir Cosmo was attracted to her and that, however pleasant he was, this was an acquaintanceship that could not possibly lead anywhere.

*I do like his voice.* She half closed her eyes. It was low in pitch. Unhurried. It had a well-modulated quality, almost musical. She noted the very slight *sh* sound he made at the beginning of words like "sword" and "saber."

". . . I go to France to train every year." She lifted her head as he laughed. "I told you it was a sport better watched than explained." She caught the pretended complaint in his tone and was horrified that she had offended.

"No, no. I was listening, intently, I only closed my eyes to see what you were saying. Some people understand from listening, but I am visual. I was trying to imagine what you would look like with an épée in your hand." She thanked God for her quick wits—this man was far too nice to snub.

"Like this!" he said. Suddenly, he turned in his chair and raised his right hand with his forearm at a ninety-degree angle to his body, his forefinger pointing at her. His left arm was crooked at the elbow, his hand pointing upward. *"In guardia!"*

*Yes, I had better be on guard,* she thought. *Perhaps there is more to this Sir Cosmo than the man sitting prompt left huffing at the enormous declarations of love and despair taking place center stage at Warwick Castle.* "I thought it was en garde!" she said.

"And so it is in France. Enough of sword fighting. So, apart from an exciting commission to make theater costumes for the theater production of *The Liars,* Cynthia tells me you are looking for a new house—for your business?"

She was taken aback for a moment. Had anyone ever referred to her shop and her dress designs as a business? It was a serious word; it belonged in the masculine world. The world of gentlemen's clubs in Pall Mall, the London Stock Exchange, and the House. Women did not go into business. Or at least ladies didn't. She wondered if it mattered to him that she was not only a divorcée but a woman of business. It didn't seem to; otherwise they would not be sitting here eating oysters and drinking champagne. *But why should I care what he really thinks?* she asked herself. *He is simply a man with good manners who has taken me out to dinner. We have nothing in common—he doesn't enjoy the theater and probably never picks up a book unless it has to do with how to catch fish.*

"The owner of our house wants it back, and in three years we have outgrown it anyway. He is being reasonable about giving us time to find another place . . . but—" She lifted her hands in pretend despair. "I want a house in Mayfair, but it's not that easy because I will be opening a shop and studio in it, and not living there, so no landlord in his right mind will want to upset the neighbors. Most of my clients are rich and titled, so it has to be somewhere elegant and fashionable so they will feel relaxed about coming to me." She realized that she might be boring him to death, but she took the risk in case he knew of a place for her "business."

"What sort of house? Larger than the one you have—or grand?"

"My vision is for a graceful house, and yes, grand would do, and since we are doing quite nicely now, we must have space to expand, rather than go through all of this bother in another three years. It is such an upheaval to pack and move, and on top of that I need another smaller, much less grand house for myself, my daughter, and my mother. Esmé is too old now to live above a shop." She ground to a halt and watched his smile turn into a laugh.

"Live above a shop—do you mean like Miss Grits, the greengrocer's daughter?" When he lost the serious look, he was almost handsome.

She laughed at his reference to the card game Happy Families. "Yes, poor little thing—very unsuitable for a thirteen-year-old girl. Not to mention . . ." On an impulse to lighten this polite exchange, she leaned forward. "The strong smell of shallots on the stairs." She invited him to play the old nursery alliterative game with her, wondering if he even knew it.

He sat up straight. "Piles of potatoes in the portico—"

"Mountains of mushrooms—"

"—under Molly's marbles."

She stopped laughing. "You lose; we don't have a Molly in our house!" A gentleman at the table next to theirs turned and stared at them through his monocle.

Cosmo whispered, "Mountains of mushrooms under Mama's monocle."

She laughed. "Very good. Oh dear, have we gone too far?"

The waiter clearly thought so; he whisked away their empty champagne glasses. Succulent slices of lamb with delicate potatoes Dauphinoise and freshly minted garden peas were put in front of them and claret poured into fresh glasses. The hard shell of propriety had cracked, and they fell into an easy discussion about houses and the fashionable areas of Mayfair, Knightsbridge, and Lowndes Square. They picked at their food and finished the wine.

At eleven o'clock she noticed the time and stared with dismay at the summer pudding looking forlornly misshapen and unwanted on the table in front of her. "Good heavens, it's after eleven. Thank you so much for a wonderful evening. If I wasn't a working girl I would have dinner out every night of the week."

Outside on the pavement he asked, "Shall we walk? Your house is quite close."

She hesitated, almost persuaded, then decided against. "No, I must get on. Would you find a hansom for me?" She put out her hand and he took it in his, but instead of shaking it, he held it for a brief moment. "Thank you for such an enjoyable evening. I hope we can do it again soon?"

She withdrew her hand. "Yes, I would like that very much . . . and if you hear of a suitable house on a long lease in Mayfair, please let me know."

LUCY STRETCHED OUT in the middle of her bed and went carefully over her evening at the Savoy Grill. There had been a few men in the past three years who had made it clear that they enjoyed her company— whenever they came across each other at their friends' houses. But no one had sought her out quite so directly or had made such an impact on her as Cosmo Duff Gordon. *He is a romantic,* she thought with more than a little dismay. *A sensitive man, self-aware and confident enough not to be a conceited flirt.* But would she accept a dinner invitation from him again? Who could say?

She organized her pillows, turned on her side, and within minutes fell into deep, tranquil sleep.

# CHAPTER TEN

*November 1899*

CELIA

Celia could barely form words, her lips were so cold. She crammed her numb fingers deep into her pockets. "So, tell me the worst, Mr. Harris. Any hope at all for the boiler?" The move from Old Burlington Street to Hanover Square had been rife with problems: they were weeks behind schedule. Their painter accused his suppliers of being behind in matching the shade of paint Mrs. W. had ordered, and now, despite days of mess and the house full of men clomping ash and cinders up from the cellar and down the hall, the boiler was still causing chilly problems. Her teeth chattered a rapid flamenco rhythm that echoed throughout the length of a room that could surely hold the entire Methodist congregation of Newcastle.

Mr. Harris wiped his hands on a cloth, his heavily featured face decorated with smudges of soot and coal dust. "Well, ma'am, the good news is that there are heating pipes from the furnace to this room. The problem is, as you say, with the boiler. It's an old 'un. Put in at least fifty years ago, which is why some of the rooms are slightly warmer by the dining room, than the ones on this side of the house. With a new boiler you will be as warm as you like—even here in this great room."

The boiler was the latest problem of the many she had solved in the past weeks, and it sounded like an expensive one. She folded her arms across her chest—like all the others, this was her problem to solve. Mrs. Wallace had made it quite clear at the outset.

"Are you telling me that the painters haven't finished yet? Celia, we can't move in with the paint still wet: the smell is overpowering—we'll never get the reek of turpentine out of the fabric or the furniture." Her frustrated boss had complained to Celia as she stared down at her drawing board, refusing to be pulled into any more moving plans. "Celia, please." She looked up, her eyes tired from overwork. "We will stay here, even half-packed, until the house is ready for us. I know you can make it work . . ."

How often had Mrs. Wallace said those words in the past months? Only the smallest part of Celia resented them. If Mrs. Wallace believed she was capable, then she was.

*It will be worth it*, she thought as she totted up the cost to replace the broken-down range in the kitchen as well as the new boiler. Hanover Square offered them more space, abundant natural light in the workrooms, and a kitchen the size of a drawing room so that all the staff could eat their midday meal together belowstairs. She had felt a heady thrill of pride as one of the painters had screwed a shining brass plate to the left of the newly painted black front door: *Madame Lucile, Court Dressmaker.*

Three weeks later the move was made in a blizzard, and now they all were frozen to immobility in the spacious icy rooms of their new atelier as Mr. Harris put the central heating through its neurotic paces.

*Why do we always manage to move in the coldest winter of the decade?* She dipped her nose into the soft wool of her scarf and huffed her breath out to warm it—she hadn't taken her coat off in days. *And now this ridiculous room, the reason for the outrageous rent we are paying, is as cold as charity.*

Mrs. Wallace had shut herself in her studio to work on her spring collection, refusing to take a break even for meals and waving away all problems. "I am weeks behind, weeks! No, please don't tell me what the latest problem is, Celia—if it's the painters again, offer them more money to get the work done quickly!"

Celia brought Mrs. W. hot soup for lunch and pried her out of the studio using Esmé's need for her mother to enforce another break in the evening. *We might end up with more clients, and articles about the most remarkable collection for the last year of this century in* The Queen *and* La Mode Illustrée, she fumed as she tried to remember the stupendous figure Mr. Harris had charged them for nursing the boiler back into the last moments of its life. *And more orders than we can keep up with, but what good will it do us if our principal, and only, designer works herself into a standstill?*

Celia's deeply practical Northumbrian nature was offended, and when her back was up her vowels were broader, her sentences were shorter, and her manner bordered on gruff. Her mistress put in more hours than lads down the coal pit, and it would be up to Celia to draw the line.

"How long will it take to install a new boiler, Mr. Harris? This house must be warm. Our girls can hardly thread a needle in this cold." She stifled resentment and frustration.

"We could scrounge up some paraffin heaters for you, if that would help."

She shook her head. "We'd never get the smell out of the fabric . . . So how soon can you get this house warm?"

He thought for a bit. Celia could see him calculating a healthy profit. "No more than three days . . . but it will be pricey." He walked across the floor and launched a kick at an ancient radiator. "These are worthless: clogged with rust. You'll need eight new ones to heat this room alone."

*Southerners—always out for a profit from someone else's misfortune!* She sighed, this time loudly and heavily as she remembered the other little matter that was silently waiting for her in her office.

Madame Lucile's smartly dressed page, Robbie, put his head round the door. "Blimey, it's like the north pole in here. Do I disturb Mrs. Wallace or will you? Her appointment is in the drawing room."

"Who is she again?"

"Miss Duncan."

It was the American dancer, and Mrs. Wallace had been very particular that she should see her, not that Isadora Duncan was important, but Mrs. Margot Asquith, who had referred her to Madame Lucile, most certainly was.

"Put her in the book, Celia," her mistress had told her. "She is one of Mrs. Asquith's finds. Her name is *Isadora* Duncan, and she has been holding everyone enthralled with her free-form dancing: without boundaries, without structure, and often without most of her clothes. I can't imagine what I should design for her, if she is going to discard bits of it all over someone's drawing room floor." She thought for a moment. "Mrs. Asquith has kindly taken responsibility for Miss Duncan's bill, but let's keep the costs down as much as we can. We must all contribute to those possessed with a desire to bare all for their art."

Celia tried to remember which fitting room had the driest paint. "Ask Grace to take Miss Duncan to the Peony Room and let Mrs. Wallace know she is here. I will be in my office if I am needed."

CELIA OPENED THE November edition of *The Queen* magazine and turned to an article titled "The Cult of Chiffon," featuring the creations of Jeanne Paquin's London salon by their house designer, Miss Vionnet.

"Nowhere today are there to be seen such delectable lines, fluid grace, and freedom of style as the gorgeous gowns designed by House of Paquin." Surely there was some mix-up at publication. Celia studied the illustration of a dress so remarkably like the peach gown the Blush of First Love, designed in the tumultuous days before they had moved to Hanover Square. She got up and went to the cabinet where she stored Mrs. Wallace's journals, which recorded every design she made. It took her barely a moment to find the one recording this year's spring collection.

As she leafed through the pages, myriad scraps of fabric pasted in the margins of each drawing fluttered light and color in the lamplight: lace, beads, appliquéd flowers, bows, silk of every kind, delicate lawn, soft woolen cloth, raised and embossed embroidery, ribbons, and feathers. The journal was fat with samples of the trimming used for each dress.

Halfway through forty pages she stopped and gazed down at the flowing lines of the dress featured in *The Queen* as having been designed by the famous House of Paquin in London.

For a moment Celia almost believed that it was a simple error made by *The Queen*'s fashion editor—some fool had attributed a Lucile gown to Jeanne Paquin. She must write a note asking them to correct their mistake. But one small element caught her eye. In Mrs. Wallace's drawing in the journal and the sample of embroidered silk ribbon pasted on the page was the detail of the cuff of the dress. Embroidered silk stitches so fine they might have been painted with a squirrel-hair brush created sprays of delicate plum red roses on a trellis of dark green that formed the cuff to the chiffon sleeves of the gown. She picked up *The Queen*. *How puzzling*, she thought. *There is no embroidery on the cuff in* The Queen. She began to doubt what she had suspected.

It wasn't possible to compare color: the magazine's illustrations were ink drawn, but it was the identical design and the fulsome description of the dress—"The softest shade of peach imaginable, the glowing silk of dawn"—that gave it away. The ruched bodice, the squared neckline, the off-the-shoulder décolleté gown that shouted "Lucile Wallace," and the layered cut of the skirt were identical to the one in the Lucile design journal. It was undoubtedly the same dress, except for those embroidered cuffs. As Celia stared down at the illustration, she noticed other slight differences: the delicate velvet latticework down the front of the bodice in Mrs. Wallace's design had been replaced in the illustration by heavy lace overlaid in a lattice pattern. Small differences that did not detract from the overall design or particularly enhance it. Had these details been changed to make the dresses appear dissimilar? She tried to recollect if Mrs. Wallace had changed her mind about the embroidered cuffs and had decided at the last minute to substitute the velvet for lace in the latticework down the front of the gown.

A cold finger ran up Celia's spine to stir the hair in the nape of her neck. She would not write a complaint to the editor of *The Queen* after all, not unless she wished to suffer the indignity of being told that undoubtedly the evening gown had been designed by the House of Paquin—the label in the dress said so! Perhaps Miss Franklin would care to step over to the offices of *The Queen* and see for herself? No, she must assume that what she was seeing was a copy of a Lucile design proclaiming itself to be part of Jeanne Paquin's collection.

She noted which team of seamstresses and embroiderers had worked on the dress before she returned the journal to its place and spent the rest of the morning catching up on paying bills that had accumulated during their move. As she wrote checks and balanced her account book, Celia's mind puzzled over how anyone who worked in the house could make such a detailed sketch of the gown. All finished models were kept in their linen sleeves locked up in the models room. Celia had a key, and so did Mrs. Wallace. The design journals were kept in Celia's glass-fronted bookcase, which was also locked whenever she left her spacious new office. Had a spy, a thief, made a detailed sketch of the dress and passed it on to the House of Paquin? Information that only someone who had worked on the dress, or had found access to the models room or the design journals, would be privy to?

Celia sat on in the silence of the room. If there was a spy among their workers, then it was up to her to find out who it was, as quietly and discreetly as she possibly could. There must be no suspicion cast until she was sure she knew if she was right in what she believed, and that she was even more sure of the culprit.

That any girl could smuggle designs to another fashion house had occurred to Celia before. And now here it was—a possibly stolen design. To have bought a design by Lucile for the peanuts Paquin had probably paid for it was like knowing the outcome of a horse race before you placed your bet.

Celia sat forward in her chair, her elbows propped on the desk and her chin in her hands, and thought through what she had discovered. In the competitive world of haute couture, provincial dressmakers copied the designs of the top houses in London and Paris every year; it was an inevitable fact of life. Their copies were produced long after the season and would always be seen as just that: imitations of last year's fashions. If Celia's suspicions were right, what mattered was that one of the most important evening gowns of Lucile's spring collection was being gushingly attributed to Jeanne Paquin in London's most prominent fashion journal.

All Celia could be thankful for was that Mrs. Wallace was too busy producing the rest of her collection to bother with anything else, and this gave her the opportunity to get to the bottom of this problem and clean up the mess before things went any further. *No room for complacency*, she thought as the kitchen cat who had forsaken the chilly basement for more comfortable quarters jumped up onto her desk. *Let's just hope you are going to catch this mouse before she sells the entire collection all over London*, Celia thought as she scratched gently behind the cat's ears. "Feed an animal," she remembered her father saying. "And it is yours for life. One day it's in the house, begging for kitchen scraps, and the next thing you know it is sleeping on your bed. Then you give it a name, and you might as well say that having a cat was your idea in the first place."

"Well, I've got a name for what's happening here," she said as she settled Cat in her basket by the fire, "and it's plain common or garden robbery." She took her keys from the desk drawer and went up the stairs to the models room. She unlocked the door and locked it again when she was inside. Long racks stood in rows with a numbered index card at the end of each rack designating the names of the clients and which dresses had been made for them.

The rack for the spring collection stood apart from clients' orders; they held the models that would be used for Mrs. Wallace's first fashion parade in the ballroom. Celia flicked through the covered hangers of fifteen evening gowns, seven walking outfits, and six visiting costumes for daytime. Until she came to the Blush. She lifted it from the rack and drew it out from its sleeve. A sighing slither of silk against silk. In the bright light washing in through the window, she held up the dress and caught her breath. It was undoubtedly the same dress as the one in *The Queen*. She lay the illustration in the magazine on the windowsill and lifted the skirt of the Blush: the fluted, layered skirt, the cut of the elongated bodice with the twist of chiffon over the cleavage, the squared, off-the-shoulder neckline, and even the sleeves, always so original in Lucile designs, were identical. But the dress she held was not completely faithful to the drawing in the design journal: there were the lattice strappings in velvet, and the embroidered cuffs as they had been created by Mrs. W. Her eyes went to the drawing. It was undoubtedly the same dress, except for the cuffs and the strapping. Vionnet had probably decided against these details—not only to reduce her costs but to disguise its provenance as well.

The breath hissed out of Celia. "Well, I'll be blowed—what a little vixen!" Her shock loud in the quiet room.

She sat down on a stool in the corner, the dress lying across her lap, catching the light from the window, its colors perfectly described in *The Queen*.

What placed Lucile head and shoulders above her competitors was her use of color. "Color is my religion, Celia," her mistress had said when she had exclaimed at the vibrant richness of winter models or the tender colors of spring combined to produce dresses as fresh and clear as they were in nature. And not simply the choice of color, but the perfect blend of different hues, tones, and contrasting shades.

*Never mind now how remarkable these models are, or the sheer genius of the woman who created them*, Celia thought. What matters is how many of them have already been copied and sold to Jeanne Paquin, the

House of Reville, or worst of all some other up-and-coming modiste desperate for the sort of success that Madame Lucile had achieved in the last six years.

THE GIRLS WERE gathered for their tea break in the old servants' hall and kitchen of the house when Celia came down the back stairs to join them. Mrs. Wallace had insisted that all their workers be given dinner at noon and then a substantial tea at five o'clock if they were working into the evening. "I want everyone who works for me to be well-fed and not worked to a thread," she had told the cook Celia had hired to provide dinner and tea for the women who toiled ten hours a day on the fourth floor of the house. "No need to go overboard. Provide simple, wholesome, fresh food, you know the sort of thing, because it would be what you would make for people like me."

Celia took her place at the top of the table, and a strong cup of Darjeeling was put in front of her with two shortbread biscuits. The girls were used to her sitting down to tea with them. She never talked shop if she joined them at either of their meals and, unless gossip centered on their clients, was content to sit with them, laughing at their jokes and enjoying their chatter.

"How's your mother faring, May?" she asked a young woman whose buttonhole work was almost invisible, her stitches were so minutely sewn.

"Much better, thank you, Miss Franklin." May nodded that her mother's toothache no longer troubled her. "She'll be having that tooth out next week, though. Lor', will she holler!"

Celia sipped her tea and glanced around the table, careful not to let her gaze linger too long on any one person. Her eyes rested on faces she had known since the start of their business. *Look at them all*, she thought, as she surveyed the chattering group. *We have nearly forty girls working for us now, and next year we'll probably have to hire at least another twenty. We'll have to start serving meals in shifts.*

Her eyes sought and found the young women who had worked on the Blush. Agnes Baxter worked under Flossie Maxwell in the blouse room but because of her ability with a needle had been included in the group who had made the Blush. Agnes was adept at faggoting together lace and net in the tucks of lawn and silk blouses. Her fine decorative stitches left the narrowest of gaps between pieced-together fabric, making anything she worked on as light and as intricate as a spider's web.

Her glance briefly touched on Molly Turner, a plain-faced, quietly spoken young woman who kept to herself and was a seamstress. The other girls joked that Molly Turner's sewing machine ran red hot by the end of a day as she whipped up the seams of underskirts. But Molly's contribution had been minimal, Celia reminded herself. It would have been hard for her to tell exactly how the finished article would have looked simply by working on its underskirt.

Laughter at the bottom of the table cut in on Celia's thoughts. ". . . and then I said, 'There are only two words I want to hear from you Bert Pritchard . . .'" Tall, blond, flamboyant Matilda finished her story of the boy she was walking out with. *That's another one who'll be handing in her notice in another year or so*, Celia thought. Madame Lucile lost more talented seamstresses to marriage than to any competing fashion house. Celia had learned too late not to hire pretty, outgoing young women; they lasted a year and then married and left to start families. If they worked again after that, it was from home, in the evening when their long day of cleaning, cooking, and looking after their children was finally over. And piece workers, as they were called, would earn half of what they made working for a fashion house.

Her gaze traveled down the left side of the table back to Agnes Baxter. Where had she worked before she came to Lucile? She had been well trained—it wasn't only a quick eye and a deft hand that created the flawless work that Agnes was capable of producing; she had been trained by an expert who had shown her all the tricks that resulted in perfection and, more important, speed. Was it at Reville that she had learned such impeccable technique? Reville's clientele were conservative and wealthy—*They have to be*, thought Celia. *Reville's prices are high—higher than ours. And they pay their workers a pittance—unless they are highly skilled.* Agnes finished her slice of pie and picked up her teacup, her movements graceful and unhurried. She turned to say something to the girl sitting next to her. Her bright eyes flashed and she nodded as she laughed at what her friend had said. *She's intelligent and self-contained,* thought Celia as she watched Agnes take part in the conversation without striving to be the only one talking.

". . . I'll have you know I am not a seamstress, Bert Pritchard, you lug . . . I am a professional . . . a modiste!" A burst of laughter from around the table. Agnes didn't even glance Matilda's way. She didn't have time for the loud, popular girls. *Just because she doesn't join in doesn't make her a thief—a spy,* Celia reminded herself as she glanced across to Molly Turner's rather sullen face.

"And I earn a jolly sight more than you do, Bert . . . so stick that in your pipe and smoke it!"

More laughter. Agnes looked down at her plate, picked up crumbs from it with a dainty forefinger, and put her finger in her mouth.

*You might very well make more money than your boyfriend, Matilda,* thought Celia, *because you manage the embroidery room, but most of the rank-and-file seamstresses do not.* Matilda and her close friend Beryl were gifted. It took more than patience and practice to embroider; both girls were blessed with a discerning eye. Celia's pulse rate picked up a little. It was Beryl who had worked on the Blush! It had been Beryl's hands that had embroidered that delicate tracery of plum roses.

*How much money does Beryl make?* Celia did the arithmetic. It was a very respectable wage for a young woman. She remembered that Beryl was a romantic. "Imagine wearing something like this," she would say, and hold up a length of the finest lace. "How beautiful you would feel!" *Did romantic Beryl yearn for clothes to wear as beautiful as the ones she helped to create for rich women?* Celia wondered. *Had someone suggested that there were ways she could make money other than stitching her youth away in the attic workrooms of Lucile's fashion house?* Now that Celia had decided she needed to investigate, she understood a hundred reasons why one of their girls could easily be talked into selling secrets, and the thought was troubling.

*What else do I know about this girl?* A shiver of memory: Beryl had been with the group of girls on the stairs in Burlington Street, peeking through the peephole down into one of the fitting rooms where Lady Robinson, the Marchioness of Ripon, entertained a "friend" to tea. It had taken daring to pick away at the rest of the wallpaper that concealed a hidden peephole. Most girls were law-abiding: they did not put their jobs in jeopardy for a naughty moment of peeking.

*But peeking is a form of spying—isn't it?* How many more self-respecting young women would not have dreamed of putting their eye to the peephole to enjoy a momentary frisson of excitement from seeing a half-clad aristocrat in the arms of her lover. Celia shuddered.

She felt tired. Drained from solving problems and feeling cold all day. She pushed her cup aside. "I am hoping that the furnace will be working in another couple of days. It will make things a lot more comfortable." She almost hated to remind them that tea was over and it was time to leave the bright warmth of the servants' hall and climb those stairs to their chilly workrooms.

She got to her feet and pushed the chair neatly against the table's edge. As she looked up she met the intense gaze of a pair of dark gray eyes. Their owner's stare was intent, almost a glare. Celia turned to look over her shoulder. Surely this baleful stare was not meant for her? When she turned back again, the young woman was eating toast and jam with such an air of innocent pleasure that Celia felt real relief. She had imagined that malignant expression.

The light in the old servants' dining room in the basement of the house was bad and her nerves were tight with anxiety and what-ifs too numerous to think of.

# Chapter Eleven

*November 1899*

Lucy

Cosmo Duff Gordon, head bowed, shoulders squared, said something so unexpected that Lucy's head came up. She must have been woolgathering, as her mother called it. She might be sitting at a table of this romantically lit restaurant, enjoying supper after the theater with Cosmo, but her thoughts had strayed throughout the evening to the dress she was working on. A dress for a young girl on the verge of womanhood: a tint of sky blue for the innocence of girlhood and the freshness of a clear morning in April, the skirt a meadow of wildflowers, a décolleté gown that displayed the flawless firm skin of youth. Try as she might to concentrate on the play they had just seen together and now the menu in front of her, her mind strayed back to the dress. *Happiness*, Lucy said to herself—it was a perfect name for the dress of a girl on the brink of her life as a woman. Then Cosmo Duff Gordon had spoken, and his words were not ones she particularly wanted to hear.

"Happiness?" he said in a tone of such delight that her eyes widened as she looked up to a face smiling in pleasure. "You would indeed give me great happiness if you said yes."

*Yes? Yes to what?* "Did I say that aloud—happiness?" His smile told her she had.

*Now what have I done? How gauche of me—I must stop blurting out my thoughts like this.* Embarrassed, she felt her ears grow hot and rushed to apologize. "Oh, Cosmo, what is wrong with me? I am so wrapped up in my spring collection, and this move seems to have gone on for months and months. I spoke aloud without thinking." She tried to laugh off her preoccupation, but what he had said, or asked, was evidently not a laughing matter.

He reached across the table and took her hand. It was the first time that he had reached for her hand in the three months that he had taken her to every play in the West End, to the opera because she loved music, for countless dinners, and last week into the country for a drive in his new electric brougham. He had helped her into and out of carriages and cabs, his arm discreetly at her elbow, and he had dutifully danced with her. But this hand stretched across the table was asking for intimacy.

She felt his fingers close over hers, and despite her shock at his words, Lucy's hand responded; it relaxed, palm open.

"You surely know how I feel about you. It can't be a surprise." His dark eyes were fixed on hers. She carefully slid her hand free.

She made herself answer slowly. "No, I don't think I really thought about it . . . seriously . . . well, not in that way. And yes, I think it is a surprise. You see . . . I . . . I like you so much, Cosmo. I thought . . . and I know we have become close friends. But . . . marriage? It is such a giant step." She thought she had had enough giant steps, where marriage was concerned, to last a lifetime.

Her gaze drifted away from his face down to the cloth, empty now that her hands were clasped tightly in her lap. *Don't be a coward. Look at him*, she commanded herself. *If he has the courage to ask you to marry him, the least you can do is to respond honestly, directly—kindly!*

She looked up. The smile had gone. His face was tense, unsure. "I don't want to be just good friends, Lucy. I mean, I always want to be your friend, of course I do . . . but I love you too. Nothing would bring me more happiness than if we were married." His voice was strong with conviction.

*Surely a good marriage is based on friendship?* Lucy asked herself. *But do I find Cosmo physically attractive enough to share a bed and to . . . do all of that?* A brief flash of what *that* involved recaptured the old dread, the humiliation that she had experienced with James. *I can't,* she thought in panic. *Not again.* She could not bear the crude reality of male physical need, the act that was described as love and in her experience had been one of pain and cruelty. What had happened between her and James had not been lovemaking—there had been no pleasure, certainly not the sort of pleasure Elinor had tried to explain to her.

She remembered how she had shushed her sister with the shameful knowledge that James had not cared to make love but had merely slaked lust, and so brutally she had wondered if he enjoyed inflicting pain. She had eventually withdrawn from any form of physicality with James, submitting only when he demanded, seeking a distant place in her mind and filling the human need for tenderness and affection by cuddling and caring for her little girl. *Yes, I find Cosmo attractive—romantically, even perhaps physically. I might like it if he kissed me, held me in his arms, but I prefer our conversation most of all.* But what man would be content with a marriage based on friendship only?

She felt the confidence that had come to her as she built her business begin to teeter. Marriage meant the loss of freedom when she had worked so hard to find herself. The sheer joy of her light-filled studio and the thrill of draping a bolt of silk across the back of the chair to explore the endless possibilities of what she would create with it.

*Answer him,* she instructed herself. *No prevarication, no coy half answers. This is a man who considers truth and honor to be the hallmarks of civilization.* A man who played by fair rules.

But there was no need to rush into explanations and excuses; this was a serious question and deserved consideration. The last time Lucy had been swept off her feet and startled into "Yes!" had been when James had sprung the question—and she had been an ignorant baby of nineteen.

Cosmo's words had thrown her into chaos, and self-doubt began to build. *Have I been so unobservant, so wrapped up in Lucile, as to not notice his feelings for me?* She prided herself on her honesty, her directness with her friends. *His attention is flattering. But if marriage is the last thing on my mind, then I am guilty of carelessness, and that is unfair, unfeeling, and selfish.*

"I am so sorry, I had no idea . . ." His forehead furrowed in concern as he fumbled for the right words. "I really thought you felt the same way . . ."

She put out her hand to him. "No, Cosmo, no, this is my fault. I have been self-absorbed and thoughtless. You see, I hoped that we were becoming good friends, and spending time with you has made me very happy, but I don't think I am made for marriage."

A terrible silence dropped like a stone between them.

Desperate to save them from this awful moment, Lucy frantically sought for another topic to rescue them. But talking to Cosmo was never an exercise in social skills, of being amusing and not allowing a lull in chatter to bog things down.

"Cosmo, things have been so frantic with this move and all our new orders that your asking me to marry you took me completely by surprise. And my response was gauche. Please forgive me."

He smiled. One hand started to reach out across the table and then returned to pick up his wineglass. "You weren't gauche; you were preoccupied. Then . . . well, you looked horrified. And I'm sorry. Timing was all wrong."

*Yes, perhaps that's it: the timing is all wrong.* But still Lucy's hesitation hung in the air as she tried to find the words to describe a life that now mattered so much to her—not just her independence but the expression of who she had become. "I have learned over the last years to stand on my own, Cosmo. I mean really stand on my own. After nine years with James, finding confidence in being independent was like learning to crawl and then find my feet and my balance to walk. In the beginning I was convinced that I would lose my house, and Esmé would be taken from me, made a ward of the court, made to live with an old spinster aunt. And then I discovered I really liked the work. No, that's not right: I love the work, I really do. I became addicted to my independence, something I had achieved on my own because I was good at what I did.

"I think . . ." She trod carefully. "I know I would make a terrible wife to you. Any dinner party we invited friends to would be a mishmash of indifferent food with a preoccupied hostess who barely had time to find the right dress to put on." She didn't dare try to find the words to describe how disappointing she would be in the bedroom, and her fear of sexual intimacy.

"You look absolutely perfect in the one you put on tonight for dinner," he said.

"Because getting dressed up for dinner with you is an occasion . . . a treat. Something I look forward to. But how often have I called off dinner with you in the last month? Three times? Four?"

"Five," he said.

"You see? That is what I am talking about." She was about to say, "Can you imagine living with that?" and decided not to. If he really wanted to marry her, undoubtedly he would say yes.

"Lucy, when I asked to share your life, I wasn't thinking of holding dinner parties or inviting friends to shoot in Scotland—the societal round." He frowned such frivolities away.

*But how else do the leisured classes live?* Lucy thought. *They entertain. Often. That's how I met him: at a country house party. I make my living by creating wardrobes for women who are married to men like Cosmo.*

In her tension, Lucy had folded and refolded the napkin in her lap. She lay her hands flat and open and willed herself to relax, to trust this man whom she liked so much and whose voice made her want to close her eyes and listen to him forever.

"I think entertaining, for people of your class, is an indelible habit," she said, smiling to soften any criticism. "What I am trying to explain is this: my entire day and often my evenings are consumed with Lucile." She shrugged as if she were helpless where her business was concerned. Lucile called and Lucy immediately answered. "I can't imagine any husband, however much he loved me, wanting to hear a list of calamities every evening, even if it was the first time he had seen his wife in a week!"

His face across the table was attentive, serious.

"Just you try me," he said. "I find what you do and how you go about it both eccentric and fascinating. It is part of who you are. How many designers actually name their dresses, consider them as part of the wearer's emotional experience? And as for the rest, the problems—well, thank God you don't move premises every year!"

*He has no idea how niggly I can be at the end of the day. How often I go to bed at night feeling guilty that I haven't read a good-night story to my daughter. How wonderful I feel when I close my bedroom that I am alone in a completely silent room.*

"Now that you have moved in, can you perhaps take some time off?" he asked. She was grateful he didn't say how tired she looked, but she knew it. Dark circles under her eyes—her mother had pointed them out in case she hadn't noticed.

"Oh no!" Lucy was horrified at the idea. "I have to start looking for young women to train to wear my clothes for the fashion parade!"

"I only meant for a few days. Give you an opportunity to rest before you launch into this new idea. Your fashion show. Perhaps a weekend in the country with Elinor?"

Lucy threw back her head and laughed. "Oh Cosmo, you have no idea how relentless my sister is. She would have me reworking her entire wardrobe. And Clayton always requires a reaction or an idea for his latest redecorating plans." She saw herself at Wardley House watching for Clayton's predatory face peering at her around a hidden door in the wainscotting.

The waiter arrived with their next course.

"Then take a day off. Stay at home and read, or take Esmé to the park!" was all he said as he picked up his knife and fork. He looked up from his plate. "I want to marry you, and I am sorry for the awful timing. I won't bring it up again unless . . . you want me to." He put his knife and fork down. "If you say yes to me, I promise that I will respect how much you love and need your business, as much as I respect how much you love and need Esmé."

She couldn't let it rest here, couldn't bear the idea that they would have to replay this distressing scene. The last thing in the world she would ever do was marry again.

"What about your mother?" She watched him flinch and felt like a brute. "Cosmo, can you really imagine how she would feel if you arrived home with a woman who earned her living as a dressmaker and told her that you wanted to marry her?" He had clearly thought about this, and it was a significant hurdle—he reached for his wine.

"And not only a woman in trade, but a divorced woman with a child." She let that one sink in too and watched him drain the glass. She prayed that panic had not made her thoughtless; the last thing she wanted was to hurt a man she admired and trusted and who had fallen for the woman she wished she was.

"Ma'am? Mrs. Glyn to see you." Robbie barely had the words out before her sister came through the door of her studio, her cheeks rosy from a buffeting by a December north wind.

"What is wrong with you?" were Elinor's first words. "How many times have I invited myself over for tea, to look at your new house, to be met with a thousand pathetic excuses?"

Lucy's head ached; her fingers felt clumsy and disobedient.

"I had to bully Robbie into seeing you." Elinor threw her hat and gloves in a corner. "Yes, thank you, Robbie, tea would be perfect—yes, bring it in here so we won't be interrupted." As the young footman left them, she said, "Goodness me, little Robbie has grown into such a gorgeous young man! No wonder your clients lounge around the place all day long to feast their eyes on that godlike profile. So, I am here for a tour and a consultation."

"Then why didn't you make an appointment?" Lucy sounded as ungracious as she felt. Her right ear was blocked, and she couldn't sleep at night for coughing.

"A consultation, my dear sister, about the ups and downs of married life, that's what. If anyone can advise me about the disasters of marriage,

I know you can. You are familiar with the routine: long silences and moodiness at dinner. Sudden disappearances to stay with 'friends' in the country. I know my husband is having an affair with Cecily Pacey-Parsons, and probably with Isabelle Eldridge too, and I could give two hoots." Elinor patted her hair into place. "It is the drinking that I worry about, because when Clayton drinks, he gambles with men who have fifty times our income." She dumped herself down in the only other chair in the studio. "You really need to have these windows cleaned—no wonder you can't see anything."

"Up, up, Elinor, you are sitting on lace that has been in Margot Asquith's family for generations." She pulled her sister out of her chair. "Sleeves . . . for a dinner dress. And I can see everything through my windows—thank you!"

Robbie returned with tea.

Lucy poured and took a long swallow to warm her scratchy throat. "I'm sorry, Elinor, I don't mean to be brusque, but there aren't enough hours in the day. We are so behind after that damned move." She remembered how generous Elinor had been with her time and her friends when she was struggling to become Lucile—and her sister was the only person she knew that she could swear in front of. "Now, darling, tell me about Clayton." She sat down and fixed her sister's gaze with a listening face.

Elinor spoke through a mouthful of cake. "It's the demon drink." She rolled her eyes. She swallowed and her voice became less flippant in tone. "Brandy for breakfast—you know all about that. And he is being evasive about . . . well, about money." Her voice sank like a lead weight in water. "So . . . I riffled through the drawers in the desk in his study—oh, please don't look so shocked! I read letters from his bank manager. Yes, I know"—a hand came up to ward off criticism—"spying." Her eyes flitted around the studio, refusing to meet her sister's. "Once again we are verging on financial catastrophe. And still he goes off for days at a time and spends our money with . . ." She reeled off a list of names. "Every one of them known for their high-stakes gambling. I don't know what to do."

Elinor's lovely face was drawn with anxiety. Her naturally restless nature had been stilled by tension. She perched on the edge of her chair: a frozen hedgerow creature when danger is near.

Lucy reached out a hand and pulled her sister toward her, and Elinor sank her head against her shoulder. She could feel Elinor's exhalation of loss: a gust of defeat and fear. She felt anger toward a man who had been so frivolous, so compulsive in his outlandish lifestyle, that his family's welfare—their security—was now precarious. *What is wrong with them?* Lucy asked herself. *It is as if they purposefully indulge in the decadence that will ultimately destroy them. It is as if they wish it. Welcome it.* Sadly she asked herself another question. *Why are women like Elinor and me drawn to this type of man?*

The trappings of Clayton Glyn's status, the house in Grosvenor Square and his country house, were luxuriously furnished and meticulously kept—apparently well beyond his means. It was as if, having failed in his ambition to become an established member of the Marlborough House set, he had decided to raze everything in his life to the ground. An act of complete annihilation that he couldn't expect to recover from. *I must not be so judgmental,* Lucy thought. *I must be kind.* Then: *I loathe the man. Loathe him.* Did it really matter why Clayton Glyn was the way he was? Surely who mattered now was the woman who was shackled to him, and their children's future. There was one thing about Clayton, dislike him as she did, that was reassuring. He might be unfaithful and profligate but he never forced Elinor, or hit her, or denied her access to her friends. Or did he? *We women never confide the worst aspects of our marriages even to our closest friends.*

"Is it just the money: the gambling, the spending?" she asked. "He doesn't . . . you know?"

"What?" Elinor scowled. "Isn't losing all our money on brandy, soft furnishings, and gambling enough?" She threw a more understanding look at her sister. "Oh, I see. No, absolutely not, Lucy. If Clayton lifted a finger I would knock him senseless." Her expression softened, her eyes wide with understanding. "And you, little sister? James did that to you?"

"No . . ." Lucy tried to find the words. "Not hit . . . not exactly. I disappointed him . . . in that way—so he . . ."

Elinor slammed her teacup down in its saucer. "What a bastard!" she said, and threw herself into her sister's arms. "Oh, darling, why did you never say?"

Lucy shrugged—because of the shame, she wanted to say. The shame of being married to a brute. "It's over now, Elinor. I am free. My life has changed. Now, what about you?"

Her sister shook her head. "Just money problems, and the drinking. It doesn't make him violent, drinking half a bottle of brandy, but he gets incoherent and emotional. It's awfully sad to see him that way."

Her sister needed reassurance that Lucy might not be able to give.

"Elinor, the only thing I can tell you is that there was nothing I could do at all to save James from himself. Even the fact that we had a child together didn't matter. They can't help it, some men; it's an affliction of the blood. I am so very sorry that you have to go through the agony . . ."

Elinor got to her feet, her arms folded tight across her bosom. "I don't know whether he drinks because he is in debt from gambling, or whether it's the company he keeps . . . or that he is terrified of facing the truth of our circumstances. I don't know. He won't talk to me, Lucy. And when he does, it's only because he has been drinking, so he is incoherent and frightened . . . and I can't make sense of what our predicament really is." She stood in the window, her head bowed. "I have to spy on him to find out the slightest thing. It's awful and I feel so helpless."

Practicalities were needed here. There was no saving Clayton, but Lucy needed to help her sister. She got up and put her arms around her sister. "How bad do you believe it is?"

"Bad enough for me to start writing, and not just for the fun of it. Perhaps I can keep us solvent by writing a novel. Heaven knows I have enough experience of life." The rock-hard set to her features dissolved with her laughter. Her wicked giggles were a release for Lucy too. And she thanked God that Elinor had the resilience she needed to face life head-on. "I was thinking of writing a romantic novel—of course I would need to find a publisher. Apparently, that sort of thing is immensely popular. Books about passion and risking all for love go down frightfully well with the female reading public. I could make a mint—if I were successful."

Lucy felt such admiration and love for her sister in that moment that it was almost like relief. They were Sutherlands, their father's daughters, and the Sutherlands never said die. Never threw up their hands in horror at every catastrophe and surrendered to the flood. She forgot how much her head ached and how long her days sometimes were. "Yes, yes! Only you could do justice to a romantic novel! I used to love your stories when we were young. So, you have an idea for a book?"

Elinor giggled. "Sort of. It's frightfully difficult to think romantically when you have gone off your husband. But there it is—we just have to focus elsewhere. I was thinking about Mother when she finally allowed herself to fall for Father. Do you remember all those wonderful stories she would tell us? A young innocent courted by a man whom she has known for years as a friend." Lucy did remember her mother's wonderful fairy tales of love. In some way they had been her downfall too—her determination to fall for James had been based entirely on fairy-tale romance. "Of course, in my story she is in love with someone else: charming, witty, handsome, so he completely eclipses the friend. And of course the man she is infatuated with is awful, simply awful. A boaster, and a show-off, with that charismatic charm that young women always fall for: thoroughly unsuitable but exciting—you know the sort of thing"—a gasp of laughter—"rather like our husbands!

"Unlike Mother, my heroine comes a cropper as she slowly discovers what this man is really like. Maybe she discovers that she is not the only woman in his life, or perhaps he has no intention of marrying her—and only intends seduction!" Elinor smiled as if she was explaining to Esmé. "When he proposes and she accepts, it's just like Mama and Papa. There has to be passion, real passion. Desire that carries her away—engulfs her; that is what sells, you see."

*Why?* Lucy wondered. *Why do we have to become brainless with lust in order to marry?* "Do you think Mother will approve, being used as the heroine of your book?" she said instead. "I mean, when Papa proposed, it was rather daring and original, when they were stuck in that leaky boat in the middle of a lake in a storm."

To her relief Elinor had recovered from her earlier pain at the collapse of her husband's fortune and constancy. She waved her sister's caution away with a series of annoyed exclamations.

"Fiddlesticks, darling, she'll never read it! When did she show the slightest interest in anything you or I have ever done—apart from whether the men we married had money?" Elinor tossed her head and Lucy realized she was already well into writing her book. "Mother lives in the past. In her mind she is still an elegant wife adored by her husband with an army of servants to do her bidding. The slightest thing throws her off balance and she resents us like mad if our lives interrupt her glorious memories of the past."

Lucy smiled. If their mother read her sister's book, she would never recognize herself. Elinor's penchant for embroidery and gross exaggeration would heavily disguise all their mother's tender moments that she still harbored in her memories of happier times. Not to mention the passionate love scenes she knew her sister would scatter, vividly, throughout her book.

Now was the time to bolster, to encourage her sister's path to financial independence. "I think writing a book is a splendid idea. It will take your mind off Clayton's money problems. But you always say you are on the verge of financial ruin . . . and then everything comes right again."

"For a while," her sister warned.

"Come on, you have interrupted my workday." Lucy took Elinor's hand and pulled her to the door. "Now you must pay the price. I want to show you around our new shop!"

"Well, that's what I really came to do." Elinor slipped her arm around her shoulders. "Goodness, darling, you had better put on your little coatee; your hands are like ice and the boiler was replaced weeks ago."

# CHAPTER TWELVE

CELIA

G ood afternoon, Celia. Unusual to see you here." Sir Cosmo took off his hat and handed it to the maid who had opened the door of Lucy's house in Molton Street. "No need to take my coat, Smithers. Only stopping for a moment; I have come to take Mrs. Wallace to lunch."

The maid glanced at Celia. "Yes, Smithers, that will be all, thank you." Celia took Sir Cosmo's hat from the maid, who scurried for safety behind the baize door.

Silence. Celia fidgeted with Sir Cosmo's hat and then put it on the hall table.

She found this tall, broad-shouldered man with his dark eyes, long, straight nose, and splendid mustache intimidating. Esmé had told her he was a sword fighter, which only made things worse for a young woman who lived and worked in a feminine world. Most conversations started with the weather—that was what these fine folks talked about if there was awkward news to impart.

"Cold wind blowing down from the north today, sir."

He nodded as if north winds were a rarity in February. "Yes, Celia— bitter out there." He picked up the *Times*, lying unread on the hall table, and glanced through the headlines.

Celia gave up on polite exchanges—*get on with it, for Lord's sake.*
"Mrs. Wallace was unwell yesterday evening, sir. We thought it was
nothing but a chill at first. But during the night, she became very poorly
indeed. The doctor is with her now."

"Poorly?" It was as if this man didn't understand the queen's English.

"A fever, sir: sore throat and a bad cough," Celia explained. "I came
over from the shop for her orders for the next few days." She lowered her
voice. "Mrs. Wallace has been working far too hard: not enough sleep,
not enough time to sit and enjoy her dinner."

The alarm on his face was startling. "Yes, I have been worried that
she was overworking."

*As have we all*, she thought, grateful that her boss was finally taking
a few days in bed. *Working like there are demons at our heels.* She glanced
up at the silent giant from under the brim of her felt hat. It was hard to
see his face, standing as he was with his back to the light from the hall
window. "Is there a message I can give to Mrs. Wallace?"

He scratched his forehead, perplexed at her news. "When did she
become sick?" he asked.

"She has been a bit off, you might say, for a week now." Overburdened with worry about how the salon would function without its
leader, she found herself saying, "But she wouldn't rest . . . and now . . ."
Her eyes filled with tears and she stared hard at the wall behind his
head, willing them to go back from where they came and not trickle
down the sides of her nose.

To her horror, Sir Cosmo walked toward the bottom of the stairs.
Surely he knew he couldn't go up there and see Mrs. Wallace. It was
unthinkable even to mention her bedroom to him. A real gentleman
would say how sorry he was, retreat, and send flowers with a note. Not
camp out at the bottom of the stairs—let alone go up them.

He stood looking up to the first landing as if contemplating his reception in the sickroom. "Yes, she has been overdoing it for some time
now. So very worrying." Now he was facing the front door and she could
see his expression. His eyes were crinkled in concern, and if he had a

bottom lip under that hedgerow on the upper one, he was certainly biting it. She rushed to reassure him.

"Just a winter cold, sir. She'll shake it off now that she is confined . . . to . . ." She couldn't bring herself to say the word "bed." This, after all, was Mrs. Wallace's gentleman friend. A man who took her out to the theater and to dinner. And who dropped by for tea with Esmé and Mrs. Kennedy.

He nodded. "And the business, how is that faring without its captain?" he asked.

"Oh, early days yet, sir. And if Mrs. Wallace rests, she will be back on her feet in no time." Ponderous steps on the stairs as the doctor came down. He glanced at Sir Cosmo. "Good morning, sir. I expect you are as concerned as I am about Mrs. Wallace's health. Severe congestion." His brows came down, as if this was a forbidden complaint, much too serious for anyone but himself to comprehend or even speak of. He turned to Celia. "The biggest problem we are facing is the patient's determination that this is simply a winter chill. Well, let me tell you, it is far from an afternoon off by the fireside with her feet up. It is bronchitis and a nasty case of it. If the patient does not stay warm and quiet, with plenty of rest, she might easily contract pneumonia. A very grave illness indeed." He frowned harder at "pneumonia." "You are Mrs. Wallace's assistant?"

Celia nodded. "Yes, sir."

"Her right hand, she says!" A tight smile.

"Indeed, sir."

"Your mistress will be up and fighting fit if she is not bothered with business matters. I am counting on you, Miss . . ."

"Franklin, sir."

"Counting on you to do whatever it takes to not worry Mrs. Wallace about her shop and all of that. Am I clear, Miss Franklin?"

"Yes, sir."

"I have left instructions with her mother, and a night nurse will be arriving at six o'clock this evening."

"Yes, sir."

"Very serious, very serious indeed. Good day to you."

And with that he clamped his hat on his head and fought open the front door. A bitter wind blustered into the hall, sending the morning's delivery of post sailing across it, before the door was slammed shut, leaving them both in shivering silence.

Celia could hardly catch her breath, she was so stricken that she had allowed Mrs. Wallace to work on, unwell, into a terrible illness. She closed her eyes and saw in agonizing vignettes her dearest Mrs. W. sinking slowly into worse health. She pulled in a deep breath to stop herself from unraveling in terrified tears. *Oh God, please not pneumonia!*

Mrs. Wallace expected great things, she exhorted everyone who worked for her to strive for perfection, but she was one of the most fair-minded and just of employers: tactful in her criticism, generous with her praise. *How will we cope if things get serious?*

Overburdened and terribly worried, Celia gave up on all efforts to squash down emotion. Two huge, silent tears raced down her cheeks, missing the corners of her mouth, to trickle down her neck and land on the collar of her gray worsted coat. She had let her mistress down. She had accepted that Mrs. Wallace was overworking and could pull on her immense reserves of energy until there were none left. Her stalwart boss, who had always said she would not work her girls to a thread like so many other fashion houses, had driven herself into her sickbed.

"I wouldn't blame myself quite so thoroughly, if I were you," said a voice from the bottom of the stairs. "Mrs. Wallace is a headstrong woman; nothing can persuade her when she has an idea firmly fixed in her head. You cannot accuse yourself if she is sick in bed. If you think she's stubborn, you should meet her sister." It was a kind attempt at lessening the mood, but it failed. Celia slid a sideways glance at the hunched figure sitting on a low chest at the bottom of the stairs. In spite of his insouciant appearance and his calm responses, Sir Cosmo looked deflated, as if he was not sure what to do next.

But his light, conciliatory tone made Celia pull herself away from blame to face the real concern. How would Madame Lucile survive the practicalities of day-to-day business? *How on earth am I to manage the orders and her client consultations?* And despair. *Not one bill has been paid in weeks—no, months. And they won't either, not until those selfish weasels leave their country house sports and come back to town for the Season.*

Frugal Celia had managed to pay the rent for the next three months. No anxiety there. But the girls' wages were huge, working as they had been to full capacity until the exodus from London in August for the Glorious Twelfth and the winter holidays. She ran through the immediate bills, the ones that were overdue: the bill for the silk merchant was staggering, and she must settle it by the end of February, leaving them very little in the bank.

"How can I help?" Two kindly eyes were watching her. She had forgotten about the gentleman friend, who had found his hat and was now turning it slowly in his hands.

Her sharp north-country humor wanted to ask him if it was embroidery that he excelled at, or was his specialty faggoting?

"Clearly there are many burdens about to land on your shoulders, Miss Franklin. There must be something I can help with. My family made all their money in the sherry business. We may look like a bunch of titled layabouts, but I promise you I know how to work. Although I have been told you are the master bookkeeper, and that Mrs. Wallace depends completely on you. But we don't want you to struggle on until you, too, fall ill."

Celia gazed across the hall at him; he wasn't quite so intimidating now that he was sitting down. Torn between loyalty and the financial mess they were facing with the crippling bills from the move and renovating the house, their bank account was almost as lean as it had been in the early days. *And what will happen if in a month or two, just as she is getting better, we can't pay our working girls? What will we do then? Badger our fine clients for payment, or go quietly under?*

Celia wondered if writing to the titled ladies whose overdue bills were still unpaid would be acceptable to her boss if the alternative was ruin. But Mrs. Wallace would be outraged. "We are not a family of coal merchants, dunning our precious customers!" A line straight out of her mother's repertoire.

"Something I can surely do to help?" The voice across the hall persisted. "Especially as my friend upstairs with the sore throat and the concerned doctor has not spared herself a single day off. After the cost of moving and making Hanover Square fit for business, I am quite sure that your bank account is a bit sparse—since all of your clients are in the country." Celia's eyes were hopeful as she heard this last practical statement. It was as if he had read her terrified thoughts. If his people had made their money in trade, he must understand how money went out and sometimes absolutely refused to come in when it was called home. *We look so good on paper*, she thought, *but one glance at what we have in the bank would wipe that pleasant smile right off his face.*

"Our outlay for the move kept exceeding the original estimate . . . and then Hanover Square needed so much doing to it. The heating, for one thing."

He nodded. "Mm . . . it's inevitable. When we expand, there are always hidden costs."

*Hah*, she thought, *not so much hidden as concealed.* Her dislike for their landlord, who had lied outright about the condition of his house, still rankled, even though Mrs. W. had waved it aside. "Too late now, Celia. I have signed a ten-year lease. We have to make it work." And "work" had been the operative word: Mrs. Wallace had flogged herself into the ground.

She looked down at the toes of her boots peeking out from under the hem of her skirt. She would never have worn such lovely clothes or put her feet into such fine shoe leather if it weren't for Lucy Wallace. She had been given a beautiful bedroom *and* her own parlor at Hanover Square—cleaned by one of the maids. She ate as well as anyone. And her life had purpose, direction, and a family she cared about. She would not let her beloved Mrs. W. recover her health only to sink under a landslide of unpaid bills.

"Most of our clients do not pay on time," she blurted into the cold, echoing hall, horrified at how loud she sounded. "Well, the Americans do. They pay as soon as a gown is ready for them to wear. But when the season is over and they go back to America, we have to rely on the other lot. I don't expect any of them to pay us until April or May. And now that Mrs. Wallace is sick, I really don't know . . ." Her voice sounded as desperate as she felt, and Sir Cosmo nodded his understanding.

"Parasites, every last one of us." At least Celia thought she heard him say "parasites," but she could have been mistaken, his voice was so low. "Inevitable, I'm afraid, in your sort of business. Has this always been the case?"

"It comes and goes. But most of our customers rarely pay a bill within six months of receiving it. And we are careful not to overextend so we can carry unpaid bills for longer if we have to. But this move has wiped out all our reserves."

He shook his head again and lit a cigar. It smelled wonderful: a warm, rich, ripe smell almost as good as a well-kept stable yard. "If I can help solve your financial problems, can you keep things going until Mrs. Wallace recovers?"

"Course I can," she said with her forthright bluntness. "But how will you get them to pay?"

He laughed. "I agree it is a problem—they will pay, of course, eventually. I think a talk with your bank would be a good idea. They can arrange a loan to carry you until the beginning of the season, when your clients will be demanding dresses made in double-quick time and are ready to clear their account with you. And if your bank manager suggests an outrageous rate of interest, then we can move your account to my bank, which, I promise you, will undertake a loan at a very reasonable percentage."

This sounded more like it! Celia was astonished that life could be made so easy, but her practical Northumbrian sense told her to be wary. She'd had no idea that banks gave out money. In her experience, they were always pulling it in or reminding you that your balance was straying in the wrong direction. There was just one little thing. "How does a percentage work when you ask for a loan?"

"A loan is negotiated on how much you are going to pay the bank for the amount you borrow. It is called interest. Put very simply, if you borrow four hundred pounds for a year, and the rate of interest is two percent, then you repay the bank the four hundred pounds by the date you have agreed on, plus an additional eight pounds for the convenience of borrowing. Of course, if it takes you longer to repay the loan, the percentage rate may increase unless you have negotiated your loan otherwise. You have to be careful how you set your terms."

Banks made money this way? Celia felt embarrassed about how little she knew of the masculine world. Borrowing money didn't sit squarely with her north-country upbringing. Who was it who said, "Neither a borrower nor a lender be?" Probably Shakespeare, as he was always being quoted.

"Would Mrs. Wallace agree to a loan from the bank?" she wondered.

He smiled. "I am quite sure she would. But it is very important that we ask her before we even visit your bank manager."

"If she agrees to this loan, then how do we arrange it at the right rate of interest?" Celia had no intention of asking Lucile's bank manager for a loan; he would bundle her out of his imposing office, fully aware that he wasn't dealing with the principal.

He got to his feet and put on his hat. His dark eyes were gleaming as if he was laughing at some inner joke. "Why, right now, Miss Franklin. As soon as you have cleared it with Mrs. Wallace." He cleared his throat. "I am sure she will understand what we are undertaking, but just in case she is feeling too unwell, are you sure you can explain how a loan works to her?"

Her foot was already on the bottom step of the stair. "She hasn't a clue about business and money," she said. "But I'll explain it so she does. I will be down directly; then perhaps you would come with me?"

He sat down on the chest and opened up his newspaper. "I'll be here."

Celia had never seen her mistress so quiet and pale. Her face was almost the color of her pillowcase, her long lashes dark against her cheeks. Celia looked at Mrs. Kennedy sitting on the edge of her chair. *Watching me as if I was about to steal the bloomin' bedpan.*

"Is she awake, ma'am?"

A nod.

"Mrs. Wallace?" The eyelids lifted. "Can you hear me?"

"Yes, Celia, of course I can."

*Not too many words: no alarm, be clear and concise.*

In minutes she laid out the state of their finances and the resolution. Mrs. Wallace watched her closely.

"The bank will do that?" she asked.

"Sir Cosmo says it is done all the time. It will be a short-term loan of six months, and"—with a flush of pride—"we will negotiate a good rate of interest."

A long sigh and the eyelids fluttered to close. "Thank you, Celia, please arrange it. And thank Sir Cosmo."

Celia reached down and took the cold hand in hers. She stroked it open and watched the fingers relax.

"Rest now, Mrs. Wallace. Nothing to worry about."

She tiptoed across the room and put her hand on the doorknob, turning it as quietly as she could.

"One moment." The ice-calm voice of Mrs. Kennedy stopped her, and with her heart beating she turned.

"Yes, ma'am."

"Thank you . . . Celia. I can't imagine how we could ever manage without you."

"I did very little, ma'am. It was Sir Cosmo . . ."

Mrs. Kennedy lifted her hand to silence her. "I mean for the last seven years, Celia, for all the years you have helped Mrs. Wallace—us."

Celia nodded. "I can't imagine working for a better mistress, ma'am. There is no need to thank me." And she left the room.

Celia was down the stairs in a moment.

"Yes, she says yes."

"What is the name of your bank manager?"

"John Forsyte of Barclay and Company."

"Then let's start with him."

YOU HAVE TO *get better,* Celia willed her boss. *You* have *to get better.* More terrified than she could remember, she dropped to her knees in her parlor and sent a fervent prayer to God. It was more of a plea. *Please, God, spare her. Please, God, make her well. Please . . .* was all her distraught mind could come up with; then she gabbled out the bits of the Lord's Prayer she remembered from the workhouse. When she was sure she had been on her knees for an appropriate length of time for a deep prayer, she got up and went about the business of keeping Lucile going: customers' requests for alterations; meetings with Alice to allocate new gowns among the workrooms; quieting the arguments that naturally occur when forty women work together. *And finally,* she said, with another quick prayer of thanks for Sir Cosmo, *I can pay the bloomin' bills.*

"YES, COME CLOSER, Celia, and sit here." Mrs. Wallace's head turned on her pillow as Celia came into her room. "How is my shop? I do miss her so!"

Celia perched on a chair by Mrs. Wallace's bed. It had been days since she had last seen Mrs. W.

"Ten minutes only." A round-faced woman draped a shawl around Mrs. Wallace's shoulders. "No excitement and absolutely no worrying her. I hope you are clear on this point, Miss Franklin."

Mrs. Wallace twitched the shawl away. "We have a lot of things to cover, Nurse; better make it twenty."

Two huge hands planted themselves on wide hips. "Ten minutes. I am starting my count from now, Miss Franklin!"

In the last weeks Mrs. Wallace had been too ill to see her, and Celia was appalled at how tiny she looked in her bed. Huge eyes stared up at Celia, and her mother's last illness came rolling in from the past to drown out hope.

*Pull yersel' together, Ceel,* she told herself. "First of all, everyone who comes into the shop asks after you and wishes you well." She smiled at the flowers in the room. "And all the girls, every one of them, ask after you—you are sorely missed, so concentrate on getting better!

"Now, about the business, don't worry yourself, ma'am, everything

is going as smooth as silk at the shop." She smiled at her little joke and
watched Mrs. W. relax.

As concisely as she could, she made her suggestions. "We can use
your spring collection to show to clients—not in a fashion parade, of
course, but on canvas dummies. Alice is more than able to adapt and
make changes to suit, and because she has worked for you so long, she
will have no difficulty with allocating which workroom will take which
orders. Do you agree? Do you think this will work, ma'am?"

A nod. "Yes, I do. Well done, Celia, five steps ahead as usual. You
can make a display in . . ." Her shoulders shook and she pressed a handkerchief to her mouth.

"The drawing room? Yes, ma'am."

A thin hand reached out for the water glass on her bed table. A few
sips. "Help me sit up."

Celia slid her hand behind Mrs. Wallace's back along the protruding
bones of her spine and the sharp wing of her shoulder blade. *How much
weight has she lost, poor creature?* "I don't want you to worry about anything, ma'am," she said as she wrapped the shawl firmly around Mrs.
W.'s lean shoulders. "Did you read Sir Cosmo's letter about the arrangement we made at the bank—the details of the loan?"

A fit of coughing, more sips of water. "Yes, and I can't thank you both
enough. Will we be solvent when all our bills are paid in the spring?"

"Yes, and since it has got out that you are sick, quite a few have paid
already!"

A little more color had come into Mrs. Wallace's face. If anything,
talking about the shop was good for her. "I think we are going to have
to put the fashion show on hold for a while. But I have already hired two
girls; what on earth are we to do with them?"

Celia was grateful they were part-timers and there were only two of
them. She couldn't imagine what they would do with five very talkative
girls all day long. "What do you think if Grace were to train them up to
work in the shop? The way you did with her—just the basics. They are

such nice, outgoing girls, I am sure they would do very well selling hats and gloves. Grace can show them the ropes. What do you think?"

Two serious eyes were watching her. Another nod. "Yes, Celia, I thought the same thing, but only if they have some idea of fashion. They were not picked for their design sense but for their looks. I am not sure how long I will be like this . . ."

Their conversation had taken all of five minutes, and already Mrs. W.'s energy was fading. "Don't even think about it, ma'am. You'll be in fine fettle before you know it, and this is the quiet time of the year, after all."

The door opened, and in bustled the bossy nurse. "Time is up, Miss Franklin. I hope you have solved the world's problems." Her remark was meant to be bright and breezy, but Celia felt her teeth meet in a bite of irritation.

Mrs. Wallace clearly felt the same. She ignored the nurse. "Keep your eye on Grace, Celia; she is a headstrong girl. Wonderful at what she does. But I want our fashion-parade girls to be ladies, not star turns in a cabaret."

Celia laughed, and so did Mrs. W., but it ended in a fit of coughing and sips of water.

"Now, Miss Franklin, the patient is tired, so off you go!"


Two weeks later and the patient was allowed up for an hour in the afternoon to sit by the fire. But Celia could see she was still far from well.

"I hope you have left all your worries at the door," the nurse said.

"Nothing for her to worry about, but there is something she needs to know."

The nurse sighed as if a burden was about to descend on her shoulders. "Five minutes," she said.

"It won't even take that, Nurse." Celia crossed the fingers of both hands behind her back.

IT HAD BEEN a long, long day. Celia pressed the palms of her hands into the small of her back. There was one more job she had to do, which made her heart thump so fast in her chest that it was a wonder the girls in their workrooms couldn't hear it. She walked the length of the fourth floor, past rooms humming with activity and chattering voices. As she walked by each open door, the chatter died away. Celia was the boss in Mrs. Wallace's absence.

She put her head into the last room, caught the supervisor's eye, and beckoned her into the corridor.

"Please send Moira to me before your tea break, Martha." And then back down the steep back stairs she went, toe first, as she had heard Grace instructing her pupils on how to walk when they waited on ladies in the shop. "Don't clump about," Grace had instructed. "And slow down; you are not in a race. That's right, walk slowly, nice and slowly. Toes are silent; heels are noisy."

"NO, LEAVE THE door open, please, Moira." Celia sat up straight behind her desk. She might not feel that she was in control of the outcome of her meeting with Moira, but she would damn well pretend she was. The cat was curled up in a tight ball in her basket, and down the corridor, steps away, stood Robbie, in case things turned nasty.

Moira stood before her, hands at her sides, her face wary. Celia opened her desk drawer and took out a notebook and a key. She put them both down on the desk in front of her and watched Moira's hand go to her apron pocket and then drop to her side.

"I have them both: the key to the models room"—Celia held it up— "that you copied from mine, and the notebook you used to record the details of the dresses there. Very accurate drawings they are too." She fanned the notebook's pages. "I think you have real talent; what a pity that you chose to use it to steal instead of showing us your work. We would have been delighted to have offered you a job here as an artist." She put the key and the book down.

Moira shook her head in pretended misunderstanding. "I don't know what you're talking about . . . That's not my book. I can't draw for toffee."

"I removed the key and this notebook from your apron pocket while you were eating your tea. I had a witness who saw me do it. Look, Moira, I have been watching the girls for several weeks now, trying to work out which one of you sold Mrs. Wallace's designs. It is interesting that you only sold them to Paquin and not to Simpsons or Reville and Rossiter too."

Moira became very quiet. In the lamplight Celia could see the white around her eyes. *Perhaps I should have asked Robbie to be in here with us.*

She continued carefully. However distasteful this was, she must not rush this. "I have one or two questions for you, and if you are straight with me I will be lenient with you. Have you ever done anything like this before?" Celia guessed that if Moira was an old hand she would have some trumped-up story, but she was hoping that she had caught her early on in her career as a thief.

Moira couldn't get her words out fast enough. "No, never, ma'am. There were just the three dresses that she paid me for: the Blush, Passion's Flower, and a carmine red day dress—I can't remember the name; it was number sixteen." Tears welled and she blinked them away.

"I see. And when you had copied the designs, how did you know who to go to with them?"

Shame and despair: Moira closed her eyes. She shook her head, her shoulders heaving with the effort not to cry.

"Just tell me, Moira; it might even make you feel better."

Moira nodded and jerked her head toward the street. "It was her, from the House of Paquin. The Frenchwoman. She takes the same trolleybus as me as far as Piccadilly, where she gets off and I stay on to go home." She pulled a handkerchief out of her pocket and blew her nose. "Then, one day, she nods hello and we got to talking. She said she was a dressmaker too, just down the street from us. About two weeks later she stayed on the bus all the way to my stop. When we got off she asked me if I worked on all the dresses or did I have just the one skill. I thought she was going to offer me a job."

"But she didn't," Celia prompted.

"No, she told me I could make a bit more money if I copied down the designs and gave them to her assistant, Mamzelle Moreau. She was very clear how I could go about it." Celia nodded. *How many of our girls did she approach looking for the right one, the one who could draw well enough and who was desperate enough?* A wave of fury, of violent anger, swept through Celia, leaving her feeling shaken and outraged. Her hands clenched in her lap, knuckles white. *What I would like to do to this wicked woman,* she thought. *Stalking and tempting our girls to sneak and steal for her.* Having made her confession, Moira was completely undone. She hung her head, her arms loosely at her sides, like a deflated balloon. In that moment Celia would have done anything to make it all right, to tell her not to worry, that she wouldn't lose her job. It had taken all her persuasion to convince Mrs. Wallace and Mrs. Kennedy yesterday not to have Moira arrested.

"Are you saying she stole from us?" Mrs. Wallace's face on her pillow looked confused.

"It's quite evident that she did. Celia, you and your private detective must make a report to the police. Yes, Lucy, it is stealing." Mrs. Kennedy's lips were tight with anger.

Her boss continued to stare up at her in disbelief. "Who did she sell them to? Why would they bother to take my designs?"

"Celia, Mrs. Wallace needs her rest—just have the girl arrested." Lucy's mother lived strictly by the Ten Commandments.

"Ma'am, please tell me what I am to do."

"Call in the police!" Mrs. Kennedy was adamant.

"No, Mama, Celia was the one who discovered all this." Mrs. W. pulled herself up on her pillows. "You are sure of what she did—you have proof?" Celia nodded. "Speak to the girl; then you will know what to do. And let me know if you need my help. Somehow I don't think you will."

Celia saw that Mrs. Wallace was still having difficulty understanding the why of it all. Why anyone would want to steal her designs when they were designers themselves. *She doesn't understand that Miss Vionnet is just in it for the money,* she thought. *She thinks that everyone who designs does it for the sheer love of being creative. It would no more occur to her to copy someone else's ideas than to fly to the moon.*

The burden of what to do about Moira had been firmly placed on her shoulders. Celia leaned forward in her chair to address the girl standing in front of her. "Thank you, Moira, for being straightforward. What was the name of the woman who approached you?"

"Mamzelle Vionnet. I only met her the once. When I had a design I was to contact her assistant, Mamzelle Moreau."

"The tall, well-dressed woman who wears a turquoise hat."

A nod. "Yes."

"Thank you for being truthful. You see, when I was sure it was you, I hired a private detective to follow you. Apparently you work under the name of Lily Wright, as a designer. Was that your idea?"

Moira shook her head. "Mamzelle Moreau told me to come up with a name—for what she called my designs." Celia's cheeks flushed with anger. What a shabby trick—everything these Paquin women had done was to smooth over the lie and make the theft palatable. *What a couple of cows!*

She made herself calm. "Unfortunately, the three of you overlooked one thing: Lucile's designs are so original, so completely hers, that anyone in the trade could spot them a mile away—and inevitably someone else would too. Of course, Miss Vionnet had to change a few details . . . sometimes the color or some of the trim, so that no one could prove the designs were not hers."

Moira lifted her head. "I know what I did was wrong. But the way they made it sound, like it wasn't really stealing. It was just ideas, Mamzelle Vionnet said, not an actual dress. And then she told me how much she would pay me. I am the only one working in my family, Miss Franklin. The only one. My husband ran off a year ago, and I've two little girls to look after, and my sister died two years ago, so I have her little boy with me too. On what I earn here I can't afford to pay the rent, feed and clothe us all. The money she gave me made all the difference between going without and having a few coppers for an occasional treat for the kiddies."

Celia looked away. If Moira had sold the designs to provincial dressmakers, she would never have been caught, but she had sold to Lucile's competitor. *Things must be very hard for them*, she thought. The old feeling of guilt that she had done well while others eked out a living working long sweatshop hours for lean wages was never far from her recognition of how luck had put her in Mrs. Wallace's house.

"It is not as if you are poorly paid, Moira. We don't lose our girls to our competitors because we pay top wages. And neither do you have to tell me about hard times. I know what it's like to go hungry." The girl began to sob. Her shoulders heaved and shook. "Please, miss." Her voice was harsh with tears. "Please don't turn me in. I'm all they have. All they have in the world. It will be the workhouse for them if I go to prison."

"Can you remember the date that Miss Vionnet approached you?"

"Last summer—it was August. She asked me about the salon, how long I had worked there, and what I did. She told me how to get copies made of keys. I would then meet her assistant in the evening and show her my sketches—they always had to be in color. With clips of the fabric. If she liked them she bought them from me."

Celia had heard as much from Mr. Merton, the detective who had followed Moira to her meetings with Moreau.

"You are a very lucky girl, Moira. I told Mrs. Wallace what you had done last night. And she asked me to make the decision on what we do next."

Moira pressed a handkerchief to her eyes. Within minutes it was soaking wet. "Please . . ." Her pleading tore at Celia's heart. Poverty was the evil here—that and Miss Vionnet's greed. Moira was just another of London's many struggling women—victims caught in a trap that hard grind and going without would not free them from. A hundred girls would be ready to fill one place in a sweatshop for wages that kept them alive enough to function in a world that made its fortune out of cheap labor. Mrs. Wallace paid her workers well, but single women with families to support were particularly burdened. It was unlikely that Moira was greedy: she was simply struggling.

"Sit down, Moira, and stop crying. Mrs. Wallace and I understand that you were weak rather than venal. She has had her own share of troubles in her life, as have I, which is why I am not going to call in the police." A fresh burst of tears and a choked thank-you. "Don't thank me, Moira. Learn from this moment. You have talents—so use them! Your work is exemplary; otherwise you wouldn't be working for Lucile. Don't jeopardize everything you have for an easy way out. Breaking the law and going to prison will only deprive your family of their only source of income, but with diligence and hard work you could earn a decent living, maybe as an artist, in time."

Celia turned her head away from the girl's choked tears. *You are encouraging her to believe in the myth told by most bosses to their workforce: work hard, be reliable, and you will be rewarded.* Unless those employees tried to join one of these new trade unions; then they were fired in double-quick time.

*So, why,* she asked herself, *do we expect working single women desperate to provide for their families to stay on the straight and narrow when no matter how fairly they are paid, they still cannot provide?* Celia knew this was a belief she could not share. She worked for Mrs. Wallace; Moira was a thief. Theirs was a world that she could not change.

Moira was still incoherently jerking out phrases of thanks when Robbie appeared in the doorway. "Here is your hat and coat. Robbie will see you out." The girl got to her feet and reached out for Celia's hands. Holding on to them, she said, "Thank you, miss, for not . . . for not . . ."

"No need to say any more, Moira. Stay away from the House of Paquin and Miss Vionnet—she's poison."

She heard the street door bang as Robbie returned. One more thought occurred to her. She got up from her chair and walked to the stairwell.

"Robbie?"

His head appeared as he looked up to her from the hall.

"A moment please."

He came into her room, barely out of breath from his rapid climb up the stairs.

"Sometimes, not often, I have seen a woman walking through Hanover Square. Tall, she wears a navy coat and a dark turquoise hat. Do you happen . . ." She got no further. He nodded, impatient to be off for his supper and a night out with his friends. "Yes, Miss Franklin. She works for the French lady at Paquin. She came here looking for work once—don't know her name."

So, Mademoiselle Moreau had been hanging around for some time now. She had even tried to get a job with Lucile. Celia put her hand up to her forehead. She could only imagine how catastrophic it would have been if they had let that creature into the salon.

Celia sat with the cat in her lap long after the light faded in the street below. Her hand rhythmically stroked along her back. She listened to the girls leave the house at the end of the day.

Gradually the house fell silent. The only sound was the cat's deep thrumming purr as Celia's hand slid along her sleek, glossy coat. From below, the pace of traffic slowed to a subdued mutter. The lamplighter made his way down the street, and blue-white light lit up her uncovered windows.

There was a tap on her door, and Cook put her head around it. "Are you having dinner or what?" She was a solidly built woman with a permanent frown. "It's roast chicken and it's getting cold."

"Is that the time? I'll be right down, Mabel." She got up and put the cat into her basket.

"Heard anything about Mrs. Wallace?" Cook screwed up her mouth. "We bin praying for her, me and the kitchen maids."

"I saw her briefly this afternoon. Don't want to get your hopes up, but I think she is on the mend." Mrs. W. certainly had a good deal to say about Madeleine Vionnet. "I saw her," she had croaked. "The woman with the turquoise hat. I saw her loitering in the street, do you remember, Celia? I knew she was up to no good!"

"And you were right, ma'am," she'd said. "The woman in the turquoise hat is Miss Moreau; she's Vionnet's assistant—they were both in it together."

Mr. Merton had accompanied Celia to the House of Paquin earlier that day to inform Miss Vionnet that they were aware that Moira had sold three designs to her; then they solemnly listened to the mademoiselle's protests that the designs had not been stolen. "But of course, I had no idea, no idea at all— *Mon Dieu*, what a lie she feeds me. She told me she was a designer, Lily something or other. And yes, of course, I bought from her . . . *Mon Dieu*, to think that they were from Lucile!"

It had taken all of Celia's self-control not to plant one on her.

Celia nodded as Cook's voice warmed to the topic of the dangers of living in a river valley, that London's thick fogs would be the death of all of them. *You'd think the whole Thames Valley was populated by consumptives, to listen to the woman,* Celia thought as she swallowed a succulent forkful of chicken, *but good Lord she knows how to roast a nice fat hen.* Celia had never quite mastered the art of making dinner.

# Chapter Thirteen

*March–April 1900*

Lucy

She was outnumbered! Lucy struggled to find the energy to argue, but the faces around her were determined. Sitting up in her bed took all her strength, so she lay flat.

"You were up for how long? Two days? Now look at you!" Her mother's face was gaunt. For the first time Lucy noticed how stooped her shoulders were.

"There will be no lying around in bed if Lucile goes under," was all Lucy could manage. "Sooner or later, Mama, I have to work!"

"Work?" said her doctor, his forehead corrugated, his heavy brows drawn down as if the idea of a gentlewoman working, unless it was to arrange his breakfast, was an alien one. He looked to her mother and then her sister for enlightenment.

"Her business, her dressmaking business," Elinor replied and scowled at her sister.

"Dressmaking is the last thing you need to take on. Your system will break down if you overreach yourself. You may stay out of bed for a few hours a day—provided you keep warm." He turned to her sister. "Vitally important that she doesn't overdo things—you do understand?"

Elinor smiled at the doctor. "You think she has ever taken any of my advice?" She sat down on the edge of the bed. "You are being terribly selfish, Lucy. Have you any idea how worried we have been? Esmé cries herself to sleep at night. Mama is so beside herself with worry, she is worn to a frazzle. And now all you can do is talk about your wretched shop. Now, for heaven's sake, listen to your doctor."

Lucy obediently looked at her physician.

He must have decided that she had lost her wits, if she had any in the first place. Because he continued to talk over her to her mother, enunciating his words as if Mrs. Kennedy were deaf. "Chicken soup, or maybe an egg custard for luncheon, or a nice rice pudding. The same for dinner. A bland diet. And she must not exert herself. She must convalesce, ma'am. It is how the body restores itself to normal function. Perhaps in a week she might spend an hour or two downstairs and join you for regular meals."

"And when may I return to work?" Lucy croaked like a tired crow from her bed.

Hammond glanced down at her as if she were an inconvenience. "My dear lady, not for quite some time." The wind outside dashed rain against the windowpanes, and he continued to talk to her mother. "She needs to recuperate in a warmer climate. Sun and sea air. Can you arrange that?"

Elinor had an immediate solution. "Monte Carlo! That is what she needs: the weather is glorious there in March and April. Warm, not too hot. Sea air. What do you think, Doctor?"

He glared at Elinor as he took Lucy's pulse. "No excitement, please. We will discuss when and where in a fortnight's time. Now, young lady, you must rest."

Lucy closed her eyes as a tidal wave of exhaustion bowled her over. She simply didn't have the energy to get out of bed, let alone get dressed.

The doctor finished listening to her heart. "There must be absolutely no worrying whatsoever. Otherwise, you will have a relapse. You may talk to your assistant when you are rested."

"Oh, thank you, how kind." Lucy barely had the energy to muster sarcasm. She closed her eyes and slept.

*5th April, 1900*

*Dear Cosmo,*
*I wanted to see you before we left for Monte Carlo (we will be there*
*for at least a month, maybe two, for my convalescence) but I am*
*told that you are in Scotland.*
    *Thank you so very much for your help with arranging a bank*
*loan for Lucile. I can't tell you how much this has helped to remove*
*a yearly anxiety. And I'm afraid it rather shows up what a poor*
*businesswoman I am!*
    *I am much recovered, certainly well enough to make the*
*journey south to the Riviera to fully recuperate.*

Lucy paused to bite the end of her pen. There was so much she had
wanted to say to him, and now her words were coming out as if she was
corresponding with her bank manager and not her dear friend. Writing
letters was a skill, and one she had no practice in. Best to be brief. She
would see him on her return in June.

    *I can't thank you enough for your help . . .*

She was about to write "dear friend," but instead she simply wrote
his name.

    *Respectfully yours,*
    *Lucy*

"IT IS STILL out of season in Monte, Mama, so it will be lovely
and quiet there in April." Elinor did her best to educate a woman addicted to the Victorian code of dress. "No need to take a really smart
or formal wardrobe—no one dresses for dinner there until May. And I
have organized your journey in stages, so that Lucy isn't overtired."

She put her arm around her sister. "You will be sensible, won't you, darling? Let Mama set the pace. I only wish I could come too, but a novel takes up so much time. If I can get away I'll join you toward the end of May." She put her arms around her mother and kissed her cheek. "Bon voyage, Esmé. You might learn to swim like your mama and me. We were little fish at your age!"

THE TRAIN TRUNDLED them out of soot-stained London into a world on the edge of spring. Lambs played in fields, and wild daffodils shivered in meadows in a strong April breeze. Esmé got over the tragedy of saying goodbye to NouNou and Minou and sang, *"Sur le Pont d'Avignon / L'on y danse, l'on y danse / Sur le Pont d'Avignon / L'on y danse tous en rond,"* until Lucy said: "No more just now, darling. What other French songs do you know?"

"MAMA, ARE YOU very tired? Grandmama says we are arriving at the Gare du Nord, so time to wake up." Esmé's anxious face was the first thing she saw when Lucy opened her eyes from her nap in her corner of the train compartment from Calais to Paris. The crossing had been rough and Esmé had been sick. Mrs. Kennedy, more irritable by the moment, announced as soon as their ship docked in northern France, "How could I have forgotten how terrible the French are? Completely mercenary and so cynical. No, my good man, *that* is your tip." She waved away a porter, who sneered after she had carefully counted coins into his hand. *"Assez, c'est assez!"*

Drained from her mother's complaints and her ferocity toward station and hotel porters, Lucy was grateful that their hotel in Paris was situated in an unfashionably quiet street and was asleep as soon as her head touched the pillow.

———

WHAT A PITY *we have to say goodbye to Paris so quickly*, thought Lucy as they gathered an hour early outside their hotel for a carriage to take them to the Gare de Lyon. *One day, perhaps I can spend more time in this elegant city.* She gazed wistfully at the early morning bustle of a culture obsessed with its food, its elegant architecture, and its superbly dressed women.

Esmé was ecstatic when they boarded the train for Nice. "Oh, Mama, would you look! Here is how this works. The seats fold up and down into beds with string sides." Enthralled at the thought of sleeping on a train, Esmé stowed away her travel case. "And here in this closet. Watch! If you tip this lid up, it is a little sink! To wash in."

"Yes, Esmé, we know what that's for—please leave it alone." Mrs. Kennedy, breathless after another sortie with their porter, counted francs into her purse, snapped it shut, and slammed the door to their wagon-lit. "The cost of everything—and we have only been away for two nights."

Lucy marveled at what a splendid bourgeois her mother would have made. "I love everything French," she said as her mother opened her mouth to criticize. "I know they irritate you, Mama, but I love the efficient porters with their comical round hats and their rapid, insolent French—they are certainly more than a match for you!"

Mrs. Kennedy would have argued, but the pleasure Lucy had taken in their journey was the first indication she had seen that her daughter was truly on the mend. "I can't imagine why you would enjoy insolence," she huffed as the door to their compartment slid open and the immaculately brilliantined head of their wagon-lit attendant appeared with bright silver, crisp white linen, and the extraordinarily tantalizing aroma of fresh coffee and warm bread.

"Because they do everything so well. When have you tasted such glorious coffee—and the most delicious crusty bread with deep-yellow butter—and this is in a train, for heaven's sake. In England we would be given a kipper and a cup of weak tea! And why is French apricot jam so much more apricotty than ours? You have to admit, Mama, the French really know how to live. Dinner last night was bliss."

Mrs. Kennedy opened her mouth to say something about the astronomical prices they had paid for three courses and perhaps decided that she would pay anything to see her daughter licking jam off her fingers with such passionate greed.

EARLY THE FOLLOWING afternoon, their train trundled into Nice in a torrential thunderstorm, throwing Mrs. Kennedy into a frenzy of worried exclamations.

"Oh, dear God, she's going to die!" She helped her daughter into the leaking carriage sent from the hotel. "No, no, don't sit there, Lucy, can't you see the seat is *soaking* wet, the rain is simply pouring in!" She paused to scold the carriage driver in scathing French as if he were entirely to blame for the deluge. "No, dear, I don't need an umbrella; *you* do—yes, even inside the carriage. You must not get wet because you will catch a chill! Oh dear, what will we do if you have a relapse right here in this terrible place with no British consulate anywhere near, *and* Marie Rogers told me that the French have the worst doctors in Europe—what were we thinking?" If she had wrung her hands, Lucy wouldn't have been surprised. "It is Elinor's fault for suggesting we come to France."

Lucy tried to reassure her. "I am as dry as toast; it's you who are wet. I think my constitution is stronger than you imagine. I am quite sure I could walk to the hotel." Lucy felt the old energy returning by the day. The leisurely train journey down through the center of *la belle* France in spring had invigorated her, the food was heavenly, and her buoyancy at their arrival in Nice, storm or no storm, was catching.

Esmé burst into song: "*Si mystérieux / De tes traîtres yeux / Brillant à travers leurs larmes.*"

"Esmé," her grandmother barked. "Stop it at once. Where did you learn that disgraceful song?"

"Mama said that I should sing another French song, and I learned this from Natalie at the hotel in Paris."

Lucy bit her lips to stop herself from laughing at the words her daughter was blithely singing: "treacherous eyes filled with tears." "Yes, lovely darling, now let's sing something else. What about 'Frère Jacques'? We can sing it as a round. Come on, Grandmama, you start."

But Mrs. Kennedy refused to sing. She cowered in a corner of the lurching carriage, sal volatile in hand. Outside, the afternoon was as black as night. Forked lightning split the rain-lashed sky, and great claps of thunder made the horse rear and buck. Esmé shrieked with delight at every crash.

"What will we do if you wake up tomorrow with a fever, Lucy?" Mrs. Kennedy cried as they were helped out of the carriage by Monsieur Chayez, the hotel proprietor.

"Welcome to Monaco. It is the beginning of hower spring, madam. Everysing will be *parfait à demain* honwards," he assured Mrs. Kennedy. "And for you, we have the very best suites of rooms with its own *terrasse*." The *terrasse* came with a cataract of water cascading down its walls and a pond-size puddle in its middle.

"Oh dear, what will we do?" Mrs. Kennedy pulled out shawls from her valise and wrapped Lucy up like a bundle of washing.

"Mama, please stop. I am not even damp!" Lucy tossed off the shawl, and her mother resorted to a quick whiff from her little bottle.

Monsieur Chayez, who had nothing to occupy his time on this wet afternoon, came to the rescue. "A tisane, that is what we shall bring for you. We make from sun-dries rose petals. It takes away the chills and the despair."

Esmé, intrigued by a tea made with flowers, followed him out of their suite but was back within minutes. "There is a cat! And she has had kittens, the sweetest little darlings you can possibly imagine, all different colors. The cook says I can play with them as soon as they have opened their eyes. Until then I'm going to think of names—they don't have any, poor things." And she sped off to organize her kitten nursery, leaving her mother and grandmother to their roselle tea.

Monsieur Chayez had been quite right about the weather. The next day, voilà! A brilliant sun had dried up all the rain and shone its warmth down on them in rich gold light.

"I have never seen a sky this blue, not even when we lived in Jersey!" Her mother flung back the curtains of Lucy's room. "Look, Lucy, what a difference." Lucy sat up in bed. "There are flowers everywhere, and the birds—have you ever seen such brightly colored birds?"

Lucy was more intrigued by her mother's enthusiasm than by the birds. She got out of bed and put on her wrap. The sodden terrace had drained in the night, and in its place was a pageant of vibrant color, the air scented with daphne. *It's only April and there are roses!* She bent down and picked a deep-gold bloom, inhaling its robust apple scent. "Mama, we are in paradise!" She put the rose in her water glass and stood quite still, the broad flagstone warm under her bare feet, to watch tiny blue and green birds flitting among the mimosa blossoms.

The glorious morning and warm sun had soothed Mrs. Kennedy's nerves. She bustled to the breakfast table and whisked away covers. "Breakfast outside, darling. Could anything be more delightful?" Lucy wondered what had happened to the crotchety traveler of their journey. *Poor old thing*, she thought as she sat down to breakfast in her wrap. *It was all too much for her.*

"How long has it been since we had fresh baguettes, Mama? Not since we left St. Helier! Mm, and still warm. And where is Esmé?"

"Drink some orange juice, dear, it will do you the world of good. Esmé and I ate an hour ago." A frown. "She is off with that wretched cat. If it scratches her it will surely go septic in this weather. Now, dear, I'm going to leave you to enjoy your breakfast and rest after that appalling journey. No, no, you stay and rest. I'll take Esmé for a nice walk along the seafront. She can practice her French and perhaps we can find a café for lunch."

*Dearest Elinor,*

*So sorry to take so long to write to you, but unpacking and settling into our pretty hotel took us a while. We have been here three days now. The sun and the sea have had an astonishing effect on Mama. She is so relaxed and, dare I say it—happy?! She chatters away in*

*French to everyone, praises the food, the service. Every morning she is off with Esmé on some jaunt to a different beach or sightseeing in Monte, which is charming. It is very quiet here, which suits me at the moment, but our hotelier says it livens up in May when the season starts.*

*You will be pleased to know that I am quite happy to sit and read on the terrace, which is a simply marvelous refuge of beauty and peace. As large as our garden in Molton Street, full of flowers and pretty little green and blue birds—the maid told me that they are called bee-eaters—they nest in the bougainvillea and hunt for insects among the roses! But the most glorious thing is that it is all ours and a lovely spot to sun myself—completely private, so you can imagine there is no need for modesty!*

*The food is quite superb, and I am getting nice and fat. I feel so well that tomorrow I am going down to the beach with Esmé so I can teach her to swim. Do you remember swimming? I mean swimming in a warm, gentle sea and not being buffeted by the freezing English Channel on an agonizing pebble beach from a smelly bathing machine? Well, not here! Esmé tells me that the hotel provides each guest with a sweet little yellow-and-white-striped tent where you change into your costume, and then you walk down the beach to the sea!*

*Elinor, if you can get away, please join us here. We can go to the casino and play roulette—we might even break the bank!*

She addressed the envelope in her swift forward-slanting handwriting and put it on the drawing room table to post. Another envelope lay there, addressed to *Miss C. Franklin at 17 Hanover Square, London*. But not so much as a pang of longing disturbed Lucy's sun-warmed lethargy. She felt too lazy to even think about her much-planned fashion parade. Still wearing only her wrap, she returned to the terrace to stretch herself out on a chaise longue in the sun, and lulled by the sound of the waves

on the sand and the chirrup of birds hunting for bees, she drifted off
to sleep.

"WE ARE GOING to swim out to sea." Esmé ran ahead, her plaits bouncing on her shoulders, as Lucy picked her way around the rocks at the
beach's edge. "No more paddling in the shallows and titchy little rock-
pools! How long does it take to learn to swim and how deep does it have
to be—ten thousand leagues?"

Lucy was delighted that she could keep up with the skinny little
figure racing ahead in her flouncy bathing costume. It was a perfectly
wonderful beach, nothing like the south of England's seaside resorts. No
bathing machines, no bandstands, no mussels and whelks stalls, and no
biting wind. The expanse of silver-gold sand and the deep blue and turquoise of the Mediterranean were tonic enough to bring even the dead
back to life.

Lucy changed into her bathing dress in their little yellow-and-white-
striped tent, kicked off her sandals, and raced to the water's edge. "Don't
stop, run right in!" she shouted as she bounced through the shallows
and launched herself into deeper water. Turning, she saw her daughter
skipping through the waves and kicking sea foam into the air.

All morning she held Esmé around her tummy, flat on the water, as
she kicked and splashed. "Now, Esmé, do you remember when NouNou
went swimming in the pond in Kensington Park by mistake?" She supported Esmé with one hand. "Try paddling like Nou did with your arms
and hands. No, it's not deep—see, you can stand whenever you want to.
Now, close your fingers, that's right, cup them, and pull yourself along
in the water. That's the way—you'll be swimming in no time at all. See
how easy it is to move along? Now, to go faster you do the same thing
with your legs. Just make your legs go round and round like your old
clockwork monkey climbing the flagpole. I am going to let go now . . .
keep paddling, keep paddling. Look, Esmé, you are swimming!"

"I nearly was until the water went up my nose," Esmé said, spluttering. "And some even went in my ears!"

"It's only salty water—fish love it. If you don't want to move forward, then paddle with your legs this time, up and down, and you will stay in one place." She held on to the voluminous skirt of Esmé's bathing costume and felt her own floating up around her waist, as large bubbles of air got trapped in its skirt. She remembered swimming with Elinor naked one summer in the shallow waters of Portelet Beach on Jersey island, until their mother found out and gated them in the house for a week.

"Let me watch you swim, Mama. Oh, you *can* go fast. Grand said we should watch for riptides in case we get carried out to sea." Bouncing in the water, she said, "Look at my fingers." Esmé held up her hands. "They're all wrinkled! Can we have lunch on the beach? I am so hungry, but I don't want to go back to the hotel."

Lucy didn't want to eat in the hotel restaurant either. They would be instantly pinpointed as English, and some old major and his wife would want to talk to them. "What is the name of the old man who puts up our tent? The man who brings you *citron pressé*?"

"Marcel—he is a fisherman too; he says he can take us out in his boat. Can we go?"

"Maybe, but we'll ask him to bring us lunch for now. How good is your French these days, Esmé?"

"*Je parle un peu*," her daughter replied, looking evasive and stubborn at the same time.

"Not enough conversation for you to tell Marcel what you want to eat? You can look at the menu and give our order to him."

Esmé wrapped herself up in her towel. "You'll have to help me because I hate speaking French."

"You won't hate it when you put some effort into learning the words. Then you'll love it! Imagine rattling away like Grandmama! Look, here is the menu. Some words are very close to our own. Read it through and see if you can spot them, while I change."

Lucy was tired by the time they had ordered and eaten their delicious shellfish. All she could think of was stretching out on the daybed on the *terrasse*. She wondered if her mother had had enough of her own company for one morning and would help Esmé learn some French vocabulary.

"Aunt Elinor's here!" Esmé leapt onto Lucy's bed. "She arrived late last night and is asleep in her room. She told me to leave her for a few minutes—but it's eight o'clock; she should be up by now."

"Esmé darling, your aunt is tired from her journey. So let her sleep. Then you can order us breakfast. Tell Chantelle we'll eat on the terrace. Remember, she doesn't speak a word of English, so it will have to be French. You might want to go and practice."

"Then can we have a picnic lunch on the beach. Grand says we can."

"*En français, Esmé.*"

"*Maman, c'est possible à prendre un pique-nique sur la plage?* Grand-mère says we can."

As soon as she was rested, Elinor took charge. "Lucy, you look like a ragamuffin; you can't possibly go to the casino in that. What can you be thinking—it's made of cotton, for heaven's sake—are you a gypsy now? You certainly look like one. Thank heaven I had your maid pack a few things. No, Esmé darling, I never swim in the morning, only the afternoon. I'll take you to a wonderful new beach tomorrow with a picnic!"

Lucy unpacked an odd assortment of what her sister considered necessary for the season in Monte. "This cream-and-black walking costume?"

"Why not? You can promenade like a duchess. Now, stop fiddling with that. Lucy, did you know that Sir Wilfred Chaddesley and his wife and son are here? Imagine the coincidence, we were on the same train from Paris. What do you mean you don't know them? Of course you do. Their *eldest* son is with them—lovely Dougie. Oh no, darling, you would remember if you had met Dougie; he is such a darling, I know you will absolutely adore him. They are staying at the Splendide. I said we would join them for dinner and then go on to the casino. Look, I brought your primrose evening gown and this pretty ice blue; they will go splendidly with your new fisherman's complexion. Why, even your hair has caught the sun."

Lucy was grateful for her four weeks of being a lazy beach ragamuffin, but now she was ready to enjoy the fashionable side of Monte Carlo, and if she was wise she would leave it all up to Elinor, whose boundless energy needed a challenge. Without their mother, who was becoming restless—missing her friends and her social round, and already muttering about going back to London—Elinor and Lucy set out for the delights of dinner with the Chaddesleys, the roulette table, and the possibility of huge winnings.

THE ENTRANCE TO the casino was impressively grand: tall marble pillars, a soaring ceiling, and long gilt mirrors lining the walls. "It's really not as large as it looks; the mirrors give the impression of a vast space thronged with people," Elinor said as her critical gaze swept a crowd of magnificently dressed men and women. Lucy was grateful her sister had brought her evening gown and so, apparently, was Dougie Chaddesley. He offered his arm to her. "Ready to break the bank?" he asked as his admiring eyes lingered on Lucy's sun-bronzed face. She dutifully giggled.

Gathered around the roulette table, Lucy watched Dougie place his bet. *He is such a product of exemplary Anglo-Saxon breeding,* she thought. With a square jaw, clear gray eyes, and the fair complexion of the northern European, Dougie, dressed in a faultlessly cut evening suit, was careful as he placed his bets and cautiously subdued when he won. All in all, a perfect English gentleman.

Lucy had no interest at all in gambling, but she enjoyed watching the well-dressed crowd as they sipped champagne, flirted outrageously, and smiled in well-bred desperation as the croupiers stripped them of their francs.

She drifted away from the roulette table, where Elinor was drawing a crowd of admiring Frenchmen. Dutiful Dougie came to keep her company. "Elinor asked us to come to the St. Cyprien beach tomorrow for a picnic. Sadly, my parents are having lunch with Freddie and Dorothy Winyates, but I'm free."

She smiled up into his clear gray eyes. "How lovely, Dougie. We are taking Esmé and her new kite! Be ready for a strenuous day—none of us know how to get the thing up in the air."

"Oh, I do!" He was delighted to be useful. "Nothing I'd enjoy better!"


LUCY'S MOTHER WAS up early the next morning and had already breakfasted when Lucy went into her room to find her frowning over three pages of lists. "I am thinking of returning home, Lucy dear. Esmé has missed so much school and she really needs to learn French properly, and not with this awful Monegasque accent they have down here." She was back to her old discontent—perhaps because it was inevitable that she must return home soon, and she couldn't bear the thought of missing the Riviera en fête. Now nothing was good enough for her. The delicious food found "simply wonderful" on their arrival was now "far too oily—so bad for the digestion. No wonder Elinor has a pimple on her chin."

Mrs. Kennedy got to her feet as the maid brought in fresh piles of laundry for her to check and tut over. "We'll leave at the beginning of next week after I have spent a little time with your sister. Now, shall we take the funicular to the top of Mont Agel? Douglas says the view is absolutely remarkable across the bay." She cast a sideways look out of the corner of her eye at her, and Lucy suspected a plot was in the making.

"I'd love to go," she said.

Her mother was ready for her. "Of course, I can't come; there is far too much to do to get ready for our journey home. And I doubt Esmé will want to drive all the way to Nice; she's playing with those kittens again. I do hope they don't have parasites. She really must learn to wash her hands after she has played with them."

Dougie took Elinor and Lucy to Mont Agel, and Elinor begged off at the last moment in a flurry of false alarm. "Oh no, the funicular car is far too tiny, and it's on such a narrow track. I had no idea it would be so steep, and I do so hate heights. Look, such a pretty little café. I'll wait for you both here. Don't, whatever you do, hurry on my account." She sat down and ordered *café* with such speed that Lucy had difficulty not laughing. It was a family plot, she realized, as Dougie, all smiles, opened the door of the funicular car and helped Lucy inside, banging it shut loudly to discourage any other passengers from joining them. With a nauseating jolt they started up the side of the steep and particularly ugly rock hillside.

Dougie's eyes shone so brightly with hope that Lucy had to concentrate very hard on the view, leaning out the window to watch the scrubby treetops below them. To her surprise, she found herself wondering what Cosmo was doing now. He would still be with his family in Scotland for the summer. Lucy saw him standing on the bank of a fast-flowing Scottish river, staring down into the shadowy water as he cast his line out across its steel gray surface: on the hunt for trout. She saw quite clearly the particularly grave expression he had when his concentration was focused: eyes narrowed, lips pressed together. She lifted her head, half closing her eyes in the glare of the harsh morning light, almost expecting to see Cosmo sitting across from her as the car ground steadily up the steep slope

". . . of course Asquith is one of the most politically ambitious of men, so that explains things." She caught the tail end of a story Dougie had been telling her about his maiden speech when he had been elected to the House and in particular his assessment of the reckless expenditure of the Liberal Party.

"Oh lovely, how clever," Lucy murmured at intervals, wondering why English members of Parliament always resorted to monologues on their successes as if the more boring and pompous they made themselves, the more attractive women found them.

There was a lunging moment as the little car seemed to lose momentum and slid back a foot or two before clanking up to an ungracious stop in the little wooden hut that housed the funicular's gears and wheels.

Dougie took Lucy's hot hand and swung her down onto the wooden platform. The view was precipitous, and Lucy felt a moment of panic and stepped back from a downhill view of jagged rocks and litter-strewn scrub. Completely in charge, Dougie offered his arm. "There is a café of sorts," he said solicitously. "We can enjoy a cool glass of lemonade, if they have any ice."

They toiled up a narrow path to its top, to discover that the café did not open for another hour. Lucy fanned herself with her gloves. The sun beat down on them and Dougie had to admit it wasn't worth the wait.

"Let's join Elinor at her café!" Lucy suggested brightly, and tried not to notice the disappointment in his face as they returned to the hut to buy a return ticket.

AT THE END of Elinor's first week, Lucy put her daughter and her mother on the train in Nice. "Now, remember, Mama, that they are expecting you at the Hotel Saint Regis and then it's the Gare du Nord to Calais. Here are your tickets. Everything is paid for, right through." She pulled Esmé into her arms. "*Au revoir, mon petit poisson.* Be a good girl for Grandmère. And give Nou and Min big kisses."

Lucy felt distracted as she waved the pair of them off: *It must be the general hysteria of French stations*, she thought, as she stood waving and waving among a demonstrative crowd saying goodbye to aunts, uncles, and cousins with cries of *"Au revoir"* and *"Bon voyage"* and detailed instructions for their arrival in Paris. The last train carriage disappeared under a footbridge, and Lucy walked out to the hotel's carriage to clatter back along the steep rocky roads along the coast to have dinner with Dougie.

"MARRY ME!" THE night air was fragrant with linden. The deep blue-black velvet Riviera night lit by a perfect crescent moon made Lucy regret that the romance of their surroundings did not in any way inspire Dougie. He bent his head to kiss her, and she clamped her mouth firmly shut.

*Cosmo would never kiss me like that*, she thought. *Jam his mouth against mine.* In a moment of infinite sadness, she realized that the Riviera was wasted on the Chaddesley clan. They were patronizing about their hotel's simplicity and the delicious fish the local restaurants excelled in preparing. They were only wholly satisfied when they were in the casino with old friends from England, gathered around the roulette table or back in the security of their hotel playing bridge. Like the delicious local wine they complained about, Dougie and his family did not travel well.

"Will you marry me, darling Lucy?" Dougie inquired again, this time with more emphasis, and Lucy felt a pang of loss for Cosmo's light-hearted company. How he would have roared with laughter to watch Dougie Chaddesley sending back the pretty pink local wine and demanding a bottle of Bordeaux, and he certainly wouldn't try to mash his mouth on hers whenever the moon slid out from behind a cloud.

In England, Dougie would read the *Times* as he ate his bacon and eggs and take a hansom in the early morning drizzle to tussle with the opposition in the House of Commons. He would eat plates of disgustingly rare roast beef in the Members' Dining Room, followed by apple tart with custard. As the years went by his face would turn a florid red when he laughed, and he would breathe heavily with the effort of bending down to give her a peremptory peck on her cheek before they turned in for the night. He would want sons, of course, as many as she could manage to produce. Esmé would be overrun with little Dougies. There would be shooting in Scotland and weekends in muddy Leicestershire at the Chaddesley country seat: dark, dreary, and drafty. *He won't approve of my wafty, seductive dresses—far too bohemian. Women should be laced up nice and tightly, until bedtime.* She shuddered at the future she saw for herself as the next Lady Chaddesley and flinched at the thought of going to bed with Dougie. She couldn't in a million years marry him. She would dance the night away at the casino, go to the ballet, and win a few thousand francs at the roulette table with him, but that was all.

"It is late, Dougie, and I am tired from the drive to Nice and back."

She said good night and went to her unfashionable hotel to fall asleep and dream of Cosmo, with his shining dark eyes, as he flipped up the edges of his mustache with a fingertip and laughed to himself about the Chaddesleys abroad.

When she woke to the bright morning sun and wandered out onto the terrace in her nightgown to the fragrance of coffee and the sweet, sharp tang of orange juice, she tried to recall her dream of Cosmo. Cosmo with his low, melodic voice and his delight in the absurd. The way he had of folding his arms, tucking down his chin to laugh silently at some inner joke. She could almost see him, sitting under the vine, his dark eyes gravely fixed on the face of someone who was telling him something he found interesting. She stretched her arms upward and turned her face to the sun; the silk of her nightgown moved over a body that had not worn a corset until her sister had arrived with the Chaddesleys. *Being here in a state of hedonistic bliss does wonders for the senses,* she thought, as she smoothed the silk over her warm belly.

Cosmo would adore this place. She shut her eyes, the better to conjure him here on her terrace. The scent of his skin warmed by the sun would accentuate the very slight trace of cedarwood that she sometimes caught when he was near. She pushed her hair back off her face, imagining it was his hand, she could almost feel the tips of his long fingers tracing the outline of her shoulder up to the nape of her neck, looping a strand of hair behind her ear. She was certain his touch would be light: every movement Cosmo made was balanced, graceful; surely his caress would be that way too. She felt the sun on her closed eyelids and imagined Cosmo's head bending down to hers. The skin on her upper arms lifted in a shiver of pleasure, and Lucy opened her eyes.

*What a perfect fool I've been. So driven to make a success of Lucile that I nearly lost everything—not because I said yes to marrying Cosmo, but because I stubbornly worked myself into the ground, determined to do it alone, to be independent.* Lucy folded her arms under her breasts, hugging herself tightly. *And now that I'm miles away, like the perfect idiot I am, it is the man to whom I carefully explained why I should never marry that I want to be with me right now.*

"DARLING, I'M OFF to Paris for a few days with Minnie and then home; after all, I am rather in the way here." Elinor had heard from her publisher that her book would be released to an avid reading public in a fortnight. But what was more alarming to Lucy was that she had decided that her second book would be based on Lucy and Dougie, in what Elinor fondly imagined was a passionate love affair—given that Lucy was eight years older than Dougie and to her readers a worldly woman of experience.

"Not to worry, darling, no one will ever guess it is you. I am going to call it *Three Weeks*. The title was Minnie's idea. Three weeks of passion."

"Minnie? So, Minnie thinks it is me?" Lucy's voice was a squeak of horror.

"No, darling, not at all. I think she believes it is *me!*" Elinor laughed, giving her sister every reason to believe that she had not spent her time alone in Monte.

Elinor had made friends with old acquaintances who had arrived from England to play at the casino, a chattering band of Lizzies, Minnies, Fannies, Eddies, and a Tommy. "Your secret is quite safe with me, and I am so pleased about you and Dougie." Elinor looked into Lucy's eyes, her own dancing with yet-to-be-written scenes and wicked plots for *Three Weeks*. "He is perfect for you. Doesn't care a fig that you are divorced. He adores you, Lucy, I can tell—and Esmé—how sweet. He'll inherit a fortune and the title."

Lucy frowned at her sister's zeal—there was no point at all in telling Elinor that she would never marry Dougie, no matter how large his fortune. "I do have my own money, you know."

"Ah yes, I'm not sure you will need to bother with Lucile when you marry Dougie!" A quick kiss and Elinor got up into the hotel carriage. She blew more kisses as the driver flicked the horse's rump with his whip. "Goodbye, darling. I'll tell little Miss Franklin you are staying on!"

Every morning since Elinor's departure, Lucy had walked along the great curve of the beach almost as far as Pointe de la Veille and back again for lunch. If she rose earlier she followed the goat track up into the pine-scented rocky hills and gazed down at the turquoise-and-blue sea. If she was lucky, the only sounds she heard all day were the waves on the shore, the early morning song of the bee-eaters, and the afternoon throb of cicadas in the hot hills. After lunch she napped on the terrace, her wrap discarded, her skin soaking up sunlight until it was time to go for a swim. Her days blurred one into another in warm, sensual, and mindless bliss.

Every night Dougie arrived on the dot of eight o'clock to take her to dinner, and when he dropped her off at her hotel he asked her to marry him. When she was noncommittal he would bend his head to kiss her. She could feel his teeth behind the hard pressure of his lips against her closed mouth. And it was this that she remembered two days later when the hotel maid, brisk with importance, handed her a telegram.

It said:

IF YOU ARE GOING TO MARRY ANYONE STOP YOU
ARE GOING TO MARRY ME STOP COSMO. ARRIVING
MC TUES.

Elinor had not only told Celia that she would be staying on; she had
evidently confided Lucy's "news" to everyone in London. That evening
Lucy told Douglas Chaddesley that she would not marry him. She could
only imagine as he left her, red in the face, that his parents would be
utterly relieved.

She turned and walked into the hotel, asked Monsieur Chayet for a
glass of the delicate local rosé wine, and sat in the cool night air of her
courtyard. Cosmo would be here in two days! She took a long sip from
her glass. They would sit together here in the evening and watch the
moon climb up into the sky, and Cosmo—her dearest, trusted friend—
would become her lover. A tender, passionate lover. She could almost
feel his warm breath in her hair, his lips on hers, and knew with exquisite surety that her life was on the cusp of blissful change.

# Chapter Fourteen

*May 1900*

Lucy

The water slid over her naked skin. *Silk*, she thought as she revolved in the sea like the porpoises she saw from Marcel's fishing boat, *cool charmeuse*. She lay on her back in the water to gaze up into a night filled with a thousand stars. Along the coast as far as she could see, the lights of the fishing villages went out one by one and the warm night sighed down on her as intimate and tender as a lover.

She plunged down deep into the sea, and when she kicked upward her breath seethed in tiny phosphorescent bubbles on the surface. "When I wake up, Cosmo will be here." She was surprised how calmly she could say that, when the thought of him in her sun-filled world made her heart beat as fast as the bee-eater's tiny wings. She was eighteen again, untouched by life, her heart alive to the beauty of the world. She ran her hands over her breasts and belly—how would it feel, the slow caress of his hands?—and heard herself laugh with delight. *Don't stay out here and catch a chill—you foolish girl. The last thing in the world you want to wake up with is a swollen red nose.* She raised her head and scanned the empty beach before she wrapped up in her robe, walked back to her room through the *terrasse*, and fell into bed to wake in the morning covered in a fine crust of dried salt.

———

"THE FRENCH ARE very respectable, you know; at least the bourgeoisie are," Lucy said when Cosmo appeared on the terrace where she was waiting for him at her breakfast table: freshly bathed, delicately scented, and wearing a light lawn blouse and linen skirt.

"The monsieur thinks I am your husband . . . which appeals to his idea of propriety . . . and to mine."

She offered him coffee, determined to keep her hands steady. "Have you had breakfast?"

"On the train very early before we arrived in Nice." He sat down and lifted the cup to his lips. It was as if he had always been here, sitting under the shade of the bougainvillea sipping coffee, his serious eyes gazing at her over the cup's rim.

Remembering her dream, she felt suddenly awkward and rushed to fill the silence. "I wish I'd had a chance to see you before I left for France. To thank you for your generosity to Celia, for your help. Did you get my letter?"

He waved away Lucile's rescue, his eyes watching her carefully. "Monte has done wonders for you—you look completely recovered . . . beautiful. Bonny and beautiful." He frowned at remembered concern. He put his cup down and she saw tears standing in the corners of his eyes. "I knew you would pull through. I knew it . . . prayed for it."

"If I came through, it was because you took away the fear that I would lose everything."

Her throat felt tight; she could hardly breathe. She reached across the table, put her hand in his, and felt his fingers close over hers. He lifted her hand to his mouth and kissed her open palm.

Her fingers curled in pleasure. His lips moved to the inside of her wrist.

"I could not bear the thought of losing you. I love you, Lucy. I can't tell you how happy it makes me to see you sitting here—glowing with health." He folded her hand in both of his. "You are not going to marry that ridiculous boy, are you?"

"Dougie? Good heavens no."

"Good—he would take up all your time and bore you to tears." He got to his feet and helped her to hers, kissing the hollow at the base of her neck. "Mm, you taste salty."

"A late-night swim," she said, as his kisses traveled to the curve of her breast.

"Ever been to Cap Ferrat?" he called to her as she took her bath.

"It sounds like a wilderness."

"Perhaps a little less relentless than the casino crowd on the Riviera. I think you would like it; you can see the entire Mediterranean from the Cap. Shall we go?" He appeared in the doorway of the bathroom and her breath leapt into her throat. "There is a house we can stay in up on the cliff looking down on the bay. How long will it take you to pack?"

It was like nowhere she had ever been before. Villa Les Cèdres was planted high above the coastline, a bird's nest in the rocky hills of the promontory that formed the Cap's farthest outcrop of rock. A breeze carried the scent of sea and mimosa, the cicadas sang in the heat of the afternoon, and below the Mediterranean stretched in a crescent of gold and turquoise.

"Whose house is this?" she asked as the caretaker threw open the heavy oak door that led off a courtyard roofed with magenta bougainvillea and into the cool shadows of the villa's hall.

"My uncle owned this house, and then it was passed on to my cousin. He rarely comes here now. When I was a boy I loved it here." They walked through tall rooms and out onto the terrace to look down at the sea. His arms came around her, and when she leaned back against him she could feel his breath in her hair.

"Down there"—his right arm pointed—"is a little café that buys the early morning catch every day. They make a fish soup—the best I have ever eaten because it's different every day."

Lucy laughed with the sheer delight of every little thing. "You sound hungry." She turned in his arms and kissed his chin.

"I'm ravenous," he said, "aren't you?"

"Starved." She lifted her mouth for his kiss.

SHE SAT ON the terrace wall, wrapped in the top sheet from their bed. It was as if she had shed a shell of leathery hard skin and her body had been released tender, supple, and new.

Cosmo came out onto the terrace, gave her a glass of wine, and sat down behind her on the wall. "There is bread, cheese, and some tapenade. A cold *soupe au pistou*, and an apple tarte."

"A feast."

He reached over her shoulder and touched her glass with his. "To Hortense, Gaston's wife. She left food for us for tonight until she comes tomorrow morning."

"I think I'll eat everything," she said as he kissed her shoulder.

"We can hire a *pointu* and putter around the edge of the coast, or stay here and go down for lunch at the only restaurant in the world to eat fish. Or we can get married," he said two days later, when they had found her suitcase, hastily left in the hall on their arrival.

"All of them, let's do all of them."

"What about Venice . . . shall we be married in Venice?"

"Oh yes, I've never been." She was wearing only her chemise, and the sight of his freshly shaved face smiling at her in the early morning light made her pull it up over her head and put her arms around him.

"Not again?" he said, laughing.

"Oh yes, please!"

From Nice the train made its lazy way along the coast to the ancient port of Genoa and then inland north and east to Verona. On the evening of the third day, they arrived in Venice at their hotel on the Grand Canal.

Cosmo appeared the next morning, waving a piece of paper, as Lucy emerged from her bathroom. "Easiest thing in the world to get married in Venice, apparently. I dropped in on the British consul, to find an old friend, Harry Fairchild, in residence. We can be married in three days and he says he would be delighted to give us luncheon after he has performed the ceremony." He unwrapped her from her bath towel.

"What about the maid?" she asked him, looking toward the door.

"I think she is quite happy to be a widow, and she's two floors below us. Do you like your room?"

"Yes, everything is carved, even the marble bath. It's vast, big enough for two. Come on, hop in."

"SIR HARRY'S CHARMING companion, the Contessa Simionato, invites you to visit and says that she would be only too pleased to help you—if there is anything you need." Cosmo took Lucy away from unpacking to have luncheon at the Lido.

Lucy knew no one at all in Venice, and the next morning paid a call to Sir Harry's charming friend in her house on the Rio dei Gesuiti.

The contessa was a vivid, vital little woman with large, expressive eyes and the genuine warmth of the Venetian. "My dear, how beautiful to celebrate your wedding here in Venezia, and in May . . . with all the jasmine and roses in bloom. We must make a lovely little party for afterward: Sir Harry and I are thrilled to make it so. Now, is there anything at all I can help you with?"

There was a good deal she could help Lucy with. Having unpacked, Lucy could see from her scanty wardrobe that nothing would do for her wedding day, not even the ice blue evening gown, which carried too strong a reminder of poor Dougie. "Do you happen to know of a good modiste in the town? Someone—"

"But of course, my own dressmaker! She is wonderful, such a perfectionist, but you are a renowned designer, so she will be honored to make your gown. We shall go at once to her house and you will see for yourself how painstaking her work is, and what exquisite materials she has to make the perfect dress." She clapped her hands together and her eyes gleamed with pleasure. "There is nothing I love more than the organization of dresses. I am tempted to order something myself for the occasion. Now, when you have made your design, let us go straightaway to the signora before you return to Sir Cosmo."

Lucy had heard that old Venetian families could be very proper about fiancés spending time together alone before the nuptials, but Giulietta Simionato was the last woman in the world to raise so much as an eyebrow, since it was quite clear that she enjoyed a very close relationship with her friend Sir Harry.

Lucy sat down in the shade of the contessa's courtyard and dedicated a careful hour to committing her wedding gown to paper. "What colors?" the contessa whispered. She had watched the drawing closely.

"Does the signora have silk at her shop?"

Giulietta threw up her hands. "*Migliaia e migliaia*—every kind of silk." She shook her head. "Each visit to her brings me closer to ruin! If you are quite ready, let us go and feast our eyes on her treasures."

The signora was a thin, dark little woman, with hands like bird claws. Her answers to Lucy's questions, translated by the contessa, were reassuring. And her hoard of silk and lace was both abundant and remarkably fine. Lucy chose a fine pale turquoise-green mousseline de soie and went over the details of the dress with the signora. "Will you tell her that the high vee neckline should finish here." Lucy pressed her finger against her chest and the measurements were duly noted. "And tell her that the tall boned lace collar of the chemisette should be three-quarters of an inch below my chin." She picked up her pencil and sketched the detail of the neck. "The décolleté is threaded through with pale blue ribbon and little flat silk roses. Yes, yes, a little rose when it has opened, like this." It took Lucy a minute to create a delicate little rose, to the admiring cries of the contessa and brusque nods from the signora.

More measurements were made, with the signora snapping off numbers to a younger version of herself, no doubt her daughter, whose face frowned in concentration at the stream of Venetian between the contessa and the signora.

"The signora approves of this dress, and I imagine there will be many versions made of it when she is quite sure that you have returned to England," the contessa murmured, and the two of them laughed over the rapacious gleam in the dressmaker's eyes as she sent her daughter scuttling off to the room where her fabrics were stored.

The girl came back holding a tray on which lay a handful of tiny emerald, blue, and dark turquoise beads. "The signora says for the front panel of your skirt. These are made of glass here in Venice. Do you see each one is a seashell? In Venice we believe that a shell is the symbol of protection, and it is used as a symbol of love in the sacred bond of marriage."

As the signora totted up how much she would charge for Lucy's gown, a young woman appeared in the doorway and stood patiently waiting to be noticed. In her outstretched palm lay a perfect rose made of coral pink ribbon with the center perfectly embroidered in a raised pattern. Lucy took it in her hands and exclaimed over its detailed perfection. "How on earth has she managed to make this so quickly? What skill! Look at the stamens, each one in gold thread!" Lucy's eyes filled with tears. "*Grazie mille. È bella!*"

The contessa pinched her upper arm and said in an offhand voice, as if the little rose was not that impressive, "Not too much enthusiasm, my dear, think of the bill. I see she has already added another thousand on to it."

"I always praise my girls if their work is fine, but I'll try and control my delight if it will save me money!"

Another exchange of rapid Venetian. *Why do they always sound so aggrieved when they bargain?* Lucy wondered as she held the silk up to the light and admired the dull sheen of soft green and turquoise. The day after tomorrow she would be married to Cosmo.

The contessa got to her feet, signaling that all was accomplished. "She says that she will have the dress ready for a fitting tomorrow afternoon, and the whole thing completed the following day. You need not worry that she will accomplish this; she is charging you a small fortune for her team to work on it."

They were escorted to the front door by half a dozen of the signora's helpers, assistants, and the embroiderer to see them safely into the contessa's gondola.

"Now tell me what you think of Venetian dressmakers—and their prices. Are they reasonable?" the contessa asked when they were on their way back to her house.

"Far more reasonable than I am," Lucy admitted.

"Well then, shall we pay a visit to my milliner? He can organize something quite quickly for you."

Lucy had thought about a hat and decided against. "I want to make a little coronet of jasmine. All I will need is some dark green velvet ribbon and sewing silk from the signora, so I can make it myself that morning."

"And your hair, let me send for my hairdresser—she is wonderful." They were seated again in the contessa's courtyard, sipping freshly squeezed limes in mineral water sweetened with honey.

"I have always done my hair myself." Lucy couldn't imagine not doing her own hair.

"Please, let Helena do it for you. She is so talented, and she will love to make you special for your wedding."

Lucy looked at the contessa's ornate hairstyle out of the corner of her eye. She couldn't imagine how she could look Cosmo in the face with such organized curls and crimped waves piled up on the top of her head as if they had been carved out of wood. And at the same time she found it almost impossible to resist the generosity of this kind woman to make her wedding day so festive. *Perhaps I can guide this Helena to do it the way I want, rather than what's in vogue in Venice today.* She smiled her thanks.

On her wedding morning, Lucy, with her hair styled simply and crowned with jasmine flowers, thanked every one of the contessa's maids and helpers and the contessa herself and ushered them out of her bedroom at Rio dei Gesuiti.

"No, really, I can manage by myself, thank you so much, it is what I am used to."

"But who will lace you?" The contessa was thunderstruck. "Who will help you corset?"

Lucy smiled as she remembered how long it had taken her to learn how to lace herself into her corset when she had had to let all her maids go. "The way it is always done, by me. Yes, even the buttoning."

Standing in her camisole, her laced corset, and her finest lawn petticoat, Lucy stepped into the silk underskirt and pulled it up around her waist. Catching her eye in the pier glass, she paused to examine the woman in the glass's reflection. There was criticism and curiosity in her evaluation as she gazed into her face: her eyes were clear and cool, her skin gleamed with health and happiness, even her hair radiated glossy well-being. She bent closer. *There is something else too,* she thought. A brief flash of Cap Ferrat, of her and Cosmo, came into her head, and she felt her knees bend with pleasure. *It's love, and the joy of . . .* She bit her lip to stop herself from laughing outright. Surely at thirty-seven she couldn't possibly have become one of Elinor's "It" girls?

She stepped into the skirt of her dress and drew it up around her waist to hook and eye it under the waist of her bodice. She closed her eyes and remembered swimming in an empty stretch of water on their last afternoon at Cap Ferrat. A small shiver of anticipation. How could she possibly have ever known that the act of love could be so ecstatic? Had she anticipated that pleasure when she had plunged down deep into the sea and felt its cool salty caress on her skin? She smoothed the lace of the sleeves down to her wrists and buttoned the tiny glass seashells.

*There is a particularly good reason for brides not to see their future husbands before they marry,* she realized. Anticipation! The skin on her neck and face began to warm as she tugged the bodice down, and then, leaning forward, she put her hands beneath her breasts and pushed them up. She hadn't seen Cosmo in two days . . . and now all she could think of was his hands on her waist when he unhooked her skirt from its bodice, his lips on her throat, his arms holding her against him. *I am shamelessly addicted*, she thought, and laughed aloud. *And I thought creating dresses was the closest I could come to heaven.*

"Exquisite." The countess was waiting in the hall, wearing a flamboyantly intricate hat. "And such a delightful idea not to wear anything but flowers in your hair—a perfect Venetian bride!"

There was a chorus of loud, heartfelt cries of encouragement from the countess's large staff as they peeked over the carved balustrade of the stairs and crowded in doorways.

"The day is a little chilly—a slight wind, that is all, but we will be protected in the gondola. But please, accept this gift for what I hope will be many years of happiness for you both." Two large sentimental tears stood in Giulietta's dark eyes and were blinked away. The contessa lifted her arms and held out to Lucy a triangular shawl of the finest point de Venise, so delicate that it quivered in the breeze from the canal like a web. "I am so honored that you are going to your wedding from my house." She draped the lace carefully over the crown of Lucy's head and nodded her appreciation.

Lucy couldn't help herself; the sight of this kindly woman willing her good fortune was too much for her. She put her arms around Giulietta's shoulders and kissed her on both cheeks. "You have come into my life at such a joyous moment that I know we will remain friends for a long time." She turned to the ever-growing crowd in the hall, and Helena the hairdresser stepped forward with a cluster of tiny ivory roses wrapped in cool, dark leaves. "Thank you . . . *grazie mille.*"

"*Buona fortuna, bella signora*," came a chorus of voices. "*Buona fortuna*," they cried, scattering rose petals for her to walk on. "*Dio sia grato.*"

Nothing about the morning was commonplace or ordinary, as the contessa's majestic gondola, decorated for the occasion with fragrant swags of ivory roses, swept smoothly forward from under the cool shadows of her house. It was as if every flower seller in the city had gathered for the occasion at the cross waters of Rio dei Gesuiti and the Grand

Canal. Old women in black called out their blessings and scattered the water with flowers.

Lucy smiled her thanks. And the contessa nodded to her: "Yes, my dear, there should always be flowers at a wedding. *Buona fortuna.*"


"READY FOR LUNCHEON?" Cosmo shook water all over Lucy from his morning swim.

"I was going to say I was too hot, but you have cooled me off splendidly." Lucy looked up from her sketchbook. "Do you want lunch at the loggia or in the hotel?"

"Don't want to go to the bother of dressing, do you?"

She put her pencil down. "In the loggia. Are we becoming too lazy for words? We hardly put on a shred of clothing from one day to the next." The Grand Hotel des Bains served luncheon to their guests under a vine-covered loggia next to the beach. "I am getting used to eating outside, and I haven't worn proper shoes in weeks." She felt a pang of homesickness for her little girl, for her mother's scolding discontent, and for the orderly bustle of Hanover Square.

She dug her foot into the sand and watched it slide between her toes. "I do love it here, Cosmo, I really do. But a part of me is yearning to be busy again . . ."

"I am amazed that you have lasted this long. If you hadn't been distracted by your wedding dress, I think we would be stepping off the train at Victoria Station right this minute. So it is back to work, then?"

She nodded. "My head is crowded with ideas—it must be the romance of Venice and its delicate architecture: the pointed arches, Venetian Gothic with a touch of the Byzantine." Cosmo had bought her a pair of Byzantine earrings as a wedding present and a week later had taken her to a jeweler to find a necklace. Both pieces of intricately worked gold had been an inspiration, and now all Lucy wanted was to feel silk under her hands and to spend an evening reading to Esmé.

# CHAPTER FIFTEEN

*July 1900*

LUCY

"Cosmo, I really don't mind in the slightest," Lucy said as she watched her husband shake his head at the turbot and glare down at his empty plate.

The honeymoon was over, and they were eating dinner alone together for the first time in weeks in Cosmo's house in Lennox Gardens. "Please, don't . . ." She couldn't bear to see him so embarrassed, and she had never seen him angry. "I dress them; I don't really need to be a part of their world—most of them are unforgivably stodgy and so dull." She forgot for the moment that she was referring to his world—his peers, his old friends.

He reached for her hand. "Dull? That's putting it kindly. The Prince of Wales's set are unimaginably and stupidly tedious. A bunch of overgrown schoolboys. I would have expected this from the queen, but from Bertie? What a hypocrite! He fancies himself as Europe's diplomat and then he pulls a stunt like this. What a damned stuffed shirt, the silly arse."

*How can I make him realize that it doesn't matter to me?* she asked herself as she gazed serenely at her fuming husband. The snub when it had come had caused her a second, no more, of agony, of hurt pride: *The palace regrets that Sir Cosmo will not be able to present: Lucy, Lady Duff Gordon, at court.* There was some vague piffle at the end of the official letter signed by Edward

Hyde Villiers, 5th Earl of Clarendon, GCB, GCVO, PC, DL, Lord Chamberlain to Her Majesty Queen Victoria's Household.

Her success as a dress designer—the creator of beauty, the transformer of ordinary women into creatures of spectacular loveliness—had been reduced by the Prince of Wales to a trade. She was a shopkeeper, a divorcée with an eye to marrying a title, someone had said—probably Lady Cunard, who had brazenly done just that. Lucy remembered HRH the Prince of Wales at Warwick Castle surrounded by his cronies: short, barrel-chested, puffing smoke over everyone and everything like a steam engine panting solidly at Platform 2. What a vulgarian he had seemed to her.

She stood up from the table—it was clear Cosmo had lost his appetite. "Let me show you what I have done with the drawing room," she said. "It will be ready for us soon. I spent an incredibly happy afternoon arranging the furniture I had reupholstered. I know you'll love it." She threw open the double doors, and there in the soft glow of gaslight were the colors of the Mediterranean.

He laughed and pulled her to his side.

"Look how tranquil the colors are in this light, Cosmo. On hot, lazy afternoons I would sleep on the terrace and dream of you." She gazed at the pale sand-gold of the linen walls, the deep azure of soft furnishings, and the lime green, indigo, and turquoise embroidered cushions.

"It *is* the Côte d'Azur. But were you really dreaming of me? I don't think so. You were flirting with Dougie Chaddesley!"

"He had nothing to do with *my* Côte d'Azur. He was Elinor's idea and I was being polite. I was indulging my senses: the warmth, the scent, and the colors. It was the Côte d'Azur that made your chilly English wife discover her sensuality." She remembered the night she had swum naked in the sea, the night before Cosmo had arrived.

He looked around the room glowing in the lamplight, the portraits of his family that had always looked so stiff and commonplace hanging on the walls. "Even my ancestors look relaxed in this room. You have a gift of making everything around you full of life and beauty." He turned her to him. "Mm, I can smell mimosa, or is it linden blossom? Now, remember the rules: we have eaten dinner with everyone we know to celebrate our marriage, and now that that is done, we accept two dinners out a week at the very most."

She laughed. "Quite sure you won't be bored?"

"Never. And are you sure you are not disappointed about not being presented at court?"

She didn't hesitate. "No, not in the slightest bit, because I have other plans." He sat down on a sofa and pulled her onto his lap. "You are so much more alive than the empty-headed nincompoops of St. James's Court."

"I *dress* some of those nincompoops and they have been very generous to me. Now, may I tell you my idea? It involves you, so beware! I am going to concentrate all my energy on my designs. Of course I will have to consult, but I have taken on a young Frenchwoman to train up as a designer. When she is ready Simone can take on new clients. And to do that, I am thinking of making Celia Lucile's manager. She ran everything while I was away, everything. She understands how to supervise that great crowd of dressmakers and seamstresses and has the gift of managing them beautifully without becoming too familiar so they ride roughshod over her. And she can also supervise the books. But I want you—no, please listen. I want you to look after the business side. The real business side, because although Celia understands the money part, I think it worries her and heaven knows neither of us understands finances beyond the simple business of paying bills. We might have gone under if you hadn't stepped in and arranged a loan to carry us. Will you do it for me, Cosmo—take over that part?"

He gathered her to him. "What do you imagine it entails, or don't you want to? Quite right, because the financial side of any business is often dull. Of course I will free you to create; Celia to manage the flow of work and your employees. I think we should form a new company with you and I as directors. It would provide limited liability for us."

"How would that work? How do we do this?"

"You, as the present proprietor, would sell your business to Lucile Ltd. There would be no real change in the day-to-day running, except that I would take care of what you call the business side, but you would be the director-owner." He went on to describe their liability as business owners, but he had lost her. She stopped listening at the words "liable up to their capital contribution" and simply enjoyed the sound of his voice, her head on his chest to listen to the resonance of his tone.

*I loved my Mediterranean days, but it is wonderful to be back*, she thought as she listened to the rise and fall of his voice. *Even if it hasn't stopped raining in four days. And who would have thought how wonderful being married to Cosmo would be?*

She lifted her head from his chest and slipped her forefinger under the band of his bow tie. "Is that a lot to take on? On top of all the other . . . bits of baggage?" she asked as she undid the tie.

"No, of course not. I was hoping you'd ask. I had a brief look at the account books and they are orderly and up to date." He slid her off his lap onto the sofa, and getting to his feet, he closed the drawing room door and locked it. "Someone should give the British Empire's highest accolade to the woman who designed the tea gown," he said. "So few buttons and thingamabobs to bother with."

THE FOLLOWING MORNING Lucy returned to Lennox Gardens at eleven o'clock to have luncheon with her mother, and later that afternoon Esmé would arrive with all her life's belongings from the Molton Street house. She would be accompanied by all the creatures she held most dear: NouNou and Minou and a chow puppy that Esmé had spent her savings on as a wedding gift to Cosmo and Lucy and that she had promised to train, take for walks, and stepmother.

Esmé's acceptance of Cosmo in their lives had been matter-of-fact and neutrally friendly. It was evident that her daughter was openly reserving judgment on what Cosmo's inclusion in their family held for the future, whereas her Mrs. Kennedy had swiftly recovered from Lucy's about-face over Dougie Chaddesley after an afternoon with *Burke's Peerage*. Assured that the Duff Gordons more than met the bill in both lineage and bank account, she was quite happy to wish them both a "long and happy life together."

"To say she is in raptures is an understatement," Elinor had confided to Lucy when she had hosted a family dinner party at Grosvenor Square to toast the Duff Gordons. "The marvelous Chaddesleys have been relegated to mere arrivistes and Sir Cosmo fêted for his ancient family."

Lucy smiled. "Anyone would think she had never met him—he used to come for tea all the time. Now she can't tear her eyes away for a moment. She actually flirts! And so sweetly too, like a little gray tabby cat, sitting neatly with her silver fox fur wrapped around her like a tail."

Elinor harrumphed—her mother had been a guest at Grosvenor Square for two days too long. "So exhausting—it's 'Cosmo says' this and 'Cosmo thinks' that all day long."

*Even frightful Clayton hangs on to his every word*, thought Lucy as she watched her family at dinner that evening. *And Cosmo, thank God, plays along and praises his arrangements and his Sèvres, his bibelots, and all the other expensive nonsense he has burdened himself with.*

The only cloud had been Elinor, or rather Cosmo and Elinor—both of them. Elinor's nose was out of joint because Cosmo had all Lucy's attention when she had once ruled the day. And Cosmo was irritated because Elinor was Elinor.

Mrs. Kennedy's family enjoyed and understood Elinor's enthusiasms, her exaggerations, and her dramas—particularly when she was in a good mood—but Lucy noticed that Cosmo found her sister's affectations maddening. Her histrionics annoyed him. Her determination to dominate any occasion even if she was being amusing grated. He managed well, smiled at her outlandish remarks, and laughed when she made jokes, but he kept out of her way, and sensitive Elinor was quick to notice, even when he had been careful to congratulate her on the success of her new book.

"The thing is, darling"—Lucy had tried to explain Elinor to her husband—"she does it to distract; it's all harmless faffle." But it was clear that they would never be friends, and Lucy thanked God that her mother and her daughter doted on her new husband and decided that in time Cosmo would see his sister-in-law's generosity and kindness. But it hurt that the man she loved so deeply did not see her sister's loving side and enjoy Elinor's lively nature.

As Lucy waited in her drawing room for her mother to come and inspect her new home, she felt the first tremors of anxiety and doubt at breaking the news to Mrs. Kennedy that she was not to be presented. News that would wound her mother quite dreadfully. It also made her begin to doubt herself. Was she really considered an upstart and an opportunist? Surely her oldest clients could not think that? If anyone would confirm her worry, it would be her mother.

"No Cosmo for lunch today?" Mrs. Kennedy pouted her disappointment like a fifteen-year-old girl.

"No, he is in Scotland on business. I will be joining him tomorrow to meet the family!"

Mrs. Kennedy patted her arm. "They will adore you. Who wouldn't, my dear? What a shame about his mother—I mean her death, of course. We all want to see our children happily married."

Lucy walked her mother toward the dining room. "You must be hungry, Mama. We have a wonderful cook and I asked her to make your favorite: veal cutlets followed by a summer pudding with fresh berries brought up from the country this morning!"

The butler threw open the doors to the dining room and Mrs. Kennedy walked into the room as if she were a duchess. "I am hungry, dear," she said, assessing the table, the silver, the arrangements with satisfaction.

"I have to say that the French are very proficient with their herbal teas. The one you brought home with you is particularly good. Now, tell me, what will you wear for your presentation at court, dear?"

"No presentation at court, Mama," she said.

"Don't be ridiculous, dear. You married a peer. Of course you will be presented. Please, Lucy, don't tell me that you think court presentations are silly and that you have decided against it."

It would be easy to tell her mother a lie and say she had decided against the pomp of St. James's Court. But it would never wash. Her mother wouldn't leave her in peace until she had jammed three Prince of Wales feathers into her hair and sent her off to Buckingham Palace.

"I may not be presented, because of Lucile. And probably, more to the point, because I am divorced. Either way, no presentation."

Her mother's eyes widened. At last her eldest daughter had accomplished something worthwhile: marriage to a baronet—at thirty-seven, no less! She had married a man with impeccable credentials, a man with a net worth of thousands—Lucy need never lift a finger for the rest of her life. That Sir Cosmo had been willing—no, delighted—to marry a woman with every intention of continuing her silly dress-designing business in spite of the stain of a decree absolute had brought nothing but absolute relief to Mrs. Kennedy.

"Then don't be a tradeswoman, Lewcy," her mother snapped. "Think of Esmé. Will she be presented at court—as a debutante? Or will she be turned away too, so she can only marry into a family in trade?"

Lucy threw back her head and laughed. "Darling Mama . . . a court presentation doesn't have quite the cachet it used to have. Truly. And I would take being in trade over all that fuss any day. But I love you for being so outraged on my behalf."

## June 1902

## CELIA

"Please, no interruptions! There are not enough hours in the day," was Lady Duff Gordon's habitual refrain. She uttered it now when Celia came into her studio with Alice right behind her carrying a bolt of fabric.

"Mrs. Asquith is downstairs for her fitting, m'lady, and you have a consultation with Lady Cunard, who is pacing in the drawing room like a caged tiger."

"Would you open another window, Celia. The heat! No one would believe this was an English summer. I'm wilting." A heat wave had started at the end of May, and already London's gardens, parks, and squares were dry and brittle.

"Now, what did you say about Lady Cunard?"

Celia repeated the remaining two appointments for the day.

Her ladyship didn't raise her head. "Ask Simone to consult with Lady Cunard, please. Oh, and let her know that we do not use ostrich feathers in this salon—or those of any exotic bird either."

Celia knew how much Lady Duff Gordon disliked the fidgety and acerbic Lady Cunard. But no one would willingly upset one of London's most prominent society hostesses, and certainly not one with a tongue like a rapier. Simone was a good designer, with an exacting eye and a deft manner with clients. Celia knew that Lady Cunard would throw a paddy and demand she consult only with her ladyship. "She made the appointment expressly to see *you*, m'lady."

"Hold quite still, Julia." Mrs. Wallace pinned a swathe of fabric around the shoulder of a young woman with a glossy rope of carnelian red hair wound around her head—one of her new mannequins in training. "No, this won't do; this silk is too heavy, too stiff to drape. It has to be fluid." She lifted her head. "It is this wretched coronation, Celia. Every woman has suddenly decided that she must have at least five new gowns. Please tell Lady Cunard that I will be with her in twenty minutes and let her think that one over. Then go back to her and ask her if she would like to see our new *French* designer, Simone, immediately—I guarantee she will say yes.

"Alice, did you bring the champagne mousseline de soie? Thank you. Anything else, Celia? I must leave by six o'clock at the latest. I don't think Sir Cosmo will forgive me if I spend another evening here. Drat this coronation!" Under her breath she added, "I can't imagine what sort of king Bertie will make."

Celia smiled. "One more month, ma'am, and all the fuss will be over. We are dressing over half of Westminster for this coronation. I don't

think there has been a season like this one ever. And Mrs. Glyn telephoned to ask if she can come to dinner tonight."

Her ladyship was tacking a swathe of mousseline around Julia's
shoulder. "Oh no, not tonight. Did she telephone, or was it her maid?"

"Her maid. Mrs. Glyn wants to talk to you about . . . Ambrosine?"
She looked for a change of expression that would give her a clue—was
this Ambrosine a new client? A famous American film star?

A long harrumph. And her boss said something unprintable under
her breath.

"M'lady?"

"Oh dear God in heaven!" Lady Duff Gordon never shouted, but her
raised eyebrows did it for her. Celia waited. "It's her book," her ladyship
muttered as she turned Julia with such a gentle hand, it was impossible
to tell that she was annoyed.

Celia waited as her boss inch pleated the delicate silk and secured it
with a basting stitch.

"I have no idea why she needs me to listen to her ideas."

Celia didn't care if an answer was expected or not. "Because she
trusts you will be candid and direct with her?" *And because she was always there for you when we were starting up and in need of rich friends to
buy your gowns.*

She thought she heard Lady Duff Gordon say, "I am sick to death of
the Reflections of damned Ambrosine."

Celia waited as Lady Duff Gordon finished pleating the back of the
tea gown into a graceful Grecian drape.

Her ladyship sighed, snipped the silk thread, and surveyed the back
of the gown. "Will you telephone Mrs. Glyn's maid and ask her if tomorrow for lunch here would be acceptable—if she is free? Lord knows
my sister has had to listen to me go on about Lucile often enough."

"Yes, m'lady. Please don't forget about Mrs. Asquith. I will put her
in Lapis. And have Simone on standby to consult with Lady Cunard in
Peony."

## Chapter Sixteen

*January 1906*

Lucy

Darling, I don't understand why you ever leased this house in the first place with this ridiculous room. No one in town has a ballroom these days. If we want to have a big party in London, we do it at the Savoy or the Dorchester. Do you really have enough clients to fill it?" Elinor had arrived in a spiky mood, but now the Reflections, or rather the shocking misadventures, of Ambrosine had been thrashed out over lunch to her absolute satisfaction, she was prepared to give her opinion on Lucy's mannequin parade.

They stood on an acre of fine oak parquet surrounded by Lucile's dove gray and dark green upholstery. Elinor made discoveries by asking questions and then beating Lucy to the answers, which popped into her head on the tail ends of her questions.

*It is exactly like watching someone talking to herself,* Lucy thought, amused rather than irritated by her sister's need to hold forth. *And when she has finished talking she always assumes that I have agreed with her.*

"Are you really going ahead with this madcap scheme?"

"Yes, it has—"

"I mean, it's years now since you first thought of it—I thought you had sensibly given it up as a bad idea."

"I think it is a good—"

"So, your models will be shown by beautiful young women who will then walk up and down to show them off, is that how it works? Do they stand around like women of the night in dark corners, waiting to be noticed, or do they approach your clients?" Elinor roared with laughter at her joke. "And where on earth do you find them?"

"This is a fashion house, not a bordello. And my clients are all women, not men looking for a good time. You asked, 'Where do I find anyone who works for me?' And the answer is by looking. The girls are very respectable. You can have the women of the night for one of your books."

Elinor giggled. "I'm sorry, really I am. But where do you find them, your girls?"

"I have one already—or rather Celia did when she employed her as our parlormaid. Grace Townsend is now my vendeuse; she looks marvelous in practically everything I make. She has a glorious complexion, dark, dark hair, almost black, and such remarkable eyes. She is in every respect a perfect Grace. Esmé for the longest time was convinced she was Snow White."

She rushed on before Elinor could barge in. "Do you realize that there are working girls all over London drudging away behind shop counters, working in florists' shops, or making hats? Lovely girls in all sizes and shapes. Of course it will take me a month or so to educate them how to walk, stand, and sit—most women simply have no idea unless they were raised by strict nannies and critical mothers. The training, believe it or not, is the most difficult part."

Elinor sat down on a sofa, her head turned to the north end of the ballroom and its new proscenium, still smelling of freshly planed pine.

"I simply don't know where you come up with these ideas, do you—?"

"It just comes, like the idea for your books." Lucy sat down next to her on the sofa. "For most of this year and last, I have been dressing actresses for West End plays. There are days when I spend more time at Daly's Theatre, the Criterion, or the Vaudeville than I do in my studio. It is from watching actresses wearing my costumes in countless theater productions that has made me realize that there is very little difference between a woman on the stage wearing a beautiful dress and one walking about a large room as if she is on the stage. The idea was there years ago; I wasn't quite sure how I would present it."

"You will have a group of girls trained to walk like ladies and dressed in your latest models. Thank heavens they are not required to speak. What happens next?"

Lucy got up and walked toward the proscenium. "Imagine this!" She threw her arm out to encompass the room. "There is Lady Robinson with her coterie, trying to ignore Lady Cunard with hers. And over here is Margot Asquith with the lovely Lady Violet Manners and her two exquisite eldest daughters. And Evelyn Willie James and the smart set, all buzzing with gossip sitting right where you are now. Certainly, Daisy Brooke is among us trying not to look daggers at the new and utterly delectable *favorita*, Alice Keppel!"

"And then?" Elinor demanded action in both her books and her life.

Lucy ignored her sister. "And over there are all my newly arrived American friends; they have come for another London season and can't wait to see what delicious gowns I have created for them!"

"Yes, yes, I see them all. The rich Americans, the dreary aristocrats, your charming bohemians, all well titled and well-heeled. But what happens next?"

"Heavens! Don't be so impatient, Elinor. I am setting the scene. *Then* the lights come up on the stage." Lucy ran up the steps to the top of the dais and stood sideways, her right foot forward, her shoulders turned toward her sister. "The audience will see the outline of a young woman through the gray gauze of the curtain, rather like a scrim—a silhouette only." Lucy struck an attitude reminiscent of the way the illustrators in *The Queen* portrayed the latest fashions. Bosom out, head up, craning on a long neck, chin tilted up. One hand holding out a furled parasol away from the body, the other resting on a hip. "The lights come up—just as they do in a play—and here she stands: a glorious vision of youth: perfect skin, well-groomed hair, and a stunning dress."

Elinor clapped.

"She steps from behind the gauze curtain as a spotlight comes up revealing her flawless beauty—but would you look at the dress she is wearing!

"She faces the audience." Lucy did so. "Gracefully light on her feet, she walks down the steps and into the room and is among us! Every single woman in the room simply yearns to be twenty again: dewy, firm, slender. 'But surely,' they think, 'if I wore *that* divine dress . . .'" Lucy was transported by what she imagined, her arms gracefully extended out to the sides, her palms upward as she turned. "The lights slowly come up in the room. And we watch the beauty in the world's most delicious gown glide down its length, turn, and walk back to the center. And then the next model arrives on the stage, another glorious gown worn by yet another lovely young woman. They will each carry a card with a number to help the clients identify the dress that they have seen on the programs they have been given. It's pure theater—so much more exciting than looking at the dress on a canvas dummy."

Elinor jumped up from her sofa. "You should say something about the dress as they walk around; otherwise all you will hear will be the clomping of feet and people whispering catty things about the vision of loveliness. Women always find fault when they see a beautiful girl." Elinor's criticism was always useful.

"Music!" Lucy cried. "That's it, music! A string quartet playing softly, but loud enough to muffle conversation and footsteps. Perfect!"

"Announce them, Lucy. Like this." Elinor ran up the steps to stand on the stage. She struck an attitude of insouciant grace, then undulated down the steps to her own announcement. "Valentine is wearing a tea gown of delicate lace over a sheath of seductive boudoir pink I like to call Yearning. The large bow at the nape of the neck is all that needs to be undone. No, I mustn't laugh, because it is a marvelous idea. Your clients and friends will love every minute."

Lucy smiled and smoothed down the folds of her skirt. "As sensational as the next drama you are going to write. You see, dear sister, the theater must be in our blood."

They stood together in the middle of the great room. "How many girls?" Elinor asked.

"I have Grace and another possibility, who is one of those stunning redheads, with thick, dark auburn hair. I think if I have six girls, each wearing four to five models, that should be enough to start with. It will be invitation only for tea in celebration of my spring collection, so don't breathe a word. The fashion show will be the coup of the afternoon."

Elinor pulled on her gloves. "When will you stage your event?"

"My only problem is time. It must be at the very beginning of the season—the earlier the better. Then we will be rushed off our feet, hopefully, with orders for the summer."

"End of March would be best . . . this year?"

A look of panic crossed Lucy's face. "I am too late to put all that together for this season. It will have to be for the autumn. I have to find the girls. Train them . . . design clothes. It must be done perfectly or not at all. The clothes will be easy. Finding and training the girls will be the challenge."


*June 1906*

CELIA

It was good to have her back again. Lady Duff Gordon's step was light, her manner breezy. *Yes*, thought Celia, who was looking forward to her own summer break, a walking tour in the Yorkshire Dales with Grace for company. *There's nothing like a change of pace for putting a spring in your step.*

"Good to see you back again with us, m'lady. And congratulations to Sir Cosmo's fencing team in Athens—we were so proud when we read in the newspapers that they won the silver medal."

"A hair away from the gold, Celia, but it was a wonderful thing to watch. And Athens was a dream come true. Now, how are our girls coming along? Did Grace work wonders while I was away?"

Together they walked to the ballroom, where Grace was putting the five girls Lady Duff Gordon had hired as potential mannequins through their paces.

They paused in the doorway, and Celia nodded toward the group around the proscenium. "I think you will agree that there has been *some* improvement, m'lady."

Lady Duff Gordon surveyed a bevy of immaculately turned-out girls. "They certainly look the part," she murmured.

A petite brunette with translucent skin and large dark eyes thumped down the three steps from the proscenium onto the ballroom floor.

"Blimey, Ange, you reelly gotter lighten up on yer feet, luv. How many buns did you have for yer tea?" shouted a tall redhead with the pearlescent skin of those who have to shelter from the sun. There was a shriek of laughter from the other three girls.

A willowy young woman with a neck like a swan and soft hair fluffed out around her face in a gilt halo of light strode out onto the stage with all the resolute energy of a milkmaid on her way to the cowshed.

"Oh dear." Lady Duff Gordon walked to the foot of the dais, her brow smooth, her face serene. "Betty, Angela, Dottie, and Madge, will you come back to the stage, please? Now, I want you all to watch Grace." Her ladyship beckoned to Grace.

No one would have guessed that Grace, born within the sound of Bow Bells, had started work as a parlormaid for Lucile and had progressed to become a salesgirl. But she was every dress designer's dream come true. And, Celia noted as Grace mounted the three steps to the proscenium, an ideal example of relaxed deportment. The girls might find Lady Duff Gordon intimidating, but Grace was one of them.

Grace moved as if she had been born Lady Grace.

She walked up the steps to the stage to stand with her head up as she slowly turned. At a nod from the boss, Grace addressed their new recruits. "There is no need to rush," she said as she faced them. "You have all the time in the world, ladies. Imagine you are a member of the leisured class: the world waits on *you*! We are not belting about in a panic, searching for one-inch nails at the back of an ironmongers or racing to answer the scullery door to the grocer's delivery boy! We walk slowly and lightly. Let's go through it again, and this time give everyone a chance to see how lovely you are. Relax and enjoy it."

"As the bishop said ter the actriss," Ange shouted to shrieks of laughter.

Grace turned her elegant head and frowned at Ange's vulgarity. "There is no need to look at your feet when you take the first step down from the proscenium. You run up and down stairs all day without looking at your feet. This isn't a steep flight of back stairs, just three shallow steps. Even if you have size nines, there is space on each for your foot." She floated noiselessly down the steps. "And toe first, never heel first. Heels carry all your weight and are noisy; toes are silent." She quoted Lady Duff Gordon, who had withdrawn with a frown on her face, motioning to Celia so they could talk in private.

"Celia, this is our third group of girls. I am beginning to despair that we will find any capable of understanding how important it is to *walk*." Her whisper rose to a squeak of panic. "Who would have thought that walking was a rare talent?"

"The last one wasn't too bad." Celia tried to find something to hang on to. Some hope.

"Are you talking about Ange? Oh dear, Celia, Ange could get a job tomorrow as a runner on the brokers' floor at the stock exchange."

"Have faith, m'lady. If Grace could pass for a lady, all of them can."


*October 1906*

LUCY


The gaslight came up on the stage. The string quartet's "Autumn," from Vivaldi's *The Four Seasons*, lifted above the chatter from Lucile's guests gathered in the ballroom, then overrode it until quiet expectancy reigned. Lucy saw, out of the corner of her eye, her boned lace collar vibrating with nervous tension.

She felt Grace step through the doorway on her right.

"Wait, wait for the adagio." Now that the audience was quiet, the quartet dropped its volume. "Grace, you are perfection," Lucy whispered as she gently shunted Grace forward with a hand in the small of her back. "Slowly, slowly, lovely Grace." And she watched her glide onto the stage.

There was a murmur of appreciation from the ballroom as Grace stood tall and poised in the Crescent of a Moon: pewter satin gleamed, now silver, now dark gray, in the spotlight. Grace turned her elegant head to gaze out over her audience, her eyes half-closed as if she was listening to the cascading notes of the music.

With superb timing she floated down the steps from the proscenium, as weightless as an autumn leaf. The floating panels of her dress flared in a circle as she turned and then dropped obediently around her waist and hips.

Lucy smiled. "She is using the music as if it were a part of her."

Grace walked out into a spellbound audience as if they were not there.

"What an actress," breathed Lucy.

"I remember the first time I heard her hail a hansom cab," Celia whispered, and Lucy nodded. "That terrible shriek?"

"I'll never forget it, m'lady. Ever. Not an exaggeration to say she stopped traffic all the way to Piccadilly." They stood, close together, mesmerized as the vision that was Grace walked the length of the ballroom and turned to stroll back to its center.

"Like she was born to it," whispered Celia. "A duchess."

Lucy squeezed her friend's hand. "Duchesses rarely possess as much poise," she said.

There was a soft, concerted moan of longing as Grace made a slow circle, arms lifted out to her sides, palms upward, to show the wide draped sheer sleeves of her dress, embroidered in silver thread, catching a thousand points of light. Lucy watched heads bend to consult programs before lifting again to devour the shimmering silver before them. "The Crescent is being well received!"

Celia nodded. "Yes," she whispered. "Cats gloating over a bowl of cream."

As Grace walked toward the anteroom exit, Lucy's next mannequin was standing at her elbow. "Phyllida." Ange had not let them down—had come through her deportment class with flying colors and had been rewarded with an elegant stage name. "How perfect that color is on you. Now, remember, take your time, let the beauty sink in." Phyllida floated forward.

"Perfect," Celia said. "Not a single clump to be heard—and she's all of five ten."

"I am wondering if that russet combined with apricot gold and pink isn't a little too strong in this light," was Lucy's only comment, as Phyllida stood with her head graciously inclined to receive the spectators' gratification.

"They don't think so at all—look at them, positively salivating." Celia had a weakness for all shades of red to pink. "I wonder how many orders there will be for Autumn Amber? All those brunettes and redheads out there will be frantic for that gown."

Lucy looked down to the upturned, delighted faces of her clients. There was not a woman among them who was not transfixed by Lucile's new collection.

*How long have I waited for this moment?* Lucy asked herself as she caught her husband's eye across the stage, as the last gown of the afternoon was received with cries of adulation and whimpers of longing. *How can life possibly be so perfect? So blissful that it almost hurts?*

"Now it's your turn, m'lady. No, no, off you go. They want to tell you how much they love your beautiful clothes." Lucy turned to the manager of her salon. *Not just Lucile's manager,* she thought; *she is my friend. My kind and loyal friend.* There were tears standing in Celia's eyes.

"We worked so hard for this moment, didn't we, Celia? I mean really hard—for years—eleven of them." She laughed. "And now look at us. Look what we have achieved—we have set the world of fashion on its heels!"

Lucy forgot for a moment how exhausting it had been finding the right girls and then praying they could train the East End out of them. *Our first mannequin parade—that'll give Charles Frederick Worth and the rest of those stuck-up men in rue de la Paix something to think about!* Celia gave her ladyship a little push. "Go on," she whispered. "They want to tell you how thrilled they are."

She walked out onto the proscenium and stood quietly in the spotlight. The Gainsborough blue velvet afternoon dress emphasized her neat figure; the boned lace collar stood up around her neck, cupping her heart-shaped face in silver filigree. She bowed to the applause from her clients and turned to look into the wings at Cosmo.

"*Bravissima,*" he called out to her. "*Brava, bellissima!*" He signaled with a salute that he would see her at home—a crowd of women rapturizing about clothes was the last thing he would enjoy.

The crystal light swam in and out of focus as Lucy walked down onto the ballroom floor.

"Brilliance, sheer brilliance, clever Lucy." Daisy Brooke waved a kiss to her.

The cold, handsome face of Gwladys Robinson, the Marchioness of Ripon, acknowledged her with a bow of her elegant head and tapped the program on the table in front of her in a we-must-talk gesture.

Mrs. Willie James breathlessly started sentences with "Oh, my dear Lucy" several times, obviously at a complete loss for words, as Lucy was surrounded by chattering, happy women, clapping their gloved hands as if Lucile had scored four hundred not out in a cricket match against the House of Worth.

Her American friends, more demonstrative in their accolades, clustered around her, their voices high with pleasure. "My dear Lady Duff Gordon—spectacular, absolutely spectacular, and what a novel idea to show us your gorgeous gowns as they should be worn, on such pretty girls." Florence Bartlett Fleming was the first to congratulate her: she leaned forward and kissed Lucy on the cheek.

Angeline Wilson, a close friend of Lady Randolph Churchill's, pressed her hand and said, "I want every single one of them—every one!"

Lucy wondered how she could absorb such praise, such delight, from women she had dressed for years. *Surely*, she thought, *surely they know what my clothes look like by now?*

"I'll *never* make another trip to Paris as long as I live," the Duchess of Rutland said with absolute conviction.

Champagne was poured by hired footmen, and rented glasses were lifted. Mrs. Willie James tapped the rim of her glass for silence. "A toast to Lucile," she cried. "Long may she reign!"

The applause died down; bright eyes fixed on her face with expectation.

*And now*, Lucy thought, *I have to show them how we can go forward from this collection.* No one wanted to go down to a country house ball as one of fifteen scarlet iterations of the Lips of Passion Flowers Kiss.

She bowed to acknowledge their praise.

"My heartfelt, truly heartful and grateful thanks to every one of you." She turned to embrace them all with shining eyes. "For years you have come to me so that I might dress you, you and your darling girls who are about to take their place in fashionable society." *And your husband's mistresses*, she said to herself. *May wives and sweethearts never meet.*

She made sure to recognize the stalwarts of her accounts receivable: the American contingent. "That you now come to London for your wardrobe is the greatest compliment you could ever pay me. Thank you."

*I must never forget the friends who supported me in those terrifying first months.* "I have this to say to old friends and to new: women fulfill so many roles in this remarkable new century of ours. Tonight I gave you a glimpse of a future that we will forge together—of the infinite possibilities we can achieve *together*." A burst of excited laughter as her friends raised their glasses to her. "The world of fashion, of dressing in a way that is original to you, has changed in two short years from narrow hemlines to softly layered skirts and floating panels. Now we can at last say goodbye to the hobble skirt!" Laughter and more hand clapping. "I am happy to show you fluidity: softer outlines with more feminine allure— that bless our figures and do not constrict them!

"Until today the clothes we wore were to please fashionable society. But what we wear today not only reflects the exciting changes ahead for us but shows us how we can influence change in the dresses and gowns we *wish* to wear—clothes that will suit our new active lives." She ignored the puzzled faces of deeply conservative dowagers whom she would willingly lose to Reville and Worth. "I truly believe that what women choose to wear will dictate the sort of lives we lead in the decades to come!"

She smiled at the crowd of faces before seeking out close friends and those who had truly inspired her by their trust and their individual taste and style. "I only hope that this afternoon's glimpse of what we can do for you as a woman of our new age will make you thirsty for the ways we can dress you as a wholly original individual!"

And then it was all over. The loving goodbyes, the cries of congratulations as carriages and electric broughams filled the street and her guests left her. Behind the scenes, dresses were put away; the mannequins changed into their outdoor clothes and came to hold her hand and to thank her over and over. "It was like a fairy tale come true, your ladyship, really it was." Flossie, whose stride was as long as Sir Cosmo's, dropped a diminutive curtsy, her back as straight as a die and her patrician profile lifted in gracious thanks.

"I should thank you, all of you. How proud you have made me! You were wonderful tonight, all of you!"

And then it was quiet; a tired Robbie walked from room to room extinguishing lights. Lucy walked up the stairs to her private sitting room on the third floor to be greeted by her mother and daughter.

## CHAPTER SEVENTEEN

*June 1907*

LUCY

Rules Restaurant was crowded with the crush of an after-theater supper party. Cosmo hesitated, frowning at the crowd. *The last thing in
the world he wants to do is thrash his way through that mob, after listening
to melodramatic fluff all evening*, Lucy thought. She flashed him a you-
promised look and stood on tiptoe to catch the eye of the producer and
director of Daly's Theatre, George Edwardes. George waved them over
and the maître d' made a path through the throng for them.

Standing next to the director of the operetta *The Merry Widow* was
its new star, Lily Elsie. Was it possible that this quiet girl with her huge
dark eyes was the effervescent and flamboyant creature they had seen on
the stage of the Daly Theatre half an hour ago? Lily was still dressed in
the costume that Lucy had designed for her performance in act three
with its immense black crinoline hat. For the first time since she had
met the young actress, Lucy felt a rush of protective affection for this
deeply vulnerable young woman.

"Lily you were quite wonderful. I knew you would be from the moment you opened your mouth. First-night nerves—" She laughed them
away now they no longer loomed. "I told you they would go the moment
you said your first line!" She kissed the young woman on her cold cheek.

"I can't seem to remember it—any of it. I was sick with nerves, over-whelmed." Lily glanced at her director, seeking his approval. But George Edwardes was too busy receiving laurels from London's haute monde for his extravagant production. "I did remember," the young woman con-tinued, "to walk slowly, and to keep my head up. To stand and sit like a real lady. Did you notice?"

"Yes, I did. And you moved with such ease and grace. My dear Lily, you were as light as gossamer. And your diction so clear. But you were far more than that—far more than diction and deportment. You were a sensation. You were Sonia."

Lily Elsie blushed. "Then it should be the other way around. I should congratulate you for showing me how. I don't think I could have done it without you."

Lucy remembered the hours of coaching they had put in to turn a pantomime performer into a versatile young actress who could move and talk like an aristocrat and feel her way into her role. "No, I merely showed you a few techniques; that is all. But you *became* Sonia so com-pletely that the audience fell in love with her and you. You can achieve anything with hard work, but you have a true talent for inhabiting your character—and that is a gift."

"It will run for weeks!" They were interrupted by a woman with sharp features who had elbowed her way forward through the crowd. "Captivating!" she shrieked to George Edwardes. "Absolutely captivat-ing!" She pounced on Lily with such enthusiasm that Lucy felt her shrink beside her. "And, my dear, you were remarkable as Sonia. Such a talent—you will go far . . . mark my words!" she cried to the dwin-dling Lily.

Lucy drew the actress aside. "She is right. This is the beginning of your career. I have never heard an audience so enraptured." She did her best to reassure her, but it was almost disconcerting to see this young woman who had swept London by storm looking so timid, so unsure of herself. *If anything*, Lucy thought, *it makes her even more appealing, even more wistfully beautiful.*

She, too, was pulled away by friends and theatergoers; the entire Marlborough set had swept in through the door, and champagne corks popped, and glasses fizzed with bright wine. Alice Keppel, the king's *favorita*, was at her side, her large gray eyes fixed on Lucy's face.

"Lucy, I simply can't believe your glorious costumes. That dress in the first act: it gleamed like liquid gold. And that stunning hat. Ah, Lily is still wearing it. What a little beauty. Congratulations, my dear, a glowing performance. And, George—well done. His Majesty was entranced."

*No, he wasn't.* Lucy smiled. Ever since the Prince of Wales had become king, Bertie made sure that there was a distraction close at hand when he had to go to the theater or opera. He snoozed as soon as the curtain went up and then left in the entr'acte for a well-provisioned room close by where he could spend time with his friends. Always back in time for curtain calls.

"George Curzon told me that she grew up playing in pantomime in Yorkshire somewhere. Who would have thought she was such a quiet little thing when she was so vibrant onstage?" Mrs. Keppel sipped her champagne, looking around her. "Can't stay . . . royal duty calls. Supper with the Cassells. But we have to talk hats, Lucy. Huge hats with wide brims laden with feathers! How very clever you are." A wave of her gloved hand and she was gone.

Lucy could hardly breathe in the press of enthusiasm and laughter around her. She looked around for Cosmo, whom she had last seen talking with Lord Curzon. Someone, somewhere—Lucy racked her memory—had told her that Elinor and George Curzon had been in each other's company for many months now. She caught Cosmo's eye as he signaled that it was time to leave. She couldn't imagine for one moment that he would want to eat supper amid this din.

"Lily"—she touched the girl on her arm—"I must go."

"Oh no, must you?" Overwhelmed by the clamoring congratulations over her performance, Lily almost clung to Lucy's arm. "Mr. Edwardes is putting me in his next play, and he suggests that I come to you for a consultation—for my own wardrobe." She smiled a tight, anxious smile. "My present one is not quite up to the mark."

"Come anytime, my dear. I would be honored to dress you."

Lucile waved to Cosmo and glanced at the exit, and they both struggled through the crush to the street. Crowds of fans stood on the pavement oohing and aahing at London's well-dressed theatergoers and hoping for a glimpse of *The Merry Widow*'s stars.

"Oof, half an hour of that bunch was more than enough for me." Cosmo emerged from the entrance to Rules, draping his white silk scarf around his neck. "Shall we walk through the park?" He took her arm in his. "You won't be too cold?"

"No, no. I need air. So, Cosmo, what did you really think of Lily's costumes?"

He guided her through a throng of hansom cabs in the street, to join other theatergoers as they strolled in the direction of the park. "I think you must tell Celia to hire some more seamstresses. And I am going to talk to our agent about leasing the house across the square. We need larger premises, my darling, after tonight's success. Are Natasha and Simone ready to take on new clients? I hope so, because Lucile Ltd. is going to be the top fashion house in London after this."

Lucy's head was still crowded with scenes from *The Merry Widow*. And the gasp that had greeted Lily Elsie's entrance as Sonia dressed in gold embroideries over oyster white satin, the dress the king's mistress had described as liquid gold. In the sweet night air, her head swam with visions of dresses to come and ideas for new styles.

"There was a young man standing by the door as we left," she said. "He is a photographer, commissioned by Edwardes to make postcards of Lily in what they are all now calling *The Merry Widow* hat. Do you know what he said to me? I don't think I will ever forget it. He told me that I was 'a delicate genius.'" She didn't mention that he had gushed. "Superior to Poiret any day."

She had made some rather offhand and silly remark to cover her thrilled confusion. She had wanted to stop and ask him his opinion of

Paul Poiret's designs, simply to reassure herself that he knew what he was talking about when he bandied about such monumental praise. *Stop it*, she told herself. *When are you going to accept that you are London's top fashion designer and not some self-taught mama working out of her dining room?*

Cosmo stopped and looked down at her. "A delicate genius, very well put," he said with deep sincerity. "You made that lovely young girl shine out on the stage tonight. She carried herself perfectly. She is undoubtedly a natural beauty, but your costumes made her shine. I'm not a huge fan of operetta, but tonight was a sensation. You know *The Merry Widow* will run for months, don't you? And Edwardes said that they were off to New York after this." They strolled on arm in arm, past St. James's Palace and into the night shadows of the park. "Too far for you in those shoes? I can look for a cab."

Lucy could have strolled through the quiet tranquility of London's Green Park on a summer night forever. "Oh no, darling. I have never felt so full of life and optimism for the future as I do now. What an extraordinary season it has been: day after day of sun; it seems as if London is thronged with the most beautiful women in the world.

"Something exciting happened to me during that performance. Not just how marvelous Lily looked in her costumes, though she was entrancing. I realized that I want to completely redesign the shape and form of the gowns we wear today. No more majestic curves and sweeping trains—and the corset has to be modified completely. It is time to create dresses that are in one piece and more streamlined and less structured—like the ones I designed for Lily. Lines that are simpler—softer. Fluid. It is such a bother for women to have to be hooked and eyed into a boned bodice attached to a skirt." She was thinking out loud, grateful that her husband was a quiet man who enjoyed her long soliloquies on dress and style, and if he didn't, politely retired into his own thoughts.

"I'm all in favor of no corsets at all. What murderous things they are," was a comment Cosmo made often.

"And you are absolutely right. At the beginning of the second act, while I was waiting for Lily's entrance, it came to me that we should not push and pull ourselves into rigid submission. I want to see women in light layers of fine silk unhampered by whalebone. I am going to design the raiment of allurement."

"That sounds dangerous."

"I really hope it is. It means revising everything we wear from the outside in. It's going to be stupendous, astonishing! How I love fashion. How I love the evolution of what we wear."

"'The outside in'?" He laughed. Lucy knew he wasn't interested in the details. Cosmo rarely took a real interest in how Lucy designed her clothes or what the process of making them entailed. He enjoyed the finished result of an exquisitely dressed woman. That was enough for him.

"I am thinking of designing a line of women's underwear. What do the French call it? *Lingère*? Yes, that's it, *lingère*. Aha, so you are listening. Yes, of course the kind I wear . . . what else is there? They are perfect for this new century of fashion. Out with the corsets that encase, the Swiss cotton pantalettes that spoil the line of lovely skirts, not to mention all those heavy petticoats. And in with delicate, flimsy little lace-edged minimals. Sadly, most of my older clients will insist on keeping their corsets; they will never wear anything less. But they must be modified from that hard casing into something that gently suppresses but doesn't contort. And something has to be done to support the bosom without it jutting out like the edge of a cliff."

He stopped as they came up to the Wellington Arch. "I think it will be a struggle to change . . . well, change everything. Surely most women will feel . . . completely unclothed." He nodded to a policeman standing on duty.

She laughed. "You do like the idea, don't you?"

She could see his eyes gleaming in the lamplight as he looked down at her. "As a gentleman, I really don't think I should know what your clients wear under your dresses. As your husband, please remind me again about those little nothings—where do they come down to? Ah yes, now I remember. I think we should hail a cab."

*August 1907*

Lucy

*When are we ever ready for one of life's jolts—its shake-ups?* Lucy closed the door of her bedroom. She stood with her back to the room until she was sure of her composure. Little had she imagined that when she had designed Esmé's coming-out wardrobe with the pièce de resistance of her frothing white lace presentation dress that her daughter would become one of the most sought-out girls of the season. Her pride, her joy, her little girl, had gone from being a lanky fourteen-year-old playing on the beach in Monaco and putting kittens to bed, to a vivacious and lovely young woman—and it seemed like it had all happened in one short summer. After weeks of chaperoning Esmé to parties, balls, and soirees and watching the same girls dance with the same young men night after night—the thing that most mothers plotted and prayed for had happened.

Three days before the Glorious Twelfth, as London society was about to tip itself into trains and carriages and race for the country to shoot down millions of pheasants, Esmé burst into her room with the startling news that she was in love with someone called Hardy Tiverton, or as his closest friends called him: Tivvy.

"Darling, whenever did this happen?"

"Yesterday night—or rather this morning, Mama, before we left Diana's party. It was the last thing in the world that I expected. I mean, I hoped he would propose. I can't tell you how happy I am!"

*She* is *happy, head-over-heels happy, bless her. Hardy Tiverton—which one is that?* Lucy ran through the hundreds of young male faces she had seen night after night. She couldn't place a Tiverton. Couldn't put a face to the name. *The Tivertons?* She suppressed a sigh of exhaustion. When the "toffs," as Grace called them, packed up and went to the country to hunt and shoot and fish, Lucy had counted on some idle time. Cosmo was talking about renting a house in Italy for September.

She made herself concentrate on the elusive Hardy Tiverton. *This, she thought, is the trouble with always being involved with new ideas, some new scheme. I have become one-track minded. My family have been so happy to accept Lucile, so I have become self-centered.* She had made the assumption that Esmé's governess, Miss Briggs, was on top of things, aware of what was going on, and that Grandmama, who doted on pretty little Esmé, might have at least some idea of whom she had a crush on . . .

"Goodness, Esmé," she said, making light of her forgetfulness. "I am sure I have met this young man, but for the life of me I can't remember where." She lifted her hands at her forgetfulness and in an appeal to be brought up to date.

Esmé's face lost the look of thrilled importance. "You don't remember, do you?" It was the old challenge, the mutiny that had begun when she had been married to Cosmo for a year. The cry of "You never have time for me. You are either working or with him," echoed in Lucy's ears. *I thought we were done with all of that when she came out. When she was presented and found her feet among new friends and couldn't go to enough balls, dinners, and concerts and take part in enough tableaux vivants.*

"There seem to have been so many young people coming and going in the last few years. Perhaps if you told me his full name it might help me remember him?" She would not be drawn into an argument about how much time she spent in her studio.

"He was at Lady Manners's dinner earlier this month—you talked to him for quite some time. His father is the Earl of Halsbury and he is Hardinge Gifford, the Viscount Lord Tiverton."

In a flash Lucy saw the confident young man standing at the entrance to the ballroom at Belvoir Castle. She had thought him too conscious of his charm as he politely chatted to one of his hostess's old friends. Now she felt the beginning of anxiety. His easy personality, that awareness of the effect he had with his handsome face, his position and title. She felt a flash of real alarm. *She's far too young to marry. She knows nothing about the world—and certainly not enough about herself.* Lucy remembered the trips to the Serpentine with bedraggled toy sailing boats. Walks with NouNou, long gone now, to the park with a kite or a ball. *She's only done one season*, she thought. *And this Tiverton has asked her to marry him?*

"Do you remember him now, Mama?"

"Yes, yes, I do darling. Quite clearly. But that was only weeks ago. I mean, you hardly know him."

"How can I possibly get to know anyone when I have Miss Briggs huffing at my heels wherever I go—or you. And your head is always in the clouds anyway. The other girls . . ."

She didn't want to know about the other girls; she only had to assume that, like all mothers when it came to daughters falling in love, she was woefully in the dark. She had prided herself that she had no intention of rushing her daughter into marriage after one season. She had watched the predatory mamas eyeing up the possibilities, interrogating one another on the lineage and means of a prospective husband with contempt. When Esmé was ready she would find the right man to marry. *Well, evidently Esmé is ready—because here she is, bursting with news and happiness.*

"I think it would be a good idea for you to get to know the man you want to marry," she said with far more severity than she intended.

"You are suggesting one of those ludicrously long engagements, aren't you? So that we can spend months with each other's families . . . well, his father spends all his time at their country estate in Devon . . . so that will be difficult, since you never leave London."

"And his mother, does she spend all her time in Devon too?"

"No, Mama, she died when Tivvy was fifteen."

*How old is this Tivvy anyway?* Lucy felt resentful. A trap had been sprung and some young man had decided he wanted to marry her

daughter—as soon as possible, it sounded like. And now she was supposed to be delighted and full of congratulations that her daughter had
caught a man with a title. And she had no idea what sort of person he
was. *I must ask Cosmo about the family. He will surely know who they are.*
"Well, darling, I think the best thing to do would be for me to talk to
Cosmo—"

It was as if a conjurer was waiting in the wings. The door opened and
in walked her husband.

"So sorry, am I interrupting?" He turned as if to leave.

"No, darling, no need to go. Esmé has news. Hardinge Gifford—
Lord Tiverton—has asked her to marry him!" She kept her voice neutral, praying that he wouldn't exclaim with delight, that he would play
it down until she had a moment to find out what he knew of the family.

"Are congratulations in order? Have you given her your blessing? Do
we drink champagne?" She could have kissed him for his tact.

"Mama is struggling to remember if she knows anything about
him." Esmé smiled at her stepfather. After some serious territorial battles, she and Cosmo had established a fond, occasionally even chatty,
relationship. Reassured by his look of encouragement, she went on.
"Tivvy, I mean Lord Tiverton, would like to formally ask for Mama's
permission to marry me—or yours if you would like to step in. I thought
that if he came over this evening, you could both meet him properly. I
know you will approve. He is a good man: kind, affectionate, and
such fun."

*He is a good puppy . . . that's exactly how Esmé described Chow-Chow
when she gave him to me as a wedding present.* Lucy fumed. She glanced
at Cosmo. "Are you free this evening, darling?"

"Of course I am. We were planning on having dinner quietly at
home. Why don't we include the happy couple?"

Esmé was already walking to the door. "Thank you"—she was all
smiles again—"I'll let Tivvy know. Oh, how lovely, three of my most
favorite people in all the world!" She stopped and danced back across the
room to put her arms around her mother. "You are going to love him; I

know you will." She planted a hurried kiss on her cheek and was on her way.


COSMO CAME INTO their bedroom from his dressing room. "How is Esmé's engagement sitting with you?"

Lucy felt anxious. Terribly anxious. Her hair would not stay up; it kept slithering out of her hands. She tried again to pin it and gave up, scattering hairpins.

"I don't know, Cosmo. I simply can't take it in. I should know much more about this man. Much more about his family. This is the trouble with not growing up around these damned people. And, of course, I have spent so much of Esmé's life working."

He picked up her hairpins and sat down beside her on her dressing stool.

"It is not your fault that you didn't grow up around these people. And if you hadn't stepped into the role of family provider, then Esmé would have been taken away from you to be raised by that old aunt of yours, unfortunately deceased before I had a chance to meet the family ogre. Perhaps it would reassure you to know that most mothers of 'our sort of people' rarely see their children. We were kept in nurseries with our nannies. Dusted off at teatime for a quick visit. I went to prep school at seven and saw my parents three times a year for school holidays. My father only took an interest in me when he taught me to shoot when I was twelve. If I had been a girl I would have been under Nanny's thumb and then in the hands of a governess until I was eighteen. There is no need to blame yourself in any way. For some reason we English believe that children are happier in nurseries than with their parents."

She could feel tears welling and blinked them away. "Do you know anything about them—these Hardinges, these Giffords—whatever their name is?"

He pursed his lips in thought. "Not a great deal, I'm afraid. They are not particularly fashionable. Lord Halsbury was Lord High Chancellor at one time. Probably still is. I have heard nothing awful about him or his son. Hardinge Gifford is an only child, I believe, and probably a couple of years older than Esmé. He will inherit—but what exactly I have no idea. What are you so frightened of?"

She opened her mouth to answer and heard herself gasp as the tears rolled down her cheeks. *I was married at eighteen, completely bowled over by an older man with good looks and confident charm. It was a disaster.*

She couldn't bear the idea of her daughter marrying someone she barely knew to suffer the same cruelties and indignities that she had borne.

"I am so terrified . . . terrified . . . that she will make a mistake."

He came to stand behind her, to stroke her hair. "Ah well, darling, there is nothing we can ever do to protect someone we love from themselves. I will do everything I can to find out more about his family—if there are any skeletons rattling around in the family closets. And tonight we will welcome him to dinner with us and see what we think. There is no need to rush into this. But I can assure you that if Esmé wants to marry him, she will."

She pulled away and blew her nose. "What makes you so sure of that?" she asked.

"Because she is just like her mother."

"So, COSMO, WHAT did you think?" She was sitting up in bed, waiting for him, when he came in through the door of his dressing room.

"He seems nice enough. Eager to please—but not too eager. He evidently cares a good deal for Esmé." Lucy felt anxiety ebb to be replaced by exhaustion.

"I found him rather, rather . . ." She searched for kind words. "He seems pleasant, open. Rather naive in a way."

He laughed as he got into bed beside her. "You are talking about a twenty-three-year-old male of the species. The product of Harrow, Cambridge, and White's club. He likes foxhunting and shooting but not necessarily in that order. He has fallen in love with a very pretty, outgo-

ing, and energetic young woman who is refreshingly herself, neither
sophisticated nor spoiled, who loves dogs and other animals and will fit
right into his pleasant, undemanding life."

He could have been describing Dougie Chaddesley. *Yes, better a
Dougie*, she thought, *than a James Wallace*. Reassured, she reached out
her hand and took his.

"Then we must invite his father to dinner? Is that the next step?"

He sighed. "Yes, we will invite him to dinner, and I will talk to him
about all the rest. While you organize a wedding!" Another deep sigh
and he was asleep.

*June 1907*

CELIA

"Now, MISS ESMÉ, your mother is at sixes and sevens about this wedding. So here I am to take your measurements. She will be in as soon as
she has finished with Mrs. Keppel."

"The king's mistress? Mrs. Keppel?"

"Is there another one in London that we haven't heard of yet? And
shame on you—nice girls don't know about those things." Celia sat
down on the fitting room's daybed and opened up a book she had kept
for the last fourteen years.

Esmé let her dress fall to her feet and bent to pick it up.

"Celia, everyone knows about Mrs. Keppel. And everyone knows
how devastated poor Daisy Brooke was when the king lost interest. She's
so devastated that she has retired to Warwick Castle and has become a
socialist, at least that's what Diana Manners says: "Potty over the lefties."
And I think it is heartbreaking: years and years as *la favorita*, to be cast
aside, just like that—poor old thing."

"Poor *old* thing? She is about the same age as your mother. So watch
what you say about 'old,' young lady! And in my day we didn't refer to

those sort of women at all—we were restrained in our manner and
didn't chatter about things we shouldn't know about. I expect it's the
fault of those suffragettes with their antics and demands."

Now it was Esmé's turn to be shocked. "Women must be given the
franchise, Celia! Good heavens, what an old stick-in-the-mud you are.
I'm not sure about some of the things they do . . . but I admired the way
they turned out in the pouring rain last February, thousands of them to
march together. We women must have the vote, and pretty soon too.
Otherwise, there will be more than just marches and pamphlets!"

Celia gazed up at Esmé's stern face and stopped herself from smiling.
As usual Esmé's curling rich brown hair was escaping and springing in
little coils around her forehead. No amount of pomade could keep it
flat. Her deep brown eyes were bright and earnest as she spoke out for
her intention to be a part of the future, to help shape it. *We are going to
design her wedding dress, for heaven's sake.* Esmé was her little girl, her
daughter, her younger sister, and there was nothing in the world she
wished more than to see her happy.

"You'll be wearing a purple, green, and white ribbon in your hat
before we know it. Now, stand nice and straight." She got up and slipped
a tape measure around Esmé's bosom. "Let me see." Celia measured,
wrote, and measured again. "Still the same as you were when you were
twenty-one—a year ago—in spite of all those cakes from Gunter's.
Look." She showed rows and rows of figures. "Here is your very first
important dress. You must have been six and off to your cousin's birth-
day party. And look, here you are at sixteen, frantic to put up your
hair. And two years later, here you are for your presentation at court—
now, that was a dress and a half, wasn't it?"

The door opened and Lady Duff Gordon came into the fitting room.
"Well, the salon is closed, thank heavens. And now we have all afternoon to talk about your wedding dress, darling. So, put on this robe and
let's have tea in the drawing room and Alice will bring some glorious
silks for us to look at." She opened her design journal. "Here is my pre-
liminary design." She turned the page. "And do you see here? I have

made the changes you wanted, but I am quite sure you will change your mind over and over again."

Celia, ever aware of her boss's mood, saw a glimmer of pride as Lady D. looked at her daughter's serious face.

*Whoever would have thought that we would be working on a dress for that little girl who lavished such love on her old Pekingese?* she thought as she followed them out of the fitting room. *It seems like yesterday that she went off to sleep under the dining room table like a little gypsy while we were making that violet dress.*

# CHAPTER EIGHTEEN

*December 1908*

LUCY

We'll call it the Rose Room, Celia—perfectly private with a few gossamer things strewn here and there. I have found the very bed that Louis XVI's Madam Maintenon entertained . . . Oh dear, Celia, please don't look so cross."

*Is she annoyed or does she disapprove?* Lucy's excitement for her new idea wavered. Celia's back was straight, her elbows turned out, and her gaze fastened an inch or two above Lucy's head. It was difficult, sometimes, to tell with this impassive little creature who had worked for her for so long what on earth went on in that head of hers.

"Not cross, m'lady: disappointed. These undergarments are . . . not what I am used to." Her manager kept her head turned away from the smoke blue silk knickers edged with fuchsia lace on the table.

*How could I have known she would be such a fuddy-duddy about underclothes?* A cold thought struck next. *Am I risking too much?* She wondered if this sort of thing would be considered something that only women of trade did—to fly in the face of convention and produce vulgar underwear? *Oh, stop it, for heaven's sake!* Her clients were married women; they *knew* what *they* wanted! If they didn't like the idea, they wouldn't buy them—yet!

"Yes, they are a bit of a change from Swiss cotton pantalettes. But you are looking at the underclothing of the future. Perhaps they are a bit of a shock at first. But you are lucky; you don't have to be caged up in whalebone corsets like the poor creatures I dress: smothered in heavy layers of cotton. This is a new century, and times are changing—albeit at a glacial pace—and in the right direction, for once." She waved a froth of bloomers in sheer lavender silk. "I wear a pair like these myself—"

A choking sound from Celia.

"In fact I spent the last three days creating a new line of pretty underclothes very like the ones I wear. So feminine, so—" She was going to say "captivating," but at the last minute she decided that Celia had had enough shocks for one day. "They will be perfect under the new style of dresses and gowns I am designing. One-piece dresses that skim the waist, flow down over the hips. The corset will be adapted to achieve a more pliant curve. Our undergarments must change too."

The manager of Lucile Ltd. averted her eyes from the lavender bloomers and the smoky blue knickers. "I can't bring myself to say *the* word, ma'am."

The *word?* Lucy wondered . . . *Lingère?* Was this because she didn't know how to pronounce the French? No, it was much more than that. With every fiber of her being, Celia disapproved.

"What word, Celia, for heaven's sake?"

"I don't know the right one for this sort of thing, ma'am. I'm not a fine lady." Sniff. "All I know is respectability and what the good Lord would deem as decent." She started to fold up the pieces of sheer silk that Lucy had spread out on the table.

"I doubt if he spends much time worrying about ladies' knickers," was Lucy's reply, hoping to lighten things up a bit. But Celia continued to freeze. Her face was one of stone, her shoulders so square and tight that it was hard to imagine a woman more morally outraged.

Lucy tried not to smile. She would never laugh at her old friend's affronted feelings. *I have asked so much over the years, and she has always been stalwartly on my side.*

"They are offensive to you? You can say."

Another sniff.

"You think they are indelicate, maybe even wrong?"

A shrug.

"You have to help me understand the real reason you are upset. Can you at least do that? Is it because you think our clients will be offended?"

"Of course they will be offended. I don't want us to lose clients." Her voice was muffled with mortification.

"Ah yes, I understand. It is a leap, I must say. But I am a dignified woman, a constant wife, and a good mother, and yet I wear things like these. And I believe that other women would love to be able to feel as unencumbered as I do."

Celia's chagrin turned to irritation. "Yes, so you said earlier. Well, good luck to you, then. Your clients may be women from all walks of life—but most of them are from old, titled families, and the grander the family the more outrageous their behavior, it seems—in private. These women behave like saints—butter wouldn't melt . . . no matter what she-nanigans they get up to when no one's looking. But the rule is do what you like on the quiet. Be discreet. Don't go flaunting it about. See?"

"But these are not flaunting. These are *under*clothes! Seen only by the woman wearing them, her maid, and perhaps her husband."

Celia put the armful of fluttering silk and lace on a small table in the darkest corner of the studio. "*Lingère*—is that the French name for 'hussy'? How about that for a word? And begging your pardon because I would never apply that word to you. What will their husbands think when they see their wives . . . tricked out like . . . well, like no better than . . . They go to their kept women for all of that, don't they?"

Lucy put her hand on her old friend's shoulder and felt her stiffen. "No, Celia, some of them don't. Well . . . husbands will either not no-tice, because they never have, and if that is the case, I hope someone else will. Or . . . imagine for a moment that their husbands will be delighted to see their wives undressed like this. Perhaps these lacy and agreeable little nothings will make husbands remember the first time they met their pretty young wives. When love was new and exciting!"

"M'lady, no man wants his wife running around with her . . . her bottom half-covered. It is indecent."

"What about stockings and petticoat? They will still be there." Lucy picked up a frilled band—more lace than anything else—with suspenders dangling. "Underneath the skirts of their lovely gowns—"

"I am just saying that she will catch her death of cold. And no husband wants to see his wife with a swollen red nose, breathing out of her mouth through chapped lips."

*December 1908*

CELIA

She kicked off the fashionable heeled shoes and put her feet up to ease the ache in her calves and her feet. Frustrated and tired, Celia took solace in the quiet of her apartment on the third floor of the salon that commanded one of the best views of Hanover Square's shady gardens.

"Quieten down, you!" she ordered her purring cat. "It's been a long day." Cat redoubled her efforts to a triple purr.

A knock on her door and the parlormaid came in with a tray.

"The cook says you've eaten nothing at all, ma'am. She sent up some lovely chicken and leek soup, and a slice of her apple tart." She set the tray down on the gateleg table. "Shall I set a place for you here?"

Celia moved the cat off her lap. "Yes, thank you. I'll go and wash my hands." She walked back toward her bedroom and its adjoining bathroom. She could hear the clatter of silverware as the maid set the table.

Looking into the glass above the vanity, she examined her face in the strong unforgiving electric light. She could remember when gaslight was considered the last word in modern living. Now there was a generator in the basement and every woman she knew looked ten years older under its penetrating light.

"Fifteen years," she said to her reflection. "And I thought I had seen everything. Now it's a display of transparent knickers in a special boudoir she wants to call the Rose Room. An entire room given over to unspeakably indecent underwear."

Not to mention Mrs. Glyn's new book, which was causing riots all over London. *What is happening to this family?* she asked herself as she trudged back into the living room. The delicious aroma of chicken soup did not tempt her. She sat down in her chair and pondered the heady excitement, the secret smirking, and the giggling that Elinor Glyn's novel of passion, *Three Weeks*, had caused throughout London and the home counties.

It was a novel so excessive in its portrayal of a woman seducing a man ten years younger than herself and teaching him the arts of love that it had been banned from bookstores, and Mrs. Glyn pilloried by the respectable middle classes as a Jezebel. *And she has the cheek to call it a romance.* Celia shook her head at the blatant immorality of London society.

It had taken her some time to understand what Mrs. Glyn's novel was actually about, until a copy of *Three Weeks* had been discovered in one of the fourth-floor workrooms by a deeply religious seamstress who had promptly given notice after glancing through its first pages.

But Cook had had a quick flip through Mrs. Glyn's novel, and her derisive remarks only caused Celia more confusion. "An old bag of thirty . . . it's disgusting . . . and as for that tiger skin . . . and all those thunderstorms." A derisive laugh as she wiped a tear from the corner of her eye. "Only the toffs would think of a stunt like that. Give me a penny dreadful anytime over this muck. I am glad that my area of operation is down here belowstairs—safely away from all the 'fine' folk, as they think of themselves. They have too much time on their hands, that's their trouble. Give me self-respecting workingwomen to feed and

I'm happy." And she had tossed *Three Weeks* into the kitchen boiler, shaking her head in disbelief.

*There's not much difference in that dreadful book and lavender knickers in the Rose Room.* Celia's smile was grim as she poured herself a cup of tea. If the respectable middle classes wanted to be appalled, they should pop in to Lucile on a Tuesday afternoon when their clients' husbands dropped in to buy gifts for their lady friends. The tea was hot; she took rapid little sips as she considered life's inevitable changes and how they had affected hers in particular. "There's only one thing you can do now," she said to Cat as she mulled over the new line of *lingère*, "and that's either go with it, or simply go." The moment she said the words, she felt not only disloyal, but a cheat.

When Mr. Wallace had run out on his wife, leaving her high and dry, she had taken Celia under her wing. Had brought her on, trained her, and made her the manager of Lucile Ltd. "We've been through some terribly worrying times, together, and finally things are coming right for us," she said as she patted her lap for Cat, but she was busy washing herself, taking fastidious care over one back leg. "And you're a right little madam too, aren't you? What a hussy."


CELIA WAS THE first woman in London, apart from its maker, to wear one of Lady Duff Gordon's new one-piece afternoon dresses. In Celia's favorite royal blue, a color she never deviated from, the dress was made of a soft wool challis. "Drape and fluidity" were words heard constantly in her ladyship's studio as the dress was made up. And because Celia did not have an ample bosom, Lady Duff Gordon had designed the dress with a crossover bodice to give her a little more amplitude, winged shoulders to give her presence, and gently flaring sleeves gathered blouse-like at the wrist.

"No train, m'lady, I can't be getting it caught up on something and go crashing headfirst down the stairs," Celia said when she first saw the dress.

"Just a little train, Celia, to give you sweep," her boss insisted through a mouthful of pins.

"One day you'll swallow one of those pins, and then where will you be?"

"Punctured. Now, turn. And yes! Look in the mirror at the smooth bodice flowing through the waist and down over your hips to the skirt. This challis is wonderful: enough weight to make it fall and give contour, yet supple enough to create a soft drape around your legs when you walk. Now Alice will have the girls make it up for you, *et puis* voilà! You can float around the ground floor of the salon and show off your elegance. Hm, wait a moment, I think we need a little crop jacket, fitted through the waist, with a double-breasted front and large black velvet buttons, and nothing else, because I know you despise too much trimming."

"Were your family Roundheads during the civil war? You really are such a puritan." There was laughter from Alice and the two vendeuses who had wandered into the studio at the end of the fitting and had gathered to watch the process.

"All you will need to go with that gorgeous dress, Miss Franklin, is a nice set of Lady Duff Gordon's new lingerie!" Alice tried out the new word with a hard *g*.

"*Lahnzshair* is the way the French say it," corrected Grace, "as in ''Ello there!' Not as in 'linger.'"

Alice ignored her. "Tell her ladyship all about that very nice American lady who spent an hour or two in the Rose Room, Emmeline. Go on." And to the rest of them, she said, "She practically bought us out of hats the last time she was here. She won't buy a thing unless Emmeline advises her."

Lucy reached out and pulled the front of Celia's bodice forward and down. "Which American lady, Emmeline?"

"Mrs. Woodall—the New York Mrs. Woodall, not the Chicago Mrs. Woodall. She is forty-something, but she looks like a young girl. Tall, stately, and you should see her in the new hats. She bought five of them last week. The ones with the really wide brims."

Lucy smiled. "Ah yes, Mrs. Humphrey Carter Woodall. I think I know where this is going. Please continue, Emmeline."

Sure of her audience, Emmeline launched into her story. "I thought she had left the salon, but about half an hour later she came downstairs and said she had some questions about the 'garments' in the Rose Room, so we returned together. She had put aside a camisole in pale primrose, which she had paired up with a pair of bloomers and a pretty lace nightgown all in the same color." Emmeline was a good mimic, and she imitated the soft voice of the American. " 'These two items'—she held up the bloomers and camisole—'they are designed to be worn underneath this tea gown, aren't they?' When I told her that camisole and bloomers were undergarments to be worn under anything, and that the other item was a nightgown, she blushed scarlet and dropped it as if it was a hot coal." A peal of laughter. " 'Oh, I see,' she said. 'So, what would you wear underneath this nightgown—when it is so transparent?'

"I realized that she desperately wanted to buy these pretty things but was possibly concerned about her husband's reaction. 'Yes, madam,' I explained, 'the point of the nightgown is that you are visible beneath it.' And before she could stop herself she said, 'But, Emmeline, Mr. Woodall has never seen me unclothed in all the years we have been together. Not once!' "

More appreciative laughter, until Lady Duff Gordon interrupted. "And did she take the nightgown?" She finished putting a tuck into the sleeve of Celia's dress. "Perfect, Celia. I am pleased with the way it looks on you. Well, Emmeline?"

"She did take it, m'lady. And what is more, her maid came back to the salon the very next morning and asked for the camisole and the bloomers for her in several other colors."

Lucy smiled her satisfaction, and with a quick sideways glance at her manager she said, "We can't make those lovely little pieces fast enough, can we, Celia?"

Celia pretended to huff. "So it would seem, m'lady. Heaven knows where this will lead. Next thing you know, they'll all be wearing a bit of ribbon to cover everything, I shouldn't wonder."

*December 1908*

LUCY

Lucy got into bed beside Cosmo.

"Everything going well at the salon?" he asked, looking up from the book he was reading.

"The new dresses are immensely popular. Margot Asquith flashed into my studio, like a bird of paradise, and talked at me as I finished a dress for her. She is so wildly opinionated. Has no time for women's suffrage—talks down to everyone about them. I sometimes wonder why I put up with her."

"H.H. is bound to be Prime Minister, and everyone says it is because Margot won't let him be anything else. She must be exhausting to live with."

Lucy plumped up her pillows to sit upright. Late-night chats with Cosmo were a favorite end to their day. "What have you got there? What are you reading?"

He cleared his throat. "Let me read you a bit of it and see if you recognize it. It might even influence you into taking off your nightgown. He cleared his throat and began. " 'Paul entered from the terrace to the loveliest sight of all. In front of the fire stretched out full length was a tiger skin and on it—also at full length—reclined the Lady garbed in some strange clinging garb of heavy purple crepe, its hem embroidered with gold. One white arm resting on the beast's head, her back supported by a pile of velvet cushions while between her red lips was a red rose not redder than they—almost a scarlet rose. Paul had not seen one as red before.' "

Lucy leaned forward. "Oh no! It's Elinor's new book. The one that is causing all this kerfuffle and fuss. No, please don't read anymore. I honestly can't stand it—I am cringing already. Is it all that bad?"

He lifted the book out of her reach. "It is just beginning to get interesting." He read, " 'She merely raised her eyes and looked at Paul through and through. Her whole expression had changed: it was wicked, and dangerous and *provocante*. Paul bounded forward but she raised one hand to stop him . . . ' " Cosmo paused to allow himself a snigger. " 'No!' " He managed a falsetto through his laughter. " 'You must not come close, Paul. I . . . am . . . not . . . safe today!' " Cosmo let the book fall back on the coverlet. "She's brilliant . . . I have never read anything like it. Such rich prose. Such extravagant declarations of passion and danger. Her protagonist has no name. She is simply called 'the Lady.' I am astonished that poor little Paul hasn't run a mile from her." He flipped through the next pages. "Ah, now here is the seduction scene. 'And outside the black storm made the darkness fall early. And inside the half-burnt logs tumbled together . . .' I think they are making love. 'Causing a cloud of sparks . . .' Yes, there's their passion. 'And then the flames leapt up again . . .' Oh, ha ha ha. 'And crackled in the grate.' " Breathless, he wiped his eyes. "Such a scene at Foyles bookshop this afternoon, with elderly men demanding that the book be burned, which will never happen in a hundred years. Nigel Forrester told me that any boy caught reading it at Eton would be thrashed." He turned his head to Lucy, helpless with laughter. "It is a sensation!"

She shook her head. "Oh, Elinor," she said. "What a lot of silly drivel. Well, she said it would cause havoc and it has. So she will be pleased at all the money she will make out of it. But it is rather awful, isn't it?"

He leaned over to kiss her. "It is superbly awful. I absolutely love it. Are you sure you want to accompany this smoldering femme fatale to New York—alone? Won't you be mobbed by thousands of randy American schoolboys when you are trying to decide whether to open a salon there?"

She curled up with her head on his chest. "Don't tease, Cosmo. Elinor has been very good to me. I promise you she is only the Lady in her imagination—not in her private life."

More laughter as he pulled her close. "She is certainly the Lady with poor old George Curzon . . . and he is not an impressionable boy like Paul."

"I know where Elinor got her tiger skin from—our old spinster aunt had one. I wonder what happened to it?"

✳

# CHAPTER NINETEEN

*July 1910*

LUCY

The last trunk was packed, and the tickets for the steamship *Maure-tania*, sailing out of Liverpool for New York, were finally located by Esmé, who had come to wish her mother all the best for her trip. "They were in your hatbox, Mama," she said as she wrapped her arms around Lucy. "I wish I was coming too!"

Cosmo stopped his pacing, and with cries of *"Bon voyage!"* Lucy, Elinor, and Cosmo got into a procession of cabs bound for Paddington Station.

"What on earth are you going to do with yourself for the next six weeks, Cosmo?" Elinor was clearly in the dangerously playful mood she so loved to bestow on the protagonists of her novels. She was a famous author on her way to one of the most exciting cities in the world. Her large, feathery hat was tilted at a provocative angle, her pointed chin nestled in the silver fox collar of her black traveling suit.

It always astonished Lucy how patiently courteous her husband was with her sister's teasing. *And she's getting worse*, Lucy thought. *The notoriety of her novel has gone to her head completely. How I wish I had known before I said yes to this trip.*

She glanced at Cosmo. He was settled back with his legs stretched out in front of him as he answered his sister-in-law's question. "Well, after you set sail for the New World, I'll catch the ten fifteen up to Aberdeen and spend a few weeks taking care of estate business in Maryculter. Been too long since my last visit. And then I am planning to spend another few days with Esmé and Tivvy—fishing. By which time I am hoping that my wife has decided whether or not she is going to open Lucile Ltd. in Manhattan. And if she has decided yes, then I will be joining her . . . and you too, Elinor, if you have the time."

*Five weeks without Cosmo?* Lucy wondered, too late, if this much time in her sister's company was such a good idea after all. "I doubt very much if Elinor will have any time. I think her fans are already assembling at the New York docks in their thousands. By the time you join me I will be sitting around at the Waldorf Hotel, twiddling my thumbs and begging people to take me to dinner." Lucy squeezed her husband's hand.

Elinor reached over and clouted Cosmo gently on the shoulder. "Oh, you love birds . . . you have both become far too settled in your ways. It will do you good to run around with me in New York, Lucy, and have an adventure or two. No need to look so concerned, Cosmo."

Cosmo's eyes crinkled at the corners. "Aye, you had better behave yersel', lassie," he said in a parody of his native Scots dialect. "Don't you e'er forget I am standing by to jump on the next ship in case you lead hur astray." His accent and ferocious glare broke the tension, and to peals of merry laughter they arrived at Paddington.

LUCY WROTE TO Cosmo as soon as her considerably large wardrobe had been unpacked, fussed over, and stowed in her room in the Waldorf's cavernous wardrobes.

*My dearest darling,*
*The shocking news of the death of the king reached us today. Elinor*
*and I instantly put together mourning, and then she refused to*

*wear hers, because she said it would be too limiting socially. She
can be so exasperating—but the kindest and most generous heart,
so I must not complain.*

*This city is sensational! Quite unlike any other I have ever
visited. There is a sense of purposeful busyness in the streets. It seems
that Americans have a perennial desire to be amused, thrilled and
surprised all at the same time! I love their generosity, their hospitality: they are such fun! My shopping Expedition (deserves a capital E)
with Clarissa Woodall was astonishing: the prices that rich women
are prepared to pay their dressmaker are unbelievable. The shops on
Fifth Avenue are crammed with luxuries—and the prices are
outrageous. There are galleries and exhibitions and crowds of
beautifully groomed women lunching and visiting. I am quite
exhausted!*

*I have been completely taken over Mrs. Payne Whitney—she is
a remarkably talented sculptor, and her husband a darling. It is
wonderful to see my American friends at home and all wearing my
gowns!*

*It would be a huge step forward for Lucile Ltd. to open a salon
here. I am still undecided about signing a lease though, and I think
you should join me here before I rush in. Not just for the business
side, but to enjoy the delights of this astonishing city and to see if
you would want to stay here for a while if we were to open a
Lucile, New York.*

*All my love to you, darling. Please bring Chow-Chow with you
when you come. He will pine otherwise.*
*Always yours,*
*Lucy*

"COSMO, YOU CAN'T imagine how much I have missed you," Lucy said
as they dressed for dinner at Delmonico's as guests of Clarissa Woodall
and her adoring husband, Edgar Edward Woodall.

She reached up to straighten his tie. "It's such a pleasure to see a handsome man after all these weeks."

"Are you trying to tell me that there are no good-looking men in New York?" he asked as he buttoned his waistcoat. "No doting followers?"

"You would never believe this, but there is not one handsome male over forty to be seen *anywhere*. They might have been once, poor things. But they all overwork making their millions. It robs them of their youth. They exist on cigars, whisky, and huge dinners very late at night, and it ages them quite terribly. Most of them look like the late king; it is really discouraging. Poor Elinor has had to put up with slender golden-haired youths of thirty. They take her everywhere. I have hardly seen her."

"Thank God, otherwise I would have had to search for you in all the decidedly seamy clubs I saw as I was coming up from the docks. Do all your clients live like kings?"

She nodded and then shook her head. "Their houses are sumptuous. Packed with servants. Your eyes will pop out of your head when we go to the Willards' for dinner—the opulence, the luxury. If you are wondering what happened to all the beautiful French furniture and fine art in Europe, wonder no more—they are all here. The way they live makes us look like shabby cousins: barely scraping along."

His minimal toilette complete, Cosmo sat back in his chair to smoke a cigarette and enjoy the spectacle of Lucy about the business of doing her hair. "Why don't you wear that lovely red more often?" he said as he helped her button the back of her gown. You were wearing this same rich garnet shade when I first saw you." He stood back to admire her. "I thought how beautiful you were then. And do you know something?" He returned to his chair and lit another cigarette. "I think you are even more beautiful now."

"More faded, you mean. I have to say that American women are immensely good at hanging on to *their* youth. So dynamic, so confident—without being brash or overpowering like our own dear Maud, Lady Cunard. Did you know she has taken to calling herself Emerald?"

"Green with envy?"

"No, darling, green for her emeralds. She is plastered with them."

He was waiting for her now, standing by the door and patting his pockets to make sure he had everything he needed. "Wasn't she from New York, originally?"

"She was born and brought up in San Francisco—miles away on the other side of this vast country. Her father made a mint in the gold rush. I think he started life as a saloon keeper and then made his pile. Everyone here knew her as the little girl who came to New York after she was jilted by some Russian ex-prince, where she snapped up poor old Bache Cunard, to make his life a living misery."

She wasn't nearly ready, so he sat down again. "Poor old Bache; he is lost without her. George Curzon says she is practically running London's social scene now. She has had a dining room table made out of lapis lazuli and only the hugely influential are welcome to sit at it."

*There is nothing*, Lucy thought, as she dabbed scent behind her ears, *like a lovely long gossip with Cosmo.* "Oh, I have missed you, Cosmo. More than I ever imagined I would. Are you ready now?" she asked, as if he was keeping her waiting.

He wound his white silk scarf around his neck and popped his top hat on his head. "Who am I supposed to be nice to this evening?" he asked as he draped her fur around her shoulders.

"Anyone, anyone you like. The men tend to congregate together, which is rather odd—and they always talk business. The women are much more fun—so articulate and well-informed. I'm sorry, darling—it will be a gentlemen-only night for you."

He put out his cigarette. "How tedious."

"How was your evening?" Lucy asked as she took off her shoes. "You seemed to talk to everyone!"

"Actually, I think you mean everyone talked to me—or rather at me." Cosmo looked up from his favorite chair by the window of their suite. "The view from this room would give anyone a nosebleed." One glance told Lucy everything. It didn't matter what he said. Cosmo had not enjoyed his evening. Not from the moment that his hand had been pumped up and down by the overly enthusiastic E. E. Woodall until the very last cigar had been crushed into a damply smoldering pulp. "Yes, sweetheart, it was a delightful evening." Cosmo got up to make himself a whisky and soda and returned to the window. "Edgar Edward Woodall was the perfect host: thoughtful, expansive, voluble. Goodness, what a lot the man knows." He sighed as he sat down in his chair to look down at the traffic coursing along Fifth Avenue. "'Opportunity' was a word I heard a great deal this evening. *Opportoonity.* I felt like Methuselah, full of ancient insights that hardly matter here. Anyway, some good investment tips. I must telegraph my broker in the morning." He stretched and loosened his tie. "There is no doubt that opening Lucile Ltd. would be a perfect business opportunity. If Edgar Edward Woodall can be relied on, and I think he can, considering the size of the motor car that took him and the lovely Clarissa off to their mansion on Park Avenue—a mere four blocks away."

"You found him tedious?"

"No, no, not at all. Well—actually, yes, I'm afraid I did. According to Edgar Edward we are on to a *stoopendously* good thing. He assured me that everything here is on the up-and-up. He absolutely guarantees success. We will see our investment triple, no, quadruple in three months of opening. But would it"—he got up and wandered into their bedroom to sit down on the edge of their bed—"darling, would it be enjoyable? I know these men love the idea of spending an outrageous amount on clothes for their pretty wives, and that they are tickled to death that they can brag that Lady Duff Gordon designed her every gown. But what happens if they find a new amusement? Imagine trying to keep the E. E. Woodalls of New York happy and amused year after year." A quick glance at his wife. "Ah yes, no need to answer that one."

"But, darling, I am not dressing E. E. Woodall. I am dressing his sweet wife—who is heaps of fun and one of the kindest women I have ever met, and she is wild about my designs."

He nodded, peeled off his tie, and unbuttoned his shirt. "Ah yes, I am sure that is what you think, and what the Woodalls think—until something more fascinating turns up."

THERE WAS CHAMPAGNE and oysters at lunch to celebrate the signing of the lease of 17 West Thirty-Sixth Street as the New York branch of Lucile Ltd.

That evening a party would be given by Mrs. Louise Whitfield Carnegie at their massive Fifth Avenue mansion. "Cosmo, did you know that Andrew Carnegie is a Scot?" Lucy asked as Cosmo finished his early morning cup of coffee.

Cosmo opened his eyes wide, and Lucy had to dig him in the ribs. "Yes, a real Scot from Dunfermline—he quotes Rabbie Burns and knows everything there is to know about Robert the Bruce and Rob Roy."

"Och, hoots mon."

"Don't tell me you found him irritating too?"

"No, not at all. He is a fascinating man—a philanthropist and one of the richest men in America. God knows I would never cross him. His wife, Louise, is delightful—I mean really delightful. So, where are you off to tomorrow?"

"Elsie de Wolfe and I spent the morning talking about the look of the salon. She is the last word in interiors. She says that it will take two weeks to have the salon ready! Can you believe it, Cosmo? Two weeks! It would take months and months in London. And the place would reek of paint for days after that. . . . We are doing all the walls in magnolia damask with oyster satin soft furnishings. I want it to have the light, airy feel of an English country house: elegant, but with a slightly modern touch to appeal to the American taste."

Cosmo harrumphed. "The walls of most English country houses are plastered with badly executed family portraits all in need of a good cleaning."

"Not the ones that our American friends are used to visiting. The idea is that the clothes are what people have come for, so they must not be overshadowed . . ." She stopped mid-sentence as her husband shrugged himself into his coat. "Cosmo, where on earth are you going— Is that a smile I see on your dour Scots face?" It was the first time she had seen him looking lighthearted since his arrival four days ago.

"The wonderful Mr. Payne Whitney has a nephew who is an épée swordsman. He was on the Princeton team, and he is taking me to his gymnasium and then afterward to dinner at his club." He swooped down to give her a kiss on the cheek and, putting on his hat, was gone.

"The relief of it," said Lucy to Chow-Chow, who was sitting majestically by, watching her and two hotel maids shaking out evening gowns from three large dome trunks for her inspection before they were repacked and sent over to the new salon.


LUCY WAS QUITE happily exhausted. Helen Whitney had recommended her staffing agency, and after four days of intense interviews Lucile New York was fully staffed with a manager, Mr. Algernon Norman, and an assistant manager, Mrs. Shirlene White, and four salesgirls who had worked for Bergdorf Goodman's department store, as Lucy had learned to call a shop that sold simply everything—rather like Selfridges in London but far bigger and much more expensive. It was Algernon Norman who rescued her from searching for a workforce by engaging seamstresses that he had filched from other dressmakers in the city.

Lucy had decided that the steady Simone Bartholomew would make the journey across the Atlantic to design models for Lucile New York. "She sailed yesterday. As soon as I know that she is ready to fully fledge I will be on my way home. Until then I can't even think of returning to London, Cosmo." She watched her husband merrily packing his suitcases. "Will you please take Chow-Chow with you? I am so busy and he does miss his morning walks. Celia will look after him when you get home." Lucy closed the lid of her husband's sparely packed suitcases. She had no need to say how desolate she would be without him.

Their evening's dancing at Delmonico's, of summer weekends spent at the houses of their friends on Rhode Island, where his never-failing courtesy had been extended to people he could not begin to understand, had made Cosmo immediately welcome wherever he went. Lucy knew she could not expect him to hang about her world like a dilettante, but neither could she bear to be without him. "If you were to buy a place in Manhattan and a cottage in Newport, then I am sure he would settle," her new friends had told her. But she was selfishly aware that New York held no interest for Cosmo. His life was London. His clubs, his fencing, his place on the International Olympic Committee for Fencing, not to mention his trips to Scotland and the estate at Maryculter. She had hoped that Payne Whitney's invitations to include him would help influence Cosmo to stay in this exciting new country. Surely sailing the Atlantic would appeal to Cosmo's appreciation of the elements? It had for a very short time.

Her husband's voice broke in on her scheming. "Of course Chow will come with me. Now that you are officially opened, and Lucile New York is such a staggering success, I will see you as soon as things are quieter here—if that is at all possible."

The opening of Lucile Ltd. on West Thirty-Sixth Street had been a resounding success. Mrs. Reginald Vanderbilt, Mrs. Stuyvesant Fish, and Mrs. Payne Whitney ranked as Lucile's most prestigious and affluent clients. They flocked to Lucile and brought their friends with them, and the magnolia walls of the salon resounded to cries of delight and exclamations of joy as Lucy's trunks of clothes were put on display and adapted by Algernon Norman's teams of skillful dressmakers to their clients' needs.

Lucy was spellbound by New York and New York society. She found it agonizing to tear herself away from her new friends. Her pretty salon buzzed with visitors and invitations for her to join the energetic pace of this remarkable city. In London she had grown into being a dressmaker and a designer—it had taken years to court society into patronizing Lucile. But in New York she had arrived, and in a flicker of an eye Lucile was an immense success—like a smashing opening night on Broadway! It had been a heady and gratifying experience.

# CHAPTER TWENTY

*June 1911*

CELIA

Celia tore open a letter addressed in her ladyship's handwriting with a sigh of relief. *Well, finally*, she fumed as she scanned the first lines announcing Lady Duff Gordon's return. Why anyone would want to go all that way to open another salon, Celia simply could not fathom. From the little she had read, America was a terrifying country full of armed outlaws who rode horses to rob trains and terrorize travelers, and hadn't an entire city been broken and razed to the ground by an earthquake?

"I see you have received a letter from Lady Duff Gordon, Miss Franklin." In Celia's opinion Mrs. Kennedy had spent far too much time at the salon since her daughter's departure for America and her granddaughter's marriage. Now she was in the kitchen laying down the law to Cook, who was ignoring her.

"Yes, ma'am, with the wonderful news that she will be returning in two weeks—such a relief." Mrs. Kennedy no longer terrified Celia. On the contrary, the old lady was respectful, even courteous, when they had occasion to bump into each other, which had been a little too often in recent months.

Cook, on the other hand, was clearly put out by the old lady's presence. She slammed her oven door shut on her steak and kidney pies and thumped down a plate of bacon and eggs in front of Celia.

Celia would ordinarily have picked up her knife and fork and laced in. But manners required that she not bolt her food down with Mrs. Kennedy still standing there, ready for more conversation about her daughter.

"I will read this letter out to the girls when they eat their noonday meal. It will put their minds at rest. We were that worried about her," she said, trying not to look at her breakfast cooling on the plate.

Mrs. Kennedy frowned. "But why?"

"Everything I've read about America horrifies me. The lawlessness for one thing—the cowboys."

"There is nothing terrifying about New York other than too much money and excess. You are thinking of the Wild West, Miss Franklin; all of that takes place on the other side of the country—thousands of miles away. I can tell you have no idea how vast America is—as large as Canada. I'll bring you my atlas this afternoon so you can see for yourself." And off she went, leaving Cook to grumble about interference and Celia to enjoy her breakfast in peace.

True to her word, the old lady arrived with Esmé's old atlas at Celia's teatime and settled herself down in her parlor. "Now, scale is difficult to understand sometimes on a map. But if you look at the British Isles and then at this area here, which is America, you can see for yourself how large the country is." A thin, crooked finger pointed on the map. "Here"—she tapped with her nail—"here is New York. Do you see: a tiny dot in this massive country, and it is a city as cultured as London. And all of this area here"—her finger ran up and down the Eastern Seaboard—"is as civilized as Britain. You are thinking about here"—her finger glided across the page—"this is where they have what you call cowboys, and it was settled much later than the East. The West is far more lawless, much more primitive really, except for a few cities like this one here." She tapped on San Francisco. "This was the city that suffered such a terrible earthquake a few years ago, but it has been rebuilt now."

"And this is all Canada up here?"

The old lady smiled. "Yes, this is Canada. Ah, the stories I could tell you. My mother was French and she married a Canadian. We traveled everywhere on sleds in winter, tucked up in furs to keep us from freezing to death!" And she was off reminiscing about the vast wastes of Canada and how she had been rescued from them by the generosity and benign kindness of her first husband, the peerless Mr. Sutherland. "We had a beautiful house on Jersey island . . . in St. Helier. The garden was absolutely lovely: full of the most stunning flowers. The happiest time of my life."

Tea arrived, and Celia poured as Mrs. Kennedy finished her reminiscences, closed the atlas, and returned to the present day. "How are our preparations for the new king's coronation coming along? Lots of orders for presentation gowns? Why, it seems like only yesterday that we were celebrating King Edward's coronation—perhaps if he hadn't eaten so much rich food he would still be with us. At least King Edward knew how important it was for a woman to dress well. This one spends all his time sticking stamps in his albums."

Celia kept her face solemn. "I don't know anything about this new king of ours, but every woman in London seems to be clamoring for new dresses," she said. "Lady Ripon has ordered five new ball gowns and countless new visiting dresses. And every client who comes into the salon talks nonstop about the Ballets Russes and this dancer Ninsky."

"I think you mean Nijinsky, Miss Franklin. He is supposed to be very handsome and very athletic."

*That would explain the obsession, then.* Celia nodded in understanding.

"I wish her ladyship were here, because she would understand what they all mean by the costumes and the set design. They keep asking for something to wear that is more . . . more authentic to the culture, and I have no idea what a sultan's seraglio is."

"I doubt very much that any decent self-respecting woman would want to see this ballet, Miss Franklin. From the little I have heard"—her lips were pursed in disapproval—"it is exactly the sort of thing one might expect in this terrifying day and age: and this dancer sounds like a complete savage."

*July 1911*

LUCY

Nijinsky, Nijinsky . . . Nijinskeeee—from the moment I disembarked, all I have heard is how marvelous the Ballets Russes is. Everyone in London is talking about it!" Lucy was almost breathless with panic. It was impossible to get tickets to this extraordinary event, which was taking place right here, in dull old London, an event that she was likely to miss.

"It is quite an astonishing thing, m'lady," Celia put in when her boss finally paused for breath. "Every lady that comes into the salon talks of nothing else—they are fixated. And the costumes must be out of this world, because they are all desperate for the Eastern look."

Celia's remark caused even more anxiety. "And I have no idea what it is they are talking about!"

"Yes, I understand that the set and the costumes are supposed to be very exotic. They were designed by Léon—"

"Bakst! Léon Bakst!" Lucy was practically salivating.

"That's right, m'lady. But the dancer Nijinsky is really the star turn, from everything I have heard. It was Lady Ripon's idea to bring them all over from Paris to celebrate the coronation, and they were such a success, they have agreed to stay on for another few days."

Lucy's panic threatened to swallow her up. "I have to go," she said like a woman possessed. "If only I had known, I would have returned sooner."

"I think it would be a good idea for you to go to this ballet, m'lady, from a design point of view, but there are only a few performances next week, before the company returns to Paris."

Lucy was barely listening; all she could think of was how she could procure tickets for this remarkable event. *I will have to write to Lady Ripon and beg for tickets.* It was unthinkable that one of London's top designers had yet to see the innovation of the Russian ballet: its style, its costumes, and the invigoration it had caused among London's chic cognoscente.

"COSMO, I HAVE a treat for you. A perfectly wonderful thing has happened. Lady Ripon has very kindly given us tickets to see the Ballets Russes, and she is inviting us to a supper after the ballet, and you will never guess who will be there."

"The Ballets Russes?" he said from behind his newspaper. "Every woman in London is behaving like a demented girl about this dancer chap, so I imagine it is he who will be at Lady Ripon's supper."

How on earth had Cosmo heard about the ballet? Lucy gently pulled his newspaper aside. "Will you come with me, come to the ballet? Yes, yes, I know you don't enjoy that sort of thing, and then to the supper afterward?"

"Wild horses wouldn't keep me away." He took great delight in this tease. "Though I must reassure you that I have no real interest in being thrilled by a scantily clad man leaping into the air. Apparently every dowager in London had to be administered to in the interval of his debut . . . most of them half-dead with shock."

THE MARCHIONESS OF Ripon bowed her head in greeting as Lucy and Cosmo seated themselves in her box at the Royal Opera House. It was full of young people laughing and chattering and there was an air of expectant excitement as they waited for the performance to begin.

The prime minister's son, and Margot Asquith's stepson, Raymond
Asquith, nodded a greeting, and his beautiful wife, Katherine, leaned
over to Lucy. "This is the third time I have seen the ballet!" Her eyes
were round with excitement. "I can only promise you that it is a simply
divine experience. I know you will appreciate the costumes . . . and"—
she fluttered her eyelashes in feigned ecstasy—"Nijinsky! Are you going
on for supper? Yes, we are too—I can't wait to meet him."

Lady Diana Manners, seated next to Lucy, pretended boredom. She
smiled politely to Lucy and Cosmo and then continued a half-whispered
conversation with the girl next to her. *Surely she is a bit young to be
watching this sort of thing?* Diana's mother, Lady Violet Manners, the
Duchess of Rutland, was rather an unconventional woman, but Diana
could only be eighteen—barely out in society. On Diana's right was her
little friend Lady Cunard's daughter, Nancy. And behind them were
seated Duff Cooper, who had a dicey reputation, and Sir Denis Anson.
Esmé had told her that Lady Diana's set were called the Corrupt Coterie
because their pranks and parties were so outrageous.

The overture to the ballet started and all chitchat and rustling died
away as the music of Rimsky-Korsakov filled the auditorium with a
lilting, melancholy melody.

"Here we go, hold on to your hats!" Nancy said, and Lady Ripon
silenced her with a cold frown.

The curtain lifted to a storm of applause and to a scene of such vivid
color and exotic opulence that Lucy held her breath as she took in the
great billowing emerald and magenta silk ceiling of the sultan's harem,
swagged with scarlet and vivid pink cords with huge brass and silk tas-
seled lamps suspended over the stage. *It is pure fantasy*, she thought.

Lights shone blue and green between arched, fretted stone pillars, and
in the center of the stage was a pillowed platform on which languished
Zobeide, the sultan's favorite wife, in a state of semi-undress. Her vivid blue
baggy pants clearly showed the outline of her limbs beneath the span-
gled silk, and the jeweled bodice, which left most of her back, her upper
breasts, and her arms completely naked, caught the light, as if anyone

could not have noticed her sinuous beauty as she lay in the sultan's lap. A collective sigh of something close to ecstasy rose from the audience as she rose from the bed and danced around the sultan in a voluptuous undulation of sensuous pleasure.

"Where's Nijinsky?" Diana Manners whispered to her friend Nancy, as a scantily dressed Zobeide rippled across the stage, her graceful arms extended to show her magnificent sparkling torso.

Cosmo leaned forward and frowned at the two girls, and Lucy gulped down a giggle. She had never seen her husband so entranced by the ballet.

Hungry for detail, Lucy absorbed the costumes of the corps de ballet as they shimmered onto the stage in shades of emerald, gold, blue, and orange: vivid colors—what was it she had heard? Yes, pagan colors. She was so swept away by the fast movement of the dancers as they whirled in a kaleidoscope of brilliant color that she was only aware that the Golden Slave, Nijinsky, had leapt onto the stage from the rapturous applause that greeted his entrance.

His body was painted gold, he wore a gold turban on his head, his naked chest was adorned with a harness of jewels, and his baggy transparent pants had all the first timers to the ballet breathless with shock and delight. He leapt into the air and seemed, for one astonishing moment, to simply hang poised like a frozen bird, before he landed to repeat the jump over and over in a circle around Zobeide, who was plainly as spellbound as the audience.

As the Slave and Zobeide danced together, Lucy found herself wondering when the intertwined bodies on the stage would ever dance a solo again. Her breath came short, her eyes fixed on the couple as the lovers entwined in a lithe pas de deux of passionate love. What was she seeing? Could it possibly be? She touched Cosmo on his knee and raised her eyebrows in question. *Are they simulating the act of love?* she asked him silently. He barely nodded, but his expression spoke emphatically: "They most certainly are!"

Beside her Diana Manners laughed, a tight, nervous little laugh, and

Lucy thought how irresponsible her mother and Lady Ripon were in allowing these young girls to watch a performance as erotic and sexually suggestive as this. As for Nancy, it was expected that the careless Lady Cunard was probably not even aware of where her daughter was tonight.

"I HAVE NEVER known you to be so quiet after a performance," Cosmo said as they walked into Lady Ripon's drawing room.

"I was no more fixated by that astonishing spectacle than you were," she answered, but Lucy wasn't really interested in after-theater chat with her husband; she cast about the room and saw a small man standing in silent reverie and surrounded by a host of women vying to congratulate him. Never one to join a crowd, Lucy stood aside to watch. The dancer occasionally turned to a large, coarse-looking man standing behind him.

"That is Diaghilev; he never lets Vaslav Nijinsky out of his sight—they go everywhere together." Margot Asquith was at her side. "They are lovers, of course." Lucy glanced at the director of the Ballets Russes and shuddered. *Poor boy*, she thought, *Nijinsky looks like a defenseless faun standing next to an immense Russian bear.*

"Are they really! But he seems to be enjoying all this female attention."

"Ego," was Margot's succinct reply. "I hope Gwladys asks him to speak. She will after she has bored us to death with prizing more money out of us for the Royal Opera House. You know that this is his last performance? You were lucky she invited you."

Lucy laughed. "Only because I went down on my knees and made a stupendous donation to the opera house."

Someone tapped their champagne glass and all chatter and exclamations of praise died away as Gwladys Robinson, the Marchioness of Ripon, took her place in the center of her crowded drawing room—Lucy noticed she was wearing Lucile, and as the great lady began to speak she counted the Luciles she could see in the crowd: *Twenty-two!*

She was about to start a tally of the rue de la Paix gowns, when Cosmo gave her upper arm a nudge and lowered his head. "Stop counting!"

Lucy concentrated on Gwladys Robinson: "Thank you so very much for coming to the opera house tonight to watch the last performance of the Ballets Russe, who we will sadly lose to Paris tomorrow. How grateful we are for their generosity in dancing for us tonight." She waited for the applause to die down. "Now, without any more from me, I have promised every single one of you that at last you will hear from the most talented dancer to ever grace the London stage, Vaslav Nijinsky!"

Unlike their enthusiasm in the opera house, the crowd, now conscious of who they were, clapped their gloved hands together in more restrained appreciation.

Nijinsky surveyed the room. *Such a delicate face—almost elflike,* Lucy thought. *High cheekbones, a large and sensual mouth, but there is*—she peered to focus—*something rather interesting about those incredible eyes—almost feral.* Nijinsky spread expressive hands and spoke in Russian. When he had finished, Diaghilev translated. "Thank you for coming to see me tonight." The large man's English was heavily accented as he translated.

Nijinsky shrugged as if lost for words as he looked them over again before he spoke. "It is good for you to see dancing, to see how body and music combine to express passions and emotions that hold us in their grip." A sigh from the ladies in the room. Lucy turned her head to see Cosmo look down at his shoes, a small smile almost hidden by his mustache.

"Please." It appeared that Nijinsky had lost his initial reserve, and Diaghilev clearly had none at all. "To ask me questions, so I enlighten."

A voice from the back of the room called out, "Where did you learn to dance?"

"At home in Kiev, naturally," came the reply.

"Where were you taught to dance?" one female voice cried out, clearly hoping for stories of wild gypsies.

"Ah yes, school. Of course school, and then I go to St. Petersburg for more training at Imperial Ballet."

"And your jumps . . . your leaps," called several voices together. "How do you achieve . . . such height?"

Nijinsky held his hands up for silence and answered in heavily accented English. "It is simple. I leap into air and stop for a moment."

Lucy heard Cosmo's delighted laugh. Margot, at Lucy's elbow, said under her breath, "I simply adore that Slavic arrogance, don't you? 'I leap into air and stop!' He doesn't need Diaghilev to translate now."

But Nijinsky had not finished. "I tell you about this leap I make. When I was boy, one winter it was cold. The river nearly frozen"—he paused—"ice moved in water. My father told me I must learn swimming." The pale eyes glanced around the room and he flexed and moved his arms to mimic swimming. "River so cold in winter, no?" A chorus of sympathy from his listeners. "And so, he threw me in river. I was nine years old. I thought I would die as water closed overhead." Lucy looked around at horrified and fascinated faces. "I sank to bottom of river, to mud." His face portrayed the fear he had felt. His shoulders rounded and he spread shaking hands in dread—he was back on the stage as the Golden Slave before he was murdered by the sultan. "Strength came to arms and legs. I raised fist." He lifted an arm straight above his head, his hand clenched. "And willed myself to leap out of river like fish. I force upwards, breaking ice to swim to bank." He looked around at the scandalized faces. "*That* is how I leap. I put myself into air. It is power of mind, over body."

Tantalized cries of awe and amazement echoed around the room.

"Gwladys says he makes this stuff up as he goes along," Margot said.

"Oh no!" Lucy would have none of it. "I am sure that really happened to him. What a childhood!"

"Hah!" said Margot. "Lucy, you are such a romantic."

She turned to Cosmo; he was smiling: his shoulders shaking with glee. He shook his head as he clapped. "Get out the checkbook, Lucy," he said. "If anyone deserves a massive donation to the opera house, it's

Gwladys. I have never had so much fun in all my life." He was so pleased with the evening that Lucy did not tell him that she had already showered Gwaldys with an astronomical sum.

"What did you really think, Cosmo?" Lucy asked as they walked home in the balmy air of one of the hottest summers in decades.

"It was a wonderous spectacle," he said, still laughing. "A spectacle that must have stirred up the passions of the British sangfroid to a record high. I don't think we shall ever be the same!"

"And Nijinsky?"

"Nijinsky? I thought he was quite mad—something about the eyes. Insane, poor chap."

# Chapter Twenty-One

*1912*

Lucy

"Has winter gone on forever? I can hardly believe it's March." A bitter wind had swept away the remnants of fog and damp. But not one bud had opened on the trees. Lucy searched for signs of spring, and to her disgust there were none to be seen. "Not even a wretched snowdrop," she complained to Cosmo as they hurried into the hall of Lennox Gardens. They were returning from a visit to Esmé and Tivvy. Lucy had spent hours playing with her little two-year-old granddaughter, Flavia.

Esmé had dressed the little girl up in one of Lucy's dresses when it was time to say goodbye. "Oh, Mama, look at her, so sweet in her pretty velvet dress. Who made your dress for you, Flavia?"

"Gamma!"

Lucy nuzzled her cheek on the baby's head. Soft, silky dark curls— Flavia was like Esmé. It was agony to say goodbye. "Why don't you come to America with me—you could bring little Flavia."

Esmé laughed. "No, thank you! Goodness, what on earth would I do there? Flavia, wave goodbye to Gamma. Who does Gamma love, darling—more than anyone?"

"Faava!"

It had been heart-wrenching to say goodbye, but Lucy was restless for New York. To her surprise as they stood shivering in the hall of their house, their eyes streaming from the wind that swept up the Thames from its estuary, Cosmo announced that he would be coming with her to America.

"You will? Oh, darling, how wonderful."

"Yes, I've already made arrangements for a little surprise. We will not be sailing on the *Mauretania*, but on White Star Line's new luxury passenger liner."

The warmth of the drawing room was deeply welcome as they stood side by side before the fire, warming their bottoms. "Can it do the voyage faster than the *Mauretania*?"

Cosmo was like a boy who could hardly contain himself with an exciting gift to offer. "She can travel at twenty-five knots an hour!"

"I have no idea whatsoever what a knot is. You'll have to tell me in days."

"Five days. . . . A half day faster than the *Maury* . . . maybe less."

Tea was brought in to them and they fell on the steaming cups just to thaw out their cold hands.

"It's cold in New York too, you know," he reminded her.

Lucy waved his words away with a sandwich. "It's a different kind of cold: dry. English cold is so dreadfully damp, it gets right into your bones."

But Cosmo wasn't interested in the weather. "White Star's ship is a hundred feet longer than the *Mauretania*. And I have booked us a stateroom on A deck! We can leave from Cherbourg after I have had time to visit my young friend Paul Ansbach, who won the fencing gold medal, while you do some shopping and criticize all the poor souls scraping a living on rue de la Paix."

Cosmo sat down in a chair by the fire and stretched his legs out in front of him to toast his toes. "You'll love it; it's a sensational ship—and this is her maiden voyage. You will never want to travel on any other ship after this," he said with absolute certainty.

"I can only imagine how expensive this boat will be."

"They are not boats; they are ships, and . . . yes, she's a lot more expensive and a lot spiffier. But it will be worth the price. First class has *three* restaurants. There is a gym, a men's smoking room, a reading room, a writing room . . ."

"You can't read in the writing room, then?" she teased. "Or write in the reading room?"

She was ignored. "There is a *heated* swimming pool!" He sat up. "And a first-rate orchestra to play all the latest dance tunes."

"Darling, you know I count on these sea crossings to put my feet up and relax. Or catch up on planning the next line."

He laughed work away as he continued to enumerate the ship's many attributes. Pulling a printed leaflet out of his pocket he read: "Twenty-four knots at her sea trials. Smoother sailing with the latest stabilizers—you will hardly know we are at sea—so no seasickness on our first day out."

Lucy bent to kiss his cheek. "Good, I'm all for it. Oh, and please book a spot for Celia. She is in desperate need of a holiday, and I know she will enjoy New York. But don't tell her yet; it will be a surprise."

"Done in the twinkling of an eye!" he said and returned to thumbing through the brochure. "She's a hundred and seventy-five feet from her hull to the tip of her four smokestacks . . ."

*He is almost as excited about this ridiculous ship as he is about his new Blitzen Benz motorcar,* Lucy thought as she searched for a handkerchief in her handbag. "What did you say its name was?" she called out to him from the hall.

"The *Titanic* . . . It means . . ."

"I *know* what a Titan is." And to herself: *Why do men always call these machines she, and why do they always have to be named after something powerful or monstrous?*


*April 10, 1912*

LUCY

"Celia, don't look down—and don't look up either," Lucy instructed. Celia's bent, shuffling figure made its way behind Lucy up the gangway from the dock at Cherbourg. The four towering funnels over their heads would be her undoing if she even so much as glanced up. "Keep walking forward and look ahead. Look, we are nearly there—do you see the officer welcoming us aboard?" Lucy looked over her shoulder. Celia's face was set in determination: every part of her was inclined forward, the sooner to gain the safety of the ship's deck. With her chin jutting for additional momentum, Celia forged up the gangway, clutching at a fold of Lucy's coat, convinced that at any moment she would fall backward to plummet into the terrifying gulf between the sheer sides of this massive ship and the dock.

*I'd forgotten how fearful she is of heights.* Lucy took her by the arm and pulled her onto the deck. "Welcome aboard—I think you will really enjoy the rest of this adventure!"

*I hope to God she isn't terrified the* entire *time.* Lucy glanced up before she walked into the reception salon: the height of the funnel above her made her head swirl. *Steady on, old girl!* Beside her she heard Celia's sharply indrawn breath, whether it was the relief of leaving the steep gangway or the sumptuous elegance of the salon she had stepped into, it was hard to tell.

Cosmo at least was enthralled. He was talking to the welcoming officer and Lucy caught snatches of marine terms: "knots" . . . "ballast" . . . "anemometer" . . . and her favorite nautical term: "abaft."

"Come on, Celia, Sir Cosmo is lost to us." She proceeded ahead into a magnificent area of rich upholstery and dark mahogany lit by the soft glow of ornate lamps and the strains of a string quartet.

"This is what Buckingham Palace must look like." Celia stood with her mouth open. Lucy smiled at her delight. "The food is supposed to be sensational, Celia. We'll have to dedicate a lot of our time to walking on the Promenade Deck."

"Sorry to keep you waiting, darling." Cosmo caught up with them.

"No, no," Lucy murmured. "No apologies necessary. I am only too happy that every single man in uniform on the boat will be able to fulfill your newfound fascination with steamships."

Sir Cosmo looked at the ticket in his hand.

"We are on A deck and Celia is three decks below on D." Cosmo steered them through the reception salon and led them to the Grand Staircase with its massive glass domed ceiling.

*Is every part of this ridiculous ship made to impress?* Lucy felt a moment of homesickness for the understated comfort of the *Mauretania*. She looked around her at the heavy wood paneling overwhelmed with embossed gilt and cut-glass sconces. The opulent furnishings muted the chatter of excited passengers to a hush. The air was softly scented. *Hyacinth*, Lucy noticed with gratitude for the simple scent of spring flowers..

A steward checked Sir Cosmo's tickets and led them up the grandiose double staircase. Lucy looked up at the heavily carved oak around a large clock at the top of the first flight. *It's a monument to new money: all those fabulously rich dollar princesses and their vigilant mamas tacking back and forth across the Atlantic between their new husband's country estates in Buckinghamshire, their couturiers in Paris, and a summer spent with their families in Newport.*

To her relief Cosmo had no interest in interiors designed to impress. He was far more fascinated with the overall layout of the ship and the beauty of its engineering. He would demand a full inspection of the boiler rooms and the bridge, and she knew he was ready to explore the ship's gymnasium. Outside their stateroom he paused and consulted his map of the ship.

"Celia, do you see that little stairwell? That is how you will find us. Three decks down and aft—that means toward the back of the ship—is your cabin. On board, the right side of the ship when you are facing the direction she is going in is called the starboard. The left side is called port. The front end of the boat is the bow, and the stern is the back end. Keep that in mind and you will be able to find your way around quite easily." He opened the door for them and again Lucy heard Celia's intake of breath.

"I thought there would be bunks," she said to Lucy.

"I am sure there are bunks in second and third class," Lucy said.

"And this is just a stateroom. According to Sir Cosmo's brochure, they have suites of rooms on the *Titanic* that are palatial." Lucy wondered what Clayton Glyn would make of all this overdone opulence. Poor Clayton; if it wasn't for his wife, he would be searching for a tenant for his beautiful country house. If anyone needed to marry a dollar princess, it was Clayton Glyn.

"And you have a bathroom too," Celia said as she gazed around her, clearly not quite sure what she should do now. Their steward came into the cabin carrying two suitcases.

"Your luggage will be delivered to your cabin, Celia. But we mustn't miss the fun. This is *Titanic*'s maiden voyage, so I imagine there will be quite a send-off. Let's go up to the Promenade Deck and see what's going on; then when we have set sail, we can help you find your cabin."

*April 14, 1912*

CELIA

It was easy for Celia to fall asleep in her little cabin: the entire ship hummed like a contented bee. It was like sleeping on a train except that on board a ship there was no shuddering to a halt at stations, no squealing brakes, and no slamming of doors. Simply the rhythmic thrum of comfort and security.

Celia had explored every part of her cabin, fascinated by her covered washstand tucked in one corner with hot and cold water, the pretty little foldaway writing desk in the other, with pen and ink and postcards of the ship and writing paper embossed in blue with RMS *Titanic*. Her bed was extraordinarily comfortable, with soft lambswool blankets, covered by a silk-covered eiderdown. There was even an electric fire, as the nights would get cold as they neared northern waters. *Why am I enthralled with this snug little cabin?* she asked herself. She had far more space at home. *Because you're on board a ship, one of the most expensive ships in the world*, she reminded herself. *It is all so perfectly organized, I don't feel cramped at all!*

Her stewardess, Gale, had unpacked and put away her clothes behind the white-paneled door of the wardrobe. Fresh towels were placed on her bed—with directions to a bathroom down the companionway. And the curtains across the porthole were drawn against the driving rain. Celia sat down to read about the ship in an illustrated magazine.

The captain's name was Edward Smith; the magazine showed a photograph of a gray-haired man with a beard. He didn't look particularly nautical. He reminded Celia of the hall porter at the Dorchester Hotel.

They would be cruising at an average of twenty knots an hour—whatever that was! *Titanic*'s top speed was twenty-five knots an hour. The boat was eight hundred and eighty-three feet long!

And she was on holiday! She could do whatever she wanted for the next five days. Read in the reading room—the ship had a library. Walk the Promenade Deck or sit and watch fashionably dressed women swan past her and try to recognize which couturier they went to.

Celia had stayed on deck to watch the *Titanic* dock in Queenstown in Ireland to take on more passengers.

"They are all immigrating to America, poor things," she heard a woman say. "God help them, there is no work for them there."

Celia had watched a long line of shabbily dressed families filing up the gangway at the back of the ship—*the stern of the ship*, she reminded herself. And now this morning when she pulled back the curtain of the porthole she saw nothing but the Atlantic Ocean filling the entire horizon with solid slate blue. They were on their way to America!

She dressed quickly, her appetite for breakfast making her fingers fly. She ran her eye down the list of restaurants in the ship's guide, embossed with its blue ensign. The main dining saloon was vast and too intimidating for a solo passenger, and all her meals were included in the price of a ticket except meals at the Café Parisien, which were extra. *For Lord's sake, Celia, you only live once—I doubt very much if you'll find yourself on this ship again—so make the most of it!*

Putting on her spectacles, she left her cabin and walked aft and up one flight to find herself back in the reception area. A steward standing at the top of the stairs directed her to the Café Parisien.

*If I eat a large breakfast I can walk on the Promenade Deck, find a little place to sit out of the wind, and read all morning!* She was taken to a small table by the window. The café was enchanting: white wicker chairs and tables, white lattice on its walls supporting the fresh glossy green of real ivy. The tables set along the walls were enclosed with ivy swags and ferns—like little bowers. Her eyes greedy for all the details, Celia fixed her spectacles more firmly on her nose to observe the heavily starched cloth napkins, the fresh pink roses in the center of her table set with white china, with indigo-blue-and-gold borders.

She was early; she was the only person here for breakfast. She gazed out of the window; the sky was overcast and the ocean a swelling, billowing gray, all the way to the thick black line on the horizon where ocean and sky met. Celia felt her stomach shift uncomfortably. Best thing to do was fill it with food! She opened the menu.

Good Lord above, breakfast covered two pages.

A politely attentive waiter appeared. "Good morning, madam."

"Shirred eggs with smoked salmon, please. And then toast with honey."

"Certainly. Tea or coffee, madam, and perhaps some Florida orange juice?" Celia recognized that this interrogation might go on for hours to include practically every item on the menu, and the prices were steep. A flash of alarm. "How do we pay for breakfast?" she asked in her straightforward way.

"A bill will be left in your cabin the night before we dock . . . You may settle with the bursar or ask your stewardess to take care of it for you." He hesitated and his eyes slid over her severe blue serge walking suit and plain unadorned hat: summing her up as a well-paid governess or companion. He dropped his voice. "Easiest to include whatever you owe in with your stewardesses' tip," he explained.

She nodded her thanks for his helpful advice.

"Thank you. Yes, I'll have a pot of Darjeeling tea, not too strong, please, with cold milk, not cream." For a moment she imagined Mrs. Kennedy with her scrunched-up brows sitting across the crisp white cloth. If anyone knew about the right sort of breakfast, the old lady did.

"May I bring you a newspaper, madam?"

Perhaps there would be news of *Titanic*'s first sailing! She asked for the *Times*.

"London or New York, madam?" He had caught her!

Pleasantly warm from a breakfast that could only have been made in heaven, Celia was ready to walk for hours. She strode round and round the ship on the Promenade Deck, until her arithmetic told her she had covered three miles, before finding a spot out of the wind to read. A deck steward unfolded a wooden chaise for her, produced a long padded cushion and laid it down carefully on its surface, and when she was situated, draped a thick tartan blanket over her knees. "Thank you," she said, wondering if he was going to tuck her up too.

At eleven o'clock she was brought a cup of hot beef tea, as she was beginning to shiver. Fortified and warmed through, she left the chaise and stood as close as she dared to the deck edge. Gripping the railings, she fearlessly peered over them to look down at the water churning alongside the ship. A terrible sense of falling overtook her and she stepped back. *Why did I do that?* she asked herself. *This deck is miles above the water.*

Celia had helped dress the rich and titled, but she had never had the opportunity to watch them at leisure before. With her scarf tied down over her hat, Celia toiled forward into a brisk wind, determined to walk off the rest of her rich breakfast before the next gargantuan meal. She saw three immaculately dressed women walking ahead of her, their huge hats flapping as they clung to one another. One of them called out, "Time to change for luncheon!" and they scuttled off through a heavy door. Celia battled on to the starboard side of the ship, where it was far less windy, and tried to identify nationality before she was within hearing distance of the fashion spectacle in front of her.

"American," she muttered under her breath as she came alongside a gentleman she heard the steward refer to as Mr. Astor. He was escorting an incredibly young woman, probably his daughter, who looked as if the voyage wasn't agreeing with her. She was dressed from head to foot in Doucet.

"English." A young woman perfectly attired in Lucile held the hand of her toddler and was accompanied by the nanny.

"French." Three ladies tried to prevent the wind from blowing their skirts against their legs. They were very young and very pretty, and everyone around them was enjoying their dilemma. Worth, Celia decided.

"English." She heard the crisp upper-class clipped consonants and drawled vowels of the aristocrat. It was the man who owned this ship. Actually owned it! Lady D. had told her his name—Ismay? And talking to him was the young chap who had designed this astonishing ship. They were both leaning their arms over the rails and enjoying the fruits of their labors as it plowed through the ocean.

Celia was not alone for luncheon in the main dining room; a mother and her daughter were seated at her table. They were American. As they argued amicably with each other about what they should eat, all Celia could think of was how fussy and ornate their clothes were. Lady Duff Gordon would have been appalled at the ornate buttons, the lacings, and the countless bows. Both of them were confined in tightly laced corsets, which were so constraining that they picked at their food like two little birds. The mother caught Celia's eye.

"We are returning from visiting my husband's family in England," she explained. "He stayed on for another two weeks. I am Mrs. Eliza Mary Compton and this is my daughter, Miss Sarah Compton. We are from Lakewood, New Jersey. Our son is also traveling with us, but he is being given a tour of the ship."

"The boiler room and the generator," put in Miss Sarah Compton.

"We bought our tickets at the very last moment—I would have thought everything would have been sold out!"

There was a pause and Celia realized that it was her turn. "Celia Franklin. This is my first trip on board a ship going anywhere!"

"How exciting!" Miss Compton said. "You are English?" A frown from her mother, which she ignored. "So it must be your first visit to America? I hope you don't think we are a mannerless bunch of colonials!"

Celia thought of all their American clients. "Not at all. I enjoy the company of American women. They are considerate, curious, and often very thoughtful." Far more considerate than Lady Cunard and the fierce Mrs. Asquith.

"Perhaps you have family you're visiting?" Mrs. Compton asked, her mental social register at the ready.

"Oh no, this is part holiday and part business. I work for a couturiere, Lucile Ltd."

A gasp of recognition and awe. "Oh my, her clothes are quite simply the last word in style." Mrs. Compton's eyes glistened. And Celia realized that she had made two friends.

## April 14, 1912

## LUCY

"Come on, quick turn around the deck." Cosmo had spent an hour or two in the gym.

"How was the gym—any good?"

"Very creditable. And hardly anyone there. Wrap up, it's chilly out there." Lucy put down her pencils and took off her spectacles. "Don't you ever stop? How can you possibly want to walk after all that exercise?"

"I don't. But if you don't get out for half an hour or so, it makes you niggly. Come on, walkies—then we can have lunch. I've booked a table in Café Parisien. So, you need at least a dozen turns around the deck to work off a few pounds before we eat a large luncheon."

*Oh Lord*, thought Lucy as she found her warmest scarf. *Once around*

*the Promenade Deck and it will be goodbye to traveling in private as Mr.*
*and Mrs. Morgan . . . or whatever our incognito is.*


*April 15, 1912*

LUCY


"Happy, darling?" Cosmo took Lucy out onto the dance floor for a
waltz. *It has been ages since we danced together!* Lucy thought as he guided
her through the rustle of silk gowns. She closed her eyes and remembered nights in Venice when the busy world had been too far away to
involve them in its excitement and disappointments. His arm tightened
about her waist and she heard him humming the refrain of the "Wedding Dance" waltz.

She tilted her forehead against his shoulder as he spun her into the
next waltz.

"There is no wind tonight," he said. "Shall we take a walk before we
turn in?"

He wrapped her up in her furs, pulling the collar up around her ears
as they walked out of the electric lifts that sped them up to the Promenade Deck. "Lord, what a night!" They stood together and looked out
across a sea of black glass, reflecting in its smooth surface a moonless
night filled with stars. Cosmo caught her around the waist, and— "One,
two, three; one, two, three! It's a perfect night for a waltz under the stars,
and we have the floor to ourselves."

She laughed and leaned back in his arms as he whirled her along the
deck. The sky spun overhead, the breeze picked up the edge of her light
skirt, and it rippled outward in a flare of silver.

He danced her all the way to their cabin and threw open the door.

"My legs are shaking," Lucy said. "I can't remember the last time we
did something as fun as this! Cosmo, will you please dance with me
every night we are on board? Promise?"

He closed the door. "Every single waltz—provided we dance them on deck."

LUCY WOKE UP; the night was still, the ship silent, and a very much awake Cosmo was sitting up, listening attentively to what appeared to be nothing at all. He swung his legs out of bed and started to put on his dressing gown.

"Darling, we've only just gone to sleep. Why are you getting up again?"

"The engines have stopped." He scuffed on his slippers.

"No, they are still going; you are just used to them now. Come back to bed." But he was halfway through the door. "You aren't going out half-dressed?"

"Just putting my head out into the companionway. Go back to sleep."

She drifted back into sleep. Then he was back again. "Strangest thing," he said as he sat down on their bed. "Went up on deck, and there was this fella leaning over the ship's railings. And he asked me if I thought the boat was listing."

She sat up. "Listing or listed?"

"Listing—leaning."

"Perhaps they do that."

He was being "calm," his voice low, almost soothing, as if he had been told there was nothing to worry about when there was. "I'm going to find out why the engines have stopped. Be back in a jiffy."

And he was gone again. Lucy thought rather crossly how much of a fidget Cosmo could be. She switched on the light and looked at the clock. "We've only been asleep half an hour." She huddled back under the covers. It was awfully chilly; she should have asked Cosmo to switch on the electric fire.

There was a knock on her door. "Oh, now what?" With all this fuss and bother, she would never get back to sleep. "Who is it?"

"Celia, m'lady." This was enough to get her out of bed and into her dressing gown. "Come in, Celia. Good heavens, you must be perished!" She switched on the little electric fire to warm them, but the coils of electric wire did not start to turn red.

Celia's face was pale. "The ship's stopped, m'lady. There was a terrible noise. It was like metal grinding on metal. You surely must have heard it? A terrible groaning sound."

"No, nothing. I was asleep."

"Perhaps we have collided with another ship?"

Lucy did her best to soothe Celia; she adopted Cosmo's calm tone. "What, all the way out here? I shouldn't think so. Probably one of the engines broke down, Celia. Goodness, you are as bad as Sir Cosmo. He's gone off to find out why the engines have stopped."

Celia shook her head. "No, it's something worse than just stopping; there was water in the companionway outside my cabin."

"Water?"

"Not spilled water, m'lady. Standing water—all along the companionway as far as I could see. It covered my slippers." She was standing in a puddle of wet wool. Lucy felt the first shiver of alarm lift the hairs on her arms.

Cosmo came through the door. "Ah good, I'm glad you are here, Celia, but you need warmer clothes." He opened the wardrobe door and started to pull out coats, throwing them on the bed. "Good thing you are a little girl. Put this on."

"Yes, Celia, put it on—you are shivering." Celia looked far more shocked at being told to put on Lady D.'s fur tippet over her fine tweed coat than at finding standing water outside her cabin.

"Gloves, and proper shoes." Cosmo threw open another wardrobe door. "Hats." He threw two onto the bed. "Lucy, put your kimono on, and then this coat, and then your fur. Can Celia fit into your shoes? Her slippers are wet."

"Cosmo, what on earth is going on? Why are we getting dressed?"

"Come on, Lucy, put these things on—and anything else you can find that will keep you warm . . . while I dress in the bathroom."

The door opened again, causing even more alarm. It was their steward.

"Sorry to barge in, Sir Cosmo. Captain's orders, sir, but all ladies are to put on their life belts and go up onto the boat deck. Do you remember where it is? Up the stairs at the bottom of the companionway and to the right. Your quickest way is through the door by the gymnasium. Starboard side." He opened a cabinet and pulled out three life belts. "No need to worry, m'lady, just a precaution. Always wise to be careful."

Lucy felt a surge of adrenaline prickle uncomfortably up the backs of her legs. Something was very wrong. Water in the D deck companionway and this colossus of a boat stopped in the middle of the ocean.

"Why have we stopped, steward?"

He was too busy showing Celia how to tie on her life belt. "Nice and snug, madam, that's the way. Now you can put your fur back on."

Cosmo appeared fully dressed. Winding a scarf around his neck, he shrugged himself into his greatcoat and took Lucy's hands. "The ship hit an iceberg." He started to take her toward the stateroom door.

Lucy stared up at him in incomprehension. He might as well have said, "The cat sat on the mat." She looked blankly around their cozy cabin, reluctant to leave its warm safety.

"Cosmo," she whispered fiercely as he threw open the door. "Is it really that bad? I thought this boat couldn't sink."

"Yes, she hit an iceberg." He looked at his watch. "Nearly an hour ago, and there is a hole along the right side of her hull. She is taking on water fast. We have to get you and Celia into a lifeboat."

# CHAPTER TWENTY-TWO

*April 14, 1912*

LUCY

Lucy shrank back from the open door onto the boat deck. The frigid night air brought tears to her eyes. For the first time in her life, Lucy knew real fear. The agonizing shriek of escaping steam from the ship's boilers blocked out any other sound, adding to chaos as people, like actors in a silent film, raced up and down the deck at a frantic pace, unable to hear instructions from the crew or each other. They ran this way and that, back and forth: their faces blank with fear, their eyes wide with terror. A woman raced past Lucy with a small dog wrapped up in a blanket. It looked like it was barking its head off. A man carrying two children, their mouths open in soundless screams, pushed his way to where a lifeboat was being lowered across from the gymnasium door. Another man was shouting at the officer who was struggling to organize the crowd in preparation for loading. A woman scuttled up the deck, her dressing gown flapping, a large velvet hat tipped over one eye, carrying a hastily packed valise. The crewman pushed her into line behind Lucy and Celia.

Cosmo put his mouth to Lucy's ear and shouted something. "I can't hear you!" She shook her head. The lifeboat in front of them was stripped of its canvas and quickly filled with women and a sobbing child, who reached out their arms to a man trying to calm its mother. A ship's officer took away a small suitcase from a woman being hoisted into the boat. Lucy noticed the mound of luggage growing in a pile by the lifeboat; a large man in engineer's overalls kicked suitcases and valises overboard.

There were too many people and far too few crew, and what crew there were could hardly keep order. The next lifeboat was lowered and men pushed women and children into it before the canvas covering had even been completely stripped away. Lucy turned her head away as a woman was picked up and tossed over the side of a lifeboat. Her head emerged, and then a leg as she tried to scramble back on board to her husband. Lucy felt Celia's hand on her arm and took it in hers.

The painful whistle of escaping steam stopped abruptly, and the cries of passengers, screaming children, and the raised voices of the crew took its place. The dog escaped its blanket in the woman's arms and raced off down the deck with his stout mistress running after him. The scene had a nightmarish quality as rescue rockets lifted up into the dark sky, casting a flickering gray light over the ship.

An officer ordered the first boat to be lowered. It jerked out over the side of the ship, and its occupants screamed. Slowly it began to descend, until all Lucy could see were rows of white faces looking up at them. A member of the crew beckoned her forward as people shuffled toward the second boat—there was a large five painted on its side. She clung to Cosmo's arm, her other hand still held tightly in Celia's grip. This time she could hear him. "Get into this boat, darling. Come on. This way." But the boat was already full and was being swung out over the side of the ship.

Cosmo walked them forward to the next lifeboat. Two crewmen stripped off the canvas that covered it, and women and children were hoisted up into it. A little girl fell, scraping her knee, and cried out. Her mother hauled her up over the side of the boat. "Look, Lottie, at the nice boat. We are going for a little ride, such fun!" The child cried and kicked her legs: "Daddy!"

"Lifeboat Three." The tall officer, the one who had welcomed them aboard, stepped forward. Lucy remembered that his name was Murdoch. He took Celia by the arm. "That's the way, madam. Wait over here." He reached for Lucy's arm, but she shook herself free. "Cosmo?"

He stood quite still, with his back to the gymnasium door. He nodded to her to follow the officer's orders. "My husband?" she said to the man.

"Women and children first. Please get into the boat, madam." He reached out to her again, and she saw his hand was shaking. He was awfully young—however terrified he might be, he was efficient and calm as he organized the passengers.

"No." She turned away from him. "I am staying with my husband. Celia, get into the boat," she ordered. Celia, her eyes wide, looked at Sir Cosmo. He nodded to her. "We'll be in the next one, Celia."

Celia shook her head. "I can't. I can't," she said. Lucy could see her lips set in a face gray with fear and knew she was close to panic. "She's terrified of heights," she explained to the officer, but he had turned away to address a short, balding man who couldn't find his wife. "Is she already in a lifeboat?" The man asked over and over again. Thin strands of hair were standing up from the dome of his pink head. "Women and children only at this time, sir," Murdoch said, as if by rote, before he turned back to them.

"Into the boat." This time it was an order. Cosmo put his hands on her shoulders, and his eyes met hers, willing her to listen. "Sweetheart, please get into the boat. Celia is terrified; she needs you with her."

The crewman lifted a woman and a little boy into the boat, and another woman carrying a large bundle in her arms. Three women were hauled up over the boat's side. One of them lost a slipper; the other wailed for her husband. "No, please. I can't leave him. I can't!" Her forceful cries strengthened Lucy's resolve. "I'm staying here," she said and took Cosmo's arm. "With you."

When the boat was full, the officer waved to the crew to lower it. Lucy watched it swing out over the water.

Celia, Lucy, and Cosmo stood with twenty or thirty others as men reassured their wives and daughters that they would be on other boats. One of the crewmen spoke to them and as one they all turned and started back down the ship toward the stern. Lucy tightened her grip on Cosmo's arm. "I will not get in any boat without you. Do you understand?" Her voice was fierce. "Cosmo, I'm not going to leave you. If this ship sinks, then I will be on it with you." She turned back to Celia. "Celia, you have to get into this boat; there is plenty of room for you. Look, it's nearly ready to lower!"

"I can't." Celia's face was set like a stubborn child's. "I can't . . . Look, it's swinging all over the place and the drop . . ."

The loaded boat had started its jerky descent. A little girl started to cry, reaching up to her father. "Sit down, Emily. Daddy will be in the next boat."

The man turned away and the officer called out, "Go back to the stern, sir. Plenty of boats down there."

*How can there be enough boats back there? There are far more people in steerage than there are in first.* "Aren't those boats for second and third class?" she asked. Officer Murdoch turned away. The clamor of human voices from the stern of the ship reached them as more distress rockets were fired into the sky. *This ship is probably not even going to sink!* Lucy told herself.

A crewman took Celia by the arm, but she still clung to Lucy. A distress rocket exploded overhead. "No, please don't make me. The water is pitch-black—so deep. I can't climb across." She was babbling in fear, her grip like a vise on Lucy's hand.

"Too late now, you silly cow." The sailor let go of Celia and ran forward to help lower the boat.

"You and Celia are getting in the next boat if it's the last thing you do. It is your only chance." Cosmo walked them forward. "Listen to me, Lucy. The ship is going down. This is not a drill—we will not be returning to our stateroom."

She stared up at him, her face blank with shock. In that moment she knew she was going to drown. She felt no fear, no panic, simply a numbed acceptance that she would die with Cosmo. How long did it take to drown? Someone had told her three minutes. Hadn't she heard somewhere that it was a painless death? *It can't be*, she thought. *The body is frantic for air as the lungs fill with water.*

Cosmo's tone became more urgent. "Lucy, listen! There are certainly not enough lifeboats. And it looks like they haven't even let the third-class passengers up on deck yet. Look, they are already stripping the canvas off the next boat." His grip tightened on her arms, his face close to hers. "Do it for Celia, Lucy; she'll do whatever you do. Now, we'll stand here quietly and wait for orders, and when they are given, you will go."

The boat was tiny, far smaller than the rest. As the crew lowered it, Cosmo took Lucy and Celia by their arms. "Mr. Murdoch, may they go in this boat?" The young man lifted a pale face empty of all expression except resignation. "I wish they would. There isn't much time; they must get in now."

Lucy shook her head. "No, Cosmo, I am staying with you." She took Celia's hand. "Celia, come on, dear, they'll help you in." Lucy pulled her forward.

"After you, m'lady." Celia's small round face was ashen against the night sky. "I can't get in that little boat alone and be swung down into the dark. Please, m'lady." There were cries of warning from the men as the boat was swung down and crashed back against the rails of the ship. Someone stepped forward and lifted Celia up and into the boat. Lucy looked up at the sky. There was still no moon, but thousands and thousands of stars shone down on them—she heard the sweet sugary melody of a waltz; it came in broken strains, carried by a faint breeze. She looked around. There was not a soul on this part of the deck but she could hear the tumult, the cries of people on *Titanic*'s port side. She held on tightly to Cosmo and looked out across the ocean. It was strangely still, the water as smooth as black currant jelly setting in a vast bowl.

Lucy looked up into Cosmo's eyes. "I want to be with you, Cosmo. Please don't make me get into that boat."

"No more arguing." The officer's voice was rough.

A sailor lifted Lucy by the waist. "In you go." Lucy felt herself hoisted up and tipped into the boat, landing on her knees. She tried to struggle to her feet, but a strong little hand held her down.

"Stay with me, m'lady, please."

The boat started its jerky descent. "No! Stop! It's half-empty," cried Lucy, fighting off Celia. "We can get more people in. Cosmo!"

In answer, her husband was pushed over the side, by Mr. Murdoch, to land in the tilting boat. He fell on his back, sprawling across the mast lying down the center. Cosmo half got to his feet. "Wait," he cried, hanging over the edge, to the crew on the deck. "If you take all this stuff out, you can get more people in—twenty easily, maybe more!" The boat was cranked down another foot. "Boathooks, coils of rope, and a canvas sail. They are taking up most of the space . . . Don't you see, man, we can get more in," Cosmo shouted to Murdoch. He stood up, and Lucy, terrified that he was going to get out and start directing efforts to make space in the boat, pulled down on his coat. "Cosmo!" she cried as her husband hoisted up the end of the canvas sail, making the boat slam against the ship's rails.

Footsteps pounded up the deck, and two men shouted out, their American accents strong. "Are we too late?"

"In you get, and you and you." Murdoch turned to a burly stoker, who got in beside Celia and turned to haul in the two Americans. "And you lot might as well get in too—there's no one else." More sailors climbed in. "Lower away," Murdoch called out. "This man"—he pointed to a young sailor at the helm—"is George Symons. He's in charge of your boat. You do exactly what he says, do you understand? Now, lower away."

As they jolted down to deck level, the officer looked down at the sailor. He couldn't have been more than twenty. "Row fast, Symons. Don't stop until you are at least a hundred yards away. You have to get clear of the ship: she'll go down any minute now. Stay far away; otherwise you will be pulled down with her when she sinks."

The boat jerked downward and stopped. It hung crookedly high above the water. Lucy put her arm around Celia. "It will be all right. Look up at the stars, see how brightly they shine." Their breath came in clouds. Ahead of them the great white glittering wall of an iceberg glowed in the starlight.

"Cosmo, supposing we hit that thing?"

His breath came in grunts of pain from his fall. "Not a chance; we'll easily negotiate any ice."

The seamen were cursing, trying to push the lifeboat away from the side of the ship. Their boat was caught between A and B decks. They worked furiously, pushing against the side of *Titanic* to free the lifeboat.

Cosmo was still fuming. "Enough space for far more . . . What a ruddy shambles."

"We need to cut the wire." A colossal man—the stoker—stood up in the boat. "You and you slide along your bench to balance me." He took a knife from his pocket and cut at the wire. The boat swung down a couple of feet and stopped. Everyone watched him saw through the last strand.

The lifeboat dropped like a stone, to hit the surface of the ocean in a spray of starlit water. She realized that the water level had risen, it was almost up to D Deck and the shining dance floor of the dining room where she and Cosmo had danced—just hours ago. Lucy felt the strong tug as the four oarsmen dug in and they pulled away from the ship. She reached out a hand to her husband as the boat shot forward.

It was only as they pulled away that Lucy understood the *Titanic*'s terrifying end.

"Oh God, look, Cosmo. Look." Now she understood that everyone in their boat was supremely lucky to be in it at all. The decks were crowded with shouting, shrieking people. Down toward its stern she heard shots fired, two of them. And a crowd surged up onto the boat deck. Cosmo had been right about the passengers in steerage. They had only just been let out from belowdecks. Where were the lifeboats for them? She stared in incomprehension as a collapsible lifeboat tumbled, half-filled, over the side of the ship and overturned in the water.

She turned and caught Celia's look of outrage. "Look how many of them there are. Oh, Lord, help them poor souls—there aren't enough boats to get everyone off!"

The officer's words, when he had given instructions to the boy sailor that the ship would sink at any minute, made complete sense now. Water washed over the forecastle like waves on a beach.

Fear on the *Titanic* intensified: tiny frantic figures surged up and down its decks in distress. *There are no more boats . . . they are going to die.* Lucy twisted around on her bench, scanning the horizon for help, for other ships. Surely help must be on the way?

"Oh my God, the front, the front of the ship is almost underwater. They're all going to die—hundreds and hundreds of people!" Overcome by the horror of what she was seeing and the slow swell of the ocean, Lucy hung over the side of the boat and vomited.

When she lifted her head again, the prow of the ship was below the water, and the bridge almost covered. The massive beast looked like it would roll over on its side at any moment.

"Row hard!" cried George to the stoker beside him on the bench. "Put your backs into it." And the two men in front bent with a will to their oars.

"Row, row! Harder! God help us all!" The boat shot forward; the rowers' backs heaved against their oars.

Lucy was transfixed by the sight of the massive ship wallowing in the water. "God save them," she whispered as the lights along the decks flashed, on and off, on and off, as if *Titanic* were sending out a frantic SOS for help. The foremost funnel wrenched free and with an almighty crash tumbled down onto the top deck before rolling into the water. Lucy closed her eyes.

"Pull," cried the stoker to the sailor on the other oar. "Pull, goddamn you."

The cries and frantic activity increased on the deck. Lucy opened her eyes and saw the spot where she, Celia, and Cosmo had waited to get in a lifeboat disappear under a wave of water. The lights throughout the ship went out.

A final rocket shot up into the sky. Lucy's head swam; saliva filled her mouth; she leaned back over the side. As she threw up into the black ocean, she could still hear the cries from the ship. She scrabbled for Cosmo and he helped to pull her upright. With her head slumped against his chest, she watched as *Titanic*'s foredecks became vertical slides.

With an almighty explosion the ship broke in half, tossing the second funnel into the ocean as the front of the ship disappeared under the water, shedding passengers and debris like a dog shaking water from its coat.

*How long can they survive in this water?* Lucy wondered as chunks of ice floated past their boat. Fear gripped her, colder than the icy air. "They are all going to die, aren't they, Cosmo? Every single one of them—they can't possibly survive in this water."

Another explosion came from deep under the water. "Cracked in two, at the waist." Cosmo was staring at the foundering ship. "Dear God, not quite in two; she must still be attached at the hull. Look at the stern."

As the bow sank, the stern began to lift, its two remaining funnels crashing down over the decks and into the water.

"Harder," the young sailor cried. "We have to get away from her! Pull!"

Lucy's eyes filled with tears as the ship's stern rose upward until it stood straight: a massively dark sentinel in the flat black of the water, its three propellers gleaming in the starlight.

There was a moan from Celia as people slipped and bounced down the vertical decks and crashed into the water. For an awful moment or two, it seemed as if the black obelisk was fixed and would stay upright. Lucy put her fingers in her ears to block the cries of those who had found a foothold or a railing and clung desperately to a few more minutes of life as the stern started to sink, slowly at first, and then, with a terrible rush, it disappeared into the boil of turbulent water.

"God help them," Lucy said and, turning, put her head over the side of the boat as it pitched and rolled in the turbulence, to be thoroughly sick.

When she lifted her head, it was impossible to tell in the silence that followed where the ship had been. Lucy stared transfixed at nothing at all, her ears still ringing, her head swimming with nausea. But the terror was not over. Out of the darkness they heard the first cries from the survivors who had bobbed up to the surface. The sound grew and grew in concert. A great wail echoed to them across the water. It was the most hideous sound that Lucy had ever heard. It rose out of the black water like a cry of doom. She thrust her fingers deeper into her ears and rocked back and forth on her bench like a terrified, witless child.

"Right," Cosmo said as soon as their boat stopped pitching in the wake of *Titanic*'s plunge. "We have to get back for the survivors. They won't last long; the water is below freezing." He got up to relieve the nearest stoker, whose shoulders were still heaving with the effort of their frantic activity to get away from the sinking ship.

The stoker lifted his head. "Siddown," he panted. "Siddown right this minute—big lug like you'll have us over."

"Then let's reorganize," Cosmo said. "One of you, the two gentlemen here, and myself, we can row back if you're blown. But we have to be quick. There is no time to lose."

Lucy felt the boat rock as Cosmo and the Americans moved out of their places in the narrow boat.

"If you don't bleedin' well sit your arse back down, you'll have us over," said the young sailor they had been told was in charge.

"Yeah, you 'eard 'im. Now, do as yer told. First Officer Murdoch said Symons was in charge, not you. So shut it."

"I most certainly won't," Cosmo said. "We are going back."

"And which direction do we row in?" the sailor said. "This boat's spun around at least three times when the ship went down, that I can count. Which direction, eh, smart-arse?"

"I can't get my bearings at all now," someone said. It sounded like one of the Americans.

The wailing reached a level of distraught panic. Lucy lifted her head. To her left and out in front she could see the faint lights of other lifeboats. Surely they must be on their way to pick up survivors? She lifted her hand and pointed. "That way. Row that way."

The stoker's voice sneered at her in the dark. "Ooh, that way, is it, madam?" A derisive laugh. "You should listen to your wife, mister," he said to Cosmo. "She sees the sense in what I'm saying. She knows they'll capsize us."

"That is not what I meant at all." Lucy found the strength to lift her voice. "There are lights—other lifeboats; row toward them. Then we can make a plan with them to take some of the survivors."

Celia began to cry. "She said to go back. We have to go back; those people are dying!" Tears slid down her face. The howl of drowning people was overwhelming.

"We can't go back," one of the Americans piped up. "There must be hundreds of them."

His friend chimed in. "But we could at least try. We can save twenty. How can you live with yourself?" he asked the stoker.

"Easy," the man said. "If we go back, they'll overturn our boat. Then we'll all die. And our orders were to stay away from the ship!"

"While she was sinking!" the American said.

Lucy could hear Celia sobbing.

"That's four of us in favor of returning!" Cosmo started to move forward. "They won't capsize us; they are frozen with cold."

"And this ain't the bleedin' House of Commons, mate. And you lose, eight to four. We stay where we are."


THE NIGHT SKY and the black of the water became one. Celia crept forward from her bench at the stern and sat close to Lucy. One of the Americans passed them a hip flask of whisky. Lucy took a sip and her stomach revolted. Celia bathed her forehead with her handkerchief dipped in icy salt water.

A voice in the dark said, "Don't drink alcohol, ma'am. It will make you sick. Here, this will help." A canteen of water was put in Lucy's hand and she drank gratefully.

"It's so quiet." Celia's hat had fallen when the boat had got caught up in its descent. Her hair was frosted in ice crystals, the starlight shining in a halo around her head.

Lucy took off her scarf and wrapped it around Celia's damp hair. "Cosmo." She tugged his arm and he turned to her. "Why is it so quiet? . . . Please tell me they are not dead."

"They have been in the water for at least fifteen minutes . . . it's probably too late. Except for those who have found something that floats." He lifted his voice. "We must go back—we might be able to save however many we can."

The stoker's voice came out of the darkness. "We go back when I say we go back."

They sat on in the dark, the waves slapping against the side of the boat. One of the Americans began to pray, his voice broken with the cold and despair.

They waited, with no way of knowing where they were or what time of night it was. Lucy could feel frost forming on her eyelashes. She gazed out into the blackness. How long had it been since the *Titanic* had plunged to its death, an hour? Two? Her legs started to shake and she clenched her jaw.

"Everything has gone." Celia's voice was a hoarse whisper. She hadn't spoken since the stoker had threatened them. Her disembodied voice sounded thin, like a ghost's in the awful blackness of the night. "All those trunks of gowns for New York. All gone."

Lucy saw delicately embroidered dresses, their sleeves floating above their bodices as they wafted their way to the bottom of the cold ocean, and shuddered. *Pull yourself together*, she told herself. *They were packed in trunks—they can't float.* But the image of watery pastel silks, mousseline de soie, and lace sailing like the lost souls of the dead never left her when she remembered the nightmare of that night. "They can all be replaced, Celia. They are just things." In her mind she saw people she had dined with, had taken tea with, and had joined on the Promenade Deck to stroll and gossip. Were they now floating on the surface of the water in their cork life belts with their pale dead faces looking up into a star-filled sky? Had they died believing that help was on the way, that soon the lifeboats would return to lift them out of the bitter cold?

"'S'all right for you rich people." The thickset stoker, who had shouted Cosmo down when he insisted they return to the dying survivors, had a strong Scandinavian accent. "Once you get to New York, you'll recover! All we had was on that ship; we have nothing left at all. Nothing. Our pay stopped when that ship went down. No kit, so no one will take us on. Don't see White Star making things right for us, do you?" he asked his mates.

Lucy would not sit quiet any longer. "But we have our lives! Surely after what we have just seen and heard we should be thankful that we at least are saved!"

"Easy for you to say, sitting there in your mink coat—must have cost your husband a packet," a sailor piped up.

The stoker laughed. "We might have been saved from the sinking. Let's just hope that the radio operators sent out an SOS and that help is on the way. Otherwise we'll all perish from exposure."


THE NIGHT CRAWLED by as they sat in the boat, huddled together for warmth, surrounded by the phantom shapes of icebergs.

"Coldest hour, just before dawn," the stoker said. Lucy couldn't feel her feet. She tried to move them, but they refused to obey, as if they were part of the wooden floor of the boat. Her body was so cold it felt as heavy as lead. In the implacable dark she wasn't sure if her eyes were open or closed. She slowly turned her head and saw a green-gold light ripple like a ribbon across the sky, its edges a dawn pink. *Celestial*, her mind said, *celestial gold with pink and green streamers*. She heard singing, far, far away: voices sweet and pure like young boys in the choir at Westminster.

"Lucy, Lucy. Wake up. You're drifting." Cosmo's voice was sharp; he jolted her forward. "Wake up. Come on, rub your hands together. That's the way, and stamp your feet. Yes, you can: stamp them. Any whisky left?" The flask was grudgingly passed back to him by one of the American businessmen. "Slowly, slowly. That's the way. Celia, move closer to Lucy and have a nip of whisky. We have to keep each other warm."

"Is that the dawn?" Celia asked. "The sky is pink over there . . . and green."

"No, those are the northern lights," one of the sailors said. His teeth were chattering, and in the green-white light his face was leached of color. "Some native tribes call them sea spirits."

"Yes," said Lucy. "They are singing . . . quite loudly."

Cosmo had his arm around her, hugged to his side to keep her warm. "They'll be coming for us," he whispered in her ear. "They radioed out our position when they knew she was sinking; we'll see the lights of the first rescue ships. They'll be here very soon, now."

Lucy thought about the people bobbing in the water again. A short distance away a light shone out and was joined by another. She could hear voices echoing across to them. Instructions given, the clash of oars against the wooden sides of lifeboats.

"They are going back now," said the stoker. "Going back for survivors."

"It's too late," one of the Americans said. "God forgive us, we left it too late."

# CHAPTER TWENTY-THREE

*April 16, 1912*

CELIA

"Dear God, help me." Celia looked up at the sheer cliff of rust-stained iron as their lifeboat slammed against the side of the ship. One of the sailors helped her to her feet. "Up you go, miss. Tie that coat around you tight with this bit o' rope so it don't flap. Thassaway. We'll hold the tail end of the ladder steady." He jostled her to her feet, but she could neither grasp the rope of the ladder nor lift her leg to the first rung. She managed to turn her head.

"M'lady?"

Lady Duff Gordon's face looked up at her. "Celia, it's up you go or perish."

She summoned her strength and climbed a rung—the ladder swung against the rusting iron, bruising her knuckles. She lifted her right leg and froze. "I can't. I can't," she cried and slithered back into the safety of the boat.

"Someone needs to go ahead of her. Go on, Cosmo. I'll follow so she doesn't feel so exposed." Her boss was talking between lips blue with cold, but the whisky had evidently revived her ladyship. "Now, Celia, don't look down or up. Keep your eyes straight ahead and take it a rung at a time. I'll be right behind you."

Lady Duff Gordon had swayed to her feet and Celia prayed she hadn't had too much whisky. "Celia, think about breakfast. It's waiting for you at the top of that ladder. Warm clothes, a comfortable bed, and a lovely cup of something hot and sweet. Go on, I know you can do it."

Celia put her foot on the lowest rung. *Coffee*, she thought, *I want coffee and some eggs and bacon to go with it: crisply fried with some bread to soak up the drippings.* She stared fixedly at the shoes just above her head and climbed three rungs. "That's the way, up you go. Right behind you." She felt Lady D.'s ice-cold hand on her ankle for a moment, urging her upward.

Slowly, slowly, they inched their way up the ladder, rung by rung, until two strong arms hauled her up over the side of the ship.

"M'lady?" She turned and in the dawn light looked back into the tiny boat that had brought them to safety. "Where is she? Where's Lady Duff Gordon?"

"Just a bump, my dear, she's all right. Look, here she is." Lady D. was being bundled up in a heavy blanket with Sir Cosmo beside her. "We pulled her up in a cargo net," a voice said. "You're safe. You are on the *Carpathia*. It's all over now. That's the way. Can you walk?"

*Walk? I climbed eighty feet or more of bloomin' rope ladder!* "Let's get something hot inside you." Celia sank her nose into the steam of the cup and took a tentative sip; the scent of beef broth would cling to her memory of that terrible night for the rest of her life.

*April 19, 1912*
*New York Plaza Hotel*

LUCY

The sweat was pouring off her. Had the boilers in the hold burst? The sound of escaping steam filled the air: a high-pitched scream that hurt her ears and made her head throb. She plunged down into dark, black water. Sharp bright knives cut into her. Her blood froze in her veins.

*Don't make me go without you.*

Lucy fought her way upward. Past delicate women dressed in pastel blues and pinks; the beaded and embroidered panels caught the lights in the sky as their arms floated up above heads, their hair streaming like silver seaweed. *Up!* she told herself, kicking her legs free of her skirt and forging upward. Up, up, and up into the starry night sky to the northern lights, folding in an undulating accordion of pink and green, welcoming her home. Long silken ribbons of light. The voices of the sea spirits sang as sweet and as clear as sirens in an endless hypnotic chant: *She's coming round, she's coming round. Round, round, round!*

The dreadful chill in her limbs began to recede. She was safe. She was home. Heavy damp cotton was peeled away from her arms and legs, and the lulling waves of the Mediterranean lapped against her stomach and thighs. The soft hands of the sea spirits smoothed her hair. *She's coming round, round, round.*

"It's the northern lights," she said. "They are watching over us. Why did they take so long to come?" She opened her eyes.

The light hurt and she closed them again. A hand took hers and held it.

"Cosmo?" She struggled to open her eyes again.

"Lower the light," a voice said, the weight of it heavy on the *el*'s. "There, my darling, you are safe. No more struggling; you are safe." The voice of her husband in the dark.

She stared up into his dark eyes. A hand slipped behind her head and a cup was put to her lips. The bliss of cool water.

"Celia?" she said. Her tongue felt too big for her mouth. "I thought you fell."

"No, my darling girl, it was you who fell, but you are safe now."

"I'm right here, m'lady. We are in New York—at the Plaza."

"Everyone?" she asked. *Is the ship large enough for so many?*

"Rest, my dearest love. Sleep and rest."

———

"WHAT DO YOU remember?" Cosmo wrapped her hands around the cup. "It's soup; drink it."

"Everything. I remember everything so clearly. Awful things." She shook her head to clear it of ugly images: of people sliding and bumping over the edge of the ship to drop into the dark water.

He sat down on the bed next to her. "Can you bear a little light?" The sun would be a blessing after the black.

Lucy nodded and the curtains were pulled open. "Now, eat your soup slowly."

"How long have we been here?"

"Not long—do you remember the *Carpathia*?" She remembered that miserable climb, with shaking legs and numb hands and feet, and then tumbling backward. "Yes, quite clearly. I felt cold, my head ached. People were so kind. But I don't remember arriving here at all."

"You fell back into the lifeboat when you were climbing the ladder. And you have been sick, a fever caused by the chill and a bang to your head when you fell. You are quite all right now."

"Yes. How many, Cosmo—are safe?"

He looked away. "They say seven hundred or so from the lifeboats. They are still looking for the bodies of the others."

MRS. STUYVESANT FISH's drawing room was breathtakingly hot. Through the window Lucy could see the fresh lime green of spring leaves quivering in the April air and put down her teacup. She couldn't breathe, and the scent of narcissi in huge pots wherever she turned her head caught in her throat.

"My dear Lady Duff Gordon, how pleasant to see you again." A large woman with a vast hat crowned with feathers was smiling at her. It was a plain, heavily featured face, but her eyes were bright with pleased recognition and her hands were firm in their grasp. "Mrs. Margaret Brown? Do you remember we met on board *Titanic*?"

Lucy's eyes slid away to the other women in the heavily decorated drawing room. A bright bevy of gorgeously attired young beauties were making a terrible noise in the conservatory, a gauzy cloud of butterflies, as they took delicate bites of cake.

"They are excited for the first assembly," the woman with the large hat explained.

*What on earth am I doing here?* A sleepwalker stumbling into the light, she realized that there was a piece missing still. The overabundant luxury of the *Titanic* was almost as suffocating as this massive room filled with overdressed women eating enough food to feed a battalion.

She shuddered: that hideous ship, with its claustrophobic furnishings, its thick, stifling carpets, and the syrupy strings of an orchestra playing the "Waltz of the Flowers." The oppressive opulence, the crushing self-indulgence. *And there were people bobbing on the surface of the frozen Atlantic in their life belts with ice crystals in their hair. Faces as white as the icing on that enormous cake on the table of this suffocating room.*

"Mrs. Brown," she said, and put her hand on the woman's arm. "It would seem that I am not feeling quite the thing." *And I don't want to make a scene.*

A searching glance. "You look very pale. Would you like to leave? I am sure they would understand."

Lucy nodded. "Yes, I think I would." *Because I don't want to be sick all over the Aubusson.*

Mrs. Brown lifted her hand and rested the inside of her wrist briefly on Lucy's forehead. "I will make our excuses. You need some air." She patted her shoulder. "I will say our goodbyes."

A woman seated near her smiled, leaned forward, and said, "Wishy fish, wishy fish."

And Lucy politely murmured, "Oh, no, thank you." *I can't even hear properly.*

And they were gone, down a staircase broad enough for a coach and four, and out through a portico as wide as the entrance of a cathedral.

The street was shady and sweet with the scent of newly clipped grass, the blessed air cool on her face. A large motorcar pulled up at the curb. "Top down, Roberts," the capable Mrs. Brown instructed. "Yes, that's the way. Now slowly through the park."

"A little too hot in there." Lucy loosened the top button of her coat. A bead of sweat trickled down the inside of her starched collar.

The woman nodded. "Yes, I have stayed in one or two of your fine country houses in England. I had to wear woolen pantalettes under my ball gown. We Americans do so love our central heating!"

The park was thronged with people enjoying the spring sunshine. "Where are you from, Mrs. Brown? New York?"

Two shrewd eyes assessed this innocent remark. "I'm from Leadville, in Colorado. You don't remember anything from the ship, do you?"

Lucy frowned. "I remember everything from the moment we went up on deck and were told to get into lifeboats, and most of the nightmare that followed. Did I miss anything?" The cool air made her feel more like herself, and she laughed. "I mean of the three days on the ship before it sank?"

"Well, not much. But someone told me that you owned a shop?"

Lucy laughed. "That's quite true. I do. Two of them actually."

"And that you design naughty underclothes?"

Lucy laughed again. "Quite true, I do." She smiled at a woman who clearly wasn't from an old family.

"My husband owned a strike called Little Jonny—a gold mine. And before that I scrubbed kitchen floors and cooked in a soup kitchen. And now I run them"—she waved around her with a large, gloved hand—"all over this town and the town I live in now, in Denver."

"I'm pleased to make your acquaintance, Mrs. Brown." Lucy put out her hand. "And thank you so much for your help. I feel so much better now."

"Don't you mention it, and we can do away with the formalities; I'm

Molly and I want to talk to you about my committee to help the families of the people on board that ship, not from first class, who did not survive." Two forthright and thoughtful eyes fixed themselves on Lucy's face.

"Were there many?" Lucy asked and was stunned by her reply.

"One hundred and eight women, fifty-six children, and six hundred and forty-eight men. A total of eight hundred and twelve did not make it into the lifeboats. They either went down with the ship or died from exposure afterward—in the water."

Lucy's scalp seethed as she heard the long, wailing cries of despair echoing across the black water.

"There are families here in America and probably in England, too, who are hard-pressed by the loss of those that perished when the *Titanic* sank—most of the passengers who died were in steerage: working people. Our committee is to help any survivors or their families find work if they have lost a breadwinner, to look after orphaned children, and to help in any way we can."

Lucy looked out across the park with its carefree walkers of the well-dressed and well-fed classes. She watched a little boy racing along the smooth gravel path after a bright red ball. *How do working families who have lost a son or a husband manage? How do children from poor families thrive if their father and mother have been killed?*

"How many of our . . . how many survived from our part of the ship?"

Molly's large chin sank down and made two more in her collar. "Oh, I can be quite sure of that number, Lucy," she said. "There were three hundred and nineteen passengers on our part of the ship—one hundred and twenty perished at sea. Yes, I see you understand what I am saying. It's the same in life, no matter what. The rich will always survive over the poor. So, what can I put you down for?" Her face beamed with good humor, and she took a pencil and a notebook out of her handbag.

Lucy smiled. "If you take me to my hotel I will give you a real cup of tea and write you a check. And I am good for eight hundred and seventy pounds. Will that be enough to start with?"

"That's an interesting number—and certainly a very generous one."

"Yes, it is how much White Star charged for our stateroom on that ship."

*April 30, 1912*
*New York*

CELIA

"I'll say this for the girls we have working for us, they know how to work. I have never seen such diligence—and they are very reliable." Celia had not stirred from the atelier in days. She had lost herself in work, grateful to immerse herself in the challenges that their new salon in this strange city offered, and delighted by the girls who worked so meticulously.

"Mm." Lucy pinned the last swathe of chiffon across the front of the skirt. "The silk warehouse in this city is vast, absolutely vast. I was spoiled for choice. Look at this lovely crepe de chine." She stood back, her head on one side, eyes narrowed. "Yes, that is so much better with the drape going that way." It was a blessing to see her back to normal. Lady Duff Gordon was at last right where she should be: standing in the workroom of her Thirty-Sixth Street salon.

A group of seamstresses, machinists, embroiderers, and scrap girls stood around in a respectful group as their boss, always mindful of an attentive audience, inspected a row of shining beauties dressed in her models. The Hanover Square mannequins had arrived from London and were being dressed for the first fashion show New Yorkers had ever seen.

"Girls, New York obviously agrees with you. You are all looking so bonny dressed in the colors of spring. How lovely you are," Lucy said, but her gaze was firmly fixed on their gowns. She lifted her arm and made a circular movement with her finger. Slowly, one by one, the mannequins turned.

"Gamela's skirt is too wide across her hips." Lucy pinched a quarter inch of fabric. "There, it needs to come in, right *here*." She walked up and down the line. "Florence's neckline should be deeper." With her forefinger she traced a horseshoe in the air over Florence's fine décolletage. "Otherwise, it will be a shameful waste of a beautiful bosom."

Celia wrote, her cheeks pink with pleasure. *This is more like it*, she thought as she scribbled down annotations to the diagrams in her notebook. *There is nothing like a bit of work to make you feel like you are back with the living again.*

Their arrival in a city mourning for its dead had been hard to bear. Shock from the disaster of the *Titanic* and the nightmare of the hours until their rescue by the *Carpathia* still echoed through Celia's days and nights. One night she had woken to the final cry she had heard before an implacable silence had descended on the black ocean as the last of the survivors had died. There had been a pause in the concerted wail for help, and then one voice had lifted among the others with determined strength: "Billeee!" the thin voice had cried out with surprising force. "Billy, whur are you?" Cold, exhausted, and terrified as she was, Celia had recognized the burr of her native Northumberland and had prayed for Billy with all her might, that he was in one of the boats that waited in the dark night. The voice had not cried out again; it had been swallowed in the whispering plaintive murmur of dying humanity who had given up hope. A whisper that Celia would never forget.

She closed her notebook and turned her head toward the light-filled windows of the atelier. *You survived*, she told herself. *God knows how or why, but you did. Now be thankful for life.* When Gamala and the other girls had arrived from London and filled the building with their bright cockney voices, their excited exclamations for the novelty of New York, it was then that Celia and her boss felt they could bear to join the living and get back to work.

Lucy stood back to admire her work again. "You look sensational. I wouldn't be at all surprised if I lose you all to wealthy old American businessmen!" She laughed and the girls joined in.

*April 30, 1912*
*New York*

LUCY

"Good afternoon at the salon, darling?" Cosmo came into their bed-room at the Plaza Hotel as Lucy shook out the sheer folds of her dress. "Mm, now, that's a glorious shade of blue. Exactly the shade that chap used when he painted the Sistine Chapel."

"Michelangelo? Yes, it is exactly like."

He wandered over to help with the buttons. "So many of them," he said as he squinted through the smoking cigarette in his mouth.

When he had done up the last one, she caught the downturned mouth. That expression wasn't about buttons. "Did you go to the gym-nasium?"

"No, didn't have time in the end. I had a letter this morning from Lord Mersey's clerk, Thomas Howard. Have to go back to England—soonest. Mersey is heading up a Board of Trade inquiry into the *Titanic* on behalf of the British Wreck Commission."

Lucy finished putting on her earrings.

"But why do *you* have to go? Do you have shares in White Star?" He had interests everywhere.

"No, not at all. It's nothing like that. They want to talk to me as a passenger. One of the few surviving British passengers—in first class." He put out his cigarette. "Are you ready? We should get going if we are not to be late. Americans are such sticklers for punctuality."

He wrapped her up in her fur. "Pretty chilly out there."

"Aren't the Americans doing an inquiry here? Can't you go to that one?"

He searched around the room. "No, my dear," he said as he found his hat. "No, they want me to give testimony at the British Board of Trade inquiry. So, I have made a reservation on the *Mauretania*'s return voyage to England."

Was it his tone, or was it the overly aloof expression on his face, that made her clamp down on inner alarm? "I hope you made a reservation for a stateroom."

"No, I didn't. You have the mannequin show and all of that—you surely don't want another sea voyage just yet? And I don't need a stateroom."

"Well, you better change it, then, because if you have to give your testimony at this inquiry, I seem to remember that I was with you on that night. So, they will want to hear from me too." She tried to sound firm, but it came out all wrong: as bossy.

He laughed. "And Celia? Will they want to hear from her as well?"

"No, Celia must stay here and manage the show next week. When are we sailing?"

"Day after tomorrow."

"Good, then I'll have time to look over the hats and I must remember to cancel my afternoon with Mrs. Goodall."

*May 5, 1912*
*London*

LUCY

Lucy woke to gray skies and cold winds in their Lennox Gardens house. Cosmo had risen early and had already gone, leaving her a note that he would be home in time for tea. *This wretched inquiry will take up hours and days of our time*, Lucy thought as she drank a cup of tea—*piping hot*—and ate her toast. *Mm, real marmalade!*

"Good morning, Browning. We will be lunching out today," she said to the butler as he opened the front door. *Everyone knows there weren't enough lifeboats on that blasted ship to begin with*, she fumed as she stepped out into a raw morning. *And no one had a clue what to do in a real emergency.* She stopped, shivering as the wind picked up along the street. *And all those poor, poor people would never have died.*

"It's more like February than May," she complained to Margot Asquith and her stepson, Raymond, when she joined them for lunch at the Savoy Grill.

Margot shook her head. "You are still looking very pale, Lucy. I can't imagine how you could get on another ship again."

Lucy stared down at her plate. "I made myself do it," she said. "I had no choice."

"Very brave of you, Lucy, but where is Cosmo? They haven't called him in to give his testimony already, have they?" Margot was at her most officious, having read Lucy's telegram informing her of their required return to London at the request of the Board of Trade. "I particularly wanted him to talk to Raymond before he spoke to anyone at all, because Raymond is involved with the inquiry."

Lucy sipped her wine. "You sound like a member of Great British Press: all they talk about is 'the inquiry.' They practically mobbed us when we got off the ship—vultures invited to a banquet. And anyway, Cosmo is only being asked a few questions about how inadequately the lifeboat procedure was handled. We could have got twenty more people into ours if they had taken out all the unnecessary stuff they had stowed in there—and had been better organized."

Raymond Asquith turned his head to order Dover sole for them and then leaned toward her. "No, Lady Duff Gordon, that is not why they have asked Sir Cosmo to return to England. It is not to give his opinion on lifeboat procedures on a sinking ship. They are getting ready to point fingers. Culprits have to be found. I'm sorry, I didn't mean to alarm. The Board of Trade are culpable of possible negligence just as much as White Star, and not just because there were insufficient lifeboats on board, but for a hundred other issues that will amount to a long, quarrelsome session." He slipped his card across the table. "Please ask Sir Cosmo to get in touch with me so I can brief him on what he is to expect."

"But Cosmo has nothing to do with White Star—he was just a passenger!"

"Nevertheless, please ask him to call me." Lucy slipped the pasteboard card into her purse. The wine in her glass tasted sour, and she huddled her fur more closely around her cold neck.

Margot's deep-set eyes disappeared under straight black brows in a frown of annoyance. "Now you have made her anxious, Raymond, and that was not the purpose of this luncheon."

Lucy folded her hands in her lap to warm them. "I am not anxious, but I would be grateful if Raymond were to tell me a little more, since I am to testify too."

Raymond nodded and put his hand on his stepmother's forearm to stop her from interrupting.

"When I say finger-pointing, I mean literally that. No one is willing to take blame. And the tenor of the inquiry will have everyone determined to fix blame somewhere else. And it seems that someone in your boat—a crew member who didn't like the Duff Gordons—is accusing you, Lady Duff Gordon, of refusing to go back to the site of the sinking to take on people who had survived it. He says you were frightened that they would capsize the boat, and that Sir Cosmo went along with you."

Lucy shook her head. *Am I hearing this right? They are saying this about me—and Cosmo?*

"That's absolutely enough, Raymond. Lucy dear, Raymond is only warning that mud is about to be slung, and not just at you and Cosmo. Certain people are trying to avoid their responsibilities. Their accusations against you both are simply a distraction—a bit of public relations—a sideshow.

"Have a little more wine, my dear, and tell me what is wrong with this hat. I went to Reville—no, don't shake your head like that; you were off enjoying a sea voyage, so where was I to go? I look like a pirate in a gale in it, don't I?"

Lucy swallowed down alarm with a sip from her wineglass and felt gratitude for good friends. "Thank you, Raymond, I will ask Cosmo to call on you." She looked across the table at her dear, fierce friend. "No, not a pirate, Margot. You look like a very imperious buccaneer." The wide brim of Margot's hat had been pinned to its crown in the front with a large, ugly brooch. The hat perched over Margot's long, hawklike nose; it made her look rather like Captain Hook.

"RAYMOND ASQUITH THOUGHT it would be useful to have luncheon so he can tell you what he knows about the inquiry. Who's involved and what is emerging so far." She kept her tone offhand as she lay back in the crook of Cosmo's arm against the pillows of their comfortable bed. *There is,* she thought, *nothing like being in one's own bed, even in what threatens to be trying times.* When she awoke, in the dark, convinced that she could feel the roll and billow of the ocean and heard the howl of despair in the dark, it was the hushed and unmistakable sound of London traffic—wet rubber wheels on tarmac—that lulled her back to sleep.

Cosmo turned his head and kissed her on the forehead, smoothing back her tousled hair.

"Raymond Asquith? Ah yes, I remember we met him at the Ballets Russes. Is he old enough to be a barrister?"

Lucy sighed. In his own quiet way, Cosmo was resisting any attempt to prepare himself for what appeared in the press to be a bun-fight going on at the Scottish Hall at Buckingham Gate over the sinking of the unsinkable ship. She lifted her head so she could look him in the eye.

"Raymond Asquith is a highly intelligent young man. He was called to the bar eight years ago and has a reputation for being a brilliant barrister. He is my dear friend Margot Asquith's stepson, and she thinks very highly of him. Anyway, he's junior counsel for the British Wreck Commissioner—so that should tell you how well regarded he is."

He turned on his side so that they were facing each other. "Darling," he said. "If it makes you feel easier, I will talk to Asquith. I don't want to bore or worry you about it all; you have enough on your plate with your new designer, Mr. Molyneux, and the upheaval he caused at Hanover Square. Not to mention what's going on at Lucile in New York."

Lucy cupped her hand around his cheek. *Why is it that he feels that nothing must worry me, that Lucile takes precedence in our lives? Has it always been this way?*

She drew back to shake her head. "Molyneux has a little too much temperament, that's all. All designers do; he hasn't learned to control his yet. He just needs someone to keep him under their thumb. Can I at least tell you what Raymond told me?"

He nodded. "Yes, yes, of course, I don't mean to be a pain in the neck."

*How many times has he apologized for the* Titanic *to me?* She plumped up her pillows so she could sit up in bed.

"Here is Raymond's tuppence worth. The Board of Trade passed the *Titanic* as fit for sea, which is why they want to hold this inquiry in the first place—to squash any murmurings against their efficiency." She put her hand on his arm. "Of course I know you know all this anyway, but I am just reiterating what Raymond told me."

Cosmo nodded her on.

"Raymond called it using the whitewash brush. Apart from protecting itself, the Board of Trade has no interest in seeing the White Star Line found negligent in any way whatsoever—or, come to that, the shipbuilders, Harland and Wolff. Any damage to White Star's reputation or balance sheet will be bad for British shipping—and there is considerable potential for both. Negligence on the part of the shipping company might pave the way for millions of pounds in damage claims and lawsuits that would tie up the courts for years, possibly break the White Star Line, and result in the loss of much of Britain's lucrative shipping traffic to the Germans and the French." As she finished she hoped that her tone hadn't been too instructive. *Why are Cosmo and I so out of kilter?* she asked herself. *It is the damned inquiry and those dreadful headlines. We feel guilty because we survived.*

He smiled. "Yes, so I understand from my friend Hamar Greenwood and our son-in-law, Tivvy. Aha, you see I have been doing some home-work after all. They are all flocking to the inquiry: the National Sailors' and Firemen's Union, the British Seafarers' Union." He thumped his pillow and sat up next to her. "The Imperial Merchant Service Guild . . . all of them, even the Union of Ships' Stewards. Everyone will want a slice of the cake."

Lucy got out of bed and put on her robe as he continued. "And since you are determined to hear the very worst, the reason I have to testify is that I am suspected of cowardice and bribery—that is probably what Raymond wants to talk to me about."

She had been on her way to run her bath, but this baldly made re-mark stopped her mid-stride. "Dear God, what on earth are they think-ing?" she cried. "Cowardice! You were thrown into our wretched boat by that officer. What was his name? Murdoch? He'll testify. He'll say that the lifeboat was down on one rope and he tossed you in at the last minute with those Americans!" Her outrage tightened her throat. It was almost impossible to breathe.

"Murdoch didn't make it—after he left us he went to supervise the loading of second- and third-class passengers: far more of them than there were in first. The shots we heard as we rowed away from the ship were apparently fired by Murdoch as he tried to keep order." Cosmo's mouth tightened for a moment. "And . . . then he shot himself . . . poor man."

"But you were not the only man in the boat—and there were more crew than passengers, for God's sake!"

"Yes, yes, I know. I am sure those Americans are probably considered as culpable of cowardice as I am, but they are Americans. I am British, and this is a British inquiry."

Lucy sat down on the edge of the bed. "I won't have it said that you are a coward! Oh my God, Cosmo, there is no more honorable man in Britain than you." Tears of anger stood in her eyes.

Cosmo pulled her to him.

"It's so wrong. So wrong," she said into his chest.

"You must hear everything, and then you won't be so frightened. You might not remember this, because you were busy being seasick, but when we were in the lifeboat, one of the men said that they had lost everything when the ship went down. Everything."

Lucy shook her head. "I do remember them saying that—that stoker said they lost all they had. He said something about not being paid from the moment the ship went down."

His face was grim as he nodded. "Yes, the crew made the point we first-class passengers would emerge from this with our livelihoods intact. Whereas they, the crew, had lost *everything* that would enable them to find another berth." He held up his hand. "Let me finish, please.

"So just before the *Carpathia* docked in New York I found those men—the seven lads who were in our boat. I remembered what they had said about their plight. So, I gave them a fiver each. To get them started."

Lucy's head came up. "And some idiot"—her chest heaved with indignation—"saw you give them the money and saw it as a bribe?"

He nodded. "Always so quick off the mark." He stroked her cheek with his forefinger. "Yes, I am being criticized for bribery *and* cowardice."

"But you didn't bribe those men to keep us safe in the lifeboat, you gave them money after we had been rescued, when we were on the *Carpathia* . . . a gift to help them out." She was on her feet again. "They are probably still in New York, looking for another berth. We have to find them and then they will clear you." She lifted her hands to her head in despair. "I wish I hadn't been so seasick. What were their names? Celia! We have to telegraph Celia. She has such a good memory. Surely she will remember their names."

"Yes, I think we might very well have to get poor Celia involved. But only if it gets ugly. I am sure it won't."

"How many men from first class survived that wreck, do you think?" Lucy demanded. "Didn't I read somewhere in the papers that there were fifty-six or -seven male survivors from first class? So why you?"

He shook his head. "Rumor. The need to blame. Perhaps because I asked Captain Rostron of the *Carpathia* if it were true that the minute that ruddy ship sank, those men were taken off White Star Line's payroll. He was not alone when I asked him for information; he was on the bridge with his officers when he confirmed it as most likely. Then I told him that I wanted to help them and he located them for me. It was all pretty public, or at least to those who were around at the time. Celia wrote them checks: seven of them for five quid each. Captain Rostron knows why I gave those men money—he knows it wasn't a bribe! But everyone who reads these ghastly London rags thinks I paid them off not to go back to pick up survivors. You know how awful people can be. So, yes, darling, of course I will speak to young Asquith—but I doubt if there is anything he can tell me that I don't already know."

"SURVIVORS OF THE *Titanic*. Sir Cosmo and Lucy, Lady Duff Gordon give their testimony at the Board of Inquiry. Today!" Lucy looked up from the newspaper. "Margot, they are calling our lifeboat the Millionaires' Boat."

The newspaper was snatched away from her. "Don't read that rubbish." Margot Asquith looked even fiercer today, in a hat that had black birds' wings on either side of her head. The Valkyrie sat forward in the back of her large motorcar, where they waited for Lucy to go into the Scottish Hall to make her testimony. Margot glanced through the paper and hurled it to the floor of her Daimler. "What a lot of tripe. Jealousy and spite. Pull yourself together, Lucy. You are more than a match for some underqualified little barrister who comes from the home counties."

Lucy stared down at the headlines glaring up at her from the floor of the motor. "Cosmo will be questioned after you, Lucy. Go in there and be gracious and calm; do not do any more than answer their questions with either a yes or a no. Do you remember what Raymond said?"

"Yes."

"Good. I will be in the gallery. And so will Daisy Brooke and Violet

Manners and your sister, Elinor. And half of the smart set if I know them."

THE PROSECUTING COUNSEL was a thin man with papery skin and heavily brilliantined hair. The sort of man whose wife jumped at his every command and catered to his irritable whims. He had a hard, tight face, and a long red nose. *He drinks*, thought Lucy, as she got to her feet. *No, don't think that! Be calm, be pleasant. And don't interrupt!*

"Lady Duff Gordon." He made a sneering little half bow. "I only want you to tell me one thing before we get to the situation of the lifeboat. Had there been offers to you to go into any of the other lifeboats?"

She heard her voice, clear and calm. "Oh yes. They practically dragged me away."

A spasm of impatience. "Dragged you away? Do you mean some of the sailors?"

Why were her hat feathers shaking? Lucy took a long, steadying breath. "Yes, the sailors. I was holding on to my husband's arm. They were very anxious that I should go."

"And you *refused* to go?" He made her sound like a fool.

"Absolutely."

A cold, sarcastic smile. "Well, eventually you did go with your husband, as we know, in what has been called the emergency boat?"

"Yes, I did."

He took the time to look up at Lord Mersey, who was sitting in his carved chair, his eyes half-closed, the ends of his long wig vibrating with impatience. Mersey opened his eyes and glared. It had its effect on the prosecutor. "Just tell us quite shortly—I do not want to go into it in any detail—but quite shortly, how it was you went into that boat. Do you remember?"

Her hat feathers were still now. "Quite well."

In a voice dripping with exaggerated patience: "Well, would you tell my lord?"

Lucy turned to Lord Mersey. "After three boats had been lowered, my husband, Miss Franklin, and myself were left standing on the deck. There were no other people on deck at all and I had quite made up my mind that I was going to be drowned, and then suddenly we saw this little boat in front of us—and we saw some sailors and an officer stripping off its canvas cover. I said to my husband, 'Might we perhaps go in that boat?' And he said, 'Yes, but we must wait for orders.' And we stood there for quite some time while these men were fixing up things, and then my husband went forward and said, 'Might my wife and this young woman go in this boat?' And the officer said in a very polite way indeed, 'Of course, of course, this is the last boat on this side. They are loading from the other side now.'

"Then somebody hoisted Miss Franklin, and I was pitched in after her. It was not a case of getting in at all because the sides of the boat were quite high. After we had been in a little while the boat was starting to be lowered with just the two of us! I called out that there was more room. And the officer gave my husband permission to get in. And then two American gentlemen arrived and were thrown in too."

Counsel held up his hand. "That will be all, Lady Duff Gordon."

"Oh yes, and there were seven crewmen who were put in too—before the boat was even lowered. Did you know that, Counsel?"

"Yes, thank you, Lady Duff Gordon. That will be all."


"POOR COSMO'S TESTIMONY went on far longer than mine, didn't it?" Lucy said as she climbed into Margot's motorcar. She had tried to avoid Elinor as she left the hall, but her sister had been too quick for her.

"Elinor, I can't talk now. I am so tired. I just want to sit quietly in Margot's car and wait for Cosmo. Perhaps we can talk tomorrow?"

But relentless Elinor only had one question. "Why did he give those sailors money, Lucy? That is the most condemning thing about this whole inquiry—it makes him look like a coward bribing his way to safety!"

Lucy put her arms around her sister and drew her close. "Elinor, please, don't stand on the pavement shouting. Cosmo gave them money for their kit—to help them buy new kit. He didn't bribe anyone." She was blushing and stuttering as if she and Cosmo had tried to buy off the entire ship's personnel.

"It is going to look so bad . . . It will look like a bribe." Lucy gave her sister a firm kiss on the cheek when she wanted to put her hand over her mouth. "I'm free tomorrow if you would like to come for luncheon, Elinor. We'll talk tomorrow!"


"ONE RULE FOR the Rich and Another for Those Who Travel in Steerage." Lucy picked up one newspaper after another, read the headline aloud, and dropped it on the floor. "What do the Americans say when things go from bad to worse?" she asked Lily Elsie, who had come to visit for tea.

"They say bad luck. And most of them shrug it off and carry on." Lily had sat up in the gallery to watch both Lucy's and Cosmo's testimony. "You did a splendid job, Lucy. And nothing will come of it; there was nothing either of you did that was cowardly. Your cross-examinations were a planned distraction from White Star's sloppiness. Twenty lifeboats for how many passengers? Two thousand two hundred and forty—and that's not counting the crew! It's ridiculous. I heard someone say that there was space on the boat deck for sixty boats! The shareholders are terrified of losing money. And then they tried to bully poor Cosmo."

Lucy gritted her teeth as she remembered how she had sat on her hands and composed her face as Cosmo had been interrogated. "Yes, they did. Round and round, the same questions asked in a dozen different ways. When did you give the men money? How much money? And that dreadful man, the stoker—the man who said he would not go back to help those crying out for help—that Hendrikson saying that *I* told him that we were not to go back to take on the survivors. He was such a brute—I can't imagine why he is the only one of the crew in our lifeboat who was able to attend the inquiry. Know something, Lily? Cosmo and I are being pilloried for surviving."

"Have you heard from Miss Franklin? Has she located the other members of the crew?"

"I hope so, Lily, I really do, because unless she does, the inquiry will only have Hendrikson's testimony. And I can't remember saying anything at all about not going back to help those poor people. I could hardly speak for being sick."

Lucy dropped the last newspaper onto the floor and rang for tea. "Tea? Or shall we have something stronger?"

Lily put a cigarette into its holder and lifted it to her mouth. "How will Miss Franklin locate these crewmen?"

"Through Mrs. Brown—if she hasn't returned to Colorado. She set up a committee for aid to the families of those who perished. If anyone knows where everyone who survived that vile night is, it will be Margaret Brown."

Lily laughed and lit her cigarette. "The Unsinkable Molly Brown. That's what the papers are calling her. Do you know there is a story going round that she took one of the oars of her lifeboat and started pulling back to pick up those poor people drowning?"

Lucy harrumphed; she was sick to death of newspaper headlines. "Yes, that is what they are saying, but she told me that she didn't do anything except sit there among the women crying for their husbands, grateful that she was at least in a lifeboat and wishing she had put on her long underwear!"

Lily smiled her sad smile. "You know as well as I do what a good headline is worth: 'Lily Elsie on the Boards from the Age of Six: The Most Accomplished Actress of the Century!' What rubbish. 'Lucy, Lady Duff Gordon, London's Top Designer, Survives the *Titanic* Disaster!' Well, at least that part is true."

Lucy shuddered. "How ugly it all is. Why are people so ghoulish, so eager for the ugly details? It was terrible, Lily, absolutely terrible. We sat in that boat in the dark and listened to the cries of people dying, with that oaf of a Hendrikson refusing to go back—wicked man. And now all the newspapers want are more victims and blame. Why? Cosmo isn't a coward—he didn't bribe anyone. Poor chap—he is returning from Scotland tomorrow for a final grilling."

Lucy poured tea and they sipped in silence, until Lily broke it. "I came up the hard way, Lucy, and there is nothing like a bit of notoriety—the horde love it when the rich and powerful are brought low and the poor rise up on their merits. I'm sorry, but there it is. The press have made Molly Brown a rags-to-riches heroine—a woman who worked in a soup kitchen in the minefields: she may be a millionairess now, but she is still untarnished and pure." Lily frowned, her face bitter. "They can break you—those newspapers. One minute you're on top; the next—" She drew her finger across her throat. Then she laughed. "Here's to Molly Brown," she said and lifted her teacup.


"Cosmo, Cosmo. Where are you?" Lucy ran into the drawing room, an envelope fluttering from her hand. "Molly Brown has written." She had to stop to catch her breath. "Sam Collins, George Taylor, Fred Sheath, and Albert Horsewill have been found. And they have testified that the money you gave them was for kit and to help through the hardship as they would not be paid by White Star. Not as a bribe. They have provided written testimony. And they said they never heard me saying we shouldn't return to help the survivors in the water. I think this means that the inquiry will not find you guilty of either cowardice or bribery. Or me of being hard-hearted and selfish. Oh, darling. Such a relief."

Cosmo walked past her into the drawing room. "A relief that I am neither a coward nor capable of bribery?"

It was as if he had struck her. *He believes that I thought him guilty of being dishonorable,* was the only thought that came to her mind. *That I believed that the money he gave to those men was a payoff?*

*He can't think that. He cannot possibly think that.* "Cosmo!"

"Yes, darling, I heard before I left Scotland. The inquiry is over, thank God. No one was to blame—for anything. The White Star Line is absolved of not providing enough lifeboats . . . even though that conceited ass Ismay had the boat deck cleared of countless untidy lifeboats to enhance the look of an unsinkable ship. Even though there was no lifeboat drill for their passengers. Even though there was some sort of bet going on about the speed that the *Titanic* could achieve to beat any other Atlantic liner. Even though the captain ignored countless ice-field warnings. All that is certainly known is that the *Titanic* was going too fast into an ice field." His tired eyes met hers. "No matter how many able seamen spoke up to say I was pushed into the lifeboat, that there was no one else on the deck to go into it—except the two American businessmen. That I was the first to say that the crew should go back to pick up drowning survivors. No matter how many people speak up that Cosmo Duff Gordon acted with honor. It is too late. Our names have been blandished across newspapers all over the world as the cowards who put their lives first. The survivors in the Millionaires' Boat."

She started toward him, her arms out to comfort, to reassure him that all would be well. But he turned away from her.

"I have made reservations for us on the *Mauretania*. We can go back to New York and join our friends there. We can set sail next week; if you telegraph to Celia, she can arrange a special showing. Do you know that our name wasn't even mentioned in the New York inquiry into the sinking? Not one single word mentioned or in print."

He sat down on the sofa and opened up the *Times* newspaper.

"You mustn't feel like that!" Lucy sat down next to him. "Yes, people repeat stupid, cruel things—without any idea if they are true or false. The newspapers love a good story—it is how they thrive. But you were absolved. We were cleared of any misdoing. Cosmo!"

He put the newspaper down. "Oh my darling, do you really believe that? Do you really believe that an exoneration in a court of law is an absolution too?" He put his arms around her. "I can almost hear you saying: life must go on. And it is true, it really must. I only wish that I had your strong sense of survival—your wonderful middle-class never-say-die attitude. But I am of the weaker species, from the privileged class: the aristocracy of an arrogant empire that believes that God is an Englishman and we were put on earth to rule the world. No one can touch my money; no one can take away my heritage and my lands in a lawsuit. And no one can touch my birthright. But they can call me a coward, a man who bribed others to save his skin. They can take my reputation, my name. No exoneration from the British Board of Trade can give me that back."

# CHAPTER TWENTY-FOUR

*May 1912*
*New York*

CELIA

Things weren't right between them—not by a long chalk. Lady D. had been a mess after that terrible night when the *Titanic* sank and almost on her way back to normal when they had been called to London. It was the Board of Trade inquiry that had put the kibosh on things. Celia knew as soon as she had seen both of them when they returned to New York that the accusations of cowardice had hit hard. Sir Cosmo was thinner and seemed to have lost his relaxed and pleasant way of being with their friends and with the staff. There was a strained quality to his manner whenever he came into the salon these days, which was rarely.

Of course, Lady Duff Gordon was her usual outgoing, laughing self, being the master of putting a good face on things that she was. Over the years she had perfected the art of being delighted to see friends and clients alike, no matter what was happening in her life: always buoyant, always encouraging others to see the bright side. But her eyes were strained, and there was a mechanical quality to her laughter and in her lighthearted welcome of whoever came into the Thirty-Sixth Street salon.

And business was brisk. Brisk to overwhelming. Everyone wanted to be dressed by an aristocrat who had survived the *Titanic. So why on earth did we need to have a reception now, of all things?* Celia circulated among their guests, introduced as the "wonderful Miss Franklin—Lady Duff Gordon's right hand." She even had the leisure to enjoy a glass of champagne.

Celia enjoyed the straightforward informality of New Yorkers; it was pleasantly refreshing after the class consciousness of the British aristocracy. Of course, the Four Hundred, or whatever it was they identified themselves as, were worse than any duke or duchess when it came to snobbery. But the wives of what they called new money were free of such snobberies. She smiled hellos to Mrs. Andrew Carnegie and her cousin across the crush.

What most amazed Celia of all the new and astonishing things she had come across in this clamoring city that flaunted its wealth like a flag was how generous American men were to their wives—and the self-made men the most generous of all. No budgets or restrictions prevented their wives from spending a fortune on their wardrobes. They ordered what they wanted, even if there were not enough hours in the day or days in the week to parade their new dresses.

Mrs. Guttenberg, looking splendid in silver, touched her on the arm. "I have been looking everywhere for you, Miss Franklin. What a delightful party. I wouldn't have missed it for the world. What a splendid idea to hold a mannequin parade of all Lucile's lovely new gowns!"

They passed a pleasant few minutes discussing bridal gowns for Mrs. Guttenberg's youngest daughter.

"I must talk to the butler about more champagne. Will you excuse me, Mrs. Guttenberg?"

"Of course, of course. My regards to Lady Duff Gordon. I haven't been able to get close to her all night, and I can see my husband is looking tired. Such a long day!"

Celia made her way to the pantry to lean up against the door to the kitchen and catch her breath. *Now, get a hold of yourself girl; it's all been a bit much. But it's back to normal.*

She stood in the doorway, reluctant to go back into the throng. From the top step of the pantry she could see Lady Duff Gordon, surrounded by a crowd of admiring women. Her face was bright with laughter, but Celia caught her quick, anxious glance around the room. She followed her gaze and sighed with relief. At least he was still here and had not left already. Poor man, how could he leave? His exit was barred by two stalwarts of the stock exchange, their broad chests expanded with conceit, as they no doubt speculated on tomorrow's investments.

Cigar smoke wreathed the air: Sir Cosmo was caught in a polite trap. Like his wife's, his face was affable, his manner pleasant, but as Celia watched he edged a little closer to the door.

*May 1912*
*New York*

LUCY

The room was overheated—she must ask one of the footmen to open the windows. And there were far too many tuberoses in the flower arrangements; their scent was overwhelming—almost funereal. Lucy scanned the crush, looking for her husband. She heard his name before she saw him. Or rather she heard the man who was talking to him.

"Musta been a damned inconvenience. Going back to England on their say-so. I mean to wait around to be questioned." The brash, hard voice cut through the overscented air. "I mean weeks of your time. Will they reimburse you?"

She edged closer so she could hear his reply. "Most inconvenient." Cosmo's voice was polite. She took stock of the group around her husband, nodding vaguely to a tall woman in a hat trimmed with mink gushing about an evening dress she had bought ready-made from the Lucile shop next to the salon. The group around her husband were the usual overconfident, expansive braggarts who had fought their way to the top. Some might say because they were quicker and sharper than the average man. Others who had tangled with them and come away bruised would shrug them off as ruthless, with no remorse for those they trampled as they made their millions.

What had Lily Elsie told her before she had left London? "The French say that the *Titanic* embodied the greed of America and the arrogance of Great Britain." Lucy had had no idea what Lily was talking about; she must have looked puzzled. "John Pierpont Morgan owns International Mercantile Marine, which owns White Star and therefore the *Titanic*! The *Titanic* might have been built by the Irish and registered as a British ship, but it was really American owned. The French love to point that out; they talked of nothing else the whole time I was there!"

Lucy wove her way through the crowd toward the ebullient laughter by the door. "I guess you showed them . . ." A heavy hand clapped Cosmo on the shoulder. She couldn't remember the man's name, but she knew he had made his pile in timber.

"Hell, I'da done the same thing!" a man who had made his in steel chimed in.

"Here is what these people have to understand: their customers call the shots, right? White Star let you down, Sir Cosmo. Not enough lifeboats and no idea how to man them in an emergency. You must have paid a packet for your stateroom, and then they have the audacity to question you about your actions as their unsinkable ship hits the bottom of the Atlantic?"

"Ah yes, you have a point there." Cosmo was elusive. He politely refused to join them in decrying the establishment and had made no effort to defend himself or White Star.

Lucy watched a lean figure on the outside of the opinionated crowd of men around Cosmo turn away, his face perplexed as he looked for his wife.

Payne Whitney. Lucy's skin prickled with outrage at Payne Whitney's snub both to Cosmo and to herself. Payne had lost his closest friend, John Jacob Astor, when the *Titanic* went down. A stalwart of the old Four Hundred, Astor had handed his nineteen-year-old pregnant wife into a lifeboat and had gone off to seek solace with men of his class. Astor would not have been surprised to see Cosmo among their number, drinking brandy with them as the water closed over their heads. Now Payne was running for the door like a scared rabbit, wondering if people would remember that Payne Whitney had become a friend of Sir Cosmo Duff Gordon.

Lucy said something vulgar about Payne under her breath. *It was my fault,* Lucy thought as she stood alone in a room crowded to celebrate Lucile. *If I had allowed myself to be loaded into that first boat, no one would have even known that the Duff Gordons had ever been on that wretched ship.* Cosmo, no doubt, would have gone down with Astor and his name mentioned with respect, sympathy, and regret. *Perhaps he would have preferred that outcome,* she thought, *but I damn well wouldn't.* What she could not bear was that by refusing to get into a lifeboat, she had in some way compromised her husband's honor.

Lucy watched Payne Whitney searching for his wife, a look of irritation on his face. Like most of New York's elite, the Whitneys could hardly claim any lineage at all. *Scratch any one of them sitting in their clubs and there is a grocer or a farmer in their ancestry.* Lucy smiled at how Old New York looked down on new money: the Fords, the Carnegies, and the Vanderbilts. She knew what it was to be on the outside of high society looking in. *None of it matters,* she thought. *At the end of the day we have to live with who we really are.*

Before she met Cosmo she had been adamant that nothing must stand in the way of the independent life she had fought hard to own, that designing dresses of emotion gave her more pleasure than anything else, other than her daughter. *And then I met you,* she thought as she looked at her husband, with his back to the door, politely listening to men he had nothing in common with, in a city he clearly disliked. *And you have always been so generous to me. I have never known such joy, such delight in friendship and marriage, as I have with you.* Cosmo had honored their agreement that their marriage would not get in her way, her need to create. *I am not a child,* she thought. *I know what is at stake now, and there is something I can do about it.*

"Darling?" She searched through the dark rooms of their hotel suite. Had he gone on to a club? Surely he would have said something. She found his coat and hat tossed over a chair in the hall, the drawing room shrouded in shadows. The bedroom was empty and so was his dressing room. The bathroom door was wide open, with its gleaming white tiles and massive tub. Their suite appeared to be completely empty.

Panic nibbled away at her determined calm. "Cosmo? Cosmo!"

Lucy found him tucked away in the corner of the drawing room, in a chair pulled up to the large window, looking down on the lights of Fifth Avenue. He had loosened his tie, and his feet were propped up on the windowsill. In the light from below he looked like a night bird, high on his perch, silently watching the world below him.

"Cosmo?" He turned, and relief washed away anxiety. His face was relaxed—more contemplative than the usual withdrawn anxiety she had seen in recent weeks. *Men like Cosmo have a habit of making light of their fears, their angst. That is what they have been taught: "Swallow down those tears, cover your emotions, m'boy, it will only make the other chaps tease you the harder."* And swallow they did. They gulped down fear, distress, tears, and hurt until they shut down completely to become functionaries only—without emotion and without forgiveness.

A polite smile, eyebrows raised in apology. "I am sorry, darling. I can't seem to shake this headache. Didn't think I would be much company tonight, didn't mean to disappear without saying goodbye."

"I'm exhausted." She tried to match his tone and kicked off her shoes. Pulling combs and pins out of her hair, she felt the weight loosen from her tight scalp. She yawned her jaw wide to relax the muscles. Cosmo returned his gaze to the traffic below, a busy stream of motorcars coming down the avenue from theaters now closed, filed by another steady stream going uptown to Delmonico's: the supper crowd.

She walked over to the window and stood next to his chair. A month ago he would have pulled her onto his lap, stroked her loose hair, and kissed her. He reached up a hand and took hers.

"Go to bed, darling. I'm not at all tired." His gentle, reasonable voice broke her heart.

He had slept in his dressing room, night after night, since the inquiry. She yearned to wrap herself around him. To go to him and hold him in the night when he tossed and turned in his lonely bed.

"Come to bed with me, Cosmo?" Her plea was honest, unembarrassed. "I'm so cold."

He got up out of the chair, stubbed his cigarette out in a brimming ashtray. "Cold?" he asked, as if they were still at sea on the dark Atlantic. "These late spring nights . . ."

They got into bed and he pulled her into his arms. She turned to face him, her mouth close to his. *Could I be any more obvious?* she asked herself as she locked her arms around his back and pushed her breasts into his chest.

His chin dropped down and he kissed her forehead. "Go to sleep, sweetheart," he said.

She awoke before dawn; his side of the bed was empty. She stretched out an arm to the pillow next to hers: the linen was crisp and cold. She swung her legs out of bed and walked to the door of the dressing room. It was half-closed. She stood there, summoning courage to push it open.

He lay stretched out on the narrow bed, his head on one side, asleep. Finally asleep.

### July 1912

## CELIA

"Celia, do you have a moment?" Lady Duff Gordon was all business this morning. She had her notebook open, her pencil hovering, and was perched on the edge of her chair. "Let's talk about the future of Lucile."

"Talk about the future . . . with me?" The words were out before she could stop herself.

"Yes, you. How do you think our manager, Mr. Algernon Norman, is doing? Are they up to snuff here, do you think?"

Celia shrugged. *Men are all alike. What matters most to them is how often their voices are heard.* "Mr. Norman does a good job, m'lady. No great talent there, but his designs are faithful to your style, which is a good thing, and he understands the importance of the empire line, as he calls it. And he is an efficient manager." *After I taught him a thing or two about working with women without making them feel like idiots.* "And he does listen to advice." *If you take every word out of your mouth and look at it first.*

"And the girls—no problems, no unhappiness? You know the usual things—do you think we have a good group?"

Celia's nod was vigorous; her smile expressed the pride she had in the backbone of the New York West Thirty-Sixth Street salon. "They are good girls. Mostly Catholic: from Italy and Ireland. Hardworking and easier to train than our girls at home." Celia had been shocked at how submissive they were—particularly toward Algernon Norman, who perhaps had it in him to be a bit of a bully.

"And you, Celia"—her ladyship's voice softened—"my old friend. How are you? Do you enjoy life in New York? Or are you homesick for London?"

Celia shook her head. "What a question to ask me," she said. "The job is the job, isn't it? Isn't that what we always told ourselves right from the start?"

Her boss smiled agreement. "Yes, we did, didn't we? But then it was sink or swim—an unfortunate expression to use these days. Now we have a choice. Where do you want to be, Celia? Here or London?"

She hesitated and then decided her boss was owed some plain speaking. "London any day of the week, m'lady—it has become my home. But I'd rather be here than in the London salon with that ridiculous Edward Molyneux . . . what an idiot!"

"Really?"

"Yes, really, m'lady. He may be a promising designer . . ."

"Oh, without a doubt he has great talent . . . but you have some misgivings?"

"He likes to show off . . . and he throws tantrums and can be spiteful. He needs a very firm hand, m'lady, and I know he gives Simone and Natasha a hard time of it. Not, of course, when you are around."

Lady Duff Gordon sat back in her chair, her gaze intent. "If you were to go back to London, who would you like to see as the head designer there?"

Celia was ready for her. "Simone, no doubt about it. She might not be quite as talented as Molyneux, but she is respected by everyone in the Hanover Square salon—and your clients trust her and like her. And Natasha is a perfect foil—they both have their own ways of expressing their vision, but they mesh."

A brisk nod, but it was clear that Lady D.'s mind was already made up. "Good, that's settled, then: you run London with Simone and Natasha as your designers, and I will take Molyneux off your hands and put him in my new Paris salon. He can travel back and forth with me between Paris and New York. I think the new Paris salon will be good for him—take some of the prima donna out of him." Celia was almost on her feet with shock. "Paris?" she said as Lady D. poured them both a glass of brandy. "Oh Lor', m'lady, not brandy. I'll be all over the place after just one sip."

"Yes, Celia, Paris. I know the Parisians say that Englishwomen have untidy hair and big feet, but what do the great houses of Worth, Doucet, Paquin, and Poiret really know about the simplicity of line and color? Good heavens above, the poor silly mutts are still putting bows on everything—well, maybe not Paul Poirot, but the rest of them are so fussy."

Celia took a sip of brandy and shuddered.

"I am going to open a salon in Paris and live in a pretty little house somewhere—maybe in the Bois de Boulogne. I am tired of hotel life and the fast pace of all this." She waved out the window at the bustling city. "It's draining and I need some peace. Some time to think. That is, if I can persuade Sir Cosmo that Paris is a better alternative to Manhattan and the unbelievable pretensions of the Four Hundred."

Celia watched her sitting there with her brandy. *She loves New York,* she thought. *So, what has changed?* Celia knew the answer; she had guessed it weeks ago when the Duff Gordons had returned from London. It wasn't the boss who needed a break from this scintillating city; it was her husband. There was nothing for him here in New York. *His loyalty to her is why he is here, and she knows that he battles daily with the hell of the* Titanic *and the humiliation of the inquiry.*

"Of course, Mrs. Kennedy will never make the move with us to Paris . . . she is determined to stay on in Molton Street, where she says she will 'keep an eye on things.' I do hope that will not make things difficult . . . for anyone."

"It never has before, m'lady."

Celia felt an immense wave of pride and affection for her boss. She had done everything she could to keep her little family afloat after she had been abandoned. Creating her beautiful clothes had been her own reward—and she had never forgotten what it was like to feel financially insecure, to worry about paying the rent. *We never lose girls to the competition; they stay year after year because she is honest and fair to them.*

It was true that Lady D. had become a bit one-track-minded when she got the bit between her teeth. And her husband had understood right from the beginning that his wife's first love was Lucile. *Now it's her turn to do some giving.* Celia took a sip of brandy and coughed, her eyes watering. "Dear Lord in heaven," was all she managed to say. "And people actually like this stuff."

"I'll ring for champagne." Lady Duff Gordon was laughing. "My goodness, Celia, when did a nice glass of Northumberland pale ale last cross your lips?"

"Never, m'lady."

The champagne came and they lifted their glasses. "Here's to your return to London and to the new Paris salon."

Celia breathed in the toasty effervescence of the wine and thought of the gentle English climate. As soon as things were settled and back to normal again, she would plan a walking tour of the Peak District with Grace—the two of them in the mild, sweet-scented air of north England.

"To Paris." She raised her glass. "After all, Sir Cosmo has always preferred the French tradition of fencing."

Lucy smiled. "And he will be able to continue as the chairman of the International Olympic Committee. I do hope I can persuade him."

"Somehow, m'lady, I don't think you will have any difficulty at all. He always says that Paris is the most civilized city in the world."

"Except Edinburgh—God help me."


*September 1912*
*Versailles: The Pavillon Mars*

LUCY

It was evening: the most perfect hour of the day. The violet hour. The garden cooled in the late September evening, and the scent of late lilies filled the air.

Lucy reached out and her hand curled around the open petals of a flower's cup, gently folding them inward and releasing their fragrance.

Cosmo came out onto the terrace. He stood there with his hands in the pockets of his evening coat, his nose lifted to the evening breeze.

"When did you get down from Paris?" he called out.

"Oh, about an hour ago. I was only a couple of hours behind you—you were taking a nap when I arrived."

"And the salon—how was your meeting?"

She laughed. "Ah yes, the salon. I completely forgot how competitive and emotional the French are about everything they undertake—particularly in the fashion business. Molyneux was in his element, and we have accounts with several silk merchants. I think we are ready to open."

He came down the steps onto the gravel paths that separated the parterres of flower beds reviving in the cool air.

"You smell delicious." He dropped his head to kiss her shoulder.

"Not me; it is the lilies. Still going strong."

"No, no." He kissed the nape of her neck and her skin thrilled to his touch.

She leaned back against him, and they stood together and watched the sky turn from yellow to gold—streaked with lavender, until it darkened to indigo to welcome the first star.

"My cousin, Angus, wrote to me today," he said. "He has agreed to sell me Villa Les Cèdres. Will we have time to go there do you think? I mean for longer than a week or so?"

She turned to face him, smiling. "Cap Ferrat in the spring?" she asked. "I've heard it is quite beautiful in May."

# AUTHOR'S NOTE

## LUCY, LADY DUFF GORDON, AND LUCILE LTD., LONDON, NEW YORK, PARIS, AND CHICAGO

Years ago, in London on a wet spring afternoon, I went to one of my favorite museums, the V&A (Victoria and Albert), and saw an exhibition of Lucile Ltd.'s dresses. Clothing, if not worn, does not do well; it lacks the warmth of a human body to fill it, the original colors fade, and over time it simply looks droopy and uninspiring. Like great works of art, clothes need to be looked after, meticulously cleaned, and, if mended, done so with infinite expertise. I was lucky that afternoon. The suits, dresses, and gowns I saw made me—almost—wish that I had lived in the early 1900s! I truly hope that my descriptions of Lucy Duff Gordon's marvelously original gowns have done justice to her considerable vision.

Divorce was a social no-no in the late 1890s for women of Lucy's upper-middle-class background. Undoubtedly her first marriage to James Wallace was a disaster and she must have been at her wit's end when she was abandoned by her alcoholic and spendthrift husband. In her memoir, *A Woman of Temperament*, she admits that she lay awake, night after night, wondering how she and her five-year-old daughter could possibly survive financially. She had no choice but to earn her own living with the only skills she had: the ability to make dresses and her natural and remarkable flair for color and line.

Lucy's fear of sexual intimacy might or might not be true as depicted in *A Dress of Violet Taffeta* and might or might not have been the reason she put off marriage to a man she clearly felt great affection for. In her memoirs Lucy barely mentions Cosmo Duff Gordon (she was too busy talking about herself), but my Lucy Duff Gordon fell in love with Cosmo when he came to see her in the South of France when she was recuperating from an illness, and they were indeed married in Venice.

Like all remarkably creative women, Lucy had a "temperament," as she called it. I have smoothed this down a little, since women of Lucy's time and class had to be stronger than most men, more opinionated than they were, and very self-exacting to succeed, which didn't always make them particularly generous or kind. My information about her life and her business were taken mostly from *A Woman of Temperament* and from the Victoria & Albert Museum's superbly illustrated book of Lucy's designs, *Lucile Ltd.*, as well as from the official records of the Board of Trade inquiry into the sinking of the *Titanic*.

Three years after surviving that harrowing night when the *Titanic* sank, Lucy booked a stateroom on RMS *Lusitania* from New York to Liverpool in the late spring of 1915. The night before she was due to sail, she canceled due to ill health. Or perhaps, very wisely, she decided against sailing into British waters when German U-boats had become aggressively active in their efforts to prevent precious food supplies and munitions coming from America to Britain. The *Lusitania* was ambushed by a German U-boat and with one well-placed torpedo was sunk off the south coast of Ireland on May 7, 1915. Of the 1,962 passengers and crew aboard, 1,198 lost their lives. Irish trawlers and fishermen rescued 764 souls, three of whom later died from injuries sustained during the sinking. Lucy certainly avoided a replay of her terrifying experience on *Titanic*.

## CELIA FRANKLIN

There are two women in Lucy's memoir, *A Woman of Temperament,* who she mentions as being of help to her when she started her business. One of them was a young girl named Celia (no last name) who was willing to learn every aspect of the dressmaking business at a very young age and who became indispensable to the building of Lucile Ltd. The other was Lucy's private secretary, Miss Francatelli, who survived that terrible night with Lucy and Cosmo when the *Titanic* sank to the bottom of the Atlantic Ocean. I have combined both these very real people into the character of Celia Franklin, as Lucy's right-hand woman throughout her career in *A Dress of Violet Taffeta.*

As a workhouse orphan the character of Celia Franklin represents the thousands who suffered from acute poverty in Britain during the middle- to late-Victorian era—25 percent of the population lived well below the poverty line. The parish workhouse was an institution that was intended to provide work and shelter for poverty-stricken people who had no means to support themselves. With the advent of the Poor Law system, Victorian workhouses, designed to deal with the issue of pauperism, in fact became prison systems detaining the most vulnerable in society and was feared by working-class people, and, in particular, single mothers and orphaned children.

The harsh system of the workhouse reflected the middle-class values of the time: that to become destitute was the fault of the individual and an indication of weak character that was mirrored in the terrible conditions its inmates endured: forced child labor, long work hours, malnutrition, beatings, and neglect. It would become a blight on the social conscience of a generation.

It wasn't until 1948, with the introduction of the National Assistance

Act that the last remnants of the Poor Laws were eradicated and with them, the degradation of the workhouse.

## SIR COSMO DUFF GORDON, 5TH BARONET

The aristocratic sportsman Sir Cosmo Duff Gordon became Lucy's second husband in 1900. He was prevented from presenting his new wife at the Court of St. James, not only because she was a divorcée but also because she was in trade. It might have mattered to Sir Cosmo that he could not present his wife, but Lucy makes absolutely no mention of this royal snub at all in her memoir. How well does this speak for the snobberies of the British aristocracy in 1900—when they prided themselves on their modern views at the beginning of a new century?

Cosmo and Lucy were on the *Titanic* when it sank, and they were lucky enough to be on Lifeboat One—a small lifeboat used as a tender for the *Titanic*'s captain. Sir Cosmo's name was completely cleared of the accusations of bribery and cowardice at the conclusion of the Board of Trade inquiry into the sinking of the *Titanic*, but he never overcame the shame of being pinpointed as a coward. He suffered from severe depression for the rest of his life.

After the trauma of the inquiry Cosmo lived with Lucy in a house outside Paris until the beginning of World War I, when he returned to live in London. His wife spent the war years in New York. He remained married to Lucy until his death in 1931, although the couple never lived together from 1914 onward.

## ELINOR GLYN

Larger-than-life Elinor was married to the eccentric spendthrift Clayton Glyn, who spent his inheritance on restoring the houses that he inherited to their original grandeur. When he lost all his money, Elinor became a novelist to support her family. Many of her books were considered "racy" in the 1900s—and today merely come across as more than a bit over-the-top with the melodramatic grand passions so enjoyed at the time. Like her sister, Lucy, Elinor had a strong personality and an appetite for success. She became involved with Hollywood's movie business, as both a scriptwriter and a director!

## THE *TITANIC*

Surely there is more than enough information about this magnificent luxury passenger liner that did not complete its maiden voyage to New York?

That the *Titanic* disaster was responsible for changing marine safety laws is surely the only good thing that came out of that terrible night when an unsinkable ship struck an iceberg and foundered.

Controversy over how and why the *Titanic* sank still abounds—all my apologies to those who count themselves experts on its sinking if they believe I have things horribly wrong in the book. It was believed at the time that the *Titanic* sank in two and a half hours; now some marine scientists have cut the time down to twenty minutes, or even five! In reading the many stories and facts about the survivors of the greatest civilian marine catastrophe of that century, I was struck that in 1912 it was far safer to be a first-class passenger than to be a passenger in second or third class. From the chilling statistics available on countless *Titanic* websites, the percentage of those who survived are as follows: 62 percent from first class; 43 percent from second, and from third class, also known as steerage, only 25 percent survived—fifty-five of whom were children.

# Acknowledgments

Writing a book during the pandemic was often a lonely and saddening experience, but I am utterly grateful that I could escape from the tragedies and suffering of 2020 and 2021 into another world. My greatest thanks and love go to my husband; without his encouragement and support I am not sure I would have finished *A Dress of Violet Taffeta*. Together we found pleasure in the simple things: long walks with the dogs, planning and cooking elaborate meals, and reorganizing all our cupboards and bookshelves!

My thanks, always, to my hardworking literary agent, Kevan Lyon. To my wonderful editor at Berkley, Michelle Vega, thank you for your keen eye and great insights—one of the kindest and most encouraging people I have met in publishing. And to the team at Berkley: Jenn Snyder, Elisha Katz, and Chelsea Pascoe.

Thank you to Debby, Nancy, Bill, and Georgia for those long Zoom and WhatsApp talks during our year of "social distancing."

*Photo by author*

TESSA ARLEN lives in northern New Mexico with her family, where she gardens in summer and writes historical fiction in winter.

Ready to find
your next great read?

Let us help.

**Visit prh.com/nextread**